ALL OF YOU

KYRA LENNON

Copyright

All Of You (Second Edition) © Kyra Lennon, 2025

Acknowledgements

This book is the product of a fourteen-year-old girl with a dream. And nobody can reach their dreams without help.

I couldn't have got this book finished without a team. That team consists of Clare Dugmore, Clare Bentley, Yvonne Eason, Claire Marta – yes, I know a lot of people called Clare! :p Your input, however big or small, helped me to make this story the best it could be.

Richard, for your neverending patience, for running around after me when the deadline was looming, and for making me laugh during the most stressful few weeks... I love you.

To Soph at Little Crow Marketing for setting me up a banging press kit and marketing campaign. Thank you also for your friendship, unwavering support, and listening to my absolutely ridiculous voice notes!

You guys are my people and I adore you!

Dedication

The one and only Mrs Bentley.

   For your patience with my messages that begin with, "Can I be a pain....?" and my "quick phonecalls", to all we have learned and endured together, to the *Friends* quotes, songs, and poetry, and laughing so hard our bellies hurt... this is for you.

Contents

Chapter 1

Shannen

I blinked a few times, clearing the fog that had nestled in my brain. It was dark in my room, and there was a distinct smell of alcohol and something else in the air, overpowering the usual aroma of clean cotton that emanated from the diffuser on my dresser.

Sex.

The bedroom reeked of it.

My eyes snapped open wide as I heard someone breathing beside me, slowly shifting my gaze sideways to make sure I wasn't dreaming. I wasn't.

I pinned the sheets close to me with one arm—a fairly pointless thing to do as he had already seen everything—and turned onto my side. The rise and fall of his chest would have been calming if I hadn't been so stunned.

At least he'd had the good manners to stay all night.

Wait. Was that good manners? Or was it just weird? Were there even rules for this kind of thing? In a moment of clarity, I recalled asking him about it when I'd brought him back to my flat, but he'd silenced me with a kiss that made me forget the question.

Oh, the kisses.

My eyes flicked back towards him. The dark stubble across his chin that had scratched against my face when he kissed me seemed a little thicker, and his black hair was sticking out in peaks, where I'd raked my fingers through it.

Oh, God.

I only went out for a quiet drink with my friend, and I'd come home with the man my mother warned me about.

Nine hours earlier

My gaze swept across the busy bar, glancing at the Friday night crowd dressed up for a few warm-up drinks before their night out *truly* began. The Lucky Jester was a small community establishment where people gathered before heading into the city to livelier, louder places.

I, however, was happy where I was. I would enjoy a few glasses of wine and some conversation with my colleague before wandering home with a clear head, and then spend the weekend ensuring I stayed ahead of lesson planning for the coming weeks.

And you wonder why people call you a workaholic...

After a long week at Oakwood Lane Primary School, Gaby had told me in no uncertain terms that my unsociable arse needed an evening out. Not that I *was* unsociable, just getting used to life in a new job, and a small part of me worried that if I was seen out on the town, it might somehow reflect badly on me.

Relax. You're having a quiet drink with a colleague, not performing a lap dance in a nightclub.

Shaking my head, I waited for Gaby to get back from the ladies' room, my eyes drifting around again. A group of young girls in short dresses and no coats—clearly unable to feel the January cold—stood by the doors, giggling at something on one of their phones. I wasn't sure if they were aware of the two young lads sitting across the room checking them out with lust-filled eyes. As I shifted my focus, my eyes landed on a man ordering drinks at the bar. Tall and well-built with short honey-blonde hair, probably mid-thirties at most. He wore black jeans with a belt and a crisp, tucked-in white shirt. Something about his profile as he turned his head seemed familiar, but I couldn't quite place him.

My phone buzzed on the table in front of me, and I looked down at it, rolling my eyes as I saw the message preview.

Jade: You won't find Mr Right in that dive. Why don't you...

I didn't bother opening it to read the rest as it would be the same self-righteous diatribe about how I needed to hurry up and find myself a 'good man'. Jade may have been my best friend, but her opinions on what I *needed* to do, especially when it came to relationships, were getting old fast. Instead of answering her, I went back to staring at the man by the bar, trying to work out where I knew him from.

"What are you looking at?" Gaby asked, catching my attention as she sat down beside me again. She offered a cheeky grin; a trademark of hers. Gaby was mischief personified.

I nodded towards the guy in the white shirt. My eyes remained on him as I tried to remember where I'd seen him before. I picked up my wine glass to take a sip as I mulled it over.

"You want a piece of that?" Gaby asked, following my gaze. "Because I approve."

"No!" I laughed, then it suddenly hit me. "Oh!" I thunked my glass down on my beer mat in victory. "I know who he is. He's Aiden Lewis's dad."

Gaby swung her head around to me so fast I was surprised she didn't get whiplash. Her long blonde hair flicked across her face, and she pushed it back behind her ears. "No way."

Aiden Lewis was the troublemaker of my class. Well, troublemaker might have been a bit harsh, but he was one of the more disruptive kids; the one who got told off the most.

"Not that I'm judging, but he doesn't look like someone who could have spawned a nightmare child like Aiden," Gaby said. "Also, Mr Lewis is *hot*." She turned back for another glimpse, smirking, and I was almost positive her gaze landed momentarily on his ass.

"Gaby! He's married. Or at least attached... I think."

Aiden's mum picked him up most days, but this man had definitely collected him several times. Unless the woman was Aiden's nanny or the babysitter... or bar guy was a helpful uncle, perhaps. Nobody had shown up for Aiden's first parents' evening, so I'd never been officially introduced to his mum and dad.

"They always are." Gaby sighed.

Gaby's struggles to find the right man were bordering on legendary in the staff room. She had no issue attracting potential partners. Her problem was finding one who wasn't concealing some kind of bizarre quirk. Amongst her horror stories were a guy obsessed with a famous pop singer and could only get in the mood if he was listening to her music, and a man who thought it was appropriate to decorate his entire flat with printed-out photos of young women in very revealing cosplay outfits.

As I took a sip of my drink, Gaby said, "So, what are the chances of me dragging you to a club later?"

A small sigh left my lips. "I'm not a club person, you know that. All those sweaty people squashed up together in a tight space." I shuddered at the thought.

"You know, you don't need to sacrifice having a good time just because you're a teacher. In fact, blowing off steam is necessary."

I rolled my eyes. "Come on, Gaby. We've been through this a hundred times. I still go out, but-"

"You go to sensible places with your sensible friends," she interrupted, fixing me with a stern look as if challenging me to argue.

And I couldn't.

"You talk as if I spend every evening knitting with a blanket over my knees and a cup of cocoa beside me," I said, but I knew her words weren't meant to offend me. "I'm here, aren't I? And I didn't even put up much of a fight."

She grinned. "That's true. So, does this mean we can do it more often?"

Smiling, I said, "Yes. It beats Jade's fancy dinner parties."

At the mention of my best friend, Gaby groaned. "Now, there's a girl who's old before her time. Twenty-five years old and the only thing she's interested in is figuring out what to cook her future husband for tea."

"That is what she *wants* for her life. I just wish she would stop trying to force me to do the same."

Gaby opened her mouth to answer me, but my attention was drawn to a man just entering the pub. Tall with jet-black hair, a sharp, stubbled jaw, and deep brown eyes. He wore faded blue jeans, a black shirt, and a black leather jacket, and he walked to the bar with a swagger. Not the type of person I would usually have been attracted to—he looked way too cocky—but something about him had made my knickers smoulder.

"You okay over there?" Gaby asked, a slight chuckle in her voice.

Swallowing hard to lubricate my suddenly dry throat, I nodded. I still couldn't drag my gaze from the good-looking guy who had caught my interest, though. He approached Mr Lewis and ordered a drink before the two of them sat at a nearby table together.

He must have felt my eyes on him because his head turned slowly towards me, and he winked, a suggestive grin pulling at his lips.

I averted my gaze way too late. He'd caught me.

Forget it, I told myself, trying to steady my suddenly racing heart and the flush I felt in my cheeks. *Look at him. Could you be any more different?*

"Do you need a change of underwear?" Gaby asked, still with amusement in her tone.

"What? No!" I rubbed my forehead with my hand as if hoping to erase the image of his filthy smile from my mind. My cheeks were burning now, and I would have happily teleported out of the pub if I could to escape the sensations of embarrassment and arousal churning in my stomach. "Oh, God. Is he still looking?"

Gaby nodded, although she didn't obviously turn in his direction. She could check out men with just the slightest movement of her eyes and still catch the attention of her target. That was Gaby. Flirting level: Expert.

"Stay cool," she said. "Have a drink. He'll come over."

"I don't want him to come over!" I downed a large swig of my wine. "Sheesh, have you seen him? He's not even my type!"

"Not your type?" Gaby raised her eyebrows. "Shannen, if you were any hornier, you'd be humping the table."

My eyes bulged at her words, but her no-nonsense way of speaking triggered a burst of laughter. How this woman was allowed to teach impressionable five-year-olds was beyond me. Or maybe it was her wild streak that made her so popular with the little ones. I often heard the echo of children's giggles when I passed her classroom. She had successfully mastered the skill of balancing learning with fun. I was more the gentle, nurturing kind of teacher, but I'd picked up a trick or two from my colleague over the past few months.

Refusing to turn in his direction again, I straightened my back. "Okay, okay. He's attractive. But that's as far as it goes. I don't want him over here."

A smirk covered her pouty lips. "Liar."

"I'm serious! I'm not looking for anything or anyone right now. I need to keep my focus on my career."

Plus, my father would have a stroke if I brought him home. Everything about him screamed 'unsuitable', at least in my dad's eyes.

Gaby held up her hands, even though her expression suggested that she thought a fling was exactly what I needed. "Okay, fine. But I bet you ten quid you can't resist turning around for another look before we need more drinks."

"Trust me, I'm winning that bet." I took another sip of my wine, still waiting for my heart to stop racing.

If I turned around, I was screwed.

Callum

"Cal. Cal!"

My mate's voice dragged my attention from the woman across the pub who'd been staring at me, and I turned back around to face him. "What?"

He huffed out a sigh—a common sound whenever I was around—and said, "Can you pick Aiden up from school on Monday?"

I nodded. "Yeah. I'll be done with the Hendersons' place by the time he gets out."

Unable to resist, I swung my head back in the direction of the hot-as-hell woman to see if she was still checking me out, but she was facing away from me, her attention on her friend.

"For the love of fuck, can you please turn your trouser radar off and pay attention?" Guy said, but when I looked at him again, he was smirking. That was the beauty of best mates. He got pissed off with me, but he still always had my back.

"Did you see her, though?" I asked, grinning. "She was looking at me."

Raising his beer to his lips, he glanced over my shoulder in her direction. "Three words, buddy. Never. Gonna. Happen."

I straightened up. "You think I couldn't?"

"Not in a million years. Did you really look at her? That is a classy woman, and no offence, but she is unlikely to fall for the charms of a painter and decorator she met in a pub on a Friday night."

He had a point. She *did* look classy. She wore black jeans and a black long-sleeved top that had some kind of thinner see-through material around the neck, and there was an elegance in the way she sat, shoulders back, a glass of red wine in front of her. However, the colour in her cheeks when I caught her watching me made me imagine how much more I could make her blush by whispering filthy words in her ear and tangling my fingers in her long, black curls.

"What, you don't think she'll be impressed by the offer of a drink and a packet of pork scratchings?" I joked.

"Only the finest champagne and oysters, I expect." Guy was still grinning as if certain I was wasting my time by even thinking about it. He looked over at her again, staring for a moment then shaking his head.

"Well, if my boss would give me a pay rise..."

Laughing out loud, Guy said, "I pay you plenty, not to mention all the favours I do for you."

Again, he was right. Guy usually was, and I owed him a lot for taking me on when nobody else would even consider me. Without him... Christ knew where I'd be.

"Fine, fine," I said, taking a drink from my beer bottle. "She might be out of my league, but we're both drinking in the same place. How posh can she be?"

"Trust me when I say, unless she's looking for a bit of rough, you've got no chance. Enough about that, though. Helen wants to know when-"

I held up my hand. "I know," I interrupted. "And soon. I promise. We just need to get the rest of my place finished up."

I'd been staying with Guy and his other half for well over a year now. It wasn't *entirely* through any fault of my own. Some of it? Yes. When I fucked up, I fucked up hard, and Guy had been kind enough to help me. He'd recently bought a small flat that I was going to rent from him, but it still needed some work in the kitchen and bathroom. It was partially on him to get things ready for me, but admittedly, I'd dragged my feet a bit. I liked living with my best mate. His woman... not so much. She straight-up hated me, actually, and she was desperate for me to get out.

"I'll get Johnny and Chris to go over there next week to sort the plumbing out, and then we'll work overtime to finish the decorating," Guy said, but then he paused, looking me in the eye. "You'll be all right, you know?"

I hated it when he got serious on me. I needed it sometimes, but the reminder of how bad things had got for me and how I'd needed someone to get me out of it when I'd promised myself I'd never need or rely on anyone made me feel like a loser.

"I know," I told him. "I'm just as ready to get out of Helen's way as she is to have me gone. But I can't live in the new place if there's nowhere to take a piss. If you ask me, you're the one slowing this down so you don't have to be alone with her again."

"Hey," Guy said, fixing me with a glare. "She's put up with a lot from you. Don't talk about her like that."

7

I knew better than to push him. Even though he'd told me himself that she could be a cold-hearted bitch, he seemed to love her, and she had helped me out more than I'd ever thanked her for. It's hard to thank someone who looks at you like you're something she just scraped off her shoe, though.

"Sorry," I said. "She's not... that bad. Sometimes."

Guy sighed. "Look, I know she hasn't always been welcoming. And sometimes she's grouchy and bitchy, but she's also cooked and cleaned for you, and-"

"I get it," I interrupted. "And you're right. Just let her know I'll be out of her way in the next week or two. We'll make it happen."

"Thank you. I'll get things in motion in the morning."

I nodded. It was time. I needed to stand on my own two feet again.

Chapter 3

Shannen

An hour later, Gaby had outlined our entire next evening out. It included a couple of our other colleagues because I didn't really know anyone aside from Gaby and Nova, who taught the year above us. She said we would all go out for an early dinner, some drinks, and then to a club. Not a raucous one, though. One of those retro types that had music from all eras to suit the varying ages of our workmates, which didn't sound so bad.

It had been so long since I'd had that kind of fun. Not since my university days, which admittedly, weren't *that* long ago. Even then, it was more pub karaoke nights than dancing under strobe lights.

While Gaby went to get another round of drinks, I sat thinking about how fortunate I was to finally have everything I wanted. Jade thought I was deranged for wanting a career instead of a rich husband and a life of leisure, but I didn't fit into *that* world anymore. If I ever had. I'd never found the 'ladies who lunch' lifestyle the people in our circles favoured particularly appealing. Teaching wasn't exactly a dead-end career, but my choice of a local primary school in Exeter instead of a fancy private school was just another way I 'rebelled against my roots,' according to Jade.

It wasn't something I did deliberately. I didn't set out to take my life down a different road, but my parents, mostly my mum, had always encouraged me and my sister to make our own choices, so we did. Lucky for me, they weren't so snooty that they thought I'd let them down.

"Mind if I join you?"

My blood seemed to stall in my body at the gentle yet gravelly tone coming from behind me. As I turned my head, I was both pleased and shaken to see the stranger who had captivated me earlier. My stomach fizzed. He was good-looking from a distance, but close-up? Holy smokes.

When he smiled at me, his face completely transformed. The arrogance he'd displayed earlier vanished, replaced by the kind of grin even a nun would have trouble resisting.

"Well, I... I'm here with a friend, but-"

He slid into the seat beside me, ignoring my idiotic stutter. The faint, intoxicating aroma from his leather jacket crept into my nostrils, and I tried hard not to breathe it in. He was close enough to let me know he hadn't come over simply to ask the time, but far enough away that I didn't feel uncomfortable. His perfect judgement was both reassuring and slightly frightening.

This was a man who knew how to snag a woman.

His deep brown eyes sparkled, making my stomach flip, and he placed his beer bottle on the table in front of him. His eyes explored my face with an intensity that sent another ripple of excitement shooting through my veins.

I'd slipped into a daze, and he had my full attention, even though a voice in my head screamed for me to back away slowly. Talking to this guy could never lead to anything good. Sensible Shannen did not get sucked in by hot men. Sensible Shannen's boyfriends were vetted by her parents, they always had respectable careers, and they wore suits to work. I doubted the man in front of me even owned a suit.

Although, if he did, he'd look incredible.

"Hey," Gaby said from behind me, placing a fresh drink on the table for me. "I just remembered, I need to be up early in the morning for... to... I gotta do a thing. So, I should go."

My heart plummeted, then rose back up and hammered furiously against my chest. I spun around on my stool and mouthed, "Don't leave me with him!"

"Yeah," she went on as if she hadn't spotted my wide-eyed freak-out. "It slipped my mind. I'm so sorry, but stay. Finish your drink."

I couldn't make my mouth move, and as Gaby leaned down to pick up her bag, she pulled me into a hug and whispered in my ear, "Talk to him. Live a little!"

Before I could stop her, she gave a small wave, a wink, and sashayed out of the pub.

Oh, hell.

I was way out of my depth; that had to be obvious to everyone, but Gaby had already left.

Slowly, I swivelled back around to face my new companion. His eyes danced with amusement.

"I can go away if you want," he said. "But you're alone and I'm alone, so we could have a drink together."

I glanced across the room to the table he'd been sitting at before. A young couple had taken the place of him and his friend.

"Weren't you with someone earlier?"

"Yeah. My mate, Guy. He had a... *thing* too."

The smirk was back, and I allowed myself to return his smile. After all, it would be rude to just walk out. "Fine. One drink. But you'd better tell me your name before this gets awkward."

"Callum. Cal to my mates."

"Callum." I let his name roll off my tongue. It suited him. "I'm Shannen."

He held his hand out to me, and I shook it, sealing my decision to stay a little longer. The friction from the rough skin on his palm sent a shot of warmth bolting up my arm, making me wonder how it would feel if he touched other parts of me.

As he released me from his grip, I reached for my wine and downed half of it like a chav at a hen party, hoping to wash away my dirty thoughts.

"What can I do to make you less nervous?" he asked.

"I'm not nervous," I answered a little too quickly.

I was never a good liar, and when Callum laughed, my cheeks flushed again.

"Okay, fine. I'm nervous. You make me nervous."

That grin of his is going to kill me and he's only been here for ten seconds. "Why? Because I look like the guy your mother warned you about?"

Swallowing, I said, "No. Because you look like the man who taught the guy my mother warned me about everything he knows."

"Well," Callum said, leaning in towards me a little, his face just a few inches from mine, "maybe you're right. But..." He shrugged and leaned back in his seat again, "...you won't know if you run away from me. We might have loads of things in common."

His eyebrow hooked upwards, and this time it was me who laughed, my nerves ebbing away a little. "Do you enjoy foreign films, sushi, and long walks in the countryside?"

"No. But you do?"

I shook my head, smiling. "I'm just messing with you. I like comedies and Chinese takeaways, and the sole reason I'd be taking a long walk in the countryside is if there was a cake shop at the end of the route."

Callum's shoulders unhunched, and he took a swig of his beer. "Thank fuck for that."

"So, what are *you* interested in, Callum?"

He paused as if he hadn't expected a question. After a moment, he said, "I'm just getting ready to move into a new flat and it's stressful, so, right now, Shannen, I'm interested in having some fun."

I felt a shiver as he said my name. I wanted to hear him say it again. A lot. Preferably while we were both naked and he touched me in bad places.

Jesus. Good-looking men had hit on me before and I'd never once thought about getting naked with them until we'd been out on an appropriate number of dates. Yet Callum was melting my knicker elastic every time he spoke.

"Fun," I repeated. "I think I remember what that is."

"Well, if you ever need a reminder..."

"I don't know about that," I said, though I was still smiling. "I usually like to get to know a man before I have 'fun' with him."

He shrugged. "So, stay and get to know me."

Callum and I sat for a couple of hours talking, flirting. Despite my initial panic, he had somehow helped me relax. It had to be part of his spiel. He could have walked up to anyone and chatted them up, but *I* was the one who'd stared at him like I was on a diet and he was a basket of fried chicken. Clearly, he was a master at knowing exactly how to get into a woman's undies, but even with that knowledge firm in my mind, I wasn't in a rush to leave.

Callum looked straight into my eyes while he spoke to me. It was alluring; every word we exchanged was charged with an energy I'd never felt before, and I let myself get swept away in the fast-paced conversations. I hardly remembered what we talked about, but the words weren't important compared to the sparks flying around us.

"It's kind of dead in here," Callum said, looking at his watch. "Do you want to go somewhere else?"

"Somewhere else?" I moved my empty glass aside and picked up my beer mat. I wasn't quite done being in his company yet, but hot as he was, I still wasn't tempted to go to a club. Plus, the responsibilities I'd planned to go home to fulfill were still waiting for me. I sighed, realising I'd dragged this odd and unprecedented evening out for as long as I could. "*I* should probably go home."

I traced the pattern on the beer mat with my fingertips, wondering exactly what would happen next. I'd enjoyed talking to him, but now what? Would he ask for my number? Would I offer him mine? Or were we destined to go our separate ways?

What did I want?

"Maybe I could walk you home," Callum said before I could tangle my brain into a knot of what-ifs. "Make sure you get there safely."

I toyed with the idea of saying yes, but the fact that I'd known him for a mere two hours was something I knew I shouldn't ignore. It wouldn't have been quite so difficult if I'd thought 'walking me home' meant just that, but the gleam in his eyes made his intentions clear.

Callum was the complete opposite of anyone I'd been attracted to before. Not so much in looks, but in his manner. He was bordering on cocky with absolutely no qualms about being obvious he was interested in me. I was used to men who took me out to expensive restaurants and wouldn't dare to expect anything beyond a kiss at the end of a first date.

In my mind, I heard Gaby's throaty chuckle at my hesitation. If she hadn't left, she'd have told me to stop being so bloody sensible and let myself act on instinct instead of planning and worrying. We'd known each other for five months, and she already had me pegged.

Callum reached forward and took the beer mat from my hands. Another spark as our skin touched.

"You're driving me crazy with that," he said with a small grin.

"Sorry." I smiled as he put it back down on the table and proceeded to do the same thing I'd been doing a second ago.

I watched his long fingers as they moved lightly across the letters.

Slow. Teasing.

My mouth went dry as I realised just how unready I was for the evening to be over. How little I wanted to put an end to this unexpected chemistry I felt with someone I barely knew.

You have a choice here. Let him walk you home. You don't have to invite him in...

My thoughts had gone rogue, and still, I watched the movement of his fingers, imagining the sensation of them gliding over my bare skin. The vision was so vivid that little goosebumps popped up on my arms, sending a shiver through me.

I don't need that. I just want a few more minutes with him... It's just a walk, Shannen.

Without allowing myself to overthink, I picked up my bag and coat. "Let's go."

Callum finished the last of his drink, and we headed outside and into the cold night air.

As I stopped to put my jacket on, he slid his hands around my waist and pressed me back against the pub's wall. His move surprised me, and my jacket dropped to the ground as my breath caught in my throat. My heart picked up its pace as I looked up at him, but when his eyes registered my shock, he remained still, reassuring me I was in control.

And that only made him more attractive. He might have looked dangerous as hell, but his intuition was spot-on.

The warmth of his hands holding me gently but firmly through my thin top quickly made me forget the early January chill and my momentary panic about his fast move. My skin burned where his fingers touched, my breath speeding again as his eyes dropped to my lips for a second.

"You're shaking," he said.

I glanced down, and my hands hovered by his waist, fingers quivering. Apparently, I'd lost the ability to function like a normal adult, but who could blame me? This man had crashed into my life mere hours ago, and my brain couldn't cope with how much my body wanted him.

My cheeks burned, and I lowered my gaze.

Yup, you are in way over your head here.

But I didn't want to move away.

Couldn't move away.

A lazy grin crossed his face, sending my pulse galloping again. He knew the effect he had on me, and instead of making the first move, he was waiting for me. Rather than scaring me away, it sparked fire in my veins.

The heady scent of his leather jacket had tormented me all evening, so I finally allowed myself to breathe in deep, my senses filling with the smell. Tilting my head upwards, my eyes on his, I took both sides of his jacket in my hands. From that angle, I noticed a tiny cleft on the bottom of his chin I hadn't been able to see before, like a scar, and I wanted to place my lips on it.

I wanted to place my lips on every part of him.

Tugging gently, I pulled him down towards me, and he needed no further invitation.

Callum's lips touched mine with a softness I didn't expect, and my heart stuttered when he pulled back after just a second. One corner of his mouth lifted into a half smile, and I couldn't take my eyes off it for a moment, my own lips still slightly parted and my breathing shallow. The moment seemed to go on forever until I dragged my gaze up to his dark eyes. The second our eyes met, he stepped into me, fully trapping me against the wall, and his mouth covered mine. A small moan fell from my lips as I slipped my hands inside his jacket and pulled him closer.

Being pressed against him after watching him across the table all evening, imagining what he'd feel like, made my head swim.

He tasted like beer, and the odd mixed scents of alcohol, leather, and whatever aftershave he'd used were causing some kind of sensory overload. His body was firm under my fingertips, and somehow, I couldn't seem to get him close enough.

Whatever he was giving me, it wasn't enough.

He gently pulled away from me after a kiss I knew I would never forget. "Sorry," he said huskily. "I've wanted to do that all night." When all I could do was elicit a tiny and embarrassing squeak, he chuckled softly. "I think I'd better get you home."

"Yeah," I croaked, then swallowed to moisten my dry throat. "I think so too."

It was a ten-minute walk from the pub to my place, but it seemed to take hours. I concentrated hard on the sound of my footsteps; I could only just hear them over my heartbeat. If I stopped for one second to think about what I was doing, I knew I wouldn't be able to go through with it. Spontaneity wasn't exactly my thing.

Then again, nor were guys like Callum.

I lived in a nice block of flats in a respectable part of the city, in a cozy two-bedroom apartment, which suited me perfectly. As I approached it with Callum, though, I wondered what people would think if they saw me bringing home someone they'd never seen before late at night.

Someone *I'd* never seen before. Someone so unlike me.

God, you sound like the upper-class moron you never wanted to be. A leather jacket isn't exactly a sign that he goes out bashing old ladies over the head.

Throughout the evening, I'd discovered Callum was a painter and decorator, and he worked for his friend—the man I'd figured out was the father of one of the boys in my class. So, granny-bashing seemed like a fairly unlikely pastime.

Once we were inside my flat, an attack of nerves hit me hard. I'd never before taken home a man I'd only known a couple of hours. What was the protocol?

I quietly panicked for a moment while Callum glanced around my living room with interest. I was just pleased I kept the place tidy. I loved the homely feel I'd created with my gigantic squishy sofa and fluffy pillows. There was a faux fireplace opposite the sofa, and I'd decorated that area with cute gonks wearing pastel-coloured hats. A string of fairy lights hung across the top of the fireplace, which, when switched on, made the room feel cosy and warm.

After a moment of standing in discomfort, I decided honesty was the best policy. "I don't know what to do now."

Callum turned his attention back to me, raised a quizzical eyebrow, and said, "You've done this before, right?"

"Sex, yes. Sex with a man I've known for just a few hours... not so much."

His brow furrowed. "Sex? I just thought you'd asked me in for a coffee."

Heat flooded my cheeks, my eyes widening. "Oh my God. I thought... I didn't mean..."

He burst out laughing, letting me know he was just messing with me, and my heart that had stopped began to beat again. Fast.

"You're a dick," I said, but I couldn't help laughing too as I put my bag down at the side of the sofa, shrugged out of my coat, and toed off my boots.

"I'm sorry," Callum said, still chuckling as he walked towards me, slipping his hands around my waist.

I still wasn't entirely convinced I was sober. Sober Shannen would never do something like this. But there was no blurred vision, I'd walked home in a straight line, and I wasn't giggling like a schoolgirl in sex education class.

Gaby's voice sounded in my head. *Stop overthinking!* I heard it as clearly as if she were standing right next to me.

What was the worst that could happen if I gave in to this? If I slept with an almost stranger? Callum was fun, he made me laugh, and I was positive he wasn't going to disappear into the night with my television.

Realising I'd been staring into space like a complete loser for the last minute or so, I shook my head, putting my focus back on Callum.

"*Did* you want a coffee?" I asked, looking up at him.

His dark brown eyes softened on me. "Maybe in the morning."

He leaned in and pressed his lips against mine, the taste of him reminding me of how incredibly hot our first kisses were.

I wanted him. Wanted this moment of doing something... *something.*

Once again sliding my hands inside his jacket, I gave in to spontaneity. To doing something *just because*.

As our lips parted, my breathing already a little laboured, I looked up into his eyes again, moving my hands upwards and pushing his jacket over his shoulders. He let go of me long enough for me to slide it off, and the second I discarded it on the back of the couch, his hands were on my hips again, his lips back on mine.

Slowly, he dragged the material of my top up. When his fingers touched my skin, I gasped. His rough hands were like nothing I'd ever felt before and he was barely even moving yet. They rested just above the waistband of my jeans, and I needed more of that. More of his hands on me. Anywhere.

Everywhere.

"Callum," I muttered, trying to figure out how to get him into my bedroom. "I... I..."

His lips dusted across my cheek and down towards my neck. "It's Cal," he murmured into my skin. "Call me Cal."

My eyes fluttered closed as goosebumps rose in the wake of his mouth. "Cal." His name came out as a breathy whisper, and I barely recognised it. Barely recognised anything about myself as I wound my arms around his neck, my fingers teasing at his thick, dark hair. "Bedroom."

"Lead the way."

With one more kiss to my lips, he took a step away from me and took off his trainers, then reached for my hand. I wasted no time leading him across the room, into the hall, and through to my room.

Once inside, Cal let go of my hand and turned to me, his dark gaze once again mesmerising me. The fact that this man was one of the most stunning guys I'd ever seen made me wonder if this was some kind of joke. If, in a second, he was just going to laugh and say, 'Yeah, you wish.'

"Relax." He said the word in a gentle murmur as he rested his hands back on my waist, his fingers brushing the tiny bit of skin he'd exposed and making me shiver.

The soft smile he gave me when I looked back up at him was enough for me. So what if the whole evening was just some well-rehearsed routine to get me into bed? So what if I never saw him again?

I wanted him now.

Perhaps it was a moment of madness. Perhaps I'd been dazzled by his looks.

But insane as it seemed and as wrong as it might have been, if I'd left him behind in the pub, the connection we'd built would have severed. This was a limited-time offer, and one I was apparently unable to resist.

I dropped my gaze for a moment before looking back up into his eyes as I reached forward to unbutton his shirt. His lips softly brushed mine over and over while my fingers deftly got to work. I fumbled slightly, my focus engaged on the way he kissed me.

The need between us was so strong I could almost touch it, yet everything was so unhurried. Each kiss was infused with lust as if we wanted to savour every second.

Delicious torture.

He pulled back from me to lift my top over my head and drop it to the floor, and I pushed his shirt over his shoulders. My gaze drifted across his chest, taking in the light scattering of hair across his pecs. He was just toned enough to let me know that he took care of himself without being overly ripped.

Cal pulled my attention back to him by snaking his arms around me, running his hands gently down my back. The roughness of his touch felt every bit as good as I'd hoped, and I stepped into him, my lips feathering kisses along his shoulder towards his neck. He gave a quiet growl and pulled me closer, the evidence of his arousal pressing into me.

The feel of it, even through his jeans, heightened my need, and as much as I was enjoying our leisurely exploration of each other, I wanted more.

My hips pressed into his, and Cal's fingers moved back up my spine, unclipping my bra. I shivered again, whether through nerves or desire, I wasn't sure. This man I hardly knew was about to see me more exposed than anyone had seen me in a long time, and it sent a chill through me.

He must have felt me shaking because he moved his hands back to my hips and leaned back a little so he could see my face, searching for signs I'd changed my mind.

I hadn't. I just needed a moment to catch my breath.

"I'm okay," I whispered, letting his chocolate-brown eyes soothe me again. Something about them seemed to ground me, and somehow, he had quickly figured that out.

"Shannen, we don't have to..." When he said the words, something crossed his face, as if surprised he'd said it, but it vanished in an instant, and he reached up and stroked my cheek. "We don't have to."

I turned my head, placing a kiss on his palm in a gesture that felt right but too intimate for the short time we'd known each other. "I don't want to stop."

When he smiled at me, my heart began to race again, and I pulled the straps of my bra down my arms, discarding it with our other clothes. His eyes dropped to my chest, and they flashed hungrily like he was ready to devour me.

I was ready to let him.

"Lie down," he said, his tone low, causing the wetness between my thighs to become impossible to ignore.

On wobbly legs, I took a couple of steps backwards, lowering my ass to the bed before pushing myself up it with my legs. The moment my head hit the pillow, Cal covered me, his lips hot against mine.

The slow exploration was over, and I let out a desperate, needy moan and circled my arms around his back while he moved one hand to my breast, gently rubbing his thumb across my hardened nipple.

His hot kisses trailed down my neck, and by the time his mouth reached the mound of my other breast, I was panting.

What. The Fuck.

As if sensing my rising need, he pinched one of my nipples between his thumb and finger while he circled the other with his tongue.

The sensations of that alone were too much, making my vision blur and my head spin. I bucked my hips, and I heard him chuckle against my skin.

Desperate for some relief from the ache building between my legs, I squirmed, hoping the friction from my jeans would give me some respite. The second he noticed, he stopped lavishing attention on my boobs, his head lifting to look up at me with the most devilish grin. I almost came just looking at him. His kisses blazed a new trail from between my breasts slowly—so slowly—down my stomach, the stubble on his chin heightening every sensation as it grazed my flesh. As he got closer to the waistband of my jeans, I writhed with anticipation, sweat beading on my skin.

"Fuck, you're sexy," he murmured as he unzipped my jeans. I lifted my hips so he could pull them down over my knees, and I kicked them the rest of the way off.

I was soaked, and when he did nothing but kneel at the end of the bed, looking me up and down, I could have cried with need.

He surveyed me with a lazy perusal, like he was drinking in every single inch of my body, committing it to his memory. Somehow, watching his eyes drift across my skin was more intimate than a touch, and I gasped slightly, unused to such focused attention. His gaze lingered on the curve of my hips, on the rise and fall of my breasts, and eventually, to my ever-dampening underwear.

My core throbbed, and just when I was considering taking matters into my own hands, he leaned over me and took his time lowering my knickers down my legs.

"Cal," I breathed. "Please..."

I opened my legs a little wider, and he grinned. In one swift move, his head was between my thighs, and I gasped as his tongue dipped inside me, gently at first, then slowly pushing deeper until my hips were bucking so hard I was surprised I didn't give him a concussion.

I couldn't recall ever being so brazen. So desperate for someone that I wanted to beg him over and over until he gave me what I wanted. I felt my cheeks flush at the realisation of what I was letting this man do to me, and while part of me wanted to hide from him, the other wanted to explore this unexpected wildness he'd created in me.

His fingers reached up to circle my aching clit, and I gasped, seeing stars as his tongue and hand worked me into a frenzy.

The fluttering in my lower belly built, my breath shallowing as my body grew tense before shattering under his touch, making me cry out so loud I was certain the neighbours would hear.

My heart hammered as I rode out the waves of pleasure, my hips still rolling a little to try and keep hold of the feeling for as long as possible. Cal moved back up my body, dusting kisses along my skin on the way.

When he was fully above me again, that gaze back on me, I swallowed thickly, trying to regain some kind of possession over my thoughts and my body.

"You taste incredible," he said, pressing his lips softly against mine.

My pussy clenched at his words. Nobody had ever said anything like that to me before. So bold. So uninhibited. Tasting myself on him wasn't something I thought I would like, but it was exhilarating, and I pushed my tongue against his lips, seeking entry so I could taste some more.

The groan he let out made me bolder, and I slipped my hands between us. He lifted his hips so I could undo his jeans and slide them down just a little, getting me another step closer to what I wanted. My fingers dipped inside his boxers just as he shifted a little and enclosed my breast with his mouth once again. His knees were at either side of me as his teeth and lips tormented my now extremely sensitive peaked nipples, and I raked my nails across his firm arse, causing him to nip harder. I gasped at the intensity of the pain and pleasure, my vision blurring again.

With one last light graze of his teeth against my skin, Cal rolled off me and pulled his wallet from his jeans pocket, then pushed his jeans and boxers down and off, kicking them to the floor.

My eyes fixed on his rock-hard dick standing proud against his stomach. I hated going down on guys, but I couldn't help licking my lips. I wanted him in my mouth, but not as badly as I wanted him inside me. I watched as Cal swiftly sheathed himself, then climbed back over me, those desire-filled eyes letting me know exactly what was about to happen. What I was about to do.

I wound my arms around his neck and pulled his face back to mine, eager for more of his kisses. More of all of him.

Shifting one leg from underneath him, I wrapped it around him, waiting until he was lined up where I needed him.

He grinned at me as he eased himself inside me, and I closed my eyes, welcoming the sensation of him stretching me.

Cal began to move inside me, so very slowly at first that I moaned my frustration, tugging at his hair. "Please," I breathed. "More."

His grin let me know he was enjoying torturing me, and I cried out again, my nails digging into his back, encouraging him to go faster.

"You're so impatient," he said, his voice husky again as his lips lowered to mine and, to my relief, he increased the speed of his movements.

I wound my arms around his back, clinging to him as he drove me closer and closer to the edge with each thrust.

"Look at me, Shannen," he commanded softly, but I shook my head. I was lost in the sensations he was creating, my eyes still closed and my head pushed back into the pillow. "Please," he said, slowing the rhythm of his hips just slightly to get my attention.

I opened my eyes, and the intensity on his face as he moved inside me made my heart race harder.

He might have been a player, but in that moment, he made me feel... wanted. Sexy.

I could feel myself getting closer to exploding beneath him for the second time, heated shivers racing across my skin, and I bucked against him, my eyes closing again.

"Stay with me," Cal said, his voice strained, and I knew he was holding on until I'd gotten my release.

My chest was heaving, my body on fire, but I wasn't sure I could handle seeing his eyes on me when I came. Making myself brave once more, I fixed my gaze on his, blue on brown, and as utter bliss shot through me from my core, rippling out to every part of me, I cried out again moments before he reached his own release with a loud groan.

Hot. Sweaty. Dirty. Fulfilled.

The whole experience had left me paralysed, and as I rode the last waves of my orgasm, I felt like something monumental had just happened. Like, somehow, I was never going to be the same again.

What the fuck did he just unlock inside me?

I didn't mean to, but I laughed out loud, and Cal sank down, his body relaxing on mine, his skin hot and slick with sweat. "What's funny?"

"I'm sorry," I said, my breathing still all over the place. "I just... that was... what did you just do to me?"

He chuckled, tilting his head so he could look at me. "I made you come. Twice. Hard."

My stomach fluttered, that arousal at him being so open sparking to life again, but now we were done, embarrassment set in as I remembered thrusting my hips against his face in desperation and begging him to go faster.

I reached over and pulled the other pillow across my face to hide my flaming cheeks. "Oh my God," I mumbled.

Cal tugged the pillow away from me and dropped it on the bed behind him then leaned up a little. Knowing he was looking at me, I covered my face with my hands this time.

Before I could run away to find something to cover myself, Cal's laugh pulled me from my thoughts. He gently pried my hands from my face, his smile fading into seriousness as he looked at me.

"You really hadn't done that before?" he asked.

I stared back at him, unsure exactly what he meant. I'd already said I hadn't had a one-night stand before. Not that this counted as one yet. Once he left, then I could count it. As things stood, he was… I wasn't sure what.

"I've never slept with someone I haven't been on at least five dates with," I said eventually.

His head jerked back just a fraction. "Wow."

"Is this something *you* do a lot?" I asked, already fairly confident I knew the answer. He had been easily able to charm me, he carried condoms in his wallet, and his confidence and skill suggested he'd had a lot of practice.

"You know what?" I said quickly. "Don't answer that." I didn't need a reason to berate myself, especially not so soon after one of the best experiences of my life.

After watching me for another moment or two, Cal leaned down and kissed me gently, something I welcomed while my brain was pulling me in twenty different directions at once.

"Let's go get cleaned up," he said. "Or, if you want, we can make the most of… whatever this is."

Whatever this is.

I didn't know what the hell it was. What I did know was that my body was both satisfied, yet still wanted more of him. And if it was only one night, why not spend it getting off as many times as possible?

Chapter 4

Cal

I opened my eyes, Shannen's warm breath gently tickling across my chest as she lay sleeping, nestled under my arm, her black curls fanned out across the pillow behind her.

Well, that's new.

Both that I'd stayed the night and that I hadn't had to struggle to remember her name.

It wasn't that I went out every weekend looking for someone to screw. However, I wasn't an angel either.

"Fuck!" I hissed.

I glanced down to make sure I hadn't woken Shannen. She hadn't moved at all. My eyes roamed around the pale purple walls, searching for a clock. I eventually found a digital one sitting on her bedside table, and it read eight forty-three.

There was no way Helen at least wouldn't have realised I hadn't gone home all night. Not that she gave a shit. If my dead body was pulled out of a river, it would have made her day, but I still should have let her or Guy know where I was. I'd just been too caught up.

My dick was already twitching as I thought about how stunning Shannen was. How gorgeous she'd looked falling apart underneath me. How good she'd tasted.

I slowly moved her arm from around me so I could carefully slide out of bed before I went too far down that road.

Thankfully, she only stirred slightly, then snuggled into the pillow. I took a moment to watch her sleeping while I covered her still-naked body with the duvet to keep her warm.

Fuck. Fuck. Fuck.

I scooped up my clothes and tiptoed like a dickhead into the hallway then the living room, closing the bedroom door behind me. Once I'd pulled on my boxers and jeans, I reached into my pocket for my phone. There were three missed calls from Guy, and one text from Helen, telling me to get out of whatever skank's bed I was in and get home.

It wasn't because she missed me. It was because she was unhappy at me shirking my responsibilities. Again. Guy was right, I owed her a lot. I never meant to take the piss, but it didn't help that the simple act of me breathing fucked her off, so it was easier to keep out of her way.

I unlocked my phone and hit the button to return Guy's call, leaning my ass against the sofa. He answered after just two rings.

"Thank Christ," he breathed. "Where are you?"

I paused before answering, and I couldn't help myself. I laughed despite knowing I'd stressed him out, mostly through shock at how things had played out. "You know that thing you told me was never going to happen? It happened."

It was Guy's turn to pause. "The posh girl from the pub?"

"Yup!" I grinned, even though he couldn't see me.

"Okay, but where are you now?"

He knew me so well. He was fully aware I typically got what I came for and then left, so I was about to blow his mind. "I'm still at hers."

"What?" he barked, but it soon turned into a laugh. "What happened after I left?"

That was a good question. When I'd approached Shannen, I thought Guy was right. It was *never* going to happen. But she was stunning, and her blue eyes had caught my attention. I wanted to find out what she was like if she would let me.

Over a couple of hours, I discovered she was way definitely out of my league, but for some reason, she didn't tell me to get lost. I was waiting for it. For her to tell me she was done slumming it with me. At the same time, though, she seemed to like me. Yeah, she was nervous of me, or of something, but the attraction between us was clear. I didn't expect it to end where it did, though.

"I don't know. We got talking. She was sweet," I said, immediately wanting to punch myself in the face for using such a pathetic word. It was the truth, though. She *was* sweet. The way she was so unsure about me and what we were doing, and yet she was also confident in herself, and beautiful and funny too. All of those things kept me hooked on her, so much that I'd wanted to drag out my time with her for as long as I could.

Guy's laugh echoed down the phone. "Okay, mate. I've known you on and off since I was fifteen and I've never heard that word come out of your mouth before."

Of course it hadn't. Because I didn't go for 'sweet' girls. I went for girls who were a sure thing. Girls who made it clear they only wanted one night. Girls who were sexy, not *sweet*.

Except Shannen *was* sexy. Not just the way she looked, but the way she blushed when she said something flirty. The way she laughed and made *me* laugh. The way a slight hint of a Devonshire accent slipped into her words when she relaxed. It wasn't strong at all, just a sign that she was dropping her defences around me.

"Fuck. Off," I said, as much to myself as to him because I didn't realise how much I'd noticed about her in just a few hours. "I know I sound like a twat, but don't worry. I'll be home soon and back to my normal self."

"Good, because Aiden's running riot. He could use some entertainment. I thought we could take him to the park."

I was about to reply when I heard footsteps, and Shannen stood in the doorway with a fluffy white robe wrapped around her, her curly hair tangled and her eyes a little bleary. Not surprising since we'd been going at it until past three a.m.

She looked entirely fuckable, and knowing what was underneath that robe was making my dick stir again.

"I gotta go," I said to Guy, not taking my eyes off Shannen. "I won't be long."

I disconnected the call, then stuffed my phone back into my jeans pocket, wondering how much of that conversation she'd heard.

Her gaze trailed up and down my bare chest for a moment, making me want to shove her back through her bedroom door for one more round, but I couldn't. I had to go home.

Shannen's eyes moved up to meet mine as if she were searching for something, though I didn't know what. "I didn't think you'd still be here," she said, her hair falling in front of her face a little before she pushed it back, running her fingers through it.

There it is. Now *she's done with me.* It was fun while it lasted. I didn't like the disappointment that came over me with that thought. Shannen was just some woman I'd met. Yeah, we'd had fun and great sex, but so what? I'd had great sex with lots of women and I'd never once hesitated to leave afterwards.

"Don't worry," I told her, shaking out my shirt, shrugging into it, and then buttoning it up. "I'm on my way."

I bent down to pick up my trainers and leaned against the back of the sofa again as I put them on.

"No," she said quickly. "I didn't mean it like that. I just..." She shrugged. "I didn't think you'd stay."

Neither did I, but I'll be gone any minute now.

This scenario was exactly *why* I never stayed. There would only ever be awkwardness when one or the other, or both, woke up sober and instantly regretted the night before. If I left before the woman woke up, it was all avoided, and we could both get on with our lives as if nothing ever happened.

24

Shoes on, I straightened up and made the mistake of looking at her. She hadn't moved from her position in the doorway, but there was a light blush on her cheeks. She averted her gaze as if I'd caught her doing something wrong, just the way she had the night before in the pub. Before I'd ever spoken to her, and way before I'd touched her.

Just go. You both got what you wanted from each other. Time to go home.

"Look, Cal," she began, and I held up my hand, unwilling to hear her telling me to get out and desperate to get away from her so I could give my head a shake.

"I'm going," I said, picking up my leather jacket and trying to resist getting another look at her. "Last night was fun."

"And that's all you're interested in, right?" she said. "That's what you said last night. That you're interested in fun."

I whirled around to face her, where she leaned her shoulder against the door-frame. Her robe had slipped a bit on one side, and the swell of her breast peeked out, making my mouth dry out.

Fucking hell. Down, boy.

"What's that supposed to mean?" I asked, making yet another mistake by looking into those deep blue eyes of hers. I wasn't sure what was happening, but the pull towards her was something I didn't need.

Guy's assessment of her had been bang on. Anyone looking at us could have seen it. She was a teacher, and I was some bellend who worked with his hands and still didn't have his own place to live. She was classy, well-spoken—aside from during sex when she said words I wasn't sure she'd ever said before. From what I could tell, she'd had a better upbringing than most. The fact she'd even considered sleeping with me blew my mind.

"Why are you being weird?" she asked. "I'm not trying to get rid of you, Cal. I just didn't expect you to still be here. I wasn't trying to say anything more than that."

"You *weren't* trying to get rid of me?" I asked, unable to keep the suspicion from my voice, and she laughed, her smile breaking through.

"I wasn't. I just... much like last night, I'm not sure what to do here. Do you just leave now? Do you want some coffee? Toast?" She shrugged, and a strange sensation began in my chest. One I didn't recognise.

You're a prick. You shouldn't have assumed she was trying to throw you out.

"I heard you say on the phone that you're going home," she went on. "You're not... married, are you?"

I barked out a laugh, which chased away the weird feeling that had been building. "No. Not married. I live with Guy. My mate. The one I was with last night. I'm just staying with him until my new place is ready."

It wasn't a total lie. She didn't need to know anything more.

Shannen nodded, straightening back up and pulling her robe back into position. "Okay. Well... I guess I'll see you around, then."

I nodded too, once again finding my eyes were unwilling to move from hers. When I looked at her, flashes of our night together flicked through my head. Flirting with her in the pub, her throwing her head back when she laughed. The sound of her voice. The sweet scent of her skin. The intensity of her kisses.

Fuck.

"Wait there," Shannen said, which was a good thing because, if she hadn't spoken, I might have stood staring at her all day.

I shook myself from my daze, reminding myself that the last thing I needed right then, or ever, was to get involved with someone. Especially someone so different from me. My head told me to leave while she disappeared into her bedroom, but I was too busy wondering why she'd asked me to wait to make my feet move.

After a minute or two, she came out of the bedroom and handed me a small piece of paper. "I'm pretty sure I'm doing this one-night stand thing wrong, but here's my number. If you don't use it, that's okay. It just feels weird for you to leave here with nothing after we... you know."

The blush came back to her cheeks, and for some reason, it lightened some of my tension.

"Thanks, but if I wanted to find you..." I leaned forward to whisper in her ear. "I know where you live."

Her face reddened further. "I never thought of that." She reached forward to take the piece of paper out of my hand, but I clenched my fist around it and pulled it over my head out of her reach.

"I think I'll keep it," I said.

"Fine, fine." Her tone oozed with fake disinterest as she took a step back from me. "You'll probably just put it in the nearest bin when you walk home."

Although she sounded like that wouldn't be an issue for her, something in her expression said different, and again, that fluttering feeling happened in my chest.

"Would you care if I did?" I asked, unsure if I wanted the answer; an unusual and unwelcome feeling when it shouldn't have mattered.

She paused as if really thinking about it. "Maybe. A bit."

I stared at her, the overriding thought in my head asking, *What's wrong with her?* What would possess a woman with so much class, so much going for her, to want *me* to call her? Did she have some kind of fetish for losers? Was I fulfilling a hidden desire she had to fuck a manual labourer? Was she trying to piss off her rich parents?

But the longer I looked at her, seeing nothing but genuineness on her face, the more tempted I was to use the number she'd given me.

I shouldn't. She's good. Too good for me. I'll only screw her up.

She smiled at me and gave a small shrug as if to let me know the choice was mine. That she wouldn't push me into a decision.

And somehow, that made it easier.

I moved closer, resting my hand on her cheek before brushing my lips across hers. "I'll call you."

The promise was made, and I wouldn't break it.

I just couldn't promise I wouldn't end up breaking her.

Chapter 5

Shannen

AFTER CAL LEFT, A weird sense of loss swept over me. Not the intense kind you feel when someone important to you isn't there anymore, but a feeling of someone walking away from you that you had fun with but don't think you'll ever see again.

Cal was going to be that for me. Just someone I met one time who rocked my world for a few hours. I wasn't sure how I felt about it.

Sex wasn't something I shared with just anyone. Definitely not someone I'd known for less than twenty-four hours. With Cal, I'd skipped over several very important pre-getting-jiggy rituals, such as actually getting to know him before-hand. With him, though, I didn't *feel* like I'd skipped them. Perhaps because he was so different from other guys I'd met. He wasn't a businessman bragging about his wealth as if it would somehow impress me when what I truly wanted was a connection. He wasn't a lawyer talking about his latest case, or a trainee doctor like my last long-term boyfriend, who obsessed over his studies so much that mine didn't matter. It was boring and soul-sucking to spend time with someone who took but gave little in return.

Cal was easy to talk to, even though we weren't talking about ground-breaking things. I would have put money on the fact that I was just another woman in a long line for him, but he at least seemed interested in my conversation. He was a breath of fresh air in my stuffy dating life, and the idea of not seeing him again caused a ripple of disappointment to rush through me.

I'd only given him my number because, like I'd said, it felt weird for him to walk out with nothing. I held a tiny glimmer of hope that perhaps he would get in touch, but I doubted it. When I'd woken up and found him in my living room, he'd gotten cagey, like he was just waiting for me to tell him to go away. I wasn't sure why, but it was the first chink of insecurity he'd shown in his otherwise confident persona. It intrigued me, yet I pushed the thoughts away, certain I would never get a chance to explore it further anyway, even though he said he would call.

Once Cal had gone, I showered, dressed, made myself a gigantic latte, and then set off for my lunch date with my best friend.

Jade and I had a recurring Saturday lunchtime arrangement; something we'd had ever since I returned home from university. Jade *absolutely* was the 'ladies who lunch' type, and apparently, I should have been grateful she carved out a regular slot of time for me. It was an honour bestowed on her oldest and best friend, but sometimes I wondered if we would be friends at all if it weren't forced upon us. Our mums were best friends, and they fell pregnant around the same time. Jade was four months older than me, so we grew up together and had even been on joint family holidays when we were kids. I loved her like a sister, but also like a sister, she often annoyed the ever-loving hell out of me. We were extremely different people, and as we got older, those differences became more and more obvious.

When I walked into the restaurant at the country club our families had frequented for years, Jade was waiting for me. She looked immaculate as always. Her shoulder-length blonde hair was perfectly straight, makeup on point, and she wore a cute blue floral print dress. I had opted for smart jeans and a long white jumper. I didn't have the energy to fancy up my makeup. I'd done the best I could to hide the bags under my eyes, and that was all I could be bothered with after getting such little sleep.

She greeted me with a smile and a wave as I approached her and took my seat at the overly adorned table. With all its decoration, it wouldn't have been out of place at a wedding.

I would have been happy anywhere food was served. Jade, however, wouldn't be seen dead in any kind of restaurant chain.

"You look tired," she said as I sat down.

Clearly, I didn't do too well with the makeup.

I tried not to roll my eyes and fixed her with a smile while she studied my face as if she were my mother and about to break into a monologue about whether I was getting enough nutrition. "I'm fine," I told her. "Just had a late night."

"Oh, right. You went out with your work friend."

I nodded, reaching over to pour myself a glass of water from the jug on the table. I had a feeling I would need something stronger, but I couldn't face another glass of wine. It wasn't that I'd had loads the night before, I just wasn't a big drinker. Plus, I was driving, and since I was already knackered, it wasn't worth the risk.

"Did you have a nice time?" Before I could answer, she continued. "Scott took me out to The Ivy, and their lobster and tomato linguine was to die for! We were celebrating his promotion. I told you about it, didn't I?"

"Yeah. You called me, remember?"

"Oh, yes! Sorry, I called so many people I lost track." The obvious joy on her face for her fiancé made me smile, even though I had very little time for him. He was eighteen years her senior, and while I had no problem with the age gap, I did have a problem with the fact that he was a pompous arse.

"So, what's it like living with a superintendent?" I asked, taking a sip from my glass.

"Well." She paused, placing her hands dramatically on the table in front of her. "Of course, the promotion came with a pay rise, so Scott says we can redecorate the living room and-"

"Wait, wait, wait," I interrupted, holding up a hand to stop her. "You only moved in six months ago! Nothing will have had time to go out of fashion already."

She smiled, peering at me from under her long eyelashes. "I want to change the colour. I liked the dusky pink when we moved in, but I want to try a blue tone this time around. And if we do the walls, we'll have to change everything. Ooh, if there's anything you want, let me know. You might want a new sofa and chairs, maybe? You've had yours for a while, haven't you?"

The woman was a whirlwind. I was used to her barely pausing for breath between sentences, but this was a lot even for her, and when her phone buzzed on the table in front of her, I was relieved for the break while she looked at it.

"My furniture is fine," I told her, though I wasn't sure she was listening as her fingers flew across the screen of the latest iPhone. "But thank you for the offer."

She waved a dismissive hand. "If I can't offer to help my best friend, what kind of person would I be?"

My skin bristled ever so slightly when she spoke this way. Like having my own place, on my own, made me a person who needed help. My finances were more secure than hers in that my money belonged to me. I'd earned and saved my whole life so I didn't *have* to rely on someone else to provide for me. If Scott left Jade, she'd be back home with her parents until she found someone else to take her on. However, I knew she meant well, even if her delivery was terrible.

As she placed her phone back down, she handed me a menu so we could browse. Honestly, it was a waste of effort for me. I always had either the chicken supreme or a lasagne with a salad. Still, I gave the impression that I might pick something different, even though I always settled for what I knew I liked.

Once we'd ordered food and drinks, Jade straightened her shoulders and fixed me with a serious look. A feeling of impending doom crept into my stomach because I knew that expression, and I also knew exactly what was about to fall from her Botox-enhanced lips.

"So, I know you keep telling me you aren't interested in dating anyone right now, blah, blah, blah." She waved her hands around again as if my disinterest in her setups was tiresome. "But I have met *the* perfect person for you."

I puffed out my cheeks to stop myself from protesting. She was gearing up to make her sales pitch, and no amount of me begging her to stop would slow her down. I twirled the stem of my glass around in my hand, waiting.

"His name is Sam, and he's a detective who works with Scott. He's a *little* older than us, but that just means he's more mature and ready to settle down, which is perfect because you don't want to wait too long before having children. You've got time to get to know him and get married and you'll still be a good age to become a mum."

"Okay, shh," I said after blowing out a breath. "You've just married me off and practically named my firstborn before telling me anything about him and why he is so perfect for me."

Not that I'm interested. Every guy she thought would be right for me had turned out to be a disaster, from the previous colleague of Scott's who cancelled almost every date because of work, to the man she'd met at one of her dad's networking events who thought it was acceptable to call me a 'filly' and believed it was fine to put his hand on my ass to steer me around the room. Jade failed to see that attractive and rich didn't equal dateworthy.

"Well, he's into music..."

"Most people like music, Jade. Does he like staying in with a takeaway, wearing his PJs, and watching trashy Saturday night TV? Does he enjoy doing things that are totally unpretentious instead of dragging me along to extremely boring work dinners?"

Can he make me come the way Cal did?

A shiver of excitement shot through me at the thought of Cal. A shiver I never got with any of the men I'd met through Jade. Or anyone, ever. He'd remained at the forefront of my mind all morning as I tried to process what had happened between us and why I was so intrigued by him. Obviously, the orgasms helped, but that wasn't all of it.

"Actually, he does like those things," Jade went on, interrupting my thoughts. "He's career-minded, like you, but not in the way Tim and Matthew were. He knows his way around a wine rack, though, and he likes to travel when he can. You want to travel, right?"

"I do, but-"

She reached over, gripping my hands and almost knocking over an unlit candle. I watched it wobble precariously as she said, "Shannen, please! Just meet him. We'll invite you both over for dinner next week."

A vibration near my foot gave me a moment to think about what she'd said.

"One second," I said, releasing myself from her grip to reach down for my bag. I blew out another silent breath under the table and pulled out my phone. It would only be Gaby, replying to the message I'd sent her earlier.

When I clicked to unlock it, what greeted me shocked me so much that I banged my head on the table as I sat up. Rubbing the top of my head, I let out a surprised laugh.

> **Unknown number: I didn't throw you in the bin :p**

Cal had left my flat more than four hours ago, so he'd had plenty of time to decide whether or not to reach out. The fact that he had rendered me uncharacteristically giddy and more than a little flustered. What did this mean? Did he just text out of politeness, or did he want to see me again?

Did I want to see *him* again?

The thudding of my heart gave me my answer.

I quickly typed back:

> **Glad to hear it. :p Just out with a friend. I'll message you when I get home x**

Maybe the kiss at the end of the text was too much, but the shock of him messaging me had made me a tad overenthusiastic.

"So, what do you think?"

Jade's voice pulled me back to reality, and I remembered what she was talking about.

I didn't know where things would go with Cal, but his presence in my life was the perfect excuse to get out of Jade's dinner.

Placing my phone on the table, I said, "Listen, Jade... thank you for the offer, but I kind of met someone last night."

Her eyes widened, and she squealed, quickly covering her mouth with her hand when people looked in our direction. "Shannen! Why didn't you tell me?"

Shrugging one shoulder, I said, "Because it's not a big deal. I'm not sure if we're even going to see each other again, but-"

"But you like him!" she interrupted, and I felt my cheeks warm. "Oh my God, tell me everything!"

I smiled. "He's gorgeous." I closed my eyes for a second, allowing myself to picture him in my mind. "Black hair, brown eyes, and this smile that just..." I trailed off, not wanting to tell her that the devilish smirk he possessed caused me to drop my knickers almost immediately.

"Oh. My. God!" she squealed, quieter this time. "Where did you meet him?"

"In the pub. Gaby abandoned me when he came over, and we spent the rest of the evening talking."

"So, what does he do for a living?"

Of course that was her first question. Not his name. Not what we talked about. And her reaction to my answer was totally predictable. "He's a painter and decorator."

Her smile dropped a bit. "A painter and decorator. Like... he owns a business?"

"No. He works for someone else."

Jade screwed her face up. "Okay, so you'll come over for dinner next week to meet Sam, then? I mean, you just said you don't know if you're going to see this other guy again anyway. Besides, you can't bring a *painter and decorator* to my wedding. What would people say?"

"Couldn't care less," I said. "Not everyone's first question is what job a person has, Jade."

"But people will ask eventually, and then what? It would be embarrassing for you *and* him."

I wish I could say her words surprised me, but this was typical for her. If a person didn't have a Louis Vuitton label hanging out of their arse, they weren't worth her time. Plus, her wedding was six months away. I didn't imagine things with Cal would stretch on for that long.

"Not everyone worries about impressing," I said. "Some of us just want to be happy."

"I'm happy!" She tilted her hand on the table, making sure her fancy engagement ring almost blinded me. "But I don't see how you could be happy with a man who isn't on the same level as you in any way."

"He's a painter and decorator, not some knuckle-dragging junkie I met on a street corner."

Plus, he's incredible in bed.

I kept that thought to myself before she booked me in at the nearest STD clinic and possibly tried to have me sectioned for losing my mind and lowering myself to such *awful* standards. Honestly, some days the snobbery in her was so strong I could almost taste it.

"Whatever," she went on. "At least say you'll think about meeting Sam."

I shrugged. "I'll think about it."

But I wouldn't. Not even for a second.

Chapter 6

Cal

I leaned back on my bed after sending another text to Shannen. She'd messaged me late afternoon after she'd got home from lunch with her friend, and we'd been texting ever since. Well, as often as I could between playing video and board games with Guy and Aiden. Now, it was just after half past seven, and I finally had some time to myself.

I hadn't been sure Shannen would text back after her earlier quick reply. I thought maybe some decent food and fresh air would have got her thinking I wasn't worth her time, but she'd proved me wrong.

When I'd got home, Guy had been buzzing to find out what had happened between Shannen and me. He still couldn't believe I'd spent the night with the 'posh bird' from the pub. When he'd said she was out of my league, he was mostly just taking the piss; the biggest shock for him was that I didn't creep home at the arse crack of dawn. She was *definitely* out of my league, though. If she hadn't realised yet, she soon would, but until then, I was going to see where the texts took us.

> **Shannen: Packing up to move is not fun, so I don't envy you. Everything hurt when I finished moving into my place. I spent a solid couple of hours soaking in a hot bubble bath once I'd got everything put away! x**

A groan slipped from my mouth at the idea of her all soaped up in the bath. I already had plenty of memories of how she looked naked underneath me, and yeah, I did eventually fuck her in her shower, but the bathtub wasn't something I'd considered.

> That's an image I'm going to have a hard time getting out of my head.

> Ha! So, I shouldn't tell you I'm about to get in the bath now, then...? x

My dick jumped in my jeans. If she was trying to torture me, she was doing a good job.

That thought was interrupted when I heard my bedroom door opening. I tore my eyes away from my phone to find Aiden standing in the doorway in his dinosaur pyjamas, clutching his brown teddy bear.

"What are you doing in here, buddy?" I asked, putting my phone down on the bed as he wandered in. "I'm pretty sure I just put you to bed."

"I'm not tired yet," he said, rubbing his eyes with one hand and yawning. His black hair stuck up on one side where, minutes before, it had been pressed against his pillow.

Smiling, I shuffled across the bed, stood, and scooped him into my arms. "You seem tired to me."

"I'm not. I want to watch TV."

He wanted to sit downstairs with Guy and Helen, but going out earlier in the day, playing football and messing around in the park had knackered him. He would be a brat in the morning if he didn't get some rest. We'd all learned our lesson about letting him stay up later at the weekends because he still woke up at the same time—usually between six and seven—and the tired tantrums when he didn't get what he wanted were epic.

"No TV," I told him. "But what if I read one of your books to you?"

He scrunched up his face as if that was the worst idea ever, making me laugh. I wasn't much of a reader either, so I couldn't blame him.

"Okay, what if we put a movie on your iPad and you can watch that until you fall asleep?" I suggested.

It wasn't ideal for him to sleep with his iPad playing. Something about the glow of the screen, Guy had said, but from the way Aiden yawned, he wouldn't be watching it for long.

"I want to watch *Toy Story*."

Thank God for Disney Plus.

I hoped Shannen wouldn't mind waiting for a minute as I carried Aiden back to his room. We were in the middle of a conversation I looked forward to continuing, but I couldn't do that with a kid in my arms.

I moved the duvet and placed Aiden on his bed, then pulled the covers back over him. He snuggled down with his bear while I took his iPad down from the shelf on the wall and got his film ready. Once it was set to go, I took it over to him and propped it up against the drawers next to his bed so he could see it.

"Okay, buddy," I said. "Enjoy the movie."

He knew it by heart. I'd introduced him to it a few months ago and he'd watched it over and over ever since. He often ran around the house shouting, "To infinity and beyond!" I'd got him a Buzz Lightyear costume for his birthday, and he'd worn it for a week straight, not even taking it off for bed.

"Night, Aiden," I said, watching him for a moment as his eyes fixed on the screen.

"Night night."

As I left the room, I hoped he'd drift off soon so we could have an easy day tomorrow. Work and getting ready to move were going to take it out of me the following week, so I wanted a quiet-ish Sunday before things got crazy.

When I got back to my room, I shut the door before sitting back down on the bed and picking up my phone to answer Shannen's message.

Would it be okay if I called her? I did say I would, after all. I wanted to hear her voice. I wanted to find out if us talking so easily had been because we'd been drinking, or if it would still be as easy now.

Part of me hoped it would be awkward, so I wouldn't have to deal with the fact that I liked the idea of seeing her again.

Although, she had just told me she was getting in the bath, so maybe she wouldn't answer anyway.

Before I could overthink it any more, I hit the button to call her. It rang once. Twice. Three times.

No answer.

If I hung up right away, I could just say I hit the call button by mistake, but...

"Hey."

Her soft voice stopped the anxious thumping in my chest. "Hi." I could hear the gentle slosh of water down the line. "So... you weren't lying about getting in the bath?" I hoped she could hear the smile in my voice.

"I wasn't," she said with a chuckle.

"And I thought you were just flirting with me."

"Well... there was an element of that too."

The tone of teasing wasn't lost on me, and that vision of her in the tub filled my mind again. I imagined her hair piled up on top of her head as she leaned back while the water covered her, a hint of her perfect tits showing above the soapy bubbles surrounding her.

"You're making it difficult for me to stop thinking about you," I told her with a lot more honesty than I intended.

"Did you want to stop thinking about me?"

I paused before answering. Not because I didn't know the answer, but because the truth of it confused me.

I wasn't cut out for dating. Especially not with someone like Shannen. If she found out about my history, she'd drop me and never look back. I was a one-night kind of guy; it was easier that way. A quick hit, then get out before they got sick of me. Before they found out who I really was.

But knowing that didn't stop my reply.

"No. I don't want to stop thinking about you."

The pause came from her end this time. "Do you... want to come over sometime? Or maybe we could go out again. If you want to."

The feeling in my chest I'd kept getting with her that morning came back with her words. I didn't know what it was or if I wanted it to be there, but there didn't seem to be any way to stop it. "Yeah. I'd like that." The intensity of the moment was too much, and I added, "As long as we can have a bath."

She laughed. "We can probably arrange that sometime. You could..." She trailed off. "Never mind."

"What?"

"I was... you can come over tonight if you want, but I expect you've got better things to do on a Saturday night."

Not unless you count packing. I had a feeling Guy wouldn't be too impressed if I left everything until the last minute, though. Things were moving forward with my new place, so if I spent most of the next few days packing, I might be able to get out for a few hours tonight.

Now the offer had been made, I really wanted to see Shannen.

"I can be there in half an hour. I just... I can't stay tonight."

"That's okay. We kinda went super-fast last night. Maybe we could just get to know each other a bit more."

I'd rarely met a woman who had any interest in getting to know me, not that I ever gave them a chance to ask. Someone getting to know me meant them digging around, trying to find out everything about me. Shannen was way too intelligent to accept me being vague or distracting her by taking her to her bedroom.

Well, maybe that might work tonight, but not forever.

But that didn't deter me from getting off the bed, putting her on speaker, and pulling on my trainers.

"That sounds good to me," I told her. "Maybe you can make me that coffee we never got around to having."

Her chuckle cemented my decision. "I can do that. I'll see you soon."

"See you soon."

It had been a lot easier to get out than I'd expected. Before I left, I'd checked on Aiden. He was already fast asleep, so I turned off the movie and put his iPad away before going downstairs to let Guy and Helen know I was going out for a couple of hours. Perhaps the fact that I'd be moving out soon was the reason they didn't protest. Once I left, they wouldn't have to do as much stuff for me anymore. Then, everything would be on me.

Shannen opened her front door wearing a white vest top and some pyjama bottoms decorated with brightly coloured cupcakes. Her hair, still wet at the ends from her bath, was thrown up messily on her head, and she was makeup-free, her feet bare.

She was cute as hell, and I wanted to skip the idea of getting to know each other and take her clothes off.

"You'll have to excuse the state of me," she said, gesturing to her appearance by waving an arm up and down her body. "I didn't have much time to get ready."

"You look good," I told her as I stepped inside, and she closed the door behind me.

The warmth of her flat enveloped me after the cold from outside, and it was helped by the way her eyes lit up when she looked at me.

She swallowed thickly as she gazed up at me, her breath catching, and I could feel a mix of nerves and anticipation coming from her so strong it made my own heart beat faster. Just as I had the night before, I met her eye and waited for her to relax. I knew she wasn't afraid of me; if she was, she wouldn't have ever let me through her front door. But I *did* still make her nervous, so if I could ease that, I would. Something about her inspired a need in me to protect her, and when she had calmed, I placed my hands on her waist and pressed a light kiss to her perfect, full lips.

I'd been messaging her for most of the day, and we'd spoken less than an hour ago, but kissing her made this thing more real. She hadn't just been a fantasy. She was right there in front of me, kissing me back, and still as intriguing now I was stone-cold sober.

When our lips parted, she smiled. "I should make that coffee."

"Yeah," I said, my voice croaking a bit.

I let go of her waist and followed her to her kitchen, which was just off to the side of her living room.

"So, you didn't have any big plans for the evening, then?" she asked as she flicked the kettle on and then leaned back against the kitchen unit, all tension gone.

"Nah. Just packing. But I can do it tomorrow. I have the whole week to get it finished. What about you? No nights out with friends planned tonight?"

Shannen shook her head. "Nope. It's fun to go out sometimes, but after last night with Gaby and lunch with Jade, I'm done with socialising for this weekend. Tomorrow, I plan to spend the day curled up on the sofa with a book."

A smart man would have asked what she was reading, but what would have been the point of *me* asking? Unless she was reading *Gangsta Granny*, I wouldn't know anything about it.

A chime sounded, and Shannen wandered across to the dining table, where her phone vibrated across the surface.

"Excuse me a sec," she said as she picked it up and read whatever was on the screen before growling and putting it back down with a sigh.

"Everything okay?"

She went back into the kitchen and grabbed two cups from a cupboard, placing them next to the kettle. "Jade, the friend I went to lunch with today, is on my case about going to her place for dinner next week. Which would be fine if it was just dinner, but she's trying to set me up with some guy her fiancé works with."

"And you're not happy about that?"

She glanced at me over her shoulder. "If you knew who she'd set me up with before, you'd understand. She just doesn't get that what she *thinks* I need isn't what I actually need or want."

Shannen turned back around to finish making the coffee, and I said, "What do you want?"

I didn't miss the flush of colour that tinged her cheeks, and she shrugged. "Not someone who wants to parade me around at corporate lunches and buy me expensive gifts to say sorry for staying at work until ten o'clock every night."

For some reason, relief ran through me on hearing she didn't want to meet another man, but from the sound of her friend, I wasn't exactly a good match for Shannen either. Not if dinner parties were the norm in her world. The closest I'd ever come to a dinner party was watching *Come Dine With Me*, and I didn't particularly enjoy that.

As she walked towards me with the drinks, I said, "I could keep you busy on Friday night if that helps."

The words slipped out, and I wasn't even sure I'd be able to make that happen, not to mention that I'd just asked her out without hesitation.

My fight or flight instincts shouted for me to finish my coffee and get the hell out of there before I committed myself any further, but I shut it down because running was unnecessary. Even if she agreed to a date, it would probably be the only one.

Shannen smiled and handed me my cup. "I'm not saying no, but that still wouldn't stop Jade. She's like a dog with a freaking bone when it comes to fixing me up with people."

I followed her into the living room, and we both sat down on the sofa. I put my cup on the coffee table and took off my jacket, slinging it over the arm of the couch. "Just tell her you met someone."

Her cheeks flushed again, but she didn't say anything, her eyes dropping to her lap.

39

I raised an eyebrow. "You told her about me, but she thinks I'm not good enough for you."

Her friend wasn't wrong.

And yet, Shannen had still invited me over.

"Cal, that's not... *I* don't think that." She met my gaze again, honesty shining through. "I think we come from very different backgrounds, but that doesn't bother me. I met you. I like you. And..." she paused. "I would rather spend my time exploring whatever we have going on here than meeting people I have no interest in."

The part of me that knew dating her would end badly told me I needed to get up and walk away now. It was better that she had good memories of who she thought I was than to be disappointed by the truth. Whether deliberate or not, I would hurt her eventually because that was what I did. I hurt people or drove them away. Usually both.

But something about her just wouldn't let me leave.

"Did we just make a date for Friday night?" Shannen asked, breaking through my thoughts.

"If you want to." I had no plan in mind yet, though. In spite of her insistence that she wasn't into fancy shit, she still probably had higher standards than I could meet.

"We could get drinks at the Quay," she said, smiling. "There are lots of places down there to go."

Her enthusiasm forced its way through my doubts, and I let myself relax. The Quay wasn't somewhere I'd visited often as it was out of the way from anywhere I'd lived, but it wouldn't bankrupt me. "We can do that."

"I'm looking forward to it already. And not just because it gets me out of going to Jade's," she added quickly. "I don't want you to think that's the only reason I'm going out with you."

The sincerity in her eyes was killing me. I couldn't figure out how she could be so classy and well-spoken, yet still so down-to-earth and... caring. Most people who met me immediately branded me as a loser, not looking at me as anything more than an unskilled worker with low ambition and lower intelligence. That judgment wasn't completely wrong, and I was a mess in so many ways Shannen didn't know about yet.

What are you doing here? She's not going to look at you like that when she knows all the things you've done.

"I didn't think that," I said, shoving the thoughts away because I wasn't ever going to let her get close enough to find out about my past. This thing would burn out before she cared enough to dig. "If you just needed an excuse, you would have picked one that wouldn't piss her off so much."

"Every time I do something she disagrees with, it pisses her off," Shannen said with a sigh. "She's overbearing."

"Then why do you put up with her?"

"Because I've known her since birth." She tucked her legs underneath her, getting comfortable. "Our mums are best friends. She and I are just not very similar. We actually have very little in common apart from our parents, but even though she's hard work sometimes..." she trailed off, shrugging. "It's hard to break a bond that's lasted so long."

"Do you want to break it?" I asked because a hint of guilt flickered in her expression that she'd said those words out loud.

Shannen shook her head. "Not really. I just want to not feel so much pressure from her and my other friends who act like I'm disappointing them."

"How could you be a disappointment? You have a nice flat and a respectable job. What more do they want from you?"

What kind of life did she come from that meant being a teacher was disappointing?

"They want me to be like them. To not want a career because I 'simply must think about finding a husband'." She slipped into a mock posh voice that made me laugh. "I've never been like that, though. I..." she stopped, a blush rising on her cheeks. "I'm making myself sound like a middle-class spoilt brat."

"Nah," I said. "I think I get it. It's crap when you're trying to do your best but you still feel like you're letting someone down. Makes you feel selfish sometimes."

"Yeah." Her eyes brightened, like she'd had a realisation or something. "But it's not selfish. You're just... trying to be happy."

I nodded.

When Shannen smiled at me, my expression quickly matched hers, wanting to shift from the seriousness. "Your friends aren't all like that though, are they? The one you were with last night wasn't."

Shannen laughed. "No. Gaby is a riot. If she hadn't insisted I go out with her last night, you and I might never have met."

"I owe her a drink for leaving us alone, even though you looked scared to death."

Her blush deepened. "I wasn't *scared*. Just... nervous."

I thought about how she'd been so uncertain about being alone with me when we met, and how she'd gone from that to bringing me to her flat, getting bolder each time we'd had sex, even taking control some of the time. Watching her confidence grow as she'd pushed me onto my back and ridden me was the single hottest thing I'd ever seen, and just the memory made me hard.

Leaning forward, I took her cup from her hand and put it on the table beside mine. "Do I still make you nervous?"

Shannen shook her head. The atmosphere changed in an instant when our eyes connected again, and I knew she felt it too because her chest rose and fell a little more rapidly. She reached for me, her hands around the back of my neck as she slid her ass further down the sofa and pulled me on top of her.

My lips met hers in a slow kiss that made my heart feel like it was going to burst out of my fucking chest. I didn't understand it. I didn't get how, even though I knew this would go to crap, I couldn't make myself stop.

She wound her hands in my hair, her fingertips teasing, and I gently stroked her cheek with my thumb. I dipped my tongue into her mouth and groaned as hers worked against mine.

We stayed there, doing nothing more than kissing and holding each other until I lost track of time.

And it was enough.

I would always want to sink my dick into her, but she was telling me without words that we didn't have to rush anything. That we could just take everything as it came, and she was so goddamn addictive that all I could do was go along for the ride.

"Shan," I murmured after a while, my hand running softly down her arm. "I thought we were supposed to be getting to know each other."

She didn't seem to mind me shortening her name. The smile she gave me lit up her whole face. "We are."

Closing my eyes, I did something I hadn't done with anyone in a long time. I gently circled my finger around the palm of her hand before linking my fingers with hers. When her hand closed around mine, I knew I was in some serious trouble.

It had been twenty-four hours, and kissing her had just become my favourite thing to do.

"In the interests of getting better acquainted," Shannen said. "I do have a question."

My body tensed, shattering my calm state. What could she want to know? What had I given away that she wanted to find out more about?

She squeezed my hand gently, bringing me back to her, her eyes holding a question of a different kind, although she didn't voice it. With her free hand, she placed a finger under my chin, on my scar.

"How did you get this?" she asked. She didn't sound like she thought it would be the result of some trouble I'd been in. It was just a simple question, like she genuinely wanted to find out more about me.

That was a scar I didn't mind talking about.

"Fell off a climbing frame when I was nine. I hit my chin on the bars and gave myself a concussion at the same time."

Her eyes widened. "Ouch."

"Can't say I remember much about it. I mostly just remember being in A&E for what felt like forever, but I think that was because I kept falling asleep. When I got home, my little brother kept taking the piss out of the way I fell."

I smiled to myself as I remembered him standing in my room, mimicking me climbing up and then over-exaggeratedly falling and screaming like a girl as he hit the ground. He was seven then, and he'd laughed hysterically every time he thought about it. Little shithead.

"You have a brother," she said, smiling, but my own grin dropped a bit.

I used to.

Once again sensing the shift in my mood, she leaned up and gently kissed the scar without asking for any more from me. When her head fell back to the arm of the sofa, I brushed my lips against hers again. If I hadn't, I would have unleashed a whole heap of crap on her, and neither of us was ready for that.

Her arms wound around my back and, once again...

We never drank the coffee.

Chapter 7

Shannen

"What the hell, Shannen?" Gaby's eyes almost fell out of her skull after I recounted the events of the weekend to her and Nova.

We were on our lunch break, and we'd tucked ourselves away in the corner of the staff room because almost everything I had to tell them was not suitable for anyone else to hear.

I had text Gaby on Saturday, letting her know that I'd taken her advice to loosen up, but she hadn't expected me to say that Cal had been back at my place on Saturday night. He didn't stay all night, but he'd left late after we spent the evening exploring each other's bodies and talking.

When I'd first met him, I was attracted to his confidence, but it didn't take long for me to see that wasn't entirely real. While we'd been tangled up on my sofa on Saturday night, and even before he first left on Saturday morning, it became clear there was a lot more to him. He was holding something back, especially something about his family. He'd almost frozen solid when I asked about his brother, but it didn't matter that he hadn't told me why. We still hadn't exchanged last names, so I didn't expect that he'd tell me anything too deep yet. I was happy with the pace we were setting and ready to listen if or when he wanted to open up.

"I don't know," I said, my cheeks warming. "Do you think I went too far on not overthinking everything?"

A laugh burst out of her, and Nova joined in. "Not at all." Gaby shook her head, her ham and cheese sandwich halfway to her mouth. "I still can't believe you didn't run away ten minutes after I left!"

Snorting out a laugh of my own, I said, "I was tempted."

"What made you stay?" Nova asked, taking a sip from her bottle of water.

I was sure my face reddened as I said, "His eyes. They're like melted chocolate, and his smile is sexy and beautiful. I just... I couldn't leave."

Nova chuckled again, and I knew she got it. She had recently got into a relationship, so she was familiar with the excitement of having a new man. "Yeah, I can understand that."

"Ha! You've got it bad, girl!" Gaby said to me, although she glanced at Nova too because, clearly, we had both been swept off our feet with little hope of recovery.

I cringed at Gaby's words because none of what had happened that weekend was like me. Not getting so googly-eyed over some guy, and certainly not spending a night and a half getting naked with him. Usually, I weighed things up, thought them through, and made my decisions in a rational way. Since I'd met Cal, being rational had flown right out the window. All I wanted to do was be around him, learn about him, and touch him. I couldn't think straight when I looked into his eyes, but getting lost in them was quickly becoming a habit I didn't want to break.

"Do you think I should slow things down?" I asked, taking a drink of my tea. "We have plans to get together tonight, but... is it too fast?" It was fast for me, but I wasn't sure my dating life had ever been normal.

"I think you should do whatever you want," Gaby replied. "Do you want to see him tonight?"

Just the idea of more time with him threatened to make me squirm in my seat. "I do."

She rolled her eyes, grinning as if the answer were obvious. "Then see him, Shannen. Don't complicate it by worrying about what's right or wrong."

"I agree," Nova said, picking at the label on her water bottle. "If Donovan was still here, I would be spending every second I could with him."

I offered her a sympathetic smile. Her boyfriend was a travel writer and had left a couple of weeks ago for a job at a fancy resort on the other side of the world. They'd only been together for a couple of days when he'd left, and I knew she was missing him.

Looking at it from that perspective, I knew my friends were right. Plus, embracing this new side of me was thrilling. It was just hard shaking off years' worth of conditioning about how things were *supposed* to be. While my family wasn't quite as 'proper' as many in their circles, certain things were still expected. A suitable husband with good prospects was one of those things. I'd already made a sideways step off the usual path by choosing to have a career instead of popping out a few kids with someone my parents approved of. My older sister, Sadie, had also gone for a career, in law, but she had married a business analyst and they had a four-year-old son. The friends I'd had growing up were either married or getting married to extremely wealthy men. That was why I'd drifted apart from most of them. I'd never been big on following the crowd, but I was still aware of people's opinions and how they reflected on my family.

"Shannen," Gaby said, interrupting my rampaging thoughts. I looked over at her, and she widened her eyes to get my attention. "Stop driving yourself insane. Here's how it is. You like him. He likes you. You enjoy spending time together, so enjoy it for as long as you can because worrying about what might happen is a waste of energy. Don't screw up what is for what might never be. This could fizzle out in a few weeks, and you'll have missed most of it by stressing out. And if it doesn't fizzle out, then you've got something real to build on."

I nodded slowly. "You're right."

She beamed. "I know, and that's why you love me. Now, come on. Don't keep me in suspense." Gaby wiggled her eyebrows at me, then leaned in closer and whispered, "How many times did you do it?"

I threw my head back, laughing at the mischief on her face. She didn't really want to know, she was just trying to stop me from driving myself insane.

I might have been slow to see it, but Gaby was exactly the kind of friend I wanted and needed in my life. Next time she wanted me to go on a night out with her, she wouldn't need to beg.

"The next card is... an apple!" I held up the picture card I'd pulled out of a brown jute bag and showed it to the class.

They loved picture bingo, but it came with a twist. Each child had picked a bingo card, all with pictures of commonly known objects on them. However, my picture cards didn't all perfectly match their bingo cards. They were only allowed to mark off the ones that were an exact pair. The apple in my picture was red, but some of the bingo cards had green apples on. It meant they had to both listen to me and look at their cards, and they responded well to it, especially knowing they'd be rewarded with a sticker for their win. The looks on their faces when they got praise for their work was what made my job worthwhile. Shaping very young minds and seeing them grow was the only thing I'd ever wanted to do, and while the job could be tough sometimes, I loved it.

Once everyone had marked their cards, I pulled out the next one from my bag. "A cat!"

"That looks like my cat!" Abigail Martin, one of my chattier kids said, bouncing in her seat as she looked at the picture I held up.

"Do you have it on your card, Abby?" I asked, reminding her of the task at hand.

Her mouth dropped open comically, and she scanned her bingo card to check. Not seeing it, she looked up and shook her head.

"Never mind," I told her. "Maybe you'll have the next one." We had to be nearing the end of the game now, and I reached into the bag again. "Who's got a yellow car on their card?"

"Ooh, ooh! Me! Bingo!"

The shout came from towards the back of the classroom, and Michael Lynch jumped up, his chair tipping over in his excitement.

"NO!" Aiden Lewis, who sat beside him, jumped up and snatched the winning card from Michael's hand, ripping it in half, his face tense with rage. Before anyone could react, Aiden shoved Michael, who fell backwards, the leg of his upturned chair digging him hard in the back. Michael let forth a scream before bursting into tears, making the other students jump. I rushed over to check on the injured boy while Hannah, my teaching assistant, led Aiden to the corner of the room because he looked ready to launch himself at Michael again. Gaby's classroom assistant, Gemma, who had popped in to borrow something from my supply cupboard, took control of the class like a pro. She distracted them by ushering them over to the carpet to the right of the tables they'd been sitting at and talking to them about something I couldn't hear over Michael's cries.

"It's okay, Michael," I said softly as he continued to sob. His t-shirt had ridden up where he'd fallen and there was a graze down his back, close to his spine, and a bruise was already beginning to form around it. "Miss Taylor," I called to Hannah. "Can you please take Michael out of here and check him over? I'll deal with Aiden."

Relief crossed her face because Aiden was practically snarling at her.

"Wait here for two seconds," I said to Michael, and he nodded tearfully. "Miss Taylor is going to look after you."

It took all my self-control not to give him the hug he so obviously needed before crossing the room to Aiden and Hannah.

Aiden's fists were clenched by his sides, a look of defiance on his face. This was far from the first time I'd seen that expression on him, but it was the first time he'd really hurt someone. Mostly, he started scuffles, pushing kids around when he got frustrated, but this was the second time he'd sabotaged his classmates' work in the last few weeks. In my inexperience, perhaps I'd been too lenient and should have contacted his parents about his behaviour sooner, but there was no way I could ignore it this time.

"When Michael's fixed up, please can you speak to reception and get them to call Aiden's parents in to see me this afternoon? Let them know briefly what happened." There was just over an hour to go until the end of the day, and I hoped they could be reached in time.

Hannah nodded. "Will do."

She gave me an empathetic smile as she left to take care of Michael.

With the rest of the class occupied, I had time to deal with Aiden, who was very slowly unclenching his fists. I knelt down so I could meet his eyes.

"I only needed one more picture to win bingo," he said before I could speak, his voice sulky. "But Michael won instead."

"Does that mean it was okay to rip up Michael's bingo card?"

"No." His lower lip trembled, but I stood firm.

"Was it okay to push him over and hurt him?"

Aiden shook his head.

"Because of this, next time we play bingo, you'll have Miss Taylor sitting next to you, and you're going to stay in the classroom at lunchtime for the rest of this week. Do you understand?"

"Yes, Miss." He looked up across the classroom. "Where's Michael?"

"Miss Taylor has taken him to be checked over."

"I'll say sorry when he comes back."

I nodded. "That's a very good idea. However, you're to stay here with me after school because I need to speak to your mum and dad about what happened today."

"I don't have a mum," he said quietly. "I don't know if my dad will come."

My brow furrowed. I guess I shouldn't have assumed the woman who picked him up and dropped him off most days was his mother. Maybe she was just Cal's friend's other half.

Oh, God. I had to speak to Cal's best friend about the behaviour of his kid. *That's sure to set us off on a great footing.* Still, I couldn't let it go unchecked any longer.

"I'm sure he will," I said, wondering what would have made him say that. I'd seen him pick Aiden up before sometimes. Maybe his job meant he worked long hours some days, getting home after Aiden was in bed so he didn't see him that often. That might have been a reason for him lashing out occasionally. Perhaps he didn't know how to express how he felt. Whatever it was, I would try to get to the bottom of it later.

At three o'clock, Hannah saw my class out into the playground, ready for their parents to collect them, while I stayed in my classroom with Aiden. I'd set him up with some paper and crayons because he said he wanted to make a card for Michael to say sorry. Michael had gone home early since it was so close to the end of the school day, so Aiden hadn't been able to apologise yet. I sat at my desk, working on some lesson plans. The room was so peaceful at the end of the day, and even though I could hear the children outside, I always breathed a sigh of relief when the majority of the noise had subsided.

After soaking up the quiet for about ten minutes, a knock on my open class-room door alerted me that my appointment had arrived.

My eyes widened in shock when I saw Cal standing in the doorway, and although I didn't register it immediately, his did the same.

He looked gorgeous in blue jeans and a black sweatshirt, his leather jacket ever-present. Although he was wearing normal clothes, I surmised he'd gone home to get changed before coming here as he had a few specks of white paint in his hair and some dried-in spots on his hands too.

"Cal? What are you doing here? You can't just…" I trailed off, realising I'd never actually told him where I worked, so unless he was stalking me, it would have been impossible for him to know where to find me.

His face paled, and his eyes flicked to Aiden, who was still engrossed in his drawing.

My brain couldn't quite process what was happening, and I blinked a couple of times, trying to kick it back into gear. Did his friend send Cal instead of coming to deal with the Aiden situation himself?

"Miss Morgan. I… think you wanted to see me," he said, then blew out a long breath as if readying himself for whatever I would say next.

But I still couldn't speak. Aiden Lewis belonged to Cal's friend, right? He and his wife or girlfriend always brought him to school and picked him up.

I glanced at Aiden. Guy and the woman who came to the school were both blonde. Aiden's hair and eyes were dark.

Like Cal's.

"Mr Lewis?" I asked as the realisation started to settle in.

This is why you should always ask for people's surnames.

Cal nodded and stepped into the classroom. His movement caught Aiden's attention. He looked up at Cal and jumped down from his chair, running to him.

"I was naughty today," he said as if he wanted to confess before I could tell Cal what had happened, his brown eyes wide.

Cal crouched down to be at eye level with Aiden. "Yeah. Miss Morgan asked me to come in to talk about it."

"I wanted to say sorry to Michael, but he didn't come back." Aiden's eyes filled with tears, and Cal reached forward and ruffled his hair.

"You can say sorry to him tomorrow, buddy. Why don't you go back to your drawing while I talk to Miss Morgan?"

"Am I in trouble?"

Cal glanced at me, but I kept my expression impassive, still trying to get my head around what was going on. He looked back at Aiden. "We'll talk about it when we get home."

Aiden nodded sadly and went back to his seat, picking up his crayon and getting back to work.

For a moment, Cal and I just stared at each other. The guilt was heavy in his eyes, and he eventually walked closer to me. My fingers twitched to reach out for him the way they'd been able to the last time I saw him, but it was not appropriate in that moment for so many reasons.

Instead of sitting at my desk, I beckoned him to follow me to the corner of the room, as far away from Aiden as possible so he wouldn't hear. We stood, surrounded by bookshelves, and I looked up at him.

"You're Aiden's dad," I said. It wasn't really a question. I had stated what was now glaringly obvious.

He nodded. "Yeah. I'm Aiden's dad."

I could feel my brow crinkling as I watched him looking almost as forlorn as Aiden had earlier when he realised what he'd done to Michael. "Why didn't you mention him? Why have I never seen you here before? What the hell is going on?"

Cal took a deep breath and let it out slowly. "That's a lot of questions."

"Well, let's start from the beginning," I hissed. I didn't mean for my voice to sound that way, but I was in some kind of shock, and all my thoughts tumbled out at once. "You never said anything about having a child. Not even a hint. You said you live with your friend and his partner. I thought Aiden belonged to them."

Cal tilted his head. "You know Guy and Helen?"

"No." I shook my head. "I don't know them. But I see them here bringing Aiden to school and taking him home every day. I recognised your friend the other night, and I put the pieces together. Incorrectly, apparently."

"So, you recognised Guy in the pub, but you didn't say anything?"

My eyes widened. "I didn't think it mattered the night we met, and it wasn't high on my list of important topics on Saturday night."

The memory of how amazing Saturday night had been crept over me, and I was sure he felt the same, as his gaze softened, his dark brown eyes a shade lighter now.

I sighed because I didn't know what I wanted to say. Words were failing me, and my stomach was churning. For some reason, this felt like a huge deal when it shouldn't have been. Not for the length of time we'd known each other. It was just... he'd kept this huge thing from me. And it wasn't huge because his child was in my class; Cal hadn't known that either. It was because he'd talked at length about him moving into a new place, about his current living arrangements, and not once had he mentioned he wasn't just *him*. I didn't mind that he had a son, I just couldn't understand how or why he'd kept the fact out of every conversation.

"Why didn't you tell me?" I asked quietly.

He reached forward as if he were going to take my hand, then dropped it back to his side. Casting his eyes skyward, he shook his head. "I don't know. I guess because if I told you about him, then I would have had to explain a lot of other things, and most of that is stuff I'm not proud of. We've only just met, Shan."

Had I been duped? Was the guy I'd met on Friday night nothing like the real him? The one I'd been getting to know had secrets, I'd figured that much out, but how big were they? Was Aiden the extent of it, or was there something deeper to uncover?

Cal closed his eyes, balling his fist and hitting it against his forehead as he turned away from me. "Please don't look at me like that."

"Like what?" I asked, growing more confused with every minute that passed.

"Like you don't..." he trailed off. "I don't know... like I let you down or something."

"I'm just trying to understand. And I don't. Even if there are things you didn't want me to know, you could have said you have a son. That would have been enough."

He didn't speak for a moment. He ran his hand through his hair, his shoulders tense. "I'm not used to telling people things about me. I'm not used to people being interested in me."

"Yeah, I've heard that about good-looking guys," I said sarcastically, and he whirled around to look at me, eyes blazing.

"You think women are queuing up to find out more about me?" He shook his head with derision. "Most are satisfied with one night."

"Well, I'm sorry for upsetting the status quo!"

This time, I was the one to turn away, hating how much it bothered me that this was how things were going. It wasn't like this was ever going to be a long-term thing, but I wasn't done getting to know him yet.

As much as I'd wanted someone different from the stuffy men who were usually introduced to me, perhaps he was just *too* different and I was fooling myself thinking we could find some common ground.

"Look, I know I must seem like the worst kind of dickhead for not telling you I have a kid, but I don't want this to be... I don't want this thing with us to be over because of it."

My heart flipped over as I turned and watched him pace. I didn't want it to be over either, which was stupid. Two nights in someone's company doesn't make a relationship. Whatever we were, we weren't that. But we were something. I wasn't ready for it to become nothing yet.

I reached out and touched his arm, halting his footsteps. He looked at me over his shoulder, his brown eyes radiating sadness.

It should have been too much, too soon. But I felt it from him. The fear of letting this connection go before we'd had the chance to explore it. I had no idea what kept drawing me to him because it couldn't just have been good looks and phenomenal sex. There was something deeper I didn't understand yet, and I *really* wanted to understand it.

"Can you please tell me everything?" I asked quietly.

He turned to face me and nodded, even though a hint of dejection lingered in his eyes. "I can, but I don't want to do it like this. Not here. I know we were going to go out tonight, but would you come over to my place instead? After Aiden's gone to bed. We can talk."

There were things in relationships I knew I didn't want. Men who were wealth and career-obsessed. Men who valued possessions over people. And men who came with more baggage than Heathrow Airport during the summer season. Cal had cleared the first two with flying colours, but he was obviously carrying around some pretty heavy stuff.

I should have said no. Closed the chapter, maybe reading it back now and again to enjoy the time we'd had but firmly shutting the book afterwards. But I couldn't make myself walk away from him. Didn't want to. At least not until I'd heard him out.

"Okay." I nodded. "Go, take Aiden home. Text me the address and I'll come over later."

Cal stared at me for a moment, like he wanted to say more. Resignation was written clearly across his face as if he were already preparing for us to part ways after our conversation later.

God, what was he going to tell me? What could be so bad that he wouldn't want me to know?

Before I could let my thoughts run away with me, Cal said, "I'll see you later."

As he walked away, I watched as he called Aiden over to him, and the two of them left, Aiden reaching for his hand.

Swiping my palm across my forehead, I had a feeling I was in for a long and turbulent evening.

Chapter 8

Cal

"Cal, you need to calm down."

Easy for Guy to say. Shannen was going to be arriving any minute, and all I could think about was whether I might say something to her that would fuck everything up. After finding her in Aiden's classroom earlier and her shock that I'd kept his existence from her, I was on thin ice.

She'd told me she was a teacher, but there were countless schools in Exeter. What were the chances she'd work at the school my kid went to and be his teacher?

I grabbed a tea towel and opened the oven to pull out the lasagne I'd made. Aiden had acted up when we got home, throwing everything off schedule. I wondered sometimes if he knew when I was already at the end of my goddamn rope and chose those moments on purpose to kick off. Guy had offered to cook even though it was my turn, but I'd needed to keep busy, so he kept out of my way and let me get on with it. I was just glad Helen was at work because I couldn't deal with her bitchiness making everything worse. I didn't need her additional reminders that I was a screw-up.

The doorbell rang, and I swore under my breath as the dish slipped, almost falling from my grip. I managed to get it on the worktop without incident, though.

"Stay there," Guy said as I put the tea towel down. "Serve up. I'll get the door."

I didn't want to be eating when she'd come to talk. It was already past eight o'clock, and I figured she wouldn't want to be home too late. I didn't want to waste any of the time I had left with her in case this was it. The last time.

Guy didn't give me a chance to argue; he'd already left the kitchen. I kept my focus on grabbing some plates and a serving spoon as I heard Guy and Shannen making their introductions. He was a charming fucker when he wanted to be.

"Cal is freaking out because we haven't eaten yet," I heard Guy say, his voice getting louder as they approached the kitchen. "I told him you wouldn't mind if he eats while you're here, but... it's Cal."

When she chuckled, my shoulders relaxed a little. At least she hadn't arrived in a mood as tense as mine.

"It's fine," she said, and I turned as they walked through the kitchen door.

I shot Guy a quick look of gratitude for putting her at ease before focusing my attention on her. In the time I'd known her, I'd seen her dressed smart-casual for a night out, naked, in her pyjamas, and then in her formal teaching clothes. This was a whole new look for her. She wore faded jeans with a pair of black knee-high boots, and a huge blue fluffy jumper that swamped her top half. Somehow, it suited her. She'd covered it with a long dark blue coat, and her hair was down, the curls cascading over her shoulders.

"Hey," she said, smiling softly. "I see you're on serving duties."

The lightness of her tone relaxed me a bit more, and I raised an eyebrow. "I'll have you know I made this."

She tilted her head slightly and gave a single nod. "I'm impressed."

"It's the Italian in him," Guy said, heading further into the kitchen and taking some cutlery from one of the drawers.

"You're Italian?" Shannen asked as I plated up the food.

"Half," I told her. "My mum was Italian."

Shannen would have registered me speaking about my mum in the past tense, but I didn't turn around to see her expression. I had more than enough to tell her about without adding that into the mix.

"Have you eaten, Shan?" I went on, more to flip the subject than anything else.

"I had a microwave meal earlier. So, yeah... I guess."

"That's not eating," Guy said. "There's plenty of lasagne if you want some."

I glanced at her as she remained in the doorway, and she nodded, breathing in deeply. "I'm glad you said that because it smells amazing."

As I caught her eye, we both smiled, and I said, "Guy, get an extra plate."

Within a few minutes, the food was served, and Guy told us he had work to do in his office, so he took his dinner in there, leaving Shannen and me alone in the dining room.

We sat opposite each other at the tableclothed round table, and I was glad it was clean. It was usually covered in splatters of Aiden's food. Guy had obviously tidied earlier because there were even table mats in place. My buddy had known from the way the evening had gone that food would be delayed and that Shannen and I would end up in here, so he'd done his best to make it look decent.

When Shannen took her first bite of lasagne, she closed her eyes, savouring it. "Wow," she said once she'd swallowed. "This is insane. What do you put in this that makes it taste like this?"

Her compliment sent a shot of pride through me, but I didn't let it show. "I don't know exactly. I just make it the same way my mum showed me when I was a kid."

Two mentions of my mum in one evening. Still, she didn't push it.

"Whatever it is, it's incredible," she said, taking another bite. "I didn't expect to be eating dinner here."

"I'm sorry. I had a hard time with Aiden tonight, and everything got delayed."

"It's fine. My sister has a four-year-old boy and he can be hard work sometimes." Smiling, she added, "He's a fussy eater, so meal times aren't the best."

"Aiden eats like he has hollow legs. I don't know where he puts it. Guy had to put the snacks up on the top of the kitchen units because we kept finding him sitting on the floor, munching his way through biscuits from the bottom cupboard."

Shannen laughed. "That boy is pretty tenacious. I saw him trying to get a second lunch in the school cafeteria once."

"Yup, that sounds about right."

As if the talk about Aiden had reminded us why Shannen had come over, we both fell silent. Firstly, my kid had done something bad at school, and I still needed to find out more about it, and secondly, I had to explain why I'd kept him a secret. I wasn't looking forward to any of it, but I also didn't want to drag it out, letting the awkwardness hang between us for too long.

"So," I began, spearing some pasta onto my fork, "shall we talk about what Aiden did today?"

She nodded. "Sure. I assume you were given a brief rundown on the phone."

"Yeah. I was told that Aiden had pushed another boy and he'd hurt his back."

Nodding again, Shannen said, "Yeah, but it wasn't just that. We were playing bingo, and Michael, the boy he pushed, won the game. Aiden snatched his bingo card from him and ripped it up, then pushed Michael over and he fell onto his chair. His back was cut and bruised. I suspect we will hear from his parents about this in the morning. Understandably, they just wanted to take him home this afternoon."

There was no judgement on her face or in her words, but I still felt like she thought I was a bad father. She had to. Only a kid with a shitty parent would behave that way. Aiden had a quick temper; something he'd inherited from me. That was a side of me Shannen hadn't seen, and I hoped she never would. I could control it for the most part, and I wasn't violent, just occasionally volatile. Aiden had seen it, the same way I'd seen it from my father, and I felt horrible about it. Even more so because now he was taking his anger out on other kids and hurting them. I never taught him to do that, but I obviously hadn't done enough to show him that it wasn't okay either.

"I can talk to them if they want," I said. "I don't know what I can say to make it better, but I don't mind if they want to discuss it."

"It's more likely that they'll want to ensure Michael is safe in my classroom. They might ask that one or the other of the boys is moved into a different class."

My defences shot up at her words. "Aiden's not a bully. He was wrong to do what he did, but he isn't dangerous to be around."

Shannen's eyes studied me, and I hated it. She was trying to get to know me, to figure me out, and I didn't want her to see the worst parts. But it felt like they were all on show and she could see every bit of me that I was ashamed of. The feelings it stirred inside me were trying to bubble to the surface, and I took in a deep breath to settle them.

"I know," she said. "But if Aiden had been hurt by another child in his class, what would you want to happen? I'm not saying Michael will be scared of Aiden now, but if he was, and Aiden was in Michael's position, would you be happy if he just had to put up with it?"

"No. I guess not."

"I can keep you updated on all of that tomorrow if there's anything to let you know about. But I need to ask you if you know why he did what he did. This is the second time he's destroyed another child's work recently. Aiden has always been quick to react to things he doesn't like, but the last week or so, he's been pushing kids around more than before. Is there something different going on that might be upsetting him?"

I dropped my knife and fork on my plate with a clatter and stood up, shoving my chair out of my way so I could pace. I wasn't upset with Shannen's questions, but it all linked into the things I needed to tell her about if I had a hope of keeping her in my life, even if just for a bit longer. Things I deeply regretted and hated myself for.

Things I was afraid would happen again.

This would be the temper you were trying to hide, you dick.

I was too wound up and afraid to look at her in case I saw something in her eyes I didn't want to see.

Fear. Disgust. Total loss of interest in me now she'd seen my true colours.

After a few minutes of my pacing and her silence, I couldn't stand it anymore. I glanced over at her. She too had stopped eating, but the only thing I could read from her was patience. She was just waiting for me to calm down enough to continue the conversation.

"I'm not very good at this, Shan."

"At what?" she asked softly.

"Being a dad. Knowing what to do in situations like this."

She watched me for a moment more, then stood up and walked over to stand in front of me. "What's going on, Cal? Help me understand."

Her blue eyes sparkled, like seeing me self-destructing caused her actual pain. But there was so much compassion in them too.

I ran my hand through my hair, letting out a growl because, even though she was looking at me that way, there were no guarantees she would continue to when I told her the truth.

What if she hated me? Or worse, pitied me?

And why did it matter? Why did the opinion of some woman I'd fucked at the weekend get me so worked up?

Why did I go back? I should have just thrown her number away like she'd expected me to because whatever we'd started was going nowhere. I was going to fuck her up like I'd fucked up everything else. Like I was fucking up my son.

"I can't do this," I said, turning away from her again and running my hand through my hair in frustration. "I can't..."

She moved around me to stand in front of me and tugged my hand down, wrapping her fingers around mine. "Cal, I don't know how to do this either, okay? This morning, you were simply a man I was trying to get to know, and this afternoon, you were a parent I'd called into my classroom. I still need to talk to you, as the person who is responsible for the safety of thirty children, because it's a part of my job. And I don't know how to balance that out with you being someone I want to... someone I want to..." It was her turn to trail off, but she didn't let go of my hand, even though she lowered her head.

"What *do* you want?" I asked.

"I want what I wanted this morning." She looked up at me again. "Before things got complicated. I want to spend more time with you, but for that to happen, you're gonna have to let me in just a little bit more."

Taking a deep breath, I swallowed hard. "I don't think you'll like what you see."

"Isn't that for me to decide? Don't take the choice away from me, Cal. Give me a chance."

My eyes landed on our joined hands. She did that. She'd just watched me freak out and she still held my hand. I wasn't sure what the hell she saw in me, but she deserved an explanation, even if I didn't want to give it. After that, she was free to walk away.

Even if I don't think I want her to go.

With a single nod, I led her into the living room. For once, there was no television on because Aiden was in bed, Guy was hiding in his office, and Helen was out. It was just me and Shannen, surrounded by my friend's overly girled-up room. I hated the chunky candles that sat on the windowsill, and the fake flowers that stood in tall vases by the fireplace. Guy had bought this house, and Helen had filled it with tacky crap and painted the walls a dark purple that made the room feel cold. Still, beggars couldn't be choosers.

I led Shannen to the sofa and we sat next to each other. She kept a hold of my hand the whole time. After another long moment of silence, I said, "I don't know where to start."

Chapter 9

Shannen

CAL'S HESITATION TO EXPLAIN his shift in mood had put me on edge, though I wasn't sure he'd noticed. I wasn't afraid of him, just surprised. It mirrored Aiden's mood shifts perfectly, except Aiden became enraged, while Cal had just gotten a little frustrated. It was like he wanted reassurance that I would still want to be around him once he revealed his secrets. But I wasn't about to make him a promise I didn't know if I could keep.

I wanted to stay. I just needed to know what he was so scared to tell me. I'd had hours to stew over it after work, and while I'd still entered his house with relative calm, my stomach swam with tension now.

"Usually, I would say to start at the beginning, but I'm not sure where that is," I said, squeezing his hand gently.

"Me neither. I can answer your question about why Aiden's been so up and down lately, though." Cal paused, then let go of my hand, placing his on his lap. I missed the contact, but I also understood that whatever he was going to say was hard for him. If distancing himself for now helped, that was fine with me.

"Aiden doesn't want to move," Cal said, not meeting my eye. "He likes living here because he has fun with Guy, and Helen has been good to him too. He thinks that when we move out, he won't see them anymore. I've told him we'll be over here all the time, but he doesn't believe it."

"Has he seen your new place yet?" I asked.

Cal shook his head. "I didn't want him to see it empty because he'll think that's what it'll be like when we move in."

"Makes sense. But you could take him out to get things for his new room. Let him choose wallpaper and bedding and stuff. It might make him feel like he's got some say in the move rather than just being taken somewhere new."

He looked up at me. "I didn't think of that. He'd like it. I wonder if anywhere sells *Toy Story* wallpaper."

I laughed. "He'd love that. He's always drawing pictures of Buzz Lightyear. They're actually pretty impressive."

A frown crossed his face. "He's never shown me his drawings."

"I think he keeps most of them at school. I'll have to slip a couple in his book bag so you can see."

There was another pause, and I said, "Cal, when I told Aiden I'd called you in so I could talk to you, he said you wouldn't come."

Cal's eyes flicked to mine. "He said that?"

I nodded.

He covered his mouth with his hand, shaking his head slowly. His eyes dimmed, and he stood up and walked over to the window, resting his hands against the windowsill.

"I thought things were better," he said. "They *have* been better, but it looks like I'm still not doing enough."

"What do you mean?"

As if he hadn't heard me, he said, "I've tried to be there for him. I feed him, I get him everything he needs. If he has a bad dream or if he's ill, I go to him, and I take care of him. I don't know... I don't know why he thought I wouldn't be there for him." After a moment, he pushed his hands off the windowsill and turned to face me. "Do you think this is just because I don't take him to school or pick him up? The only reason I don't is because of work. Does he think I just don't want to?"

"Maybe. You could talk to him about it and see what he says."

He shook his head. "I don't know if it's obvious, but I'm not very good at talking."

When I chuckled, his expression brightened, and a small smile crossed his face.

"The stuff I have to tell you makes me feel like shit," he said, his smile fading again. "Guy is the only person who knows everything about me, and that's because he's known me most of my life on and off. He's the only person who hasn't written me off." He heaved out a sigh. "I still don't know where to start."

I reached my hand out, beckoning him to come and sit next to me again. After a moment, he walked back towards me, taking my hand as he sat. His eyes fixed on mine, like he was looking deep inside for a sign I was getting ready to bolt. He didn't find it because it wasn't there.

When he'd got the confirmation he needed, he said, "Aiden is the result of a couple of drunken nights with a woman I met in a pub. I was twenty-four, when all I did was spend my benefits money on nights out. I didn't work back then, I just messed around. Until Katie came looking for me to tell me she was pregnant. Like the dick I was, I told her she was wrong and it was nothing to do with me. We *always* used protection. But once Aiden was born, I did a paternity test to find out for sure since she wouldn't leave me alone. Neither of us had anyone but each other, so she and Aiden moved into my flat and we tried to make it work."

He hadn't looked me in the eye since he'd started talking, and I was glad because I wasn't sure what reflected on my face. I hoped my expression was impassive, but hearing that he'd initially dismissed a woman who'd said she was carrying his child wasn't showing him in the best light. However, I still knew so little about him and his life back then. Didn't know what circumstances had led him to live like that.

"It was hard work," Cal went on, breaking through my thoughts. "We didn't have much money, and neither of us had a clue how to look after a baby. We were both winging it, and then, when Aiden was a year old, Katie left. I'd taken Aiden out in his pushchair because he wouldn't settle, and I walked around for hours with him until he calmed down and fell asleep. When we got home, she'd taken her stuff and left a note saying she couldn't handle being a mum anymore. She never said where she was going, and she never came back."

"Wow," I muttered. It sounded like they'd struggled hard, but how could someone walk away from their child and never try to find out how or where they were? And especially not knowing if their remaining caregiver would be able to cope alone.

He finally looked at me again, and I kind of wished he hadn't because the pain in his eyes hit me square in the chest.

"I couldn't handle it either," he said quietly. "I tried, Shan. I really did, but he never slept. He cried all night, every night, and I was exhausted trying to figure out what he needed with nobody to help me. And then..." he paused, taking a deep breath. "I started drinking. I just wanted to escape from it all. Something to take the edge off the crap that my life had become. The days all started to blur together. I was still looking after Aiden, but only just. When he was eighteen months old, someone reported me to social services, and because my place was such a shithole and I could barely keep us alive, they took him away and put him into foster care."

His eyes glistened, and he swallowed down the lump I was sure was in his throat.

"I was allowed to see him. At first, it was just once a month, and then after three months, it was every two weeks. The couple that had him was so understanding. They loved him, and they helped me learn how to take care of him. They helped me ease off on the drinking too because they saw how I was self-destructing after losing Aiden. I was never dependent on alcohol. I drank because I was drowning, but once the pressure eased and I could see Aiden was better off somewhere else for a while, I stopped. I didn't crave it and I didn't miss it. But it wasn't until I bumped into Guy completely by chance that things changed. I'd known him at school. He's a few years older than me, and we used to play football together. He moved away for a while after he left school and we lost touch. When I told him what had been happening, he whacked me across the face so hard I saw stars. Then he hugged me and told me I needed to get it together for my boy. He gave me a job, asked me to move in with him and Helen, and he helped me get Aiden back. He's been here for almost a year now. We still go and visit Angela and Simon, his foster parents, sometimes, even though I sometimes think he won't want to come home."

Suddenly, things made a lot more sense. Aiden's behaviour for one thing. He was still getting used to being in a different place after living with the same people for as long as he could remember, and then the change of starting school too. It was a lot for someone so young to deal with at once.

"So," Cal said, letting go of my hand and leaning away from me slightly. "You can see why I didn't want to tell you."

"Because you thought I'd judge you?" I asked.

"Because I probably seem like a different person now."

"Does that have to be a bad thing?"

"How could it be good?"

I took a moment to consider what I wanted to say. Was I happy to know he once did nothing but drink and screw around? No. Was I impressed that he used to be a man whore? Of course not. A different person might have listened to his story and only seen the bad. But I saw more. Perhaps because I'd seen things like this in my time as a supply teacher at various schools. Scenarios where children had been left in foster care, whose parents straight-up couldn't take care of them anymore. But Cal hadn't let Aiden go forever.

"Cal, I don't know how you ended up in a place where you had nobody to lean on, but you did the best you could for Aiden. And that includes letting him go somewhere he was safe. Many people would have given up, but you picked yourself up and turned things around to get him back. You fought for him."

"If I hadn't fucked up, I wouldn't have had to."

I shrugged. "And if you hadn't met his mum, you wouldn't have had him, and if I'd stayed home on Friday night, we wouldn't be having this conversation now. But those things *did* happen. Maybe you could have played the hand you were dealt better, or maybe you did the best you could with what you had. Thinking about what might have happened won't change it, though. In the time Aiden didn't live with you, you kept on seeing him. And then you brought him home. That tells me more about you than the mistakes you're holding on to."

Cal stared at me for a long moment, and I waited. Eventually, he said, "I can't decide if you're insane or amazing."

"I'm neither. I just think you need to give yourself a break." I reached over and placed a hand on his thigh, and he sighed again.

"Maybe not. He thinks I won't be there for him. How do I fix that?"

I paused. I had some ideas, but I didn't want to overstep. I wasn't even sure if he was actually asking or musing out loud. As if he heard my thoughts, he said, "If you have advice, I'll listen."

"Well... is there any way you could make it so you can collect him from school sometimes? If that is part of the problem, it might help him feel more secure."

Cal shrugged. "I could talk to Guy and see if that's possible. Helen was still going to look after him for me after we move because it seems to work for everyone, but maybe if there were some days I could get him myself..."

"You need to talk to him. Find out what made him feel that way."

His eyes darkened a little as if my words had annoyed him. Like I didn't understand.

"How am I supposed to do that? He doesn't even call me dad."

There was no disguising the way my eyes widened in shock, and he stood up again, my hand dropping from his thigh into the space he'd vacated.

"When he learned to talk, he used to," Cal said, starting to pace slowly. "He knows I'm his dad, but he calls me Cal. When he didn't see me often, and he heard Angela and Simon calling me Cal, he just picked it up. Even though they tried to encourage him to call me dad, he wouldn't. And he still won't."

This time, he turned all the way away from me.

What the hell have I walked into?

Things were weird enough when I'd found out Cal had a son, but it was so much more complicated than that. This was a man I hardly knew telling me that his life had been rough, and that his relationship with his child still was. We'd gone from having fun together to me having to figure out whether I wanted to take all of this on too. I knew too much now for this to be just a casual thing. *And* I was Aiden's teacher.

As I looked at Cal, still facing away from me, I saw a man who was trying his goddamn hardest but who still hadn't forgiven himself for the past. A man who, for whatever reason, no longer had a family.

But I also saw strength. The kind that had kept him fighting for his child.

"I'm scared, Shan. I'm scared that once we're on our own, I won't cope and he'll get taken away again. I'm afraid he'd rather live here or back with his foster family than with me. And I'm scared that all of this stuff..." He paused, and his shoulders sagged. "I hate that you're seeing it and that I'm throwing all this shit on you."

Without a word, I stood and walked over to him, reaching for his arm and gently turning him to face me. His eyes didn't meet mine, though. He kept his gaze over my head. His jaw was clenched, his eyes a little misty. Everything about him told me that he wished he could take back all he'd confessed.

"Cal, if today hadn't happened... if I wasn't Aiden's teacher and we'd kept seeing each other, at some point, this would have had to come out."

He shook his head. "You would have got tired of me before it was even an issue."

My forehead wrinkled into a frown. "You can't possibly know that."

"I can because, at some point, I would have made sure you did."

"So, that's your MO? Find a woman you like having sex with and then push her away when she gets too close? Well, newsflash, Cal. Because of everything that's happened today, I'm already too close." When he still didn't look at me, I took a step back, shaking my head. "You can't have it both ways. Earlier, you said you didn't want whatever this is to be over. But why if you were going to end it at some point anyway?"

Still nothing. His jaw remained clenched, eyes still looking over my head.

My heart sank. This was it. The point when it ended. Disappointment weighed heavy on me, even though I didn't understand why. It shouldn't have made me ache to walk away from him, but as I took a step away, everything in me hurt. It hurt for everything he was going through, and for how lonely he was going to be if he continued to push people out of his life. It hurt for the connection he seemed hellbent on severing.

I didn't want to go. But I couldn't keep standing there when he didn't want to talk anymore.

I made my way to the living room door, and just as I was about to leave, he said, "I'm a fucking mess, Shan." I halted but didn't turn around. "It was better when you didn't know that."

Glancing at him over my shoulder, I said, "You're not a mess. Seems to me like all you've ever done is fight to keep hold of your son. And you won. So what if you slip up sometimes? So what if things aren't all the way together yet? You're trying. That's a lot more than some people do."

He squinted, like he was trying to keep unshed tears from falling. "You sound like Guy."

I turned back around and walked over to him. The second I was close enough, I slipped my hands around his waist, and his whole body relaxed against me. He rested his hands on my hips, then circled them around me, pulling me in tight and resting his chin on the top of my head.

"Can you please promise to stop pushing me away?" I asked into his chest.

Cal breathed in deep, holding me even tighter. "I'll try."

I closed my eyes, inhaling his scent and no longer caring that we had skipped another bunch of getting-to-know-you steps. It seemed whatever this was, it was fast and intense. It didn't scare me the way it should have because as illogical as it was, I *got* him. And he seemed to get me too.

"Where do we go from here?" he asked, and I pulled back a little so I could look up at him.

"I guess we keep doing what we were doing. We go out, spend time together. This doesn't have to change everything, Cal. All it means is that I know you a bit better. That's not a bad thing."

"There's so much more, Shan. So many things you need to know."

"I know. We don't have to rush, though."

He nodded. "We've probably done enough of that."

I chuckled. "Yeah, I would say so."

After looking into my eyes for a moment as if checking it was okay, he leaned down and brushed his lips against mine. I closed my eyes, the feel of his mouth against mine making my heart beat faster, just like it always did. Although, this time, it felt more like he was starting my heart again. It had been frozen in my chest the whole time we'd been talking, unsure if we were going to crash and burn.

As our lips broke apart, he leaned his forehead against mine. "Thank you. For not walking away."

"I'm not going anywhere, Cal. I promise."

And in that moment, I was sure it was a promise I could keep.

I stayed with Cal for another hour, until everything was a little more normal again. He re-heated our lasagna, and we finished eating, talking about far less serious things, and when I left, although exhausted, I was a lot more at ease than when I'd arrived.

Before I drove away, I sat in my car for a few minutes while the heater kicked in, just thinking about all I'd learned.

I didn't just find out about some of Cal's past, I got a much deeper insight into where his head was at. What things he was dealing with. That flicker of insecurity I'd seen over the weekend was much clearer now. As much as he'd hated showing it all to me, I was glad he had. Communication might not have been his strong point, but he was trying, and could I really ask for any more so early in our... whatever we were? Somehow, after all that happened, it felt like we were speeding our way into a relationship.

Everything since the night I'd met him had been completely alien to me. We weren't formally introduced, we'd eyed each other across a pub. He hadn't asked me on a date, he'd taken me home and ravished me all night. We hadn't spent countless hours together figuring out if we were compatible, we'd flirted via text message and then had sex again. It was overwhelming in the best kind of way, and even knowing there were things in his life he wasn't proud of didn't matter. He'd fixed them, so what was the point in looking back?

On paper, Cal and I made no sense whatsoever. Social norms suggested there was nothing we could possibly have in common, and most everything he'd revealed that evening should have backed that up. He had no family around him. He had a 'normal' job. His education was likely basic at best, and he hadn't grown up with any expectations of who he should be. No country club memberships or learning how to network years before networking was necessary. We could not have been more different.

And yet there was something between us that worked. Something that made more sense than it should have. When we'd been talking on Saturday night, Cal had hit upon a truth I'd been slow to see the importance of. That, regardless of where we came from, both of us had found ourselves constantly struggling to be what other people thought we should be. For me, it was fighting against the belief I should have done better with my career choice and be on the constant search for a husband. For Cal, it was trying to fight against judgement and shake off the feelings of inadequacy. We were facing the same issue from different directions, and we'd met in the middle.

A knock on my car window made me shriek and jump in my seat. I turned my head to see Guy's face looking apologetically at me, and I put my hand on my chest, relieved it was him and not some random weirdo.

I pressed the button to open the window a little—it was too cold to open it all the way.

"Sorry," he said, grimacing. "I didn't mean to scare you."

"It's okay." I laughed. "Serves me right for lurking outside your house for so long."

Guy smiled. "It's fine. Listen... I don't know exactly what you and Cal talked about tonight, but whatever you said to him, he looks a lot more relaxed than he did earlier. I know you had some trouble with Aiden today."

I nodded. "Yeah. I'm hoping it will all blow over quickly, though. I think my heart stopped when Cal walked into my classroom earlier."

With a chuckle, Guy said, "Yeah, that was how he felt too." He blew out a breath. "Shannen, Cal can be a lot of things sometimes. Irrational, hot-headed, a fucking idiot... but he's decent. He hasn't cared about anything other than Aiden in a long time. I could tell from the way he flipped out earlier that he likes you, and I'm thinking from the way you look at him, you feel the same."

My cheeks warmed. "I do. And I get it. Sounds like he's been through a lot."

"He has." Guy paused, then said, "I just wanted to say that... if he sometimes finds it hard to tell you what he's thinking, or if he shuts down, it's not because he doesn't care. It's the opposite. He can be hard work sometimes, but he's also loyal as fuck. Just... be patient with him."

I nodded. "I can do that. Thanks, Guy."

"No problem." Guy smiled. "I'd better let you go before you let all the warmth out of the car. It was nice to meet you."

"You too."

As Guy walked away, I got the feeling I had a brand new ally. He didn't say it with words, but I heard the subtext. He was letting me know that he had my back, and that if I needed any help figuring Cal out, he'd be there.

I had a feeling I was going to need him.

Chapter 10

Cal

After checking Aiden was asleep—and thankfully, he was—I'd gone to my room, got changed, and got into bed to think.

Seeing Shannen in that classroom earlier had almost finished me. And when she'd agreed to come over to talk, the only way I could see that going was badly.

We hadn't spent much time talking about the differences between us. In fact, she usually played them down, but everything I had to tell her would make them more obvious. Shannen had a good upbringing. My family was just... normal for some of my life before it all went to hell. But hers was well-off, and they did fancy shit that made no sense to me. Telling her I'd fucked about for most of my life, living off benefits and drinking too much was one of the most humiliating things I'd ever done. And instead of walking out, she waited. She just waited for me to explain the mess I'd made of everything. Even knowing I still had more to tell her hadn't made her back off. She'd said things only Guy had ever said to me, but he was my best mate. He had to be nice to me.

Shannen had no reason to, though. If anything, she had less reason than anyone. Okay, she was Aiden's teacher, so maybe that went some way towards her level of kindness, but she refused to walk away from *me*. A man she barely knew but seemed to want to get to know better.

In the dark, I let out a long sigh, unsure what I'd done to deserve that. Would she still want to stay around when she'd had time to think over everything I'd told her? When she wasn't looking at me?

A knock at my bedroom door interrupted my thoughts, and I said, "Yeah?"

Guy peered around the door. "Can I come in?" When I nodded, he stepped inside. "Are you okay?"

Nodding again, I turned onto my side to look at him, eyeing him for a moment. "Yeah. I think I am."

"Do you feel better now she knows?"

That was a big question. In a way, yes. That was one less thing I was keeping from her. In another way, I was afraid she was going to call me in the morning and say she'd changed her mind about me.

"She took it pretty well," I said. "So... yeah. I guess so. I'm just not sure how things will be between us now. Whether she'll still see me the same way."

Taking another step into the room, Guy said, "You offloaded a lot on her. I don't think she'll see you in the exact same way, but that doesn't mean she'll like you any less."

"She said it just means she knows me a bit better, but they aren't the best things to know about me." I sighed, doubts creeping over me. Should I call her? Make sure I hadn't misunderstood anything? Fixing my eyes on Guy, I said, "Maybe you already know what she thinks. Is there any reason you went outside to talk to my... to Shannen?"

Guy raised an eyebrow. "You saw that?"

"I was closing the curtains and I saw you talking to her, yeah." I wasn't sure why he'd gone out there, but I didn't care that he had. What I didn't know was whether he'd intended to tell me, and now I'd taken the decision away from him.

He looked down at the floor, taking a deep breath before looking up at me. "Not gonna lie, I was worried about you. And about what she might be thinking. But as it turns out, there was no need. You were right about her, Cal. She *is* sweet."

I threw him a small smile. "Yeah. She is. What did she say?"

"That she likes you and she understands why you didn't tell her the truth right away."

That helped to ease my worries a bit, but it had all only just happened. In the morning, or in a few days, would she feel the same?

"Do you think me being involved with her is a mistake?" I asked, leaning up on my elbow. "She's a teacher with a posh family, and I'm just some idiot with a long line of mistakes following me around."

"That's not how she sees you." Guy shook his head as he spoke. "When you told me what little you know about her family, I thought maybe she was some spoilt brat looking for a bit of fun with someone she considered beneath her before getting married off to some rich man with a fancy house. But she isn't that. She really does like you. So... give her a chance. Don't let what *you* think about everything that's happened ruin it."

I nodded slowly. "I think you two might be related. You both say the same kinds of things."

Guy laughed. "Well, maybe if there are two of us telling you, you'll listen."

I pulled my face into a sceptical grin. "Don't count on it."

But I couldn't stop myself from chuckling too. I'd got through one of the roughest conversations I'd ever had. If Shannen could handle that, maybe she could handle everything else I would have to tell her in time.

⚜

The few days that followed were the craziest I'd had in a long time. My workmates and I spent most of the week getting my new place ready for us to move in on Saturday. Guy knew people who could sort out the plumbing in the kitchen and bathroom. He didn't do as many hands-on jobs anymore, but he helped me with the decorating, and even though it was still furnitureless, it was coming together nicely.

Guy and I stood in my new living room, breathing in the scent of new carpet and the slight lingering smell of fresh paint, and he grinned at me.

"Are you ready for this?" he asked.

The truth was, I hadn't been sure about it. I knew I wouldn't be until everything was moved in and I'd gotten used to being the one solely responsible for Aiden again. But at that moment, looking around at the geometric grey and silver wallpaper and the pale grey-painted walls around me, it felt great knowing this was my space now. My own place.

"I think I am," I said with a nod. "I just hope Aiden settles down okay." He still hadn't seen the flat since we'd only just finished it. I had taken him shopping after school the day before, and while we hadn't been able to find *Toy Story* wallpaper, we did find some posters from the movie, which Guy had framed and they now hung on the light blue walls in his room.

Since the incident at school on Monday, Aiden had grown increasingly restless, both at school and at home, although he hadn't hurt anyone else. The parents of the kid he'd pushed accepted our apology, and the boy didn't seem too worried about being around Aiden again. But Shannen had let me know that Aiden was getting frustrated over small tasks in class, and he'd been the same at home.

I still hadn't found a way to talk to him about it, which led to my own frustration, and Guy and Helen had both said he was probably feeling my stress on top of his own. All that did was add to the feeling of being a shitty dad.

"He'll be fine," Guy said, slapping me on the shoulder. "You're going to pick him up from school in a bit, right?"

I looked at my watch. I had about forty-five minutes before I had to set off. This would be my first time picking him up. I'd told him that morning I'd be there, and he'd just nodded. It didn't feel like he didn't believe me, but he didn't seem especially excited about it either.

"Yeah," I said. "I thought we'd go and have a kick about in the park for a bit. Tire him out so he'll go to bed on time."

Wiggling his eyebrows at me, Guy said, "And are you looking forward to seeing Shannen tomorrow?"

I rolled my eyes at him. "We're going out for a drink. No need for the eyebrow wiggling."

If my dick could have groaned at that fact, it would have. I hadn't seen her all week because we'd both been busy. Me with the new flat and her with work. The night she was available was the one night neither Guy nor Helen could watch Aiden. Okay, it had only been three days, and we'd spoken on the phone every night, but... fuck, I'd missed her.

You haven't even known her for a full week yet, you prick. Missing her should not be possible.

But somehow, it felt like I hadn't seen her in years.

"If it wasn't for the fact that Aiden doesn't know about us, I'd have said she could come over to your place, but I can't risk him waking up and seeing her there."

It was something Shannen and I had talked about because I wanted to do what was right for Aiden. He was still getting used to *me*. Aiden and I had a long way to go until we were the picture-perfect father and son. And with Shannen being his teacher, we didn't want him to be confused by it all. It would be weird for him knowing her as one thing during the week and someone else at the weekend. For the time being, Shannen and I just wanted to focus on getting to know each other without involving Aiden, just in case something went wrong.

"We don't mind you going out tomorrow night," Guy said. "It'll be the last time you can easily do so for a while, so make the most of it. We'll keep him happy."

I looked at Guy. "*Is* he happy? I mean, really happy. You've seen how he's been this week. He doesn't want to leave you and Helen."

Guy's eyes flitted around the room. "It's a shame the sofa and chairs aren't here yet, then we could sit." After a moment, he shrugged and sat down on the floor, then gestured for me to join him. When I did, stretching my legs out in front of me, he said, "He's been through a lot, Cal. It's not about leaving me and Helen, it's about moving to another place and things being different again."

I shook my head. "It's not just that. Sometimes, I think... I told you what he thinks. He doesn't think I'll be there for him."

"But today you're going to show him that you will be. You're going to be getting him from school on Mondays, Thursdays, and Fridays like you promised him, and Helen will get him the other days as normal and take him to ours until you've finished work. You have to build the trust. And you need to talk to him and find out what's made him feel like that because you haven't let him down. You've always done what's best for him."

"I've tried to, but that doesn't mean it was always enough."

Guy leaned back on his hands, his eyes on me. "Cal, that little boy loves you. When you're playing together, his eyes light up. He likes being with you. But you need to..." He trailed off, shaking his head.

I knew why. Guy was always the person I went to for advice, but I wasn't very good at accepting it when I didn't ask. Especially on a subject like parenting; something he hadn't experienced himself. He was great with Aiden, but I couldn't pretend I didn't sometimes shut down when someone was telling me what I should be better at. It wasn't like I didn't know already. I just didn't like hearing it because if other people could see it, it was just another way I was screwing up.

"I know," I said, looking at him. "I know."

I needed to be better at talking to him, and doing things with him when he asked me to, and finding out what was bothering him, and making him understand I would be there for him.

I needed to be less like an uncle and more like a dad.

"You won't be on your own, Cal," Guy said. "We're still here for you anytime."

Guy really meant what he'd said, but it was time for me to stop relying on him. It was time for me to figure out how to be the best father I could be. I just hoped I could do it without my temper and doubts getting in the way.

Chapter 12

Cal

When I pulled the van up outside Guy's house, I could already feel the headache coming on. All the way home, I'd prepared myself for the epic tantrum I knew was waiting for me. I should have been out with Shannen. Should have been enjoying a couple of hours with her before the craziness of moving out of Guy's place. Instead, I was called back to face yet another fight with my son. Another conversation we'd had over and over yet did nothing to make him feel better. I was out of ideas and words, but that didn't matter. I still had to try again, even though every repeated discussion sucked the life out of me a bit more.

I turned to look at Shannen. On the drive back, she hadn't said much. She'd just kept her hand on my leg as if to remind me she was there. She seemed to know without me telling her that I didn't have it in me to make random small talk. I was preserving the limited energy and patience I had left for when I went inside.

"I guess we'd better say goodbye here," she said, offering a sad smile.

I nodded. I would have done just about anything to have an hour with her. Even ten more minutes would have been better than what we had.

When she'd said earlier that she'd missed me, it surprised me. I never thought it was possible to miss someone after just a few days, especially since that was about the same length of time we'd known each other, but she'd proved me wrong. I'd nervously anticipated seeing her all day, wondering if she only wanted me to go to her place so she could end things with me face to face. She'd shown no signs of it when we'd spoken, but she was polite and thoughtful, and maybe in her world, you just didn't dump someone over the phone. Guy had found it fucking hilarious to see me so wound up, and I was dangerously close to giving him a black eye. None of this was like me. Not seeing a woman more than once, and definitely not giving a fuck what they thought about me. Knowing she'd missed me too had calmed me down, while also making me wonder again what the hell she saw in me.

I unclipped my seatbelt, then leaned over and did the same to Shannen's. I moved across to the middle of the seat to get as close to her as I could. "I'll make this up to you as soon as I can," I told her, kissing her gently.

She shook her head. "You don't need to make anything up to me."

"Bet you wish you'd gone on Jade's blind date now." I was mostly joking, but a small part of me wondered how much of my shit she would put up with before realising she could do better. She had the chance to be set up with someone who could give her the kind of lifestyle she was used to, but she'd turned it down, and all she'd got instead was a ride in my van.

Shannen's mouth brushed over mine again. "Forty-five minutes with you, even if it was mostly driving around, was better than anything she could have planned for me."

I closed my eyes, letting out a sigh. I had to stop myself from sitting back in my seat and driving away with her.

"Come on," she said, kissing my cheek. "You'd better get inside."

With another deep exhale, I moved back across to my side and we both got out of the van. When Shannen walked around to the path where I was waiting for her, she took my hand as we headed towards the house. At the door, I said, "I would invite you in, but..."

She nodded. "I know. I can wait here."

I wrapped my arms around her, wishing I could keep her curvy frame against me for longer, and she hugged me back tightly. "I'll call you once I get Aiden settled, okay?"

"Okay." She smiled up at me. "Everything will be okay, you know."

"I hope so." I kissed her one more time before letting her go. "Guy won't be long."

I took the two steps up and opened the front door, and two things happened at once.

Helen shouted, "Aiden, stop!" and Aiden barrelled into me in his dinosaur pyjamas, running straight into my legs before I could get inside.

"Whoa," I said. "What's going on?" I attempted to pick him up, but he wriggled out of my grip and turned to glare at Helen.

"He saw the van out the window and he was about to run out of the door when you opened it," Helen said, her face flushed with panic. He'd never done that before, and she was right to look stressed. If I hadn't been in the way, he could have run into the road.

"I guess we need to start locking the door," Guy said, appearing behind Helen.

I looked back down at Aiden, ready to take him back into the house, but he was staring at Shannen.

Oh, for fuck's sake.

"Hi, Aiden," she said, crouching down in front of him.

"Why are you at my house?" he asked. His tone wasn't as rude as I was expecting. It was as if her presence had distracted him from his rage.

She glanced up at me, unsure what to tell him.

I lowered down to their level too and said, "Miss Morgan is my... friend." I flicked my gaze to her, and she smiled.

"Are you here because I was naughty?" he asked her, and she shook her head.

"No, sweetie. I just came to see your daddy."

"Oh. Okay. You can come in then."

Aiden walked back into the house, leaving the rest of us looking at each other in surprise.

"What just happened?" Guy asked.

"I think my being here shocked him," Shannen said, standing back up, and I did the same. "But I should go and leave you to it."

"No," I said quickly. "I mean, you can go if you want to, but... Aiden has seen you now. Maybe you could stay for a while."

She drew in a breath. "I'd like to, but I don't know if it might be too much for him. There's already so much going on."

I hadn't turned around to look back into the house yet, but I could feel Helen's stare piercing the side of my head, warning me not to let her come in for the exact reason Shannen had said. It *was* too much. Aiden needed to go back to bed, and I had to make sure he calmed down, but once he had... why *couldn't* I spend time with Shannen? If I had to stay in, why couldn't she be with me? It wasn't how the night was meant to go, but like I'd said, Aiden had seen her. He didn't know we were dating, but he didn't seem traumatised by her being at the house.

"Please, Shan," I said, no longer caring if I sounded like I was begging. We'd both been waiting all week, and I knew she didn't want to leave yet either. "Please."

Her eyes softened, and she nodded. "Okay."

I reached for her hand and led her inside. Guy had already gone back into the house, but Helen remained by the door, watching Shannen and me closely. Her expression wasn't welcoming, but she moved aside to let us in.

Once we were in the hallway, the door closed and locked, Shannen's apprehension was so strong I could feel it. She had spotted Helen eyeing her, and it clearly made her uncomfortable.

"Come on," I said. "Let's go into the living room."

She smiled up at me, and I took her coat and bag, then removed my jacket and hung them up on the hook beside the shoe cupboard before walking down the hallway, Shannen's hand in mine again. I should have offered an introduction to

Helen, but I didn't like the way she was looking at Shannen. Besides, it wasn't as if they didn't know who the other was.

In the living room, Aiden was trying to pull out a board game from the cabinet under the TV, and Guy was asking him to put it back. As Shannen and I entered the room, Guy looked up at us and shrugged, at a loss for what to do. Usually, Aiden listened when one of us told him to do something. It often led to some kind of tantrum, but he still always did what he was told, even if there was a fight about it. He never ignored us, though.

"Aiden," I said. "Put that back, please. We're not playing now. It's bedtime."

He continued to act like I wasn't there, sitting on the floor with the box on his lap. Contempt was written all over his face, and Guy stepped around him, leaving me to it and joining Helen in the kitchen.

"Aiden," I said again, a little more firmly. "Stop pretending you can't hear me. Put the game away."

When he lifted the lid off the box, my temper flared. My shoulders tensed and my jaw clenched, but I breathed through it. I hated shouting at him, and with Shannen there, I really didn't want this to be the time my anger got away from me. I had never laid a finger on Aiden, but yelling at him wasn't good either. That was something I'd been guilty of when things got too much in the past, and I was working hard on changing it.

For days, I'd tried to get him to calm down, to accept the move. To just freaking behave. But he'd become increasingly difficult as the week went on. I was at the end of my rope, not helped by being called back home when I was trying to have a couple of hours to myself before everything changed in the morning.

I walked over to where he sat, picking up the box lid with one hand and attempting to take the game from Aiden's lap with the other. As I did so, he whacked the bottom of the box with force from underneath. His move caused the game board to fall and the game's pieces to fly up in the air and then scatter across the floor, showering us in coloured counters, some of which hit me in the face.

I tugged the box from his grip and flung it onto the floor behind me, the rest of the pieces tumbling out onto the carpet. "Get upstairs, now," I snapped, trying to cling onto what was left of my composure, which wasn't much.

"NO!" Aiden shouted as I straightened up. The glare he gave me hurt me as much as it angered me. He looked at me like he hated me, and it wasn't the first time. I had no idea if other kids looked at their parents that way when they weren't getting what they wanted, but it made me want to smash the house up in frustration because... why wouldn't he just listen?

Why did he hate me so much?

Did he hate me?

"Aiden." I lowered down to his level to meet his eye, my tone tense. "Go to your room."

His glare held firm as he screamed out, "No!" then picked up a handful of the fallen counters and launched them at me.

None of it physically hurt me, but the disrespect and clear defiance pushed me over the edge, and I turned away from him, anger threatening to explode, just as he stood up and ran out of the room.

When he was gone, I kicked the board game across the floor, flinging whatever pieces were left in the box all over the place. My heart was pounding furiously, and as I turned, I caught the look on Shannen's face.

I could tell from the way her chest was rising and falling rapidly that my outburst had scared her, but she didn't *look* afraid. She looked... pained. Like what she had just witnessed had hurt her, and I hated it. Hated that I'd upset her and that she'd seen me losing it. Hated that I had no way to deal with Aiden when he kicked off like this.

"Are you gonna report me now for being a bad father?" I sneered, unable to stop the asshole in me from slipping out when what I'd meant to do was apologise. To go to her and tell her this wasn't me. This wasn't who I was, but why would she believe me? Seven days wasn't enough to show her that.

It wasn't as if I hadn't warned her what a disaster I was, though.

"Don't do that," she said, her voice shaking slightly. "Don't use my job against me because you lost your temper. That's not fair."

"That's what you people do, though, isn't it? Do-gooders who report every little thing."

What the fuck is wrong with you?

I didn't mean a single word that fell from my mouth, but it was too late. They were out there and I couldn't take them back. It was as if my brain had gone into freefall without my permission, trying to force her away because that was my go-to. Never letting anyone get close to me because it wasn't worth the eventual pain it would cause. I didn't want to do that with her, but something had taken over, reverting to my typical way of handling things.

I watched as she silently seethed on the spot, taking a few deep breaths before she spoke. "I know you've had a tough time, but do not use me to vent your lingering anger at the people who took Aiden from you. I am *not* them. And if you're afraid I'll see something that could get you into trouble, then stop doing those things."

The tears sparkling in her deep blue eyes brought me to my knees in a way I never thought possible, and I shook my head. "Shan, I swear to God, I have never, ever hurt Aiden. I wouldn't do that to him. And I wouldn't hurt you either."

A single tear dripped onto her cheek, like the shock and speed of my outburst was sinking in, and I walked back to her, my chest aching.

"Shit," I huffed out, shaking my head again. "I'm sorry. I'm so sorry."

Shannen dropped her head back, blowing out a breath to calm herself before looking at me. "Don't ever speak to me that way again, Cal. Please." She paused, exhaling slowly one more time. "I won't be blamed for things that happened to you that have nothing to do with me."

I swallowed past the lump in my throat because her shining blue eyes were cutting into me so much that I could barely stay upright. "I don't even know why I said that. Everything just... it's too much sometimes, you know? The last few weeks have taken everything out of me. And sometimes, it's just easier to be a prick because then there's nobody around for me to disappoint."

"And what about Aiden? Are you planning to push him away too?"

She was calling me out, and I didn't want to hear it. Didn't want to hear the same things Guy and Helen had said to me so many times. They had never been in my position. And neither had Shannen. They didn't know how fucking much I wanted to do the best for my kid after I'd let him down so badly when he was a baby. How much I wanted to have a better relationship with him. I just couldn't figure out how to make it happen, and it was turning me into an angry dickhead.

"I don't want to push him away," I said through gritted teeth.

And I don't want to push you away either.

I took a small step closer to her, hoping she wouldn't move away. When she didn't, I reached out to brush a tear from her cheek with my thumb. As I went to pull my hand away, she caught it in hers, holding it in place against her face.

"Cal, I am stubborn as hell, and I won't be pushed away. But I won't be your whipping boy either. I can deal with you shouting, and I can even deal with you shutting down if it helps you to figure out what you want to say. What I won't put up with is you making assumptions about what I'm thinking and treating me like I'm the enemy because of my job. If I thought for a second that Aiden or I were in any kind of danger, I wouldn't still be here. But you didn't hurt him. You didn't touch him, and you didn't yell at him."

"I lost my temper. I shouldn't have thrown the game."

"No. You shouldn't. He doesn't need to be seeing that. But I'm not concerned for his safety. I'm concerned about you."

Relief rushed through me. She had more understanding than I deserved. Even though we were opposites in so many ways, she wasn't judging my piss-poor behaviour. She wasn't looking down on me. If anything, it was like she was looking past what I showed on the surface to see if there was something in there worth sticking around for. For whatever reason, she'd decided there was.

I just wasn't sure if she was right.

"We can talk later," she said gently. "Right now, though, you need to go and sort things out with Aiden."

I was about to speak when a loud crash from upstairs made us jump. Instinct made us both run out of the room and up the stairs, crashes continuing as I rushed down the hallway to Aiden's room. We skidded to a halt at his door. Although Aiden and I were moving out, we'd agreed to leave some of his stuff behind so he still had his own room at Guy and Helen's. While most of his toys and clothes had gone to the new place, there was plenty remaining, and the first crash had come from him pulling his toy chest over. The rest came from him standing amongst the debris, throwing handfuls of Lego and action figures at the walls and the wardrobe, and he was about to fling a hard rubber ball at the window, when Shannen said, "Aiden, stop."

My head was still pounding from what had occurred downstairs, and I was glad Shannen took control because I'd run out of... everything.

Aiden spun around, hand still up, poised to throw the ball. Angry tears streamed down his face, rage in his gaze as he looked at Shannen and then me. Deep in his brown eyes, though, I could see his frustration and sadness, and it broke my fucking heart.

Aiden threw the ball down hard, but it just bumped against the mass of toys at his feet, and he dropped down amongst them, his little chin wobbling, even though he was clearly still angry.

I slumped back against the wall beside his bedroom door, casting my eyes upwards. I didn't have the strength left in me to go another round with him. He could keep yelling all night and I didn't know how to stop it. I wanted to go into his room and talk to him, but I was exhausted.

Nobody tells you how hard parenting is. Especially if you have to do it alone. The truth was, if it weren't for Guy and Helen, I wouldn't have been able to get Aiden back, let alone keep him. Without them, he'd probably have been back in foster care. Not because I didn't want him but because being everything for someone who is dependent on you... it's a challenge, and one I never expected to take on. I'd been holding it together for weeks, and the last seven days had seen the rope I was clinging onto fraying dangerously. I wanted to fix things with my boy, but sometimes I wondered if the distance between us was too wide to bridge.

Shannen lightly touched my arm. "Please can I go to him?"

I nodded without looking at her, grateful but unable to express it. She squeezed my arm like she understood why I'd frozen before stepping into Aiden's bedroom. After a moment, I heard a soft crunching sound, like plastic under her boots, and then a shuffling sound as if she'd sat down amongst the wreckage.

"Go away," Aiden said, though there was no strength to his words.

"What's going on, sweetheart?" Shannen's voice was soft. "Why were you throwing your toys around?"

"Cal told me off," he muttered.

Cal. Every time he called me that, it was like being punched in the gut. I was his dad, for fuck's sake. Even if he didn't like me sometimes, that was who I was. I hated my father, but I still called him Dad. If I'd called him by his first name, he'd have knocked my head off.

"Why did he tell you off?" I heard Shannen ask.

"Because I didn't do as I was told."

"Look at me, Aiden." I could picture his face in my mind. His chin trembling as he tried to pretend he wasn't upset. I'd seen it before a thousand times. "You know you shouldn't throw and break things when you get angry."

"Cal threw my game because he was angry."

I winced. He wasn't wrong, and guilt crashed over me. I was setting a crap example. How could I expect him to behave well when I was throwing things around too?

"And that was wrong of him," Shannen said. "He owes you an apology, but you need to say sorry to him too for your behaviour."

"He deserved it!" Aiden snapped. "He's ruining everything!"

Tears pricked at my eyes, and I blinked them back.

Don't cry, you fucking wimp. Grow up! My dad's words beat at me, and I took some deep breaths, trying to make them stop pounding at my brain.

I was just like him. A short fuse that could spark at any second. The difference was, I would never lay a hand on my kid, and I would never tell him not to cry.

But then... could Aiden tell when I was trying not to be upset? Was that why he did the same with me? It wasn't that he never cried in front of me, but when he got like this, so out of control, he resorted to rage first. Was that something I'd unintentionally taught him?

I'd never felt more useless. I didn't deserve to be his dad when I couldn't even get myself under control.

"What do you mean?" Shannen asked, distracting me.

"He's making us go to a different house!" There was a light crashing sound, like he'd thrown something small; probably some Lego bricks. "I don't want to go!"

"Why not? Your daddy told me that in your new place, you're going to have a *Toy Story* bedroom and a special new bed that's high up. And all of your favourite toys will be there."

Her words elicited a little bit of warmth inside me. I'd upset her, made her feel shitty, but she was in there doing me a favour. It wasn't all for me, I knew that. She was there for Aiden more than me, but she hadn't written me off yet.

"I like it here." There was a moment of quiet, then he let out a loud sob that stabbed at my chest.

There was a short pause before Shannen said, "It's okay to be sad, Aiden. Everyone gets sad sometimes." I didn't hear what Aiden said, but Shannen continued, "Oh, yes, they do. Do you know what makes me sad?" Another pause. "When I don't have any chocolate ice cream left. That makes me *really* sad."

The sound of Aiden's laugh, even if it was a little one, was the best sound I could have heard in that moment. "That makes me sad too," he said. There was a slight shuffling sound, and then Aiden said, "Miss Morgan?"

"Yes, sweetheart?"

"I'm frightened."

I braced myself, waiting for him to say he was afraid of my temper. Afraid of me when I shouted at him. I really had never laid a hand on him. I didn't even get angry in front of him that often, but maybe the few times I had were enough to make him not want to be with me.

"What are you frightened of?" Shannen asked.

"Before, I had to go away from Cal. But when we lived with Guy and Helen, we could all stay together."

Brow furrowed at his words, I finally peeled myself away from the wall and turned to stand in Aiden's bedroom doorway. The floorboards creaked beneath my feet, and Shannen looked up and saw me. Aiden was sitting on her lap, curled into her, and she held him tightly.

Katie had never held him that way. At least not after the first six months or so. He was a novelty in the beginning. Something cute to show off when she was in town. People often wanted to look at a new baby and talk about how cute he was, and she liked that. But after a while, she got bored of him. People were less interested as he got bigger, and she even said once or twice how dull it was to have a baby. I never thought she would walk out on him, though.

Yet there was Shannen, holding my son while he snuggled into her, upset and afraid. I guessed it was easy for her to be that way with him since she already knew him. As I looked at her taking care of him, some of the ache in my chest eased.

She offered me a small smile before turning her attention back to Aiden. "What do you mean?"

"When I was little, I lived with different people. Angela and Simon told me my daddy couldn't look after me, but then we lived in Guy's house and nobody took me away. I don't want to go away again."

Another sharp pain hit me in the chest. Was he saying that it wasn't me he was afraid of, but that he didn't want to be taken away from me again? I wasn't sure how much he remembered or understood about the time he was in foster care, but it was likely a lot more than I'd realised.

Shannen glanced at me again, gesturing for me to go in and talk to Aiden. To tell him what he needed to hear. I shook my head.

I wanted to go to him, but I didn't know what to say to him. Didn't know how to talk to him about important stuff like this. I couldn't go in there and promise him that he wouldn't get taken away from me because... what if I actually couldn't cope? Then I would just break his trust in me all over again.

"Please," Shannen mouthed.

With apprehension, I walked into the room, and when my foot caught on a toy, Aiden's head whipped up. His eyes were red where he'd rubbed them to dry his tears.

I lowered myself down to the floor beside Shannen and held my arms out to Aiden. Aiden shuffled across to me and sat on my outstretched legs, on my knees, facing me.

Shannen pushed herself up from the floor, ruffling Aiden's hair and giving me a comforting smile before she left the room.

The second she was gone, I wished she hadn't. Now it was just me and Aiden, and I was stuck in the same position I always was. Not knowing how to talk to him. Shannen had got him to open up immediately, and I had no idea how she did it. I'd asked him so many times why he didn't want to move. He always just said he didn't want to leave Guy and Helen and he liked his bedroom. He'd never mentioned being scared of getting taken away from me.

What was I doing so wrong that he couldn't have told *me* that? And if not me, why not Guy or Helen?

I reached out and pulled him a bit further towards me. As I did, he came even closer, twisting around to the side so he could sit on me the way he'd sat on Shannen, his head resting against my chest. He pulled his knees up to his chin and wound one arm around my neck.

He hardly ever did this. It was another thing that had got lost after he was taken away. Even though I'd seen him the whole time he was gone, hugs had been rare. I was scared he wouldn't want them from the man who gave him up, so I never tried. Even though we played together and I was allowed to take him out to the park eventually, all that time, I hardly ever reached out beyond giving him a kiss on the cheek or the head when I arrived and left. Then, when he moved in with me, Guy, and Helen, I wanted to fix that gap between us, I just didn't know how. We'd progressed to him holding my hand when we were out and him sitting on my lap to play a game or watch a movie, but nothing like this.

But how could he be like this when I never let him know it was okay to want a hug sometimes, especially when he was sad?

Useless, useless, useless.

I wrapped an arm around Aiden, relishing the moment of affection from my boy. "I'm sorry, buddy," I told him.

He lifted his head to look at me, his brown eyes still glistening a little with new tears. "I'm sorry for not listening and for making a mess."

"It's okay." I took a deep breath, realising just how much he'd grown. I knew he was growing physically by how often he needed new clothes, but it was the little overlooked things I hadn't seen day to day. His eyes were a shade darker, and in them, there was so much. Things he'd learned, things he was thinking, things he didn't want to share. Things that weren't in them when he was so small because he hadn't had as many experiences. I hated that I'd contributed to some of the bad. It cut me to the core that I'd been so slow to see that he had opinions now. And that he hadn't felt like he could come and tell me about them.

"I heard what you said to Miss Morgan," I said, stroking his hair. "The thing is, though... this isn't our home. Guy helped me to get a new one just for me and you."

"Doesn't he want us to live here anymore?"

I shook my head. "No, it's not that. It's just that, you and me, we need to have our own place now. It's different than before. When you were a baby…" I paused, taking another deep breath. I didn't want to talk about Katie. He had asked Helen about his mum when he discovered other kids had a whole different family unit than he did, and she'd told him that his mummy lived in a different place. He didn't ask any more, and I didn't know how to explain it. He seemed too young to understand. One day, I would have to tackle it, but this wasn't the time. "When you were a baby, I didn't have a job or a nice place to live. I didn't have enough money to take care of you properly. I didn't want you to go away, I just couldn't look after you, and Angela and Simon could. But it's different now. I have a job, and our new flat is awesome. I promise that, even though we won't live with Guy and Helen anymore, I will never let anyone take you away again."

As much as I had been, and still was, afraid to make him a promise, I realised I had to. Not just for him, but for me. I had to grow up and be what he needed. And what he needed was someone who could reassure him when he was afraid.

"You promise?" Aiden asked, his eyes wide with hope. "Because I like living with you."

His words made me smile, and I kissed the top of his head. "I like living with you too, little dude. And yes, I promise."

Aiden stared up at me for a moment as if looking for a sign on my face that I was lying to him. After a while, he nodded and snuggled back into me again.

I rested my cheek on top of his head as I held him tight. I wasn't stupid enough to think that everything between us was fixed now or that he was going to be totally relaxed about the move. But a tiny barrier had broken down, and I knew now that he wouldn't prefer to be with someone else.

Had he been testing me the whole time? Did he think that if he pushed me hard enough, I'd give him up again? Was that what he'd been doing with me, especially over the last few weeks?

I hoped my inclination to do the same thing wasn't rubbing off on him, but… maybe I was doing it to him too. Not testing him, but fighting against getting closer to him in case it all went to shit again.

In case I lost him again.

Wasn't that what Guy had been trying to tell me? That I needed to reach out to Aiden. Not just for the fun stuff, which was where I excelled. That I had to talk to him and find out the deeper things he was worried about.

I was the adult, and I was letting my son drown in his worries because I was as afraid as he was.

"Aiden," I said, unwrapping my arms a little and leaning back so I could look at him. "If you ever get frightened or sad again, it's okay to talk to me about it so I can try to make it better."

He nodded and gave me a little smile. "Okay."

A huge wave of love for him washed over me, and I kissed the top of his head. "Now, we need to get these toys tidied and get you to bed."

Chapter 11

Shannen

I couldn't remember ever being more relieved for Friday to roll around. It had been a long week between finding out about Cal being Aiden's dad, Aiden acting up in class, and my general workload taking over. All I'd wanted to do the whole week was see Cal, even if only for an hour, but with him getting ready to move, it had been impossible.

As I finished getting ready, dabbing on the slightest bit of lip gloss, I couldn't help reeling a little at the whirlwind of the past seven days.

At that exact same time one week before, I didn't even know Cal existed. One evening of conversation followed by a night of never-ending orgasms and then one hell of a bombshell on Monday had taken me from *single* to *it's complicated* in a freakishly short time.

But it wasn't really *that* complicated. I'd spent a lot of time trying to figure out why I hadn't backed away from Cal. It wasn't until I called Jade on Tuesday to let her know that I wouldn't be going to her 'dinner party' that it became clear.

Maybe the guy she'd picked this time didn't sound as bad as the others, but it was still the same drill once you started to date someone in my usual social circles. Dates were often unnecessarily lavish, and the moment anyone got wind of it, the questions began. *Is it serious? Do you think he's the one? When do you think he'll propose?* Even though the process of dating was slow, the whole world wanted to rush it ahead so the next big wedding could be organised and new connections could be made. With Cal, it was a different kind of speedy. Things had moved so fast that my head was still spinning. It was exciting, even though the things I'd learned about him were pretty heavy. We weren't being forced together, we were drawn to each other. Spending time together because it felt good and not because people were trying to hurry us down the aisle. I didn't have to worry about whether I was making the right impression on an eligible bachelor; I could just be me.

Jade had been fuming when I'd told her I'd chosen to spend the evening with 'the painter and decorator' over her detective. So much so that she cancelled our regular lunch date on Saturday. It was as if she thought doing so would make me change my mind, but she severely underestimated the pull of a simple drink with a man who didn't bore me senseless.

The knock at my door made my heart flip and butterflies flapped around in my stomach. My heart rate picked up as I walked to the door, and I took a couple of deep breaths to calm myself down. The effect just thinking about Cal had on me was intense, and when I finally saw him after what felt like forever, a sigh of relief slipped from me. He stood there in black jeans and a dark green shirt, his leather jacket over the top, looking and smelling utterly delicious.

Cal flashed me the half-smile I was growing to love so much. "Hey. You look incredible."

I'd dressed pretty casually in blue jeans, a close-fitting grey jumper, and my trusty black knee-high boots, but the way he was looking at me made me feel like I was the best thing ever.

I grinned up at him. "Thank you." I stepped aside so he could come in, and the moment the door was closed, he pulled me against him, his hands on my ass as he held me close. I rose up on my tiptoes to circle my arms around his neck. Taking me by surprise, he lowered his hands a little then lifted me, wrapping my legs around his waist as he pressed his lips to mine. I giggled against his mouth. I'd waited for this all week, and joy radiated from me just from being close to him again.

I was like a giddy teenager, but I simply did not care. Because when our lips parted, the sparkle in his eyes told me I wasn't feeling it alone.

"I missed you," I whispered.

He swallowed hard, his eyes on mine. Nodding once, he said, "I missed you too."

Something about the way he was looking at me made me think that had been hard for him to say. Not because he didn't mean it, but because... maybe it was something he hadn't said or felt too often. Without making a big deal of it, I brushed my lips against his once more before he lowered me back to the ground.

"So, are you ready to go?" he asked.

I nodded, grabbing my jacket from the hook by the door and shrugging into it. "I am."

"I'm sorry this will only be a quick one. I just don't want to leave Guy and Helen watching Aiden for too long. I put him to bed before I left, but I don't know if he'll stay there. He was in a horrible mood after school. He's still stressing out about the move tomorrow." Cal's expression fell somewhere between guilt at going out and disappointment that he couldn't stay with me for longer. As much as I wished we could repeat the events of the previous Friday, Aiden had to come first, even more so since he was struggling.

"It's okay," I told him, reaching for his hand. "Let's just go and enjoy the time we have."

He smiled and squeezed my hand. "Yeah."

I picked up my bag and pulled out my keys to lock the door behind us. As we stepped outside, Cal said, "I hope you don't mind going out in my van tonight. A car is the next thing I want to get after the move, but until then, all I have is my work van. Unless you want to take your car."

Laughing, I locked up and put my keys back in my bag. "I've never been in a van before, but I'll go with it."

"It's clean." Cal took my hand again as we began to walk down the stairs. "At least in the front. I even took out all the empty crisp packets before I came over."

When he grinned, I laughed again. "I appreciate it. Although, my own car isn't totally crisp packet-free. And maybe the occasional chocolate bar wrapper gets left behind."

"Ohh." Cal chuckled. "So, Little Miss Organised isn't so organised after all!"

Due to my job, I *had* to be organised, and Cal had been amused when I'd told him how everything down to the emails on my laptop were arranged so I could find them easily. Keeping things tidy simply made my life easier. That just didn't necessarily extend to always throwing out junk food wrappers from my car.

"I have my moments," I said, shivering as we stepped out into the cold night air. Cal let go of my hand and wrapped his arm around me. I snuggled into his warmth, breathing in his scent as I did.

He led me to a red Citroen Dispatch van emblazoned with Guy's company logo Hue Got It.

"Good name," I said as Cal unlocked the van and opened the passenger side for me.

He helped me up the step and inside. "Can't say Guy doesn't have a sense of humour."

"That's for sure."

While Cal shut the door and walked around to the driver's side, I couldn't help but be impressed by how tidy it was in there. There was also a car air freshener hanging up that smelled like leather, and I leaned forward to inhale it as Cal got into his seat.

"You really like the smell of leather, huh?" My cheeks warmed, and he laughed. "Don't think I don't see you sniffing my jacket."

"It's a nice smell," I admitted, my gaze meeting his. "Kinda... sexy."

His eyes flashed in the darkness. "Are you sure you want to go out tonight?" A smile played on his lips, and for a second, I was tempted to get out of the van and drag him back upstairs.

"I would like to take you back inside, but then I *really* wouldn't want to let you go," I told him, leaning in to kiss him.

Being close to him was an instant turn-on, and while we'd spent a lot of time the previous weekend having sex, we'd evened it out over the last few days just talking on the phone because we couldn't see each other. We'd needed a breather after everything being so intense, but now I was craving the physical side again.

He moved across to the middle of the seat, his hand on my cheek, stroking gently with his thumb as his tongue pressed against my lips, seeking entry. I wound my fingers in his hair, deepening the kiss. My body reacted instantly as he moved his hand to the back of my neck, drawing me closer, and I squirmed, shuffling nearer to him.

His lips, his scent, his fingers on my skin. All of it combined to make me a mess of neediness. I just wanted to climb onto his lap and ride him, and the thought of it only made me hotter.

What the hell is this guy doing to me?

I was never a prude, but I'd also never wanted someone so badly I would have considered a quickie in a van, especially not with my home so close. With him, though, those few steps were just too goddamn far.

"Shan, you're killing me," Cal murmured, his forehead resting against mine and his breath hot against my cheek. "I wanna go back inside, but... you were right. If we do, I won't want to leave."

A small whimper of frustration left my lips. "I know. I know."

As I looked up at him, we both knew it was going to be a while before we'd get a full night together. But I also wanted more than rushed sex and him leaving straight after.

I pressed my lips to his once more before we reluctantly back to our seats. Cal wriggled a little, adjusting the position of his no doubt rock-hard dick. The thought made me squirm again, and I blew out a breath in the hope of shifting my mind elsewhere.

"Soon," Cal said, his voice gravelly. "I promise."

I nodded, then buckled my seatbelt before resting my hand on his thigh.

Within minutes, we'd pulled out of the car park and were on the road to the Quay. It was one of my favourite places to go for a calming walk or a night out. There were some amazing pubs down there, and it looked so pretty in the dark with the lights shining out on the water. On the way, Cal and I talked about which pub we would go to, and we settled on On The Waterfront. Too bad I'd already eaten, as they made exceptional pizzas. Another thing on the mental list of things to do with Cal soon.

Second only to actually doing Cal.

Just as we were approaching the car park at the Quay, I felt a vibration coming from Cal's pocket.

"Can you just see who that is?" he asked, and I nodded and pulled the phone out.

"It's Guy."

His shoulders tensed as he carried on into the car park. "That's what I was afraid of. Could you answer it and put it on speaker, please?"

I did as he asked, and Cal didn't even get a chance to say hello before the sound of Aiden shouting echoed out into the van, so loud it made me flinch.

"What happened?" Cal asked.

"Mate, I'm sorry. Aiden woke up about five minutes after you left, and he's having a meltdown. I don't know what set it off, but he was in your room trying to unpack your boxes. I took him out and he went apeshit. No doubt you can hear him."

No kidding. The words weren't decipherable, but the yelling was unmissable, his tone full of rage.

"Can you calm him down?" Cal asked, driving slowly around the car park. We both knew there was no point stopping in a space because there was only one way this was going to go.

"Helen's trying," Guy said, "but you need to come home."

"Has Aiden even asked for me?"

Guy paused, which said more than any words. "Cal, he needs you."

Cal's jaw clenched. "What do you think I'll be able to say to him that will make this better, Guy? We're moving tomorrow. That's not going to change."

"No, it's not. But he needs to hear from you that the move will be a good thing."

"And you think there's a different way any of us can say that? Come on. We've told him over and over that he'll still be coming to yours after school most days, and that he can stay over sometimes, and that we'll still all do stuff together at the weekends." He sighed, his knuckles turning white on the steering wheel. "Look, I'll be there as soon as I can, but I need to take Shannen home first."

I opened my mouth to tell him I could easily get a cab back, but he shook his head before I could get a word out.

"I'll take her home. Just get back here now."

Cal hit the button to disconnect the call then slid his phone back into his pocket before running his hand through his hair. He slammed his palm against the steering wheel. "Maybe I shouldn't have come out tonight, but..." he trailed off and sighed.

In that moment, I knew that as much as he'd wanted to see me, there was more to it than that. When we'd spoken during the week, I could tell there had been some especially tough days and he'd admitted he needed to get out of the house. Even though he physically looked good, emotionally, he was tired. Just hearing

Aiden down the phone had flicked his whole demeanour from calm to stressed out.

"You needed a break," I finished for him, and he flicked his gaze briefly to me as he drove us out of the car park.

"That's bad, isn't it?" he asked.

"Nope." I put my hand back on his thigh. "Everyone needs a break sometimes. Sounds like it's been hard the last few weeks."

"Weeks. Months. It's all hard."

The tension still hadn't left him, and I wished we could stop the van so I could talk to him face to face. Look him in the eye and find out what was going through his head. All I could do where we were was give his leg a reassuring squeeze.

"I don't want to go home, Shan. I'm not in the mood to deal with Helen's 'I told you so' on top of Aiden's screaming."

"I thought you, Guy, and Helen had all agreed on you going out tonight for a couple of hours."

"We did. But she also thinks I shouldn't go anywhere apart from work or out with Guy. She seems to have forgotten that until tonight, and last Saturday, that was exactly what I did. I've been with Aiden every single day. She's acting like I've abandoned him. And I know... I know maybe tonight I should have been with him, but he went to bed fine. I thought he'd be okay."

Nothing much I'd heard about Helen had been good, aside from that she seemed to care about Aiden. When it came to Cal, though, she clearly had issues. It hurt my heart that he'd gone from happy to so drained over what he was about to face. Maybe his saying he didn't want to go home should have made me think badly of him, because what kind of parent doesn't want to comfort their child? From the things he'd said to Guy, it could have sounded like he didn't want to be there for Aiden, but I didn't think that was it. He was tired and at a loss for how to fix things.

"You weren't to know he would wake up, or that he'd be flipping out," I said. "It's very easy to be judgmental when you don't have kids of your own."

He flicked his gaze to me again. "You manage it pretty well."

"Well, I might be new to teaching my own class, but I've worked in schools for a couple of years. And one thing I've learned is that there are no perfect parents. Just parents who are trying to do their best for their children, no matter what their circumstances. It's not my place to judge. It's my place to teach. And to help if I can."

"You might end up regretting those words, Shan." Cal sighed. "Because I'm going to need all the help I can get."

Chapter 13

Shannen

I sat in the hallway outside Aiden's room, listening to Cal talking to him, my head resting against the wall.

The evening had been a whirlwind, from almost having a quickie in the front of Cal's van to this moment. He and I had barely been together for an hour and a half, and yet so many things had happened.

At the forefront of my mind, I saw Cal throwing Aiden's board game across the room as his temper got the better of him. I could have lied to myself and said that it didn't scare me to see him lose it like that, but what would be the point? For a moment, my heart had stopped beating as I saw something emerge in him I hadn't seen before. It wasn't sudden, like the flip of a switch. It was a build-up of everything he'd been dealing with finally exploding, not that the fact made me feel any better. I didn't like that side of him. Didn't like that it existed, and I was sure I wasn't going to like the reasons for his inability to handle his emotions either. I'd seen him frustrated before, and it was unsettling, but he'd been in control of it then. This was different. I knew Cal was under a lot of pressure and stress with the move and Aiden's behaviour, and I knew he'd been struggling to handle it all, but what could he be capable of if he really lost it? Was throwing things the worst it ever got, or was there a hidden violent side I'd yet to discover?

The idea made a chill run through me, but it somehow didn't ring true. Even after such a short time with him. He had the look of a bad boy. The swagger of a bad boy. And just a small dig under the surface told me he had a whole bunch of issues.

Yet, for reasons I couldn't explain, I had this bone-deep belief that I was safe with him. Cal was rough around the edges, with signs of some unresolved past trauma. But even realising that, no part of me thought he would hurt me or Aiden when he went off.

Could I be with someone who was so volatile, though?

"Shannen?"

At the sound of my name, I looked towards the stairs. Helen stood at the top. She was no longer glaring at me. In fact, there was a glimmer of kindness in her eyes that had been missing when I'd arrived. She had straight, dark blonde hair that hung around her shoulders, highlighted with some lighter blonde streaks making it look almost sunkissed. Her eyes were a soft blue, and she was attractive, but the almost-permanent scowl on her face made her look pissed off and somewhat unapproachable.

"Can I talk to you for a sec?" she asked.

Nodding, I pushed myself up from the floor, and she opened the door beside her, gesturing for me to go inside. She flipped the light on in her and Guy's bedroom and closed the door over.

For a moment, she watched me as I stood awkwardly near the bed, unsure what she was going to say. After what felt like forever, she took a deep breath.

"I'm sorry we didn't get a chance to be introduced properly earlier," she said. "I know I wasn't very welcoming, but tonight, I just... I thought the last thing Aiden needed was someone else in the house. Cal can be selfish, and he was putting himself ahead of what Aiden needed."

Her words made me bristle slightly because selfishness wasn't something I associated with Cal. However, until that evening, I hadn't seen him fly into a rage either. She knew him better than I did, so I didn't say anything. She clearly had more to say, so I waited for her to continue.

"I have no doubt that Cal's told you about Guy's bitch of a girlfriend, and I'm not even going to pretend that I've ever had a lot of time for him. The two of you... honestly, it makes no sense to me, but I saw the way he was with you outside. I've never seen him like that before." She paused as if lost in thought for a moment before taking another breath. "I heard what he said to you downstairs too. He can be an absolute arsehole sometimes. But the thing is... as much as I dislike him, I want you to know that if there was even a hint of him doing anything that would hurt Aiden, Cal would be out on his ass and I'd make damn sure he never got near Aiden again. He's a lot of things, but he isn't an abuser."

There was fire in her words, and I already knew from the way Cal had talked about her that she couldn't stand him and vice versa. But as much as she hated Cal, she loved Aiden. Despite her distaste for Cal, she still stepped up for him when it mattered because she knew that Aiden being with his dad was more important than how she felt about him.

"Thank you," I said. "Thank you for saying that. Honestly, I never thought Cal would hurt him. I just... I didn't expect him to take his anger out on me."

"That would be the arsehole side of him I mentioned. Shannen, I'm not here to sing Cal's praises to you. If he loses you over this, that's on him for behaving like a dick. You hardly know him, and nobody would blame you if you didn't want to take on all of his shit. I just wanted you to know that Aiden's safe with him and you are too."

It was there again, unspoken in her eyes. It almost pained her to say anything pro-Cal, but her need to speak up for Aiden's needs won out in the end.

I nodded, thinking about what she'd said. There had been a moment down-stairs when Cal had verbally lashed out at me that I didn't want to take any of it on. Not his anger, not his baggage, and not a child who didn't need any extra confusion in his life. It wasn't just Cal's apology that stopped me from walking out. It wasn't even the absolute sincerity in his eyes, although that did go a long way to helping my decision. It was the way he didn't hide his feelings when I called him out for pushing Aiden away. He let me see the guilt, the pain, and the fear. But mostly, he let me see that he wanted to change it. That he was desperate to make things better. I could see beyond all the issues to the little hints of vulnerability that lay beneath his tough exterior that I wanted to know more about. I saw the man I'd spent hours talking to, the man who made me feel... alive.

"I know I haven't known him for as long as you have," I said. "But I think maybe you still see him as whatever mess he was in when he first landed on your doorstep. He's holding down a job, he got Aiden back, and he's not getting drunk every day. You and Guy are a big part of how he got to where he is now, but he's still done it. Does he not deserve credit for that?"

She shrugged with more condescension than I liked. "You've known him for seven days. He's mostly showing you the best parts of him."

I laughed out loud. "Are you kidding? This week I've seen him get frustrated and angry and say things to me that were completely unfair. And you know that because that's why you're talking to me right now. He's told me about some of the worst times of his life, and you think he's only showing me the best parts?" I shook my head. Even though this talk of hers was well-intentioned for the most part, she still couldn't resist pointing out his flaws. I couldn't help but wonder what the hell it was about him that got her so riled up.

"So, what's keeping you around?" Helen asked, leaning back against her chest of drawers. "Because you could definitely do better."

"How do you know that?" I challenged, standing a little straighter. "You know I'm a teacher, but that's all."

Helen laughed again. "I know you come from a rich family and that you have a nice flat in a good area. I know you have a friend who tries to set you up with men you aren't interested in, and a friend from work who is a bit crazy. You like lattes, prawn cocktail crisps, Chinese takeaways, and you would rather stay home and watch TV than go out on the town. Wine is your drink of choice, preferably red, but you like white too. You have a great sense of humour, but you're also good at listening when things are serious. And I know all of this because Cal talks about you whenever he gets the chance."

My cheeks warmed, and my lips twitched into an embarrassed smile. "Wow."

Helen held a hand up, although a hint of a grin crossed her face, like something had broken through her hard outer shell. "Don't. Don't get all mushy over that. Because that doesn't make anything I said about him less true."

"So, did you come up here to talk him up or to warn me off him?" I asked, genuinely curious.

"I came to reassure you that Aiden's in good hands. What you do about Cal is your choice." She pushed herself away from the drawers she'd been leaning on. "Guy was right about you, though," she said. "You're all right."

I chuckled. "High praise, indeed."

This time, a full smile broke through, taking away the harshness of her features. "What he actually said was that you're kind and understanding, and that even with the differences between you and Cal, something about you both makes sense."

That was exactly how I felt about him.

"Well, for what it's worth," I said, "I think Cal might have been wrong about you. You're also all right."

She laughed out loud. "I can't wait to throw that in his face," she said, though I knew she was joking. Or at least I hoped she was.

A knock on the door broke the moment of understanding between us, and Cal's head peered around the door. On seeing the two of us together, he frowned slightly, and I wondered how much he'd heard.

"I'll leave you to it," Helen said, looking between the two of us before walking to the door. Cal stepped aside to let her pass, and I followed her out into the hallway, closing the door behind me.

"What just happened?" he asked, his brow still wrinkled, and I chuckled.

"Helen just surprised me."

"How so?" He almost looked like he was holding his breath in anticipation of what I was going to say, though he should have guessed from my expression that she hadn't put me off him.

Looking up at him, I said, "She said something nice about you." Cal's eyebrows shot up so high they almost disappeared into his hairline. "You might want to thank her later."

Her kinder words about him affirmed what I had already been pretty sure about, and I'd filed the not-so-kind ones away. Her experiences with him weren't mine. Cal wasn't the same person now as he was when she first met him. If, at some point, I discovered he was a self-centred arse, I'd learn it firsthand, not from someone else's bias.

"Is Aiden okay?" I asked, and Cal nodded slowly. "And you?"

His dark eyes searched my face for a moment. "I don't know. Are you... are we...?" Unable to find the words, he just looked at me, his gaze asking the question.

I lifted my hand and slipped it around the back of his neck, my thumb softly stroking his skin. "We're good."

Cal closed his eyes as if relaxing under my touch. "Do you still want to stay for a while?"

"I do."

He nodded and took my hand, leading me into his room and flipping the light on. The bedroom was pretty much bare of furniture aside from his bed, a pine wardrobe that stood beside the door, and a matching bedside table with a drawer. Everything else was packed away, and there was some evidence of the boxes Aiden had tried to open earlier. One or two of them had holes in, and a couple more had been punched through, but the contents remained inside.

Cal let go of my hand and sat down on his bed, shuffling across, then holding his hand out for me to join him. I unzipped my boots and took them off, and he pulled me in tight to his side, his arm wrapped around me. I snuggled into him, resting my head against his chest and my hand on his stomach. I breathed him in, that amazing scent of his cologne and leather so familiar already.

"You were right," he said after a while.

"What about?" I asked, my hand moving around to his waist, wanting to be as close to him as I could.

"Aiden. About me pushing him away. I wasn't doing it deliberately, but I *was* doing it. What I realised tonight was that, even though he said he likes living with me, that doesn't mean he trusts me. He knows there was a time I had to give him up, and there's a part of him that's worried it'll happen again. Not just because we're going to live on our own tomorrow. I think he's been worried about it most of the time he's been back with me."

That made sense. I'd figured that Cal had the same fear, even though everything was going pretty well most of the time. Somewhere inside him, he doubted he had what it took to keep Aiden with him, and with both of them holding on to that same worry, it had created a barrier between them.

"I heard some of what you said to him," I said, lifting my head to look at him. "For someone who says they aren't good at talking, you did brilliantly. You gave him the reassurance he needed."

He nodded. "I tried to. He was much happier when he went back to bed. He's asleep already. I think all the shouting and crying wore him out." Cal reached out to run his fingers through my hair. "You've been brilliant tonight. You didn't get pissed off because we couldn't go out, and you came here even though it could have been awkward, and you were amazing with Aiden." Drawing in a deep breath, he added, "I really am sorry about what I said earlier. I..." he trailed off again, and his hand dropped from my hair.

I shifted my position, twisting around so I could see him better and taking his hand in mine. "What is it?"

Shaking his head, he said, "This time last week, I'd only just met you. Now, you're here with me, dealing with me and my kid, and... everything has been so... serious."

Nodding slowly, I said, "Yeah. It has been pretty intense. I probably shouldn't know so much about you this fast. If I weren't Aiden's teacher, I wouldn't."

His eyes fell on mine as if he was trying to figure out what I was thinking. "Why did you stick around, Shan? Why didn't you just call it quits when you found out I hid that I have a child?" He didn't ask the question in an accusatory or judging way. It was more like he was truly curious, and the question in his beautiful eyes made my heart hurt.

"Because, when you told me everything, I understood why you didn't tell me about him right away." I squeezed his hand. "If you had told me about him without all of the other things, then all you would have been thinking about was whether or when to tell me the rest."

"I also told you I didn't plan to keep you around for long enough to tell you."

I nodded again. "Yeah, you did. But then you asked me to stay. You asked me to stay on Monday, and you asked me to stay tonight. If you wanted me gone, I wouldn't be here."

"I want you here. I just... I haven't wanted that with anyone in a long time. Or ever. I hate that I haven't been able to take you out on a date or even spend much time with you where all of my fuck-ups haven't been the main topic of conversation." His hand raked through his hair the way it always did when he was getting stressed.

Letting go of his hand, I shifted my position again, moving my leg over both of his so I was straddling him. I wanted to look him right in the eye, and I placed my hands around the back of his neck to make sure he was focused on me. "Cal, listen to me. I'm pretty sure if anyone was to look at me and you and the way our lives have gone, nobody would ever dream of putting us together. And yet, we met, and however nonsensical, there's something between us. So, as long as you can promise not to lie to me, cheat on me, or keep anything important from me, I really don't mind that we haven't been on a real date yet. I can wait."

Cal's hands slid around my back, pulling me tighter against my chest before pressing his lips to mine. "I can promise that."

Smiling softly, I kissed him again, and his muscles relaxed beneath my fingers. As our mouths moved together in a perfect rhythm, my own tension ebbed away, and I lost myself in him the way I'd wanted to when he arrived at my flat earlier. We weren't in a rush to be anywhere now, and his lips danced with mine with a slowness and sensuality that sent my heart racing and my body melting against his.

I never want this feeling to stop. It was consuming, the way his soft lips touched mine over and over. Hungry but not hurried. Passionate yet tender. I'd never felt how much someone wanted me through a kiss until Cal, and I wasn't sure I'd ever put so much of myself into a kiss either.

His hands moved up my back, and I shuffled my hips forward, needing to be as close to him as I could get. We finally had some time alone, and I wanted every second of it to be spent with us glued together.

Cal's lips drifted across my cheek towards my ear. "Stay," he murmured against my skin. "Stay with me tonight."

My heart pounded harder at the possibility of an unexpected night together. "I want to," I said, closing my eyes as his lips lowered to my neck, making me shiver. "But... tomorrow... you... you have to..."

My point that he needed to be up early in the morning fell completely out of my mind when his mouth found my collarbone.

He paused, looking up at me, the need in his eyes almost flooring me. "We'll wake up early and I'll take you home before anyone else gets up."

Cal's lips went back to my collarbone, feathering kisses there as his hands slipped underneath my top, his rough fingers on my back.

"I don't... I don't have anything to..." His teeth grazed my neck, his hands working higher up my back to my bra strap.

His throaty chuckle sent another shiver through me, his breath hot on my neck. "Be a rebel, Shannen. Go home with your knickers in your pocket. Nobody will ever know."

His husky tone and dirty words caused my skin to heat and the fluttering sensation to stir in my core. His ability to read my thoughts and counter my protests was sexy as hell. When his fingers unclipped my bra, I raked my hands into his hair. "What kind of girl do you think I am?" I teased, tugging to pull his face back to mine.

He smirked, then brushed his lips against my own. "The kind who's going to let me spend several hours inside her, then fall asleep beside me, fully satisfied?"

I tilted my head to the side as if thinking, and he flipped me over onto my back and climbed on top of me, making me laugh.

"Say yes, Shan," he said, smiling into my eyes. "Please."

Winding my arms around him again, I said, "Yes. I guess I am that kind of girl."

Chapter 14

Cal

"Will Miss Morgan be here soon?"

Aiden was sitting on a stool at the kitchen counter, watching me as I put some garlic bread in the oven and kept an eye on the spaghetti that was simmering in the pan on the hob.

"Five minutes," I told him, turning to face him and leaning back against the counter. "Remember, though, when she's here, you're allowed to call her by her first name."

It wasn't the first time he'd heard that, but he'd been calling Shannen 'Miss Morgan' for the last six months, and he still wasn't used to seeing her outside the classroom.

Aiden frowned. "It's weird to call her that."

I chuckled. "I know, but she isn't your teacher at the weekend. She's just a person."

Aiden's eyes turned mischievous, and he giggled. "She's your girlfriend."

The reality of that still hadn't sunk in. Shannen and I had been seeing each other for six weeks, and we hadn't put a label on what we were. The first week we met had been more intense than anything I'd ever been through before, and in spite of all the ugly parts of me she had seen, she'd stuck around.

I didn't think she would. Or maybe I thought she would for a couple of weeks before she made her excuses and ended things.

But that didn't happen. We'd kept on seeing each other as often as we could, talking on the phone for hours when we couldn't, and it was working. She was still too good for me, and that was never going to change. If I allowed myself to overthink it, it made me want to end it before she inevitably dumped me, because there was still so much about me that she didn't know. That I wasn't ready to tell her. And when I did, I was pretty sure her understanding would come to an abrupt end, just like our relationship would.

A better person would have broken it off, just like I always planned to. But I wanted her. Couldn't get enough of her. So much so that she was coming to stay at my place for the first time with Aiden's knowledge.

Shannen had spent a few nights with me, coming over after Aiden had gone to bed, and she'd snuck out way before he woke up. There had also been a couple of times she'd spent a few hours with me and Aiden over weekends too, but this was something new. This was Shannen spending the evening with us, then sleeping over, and spending most of Saturday together too.

Fucking hell. I was making a spaghetti bolognese for my girlfriend, who was coming over to hang out with me and my son.

And I was okay with it. I was okay with being in a relationship, even if neither of us had said out loud that that was what it was.

There was a knock at the door—Shannen already had the code to the building—and I turned the hob down and told Aiden to wait where he was while I got the door.

Shannen smiled brightly as I opened it, and I stepped back so she could enter. Once the door was closed, she dropped her overnight bag and coat down, and I paused for a second to take her in. Her curly hair hung loose, and she wore a close-fitting dark green jumper that highlighted her curves, with blue jeans, and black ankle boots.

As grateful as I was for my son, I wished he was already in bed so I could take Shannen to my room and fuck her until the sun came up.

I was about to speak when footsteps padded towards us and Aiden stood in the doorway to the living room. His earlier mischievousness had vanished, and he fiddled with the bottom of his t-shirt as he watched us.

Shannen glanced at me, and I smiled before she turned her attention to Aiden.

"Hi, Aiden," she said softly. She paused, exaggeratedly sniffing as the aroma of the food drifted out to us. "Have you been cooking? Because something smells yummy."

Aiden's cheeks flushed, and he giggled. "I wasn't cooking. Cal made sketty bolognese."

I tried to control the flinch. The two of us had had our own place for over a month, but I was still Cal. Still not dad. I was beginning to wonder if I ever would be.

We had become somewhat closer after the talk we had before we moved out of Guy's house. Aiden still got frustrated when he was upset about something, as if he wanted to tell me what was bothering him. Sometimes he did, and other times he would shout and stomp to his room. Those times, I never pushed him to talk, and I didn't know if that was the right thing to do, or whether I should have tried to find out more. I was on a steep learning curve and I knew I was still getting things wrong. I didn't always cook him a healthy meal if I was knackered, and I'd been late picking him up from school a few times. I was still crap at showing him affection. Better, but I needed to work on it. Maybe, one day, if I could get it all together, he would be happy I was his dad.

"It's almost ready," I said, pushing my thoughts aside. Aiden cheered and ran out of the hallway and back to the living room.

Shannen chuckled as he sped off, but she shuffled her feet slightly.

"Are you okay?" I asked. It wasn't like her to be nervous—not these days.

She nodded. "Yeah, it's just... this is a big step. My first time staying over with Aiden being aware of it. He seems okay with it, though."

I snorted out a laugh. "Just before you got here, he was teasing me about you being my girlfriend, so he's fine with it."

A light blush covered her cheeks, another thing I didn't see in her too often anymore. "Is that what I am?"

There was no getting away from it now. The things I'd thought about earlier were out in the open, and even though my chest tightened with the need to run, that wasn't what I wanted. I wanted this. Her.

"Yeah." I nodded. "You're my girlfriend."

Her grin widened, and the tightness in my chest eased. This didn't have to be difficult. It didn't have to be a bad thing. It *wasn't* a bad thing. I just needed to get a handle on the bits of my past I *could* tell her about. Had to get comfortable with knowing I would have to tell her eventually.

But not now. Not tonight.

"Come on," I said, taking her hand. "Let's go and eat before I burn the garlic bread."

After the initial nerves, once dinner was eaten, everything settled and the three of us spent some time playing board games together. This time, nobody threw anything, and I could see my boy enjoying having Shannen over more and more. She was amazing with him. Maybe because she already knew him and she was a teacher, so she was naturally good with kids. She seemed to have a knack for calming him before a meltdown occurred, something she had previously assured me was a lot harder in a classroom setting when there were so many others to juggle. But one to one, she saw the signs coming and diverted it before it took hold. I'd seen her do it a few times before when she'd been with us, and although she assured me it wasn't magic, I still hadn't quite figured out how to do it. I suspected it was because she was all-around calmer than me. She didn't have the pre-stress I had when dealing with him.

"Please can we watch a movie?" Aiden asked after we'd played several games of Connect 4, Guess Who, and Snakes and Ladders. Usually, I'd be trying to get him to wind down before bed around now, but I figured a movie would do that just as well. He would go to bed a bit later, but it was Friday and we had nowhere to be in the morning. He could nap later if necessary.

I looked at Shannen. "Is that okay with you? We have hot chocolate and marshmallows."

She smiled. "That sounds perfect."

Not needing to be asked twice, Aiden rushed to the kitchen, eager to get his drink made. Shannen and I smiled and quickly followed him. Aiden was climbing up onto one of the stools as we joined him.

"Okay, little dude," I said. "What do you want to watch tonight?"

"*Toy Story 2*!"

I groaned. We could both recite *Toy Story 1* and *2* in our sleep now. I didn't even have to be focused on it, the words just filtered through to my brain, unstoppable. It was a great movie, but having seen it so many times, it was wearing thin.

"Can you pick something else just for tonight?" I asked, and he shook his head.

"It's my favourite."

"Don't I know it," I murmured. "You'll never find another favourite if you keep watching the same thing."

"I looked on Disney Plus and Netflix and it was all rubbish!"

"You never tried any of them," I pointed out, and Aiden pouted.

"May I make a suggestion?" Shannen asked as I pulled out some mugs.

"Sure," I said. *Anything to avoid another showing of Toy Story.*

"When I was your age, my mum introduced me to a movie that none of my friends had ever heard of. While everyone else was obsessed with Disney movies, I was watching the one my mum showed me. And... if you want to try it, I brought it with me. Just in case."

My eyes fell on her. She hadn't mentioned bringing a movie with her, but she was well aware of how over the Disney/Pixar classic I was. While I doubted Aiden would go for it, I threw her a grateful smile.

"What's it called?" Aiden asked.

"*The Brave Little Toaster*."

Aiden's eyes narrowed. "It's about a toaster?" His words dripped with cynicism, and Shannen laughed.

"Sort of. It's not a real toaster, it's a cartoon. There's also a hoover, a blanket, a lamp, and a radio. They got left behind when the owners of the house moved, so they go on an adventure to try to find them."

There was no improvement in Aiden's enthusiasm, and Shannen laughed again. "It's scary in places too," she added, raising an eyebrow.

That got his attention. "Really?"

"Only a bit. It's an adventure and it's fun. Do you want to try it? If you don't like it, we can watch something else."

"Not *Toy Story*," I added, and Aiden huffed but turned his focus back to Shannen.

"We can watch the toaster," he said. "It better be good, though!"

Forty-five minutes later, Aiden was engrossed. He sat in between Shannen and me, slightly snuggled into my side. My arm was across the back of the sofa, and as the movie played, I softly ran my fingers across the back of Shannen's neck, occasionally twirling my fingers through her hair. Now and again, she gave me a smile, and I knew if Aiden wasn't between us, she would have been curled up beside me, and I'd be breathing in the honey scent of her shampoo. Any movie we watched would have likely been forgotten after five minutes, but this was not that kind of night. This was a snippet of what life could be like if Shannen could deal with the excess baggage I carried.

When are you going to tell her?

I forced the question down. I was going to tell her the part that would cause her the least stress soon. I knew she was curious about my family and why I didn't have any, but she never probed. I saw her taking in anything I let slip, but she still didn't know where they were. What had happened to them.

How it was partly my fault.

Aiden jiggling in his seat to one of the songs on screen pulled me out of my thoughts, and I smiled down at him. Shannen laughed, and I could see her mouthing the words.

"You've watched this as many times as Aiden has watched *Toy Story*, haven't you?" I asked, and she nodded.

"I know this movie inside out."

"Yeah, well, I think this will be another one for Aiden's obsession collection too."

"Ssshhh!" Aiden said, still dancing. "I'm listening!"

He leaned over, snuggling against Shannen's side this time, and she glanced at me in shock. She'd cuddled him when he was upset, but he'd never gone to her and just snuggled up to her like that. We'd all watched TV together before, and we'd sat close together playing video games, but this was new. Her arm was trapped where he was leaning, so she couldn't put it around him, but her eyes softened as she glanced down at him, his head on her shoulder. With her free hand, she softly ruffled his hair before looking back at the television.

I wasn't sure what this woman was doing to me; I'd never met anyone like her before. Okay, sure, I'd purposely avoided getting close to anyone until I met her. But something about her had got hold of me and hadn't let go from the first time we'd spoken.

I was a fucking idiot if I thought I'd be able to keep her forever, but she made me want it. She made me *want* forever.

As I wound my fingers gently in her dark curls again, her eyes closed briefly, a look of bliss on her face. She was happy here. I was making her happy.

That was what that feeling was in my chest. The weird fluttering sensation that happened when I was with her. When I heard her voice. When I saw her smile. I hadn't experienced anything beyond basic contentment in so long that I hadn't recognised what it was. It wasn't the kind of high that comes from illegal substances; not that I was ever big on that. It wasn't the buzz of alcohol trickling through my veins. It wasn't being satisfied that I now had a place to live and a steady job. All of those things were nothing compared to having Shannen look at me like I meant something.

I was fucked. Because if anything took her away from me now... I wasn't sure how I'd survive it.

Chapter 15

Shannen

I took a couple of deep breaths before getting out of my car. It was Saturday afternoon, and as much as I should have been excited about an afternoon with my best friend and our mums, I couldn't muster the enthusiasm. Frankly, this two hours couldn't pass quickly enough so I could get back to Cal and Aiden. I'd loved being with them, and it had given me a small insight into how life could be. Everything had aligned, and Aiden was having a good weekend. It probably wouldn't always be so simple. But I liked the snapshot it had provided so far.

Jade had booked a 'VIP Experience' at one of Exeter's best bridal shops, The Bridal Loft, which meant the store was closed to everyone but us while she tried on wedding dresses. Jade's mum and I would be looking for our own wedding outfits too, as they also catered for bridesmaids and mothers of the bride, but it was mostly about Jade.

Honestly, I was shocked she hadn't pulled my role of head bridesmaid from me, but she frequently reminded me that she expected my 'fling' with Cal to be over by the time the wedding rolled around in six months.

In reality, there were no signs of that being the case. Despite the bumpy start, Cal and I had got through it and things were good. Better than good. Because Aiden had seen us together so soon, I spoke to the principal at school and let her know I was seeing Cal. It wasn't an issue since Aiden wouldn't be in my class forever, but while he was, I wanted to be upfront about it. The upside to Aiden knowing about us was that we didn't have to work around him *quite* as much. We were only just spending our first weekend all together, though, and I would be going back to Cal's later as we were going to Guy and Helen's for a takeaway in the evening.

I opened the door that led upstairs to the boutique. As little as I was looking forward to this, Jade was still my friend. The least I could do was support her and be the dutiful bridesmaid. Plus, I'd get to see my mum, and since she and my dad had moved to Plymouth almost two years ago, we didn't get to visit each other as often as we used to. Jade's mum, Judith, still lived nearby, but I hadn't seen her in a few months either.

"Shannen!" Jade squealed, rushing towards me. "You're here!" This was the most enthusiasm she'd shown for me since Cal came on the scene, and I guessed any annoyance she had was outweighed by the reality of her wedding getting closer.

I laughed as she ran to me and wrapped me up in a hug. "Excited much?"

She grinned. "SO excited!" She spun around and handed me a glass of champagne that was set out on the front counter. I could see just through the archway to the other side of the shop that there were some white sofas and a low table that held cucumber sandwiches, vol-au-vents, and various other fancy finger foods laid out just for us.

"Shannen, this is Tegan and Emma, and they'll be helping us out today," Jade went on, gesturing to two well-dressed ladies who stood by the counter, ready to leap into action. We exchanged greetings just as Judith and my mum entered.

Jade squealed again, rushing to them, and I took a small sip of champagne. As she ushered her mum over to the refreshments, my mum came over to me, a bright smile on her face. "Hello, darling," she said, and I hugged her tight.

Although I may have been biased, I thought my mum was beautiful. She had recently turned fifty-three, but thanks to her dedicated skincare routine, she could have easily passed for early forties. I got my thick, dark hair from her, but she kept hers cropped short these days. She was a glam mum, and I hoped I looked as stylish as her when I reached her age.

My penchant for cakes and other junk food suggested I might not be so lucky.

"Mum," I said, smiling at her. "It's good to see you."

"You too." She held onto my shoulders, looking me up and down. "You look great."

"So do you! How's Dad?"

She rolled her eyes. "You know your dad. Always busy."

My father was a surgeon, and as such, he worked a lot of hours. However, it did help to pay for their lifestyle, and it would also afford him a healthy retirement package one day.

We stood chatting for a few minutes, catching up. Mum and I spoke on the phone every week, but it was so good to be with her in person for a change.

"Okay," Jade said, clapping her hands, and my mum rolled her eyes again, making me laugh as we all turned in Jade's direction. Her eyes were alight with excitement. "I think it's time for us to have a look around. Mum and Annie, Emma is going to show you to the mother of the bride outfits, and Shannen, you're coming with me to look at wedding dresses. We will look for your dress after I've found some for me to try on."

Once we'd been given our orders, we went off in all directions to look around.

I had to admit, it was nice to have the place to ourselves. I wasn't sure how much Jade had to pay for the privilege, but it felt special to be the only ones in there.

After forty-five minutes, Judith had found and bought her outfit, Jade had made her selections, and I'd found a couple of dresses she approved of to try on.

"Is it possible that the first dress I try on is the one?" Jade asked from inside the dressing room.

"Knowing you, probably not," I teased, making Mum and Judith laugh.

"I don't know. I really like this one."

"Well, don't keep us in suspense, darling," Judith said. "Come and show us!"

Judith and Jade were so similar it was painful. The snobbery ran deep in their family, and although Judith was pleasant and easy to talk to, all that truly mattered to her was their social standing. Jade and Scott's wedding was going to set Judith and her husband, Hugh, back a small fortune, but it was nothing to them. Anything to mingle with the wealthiest people in the city. A wedding was as much about trying to outdo the last big event as it was about the actual marriage.

As Jade pulled the curtain back, Tegan behind her straightening the train, Judith gasped.

"Oh, wow," I said as she stepped forward with a wide smile on her face.

I'd never envisioned Jade in a dress with a full skirt, but she looked stunning in a white gown that flowed behind her, the bodice made of delicate lace with a halter neck. My eyes prickled with tears at seeing my oldest friend looking so beautiful and happy. As children, we'd spent hours talking about our wedding days and how we would be each other's bridesmaid. We'd come a long way since then, and seeing her dream come true was amazing. She irked me with annoying regularity, but we'd also known each other forever, and this was a huge moment for her.

"I love it," she said, her eyes wide with excitement.

Judith jumped up and rushed over to Jade, examining each aspect of the dress more closely through teary eyes. I exchanged a smile with my mum before turning my attention back to my friend.

"Jade, you look incredible."

"You really do," Judith added, staring at Jade with pride. "And if this is the one, it's a perfect choice. But you must try on the others you picked just to be sure."

Jade nodded, looking down at herself as if she were Cinderella and the clock was about to strike midnight.

"Okay," she said. "But I'm telling you, this is the one I want."

As Jade stepped back into the cubicle, Judith returned to her seat, turning to me. "Shannen, our wedding planner is getting started on table plans soon. Have you decided who you're bringing as your plus one yet?"

I spluttered into my champagne. I hadn't seen that coming. With Cal being a touchy subject with Jade and having not mentioned him to my mum yet, I wasn't sure what to tell her.

"Do *not* say you're bringing your boy toy," Jade called out, making Judith and my mum look at me in surprise. "I'm not having some manual labourer trying to order packets of peanuts and cheap beer at my wedding!"

I drew in a long breath as Judith tilted her head. "What's this? Are you seeing someone?"

"Yes. I've been seeing someone for a few weeks. I just... I wanted to see how things would go before I told everyone."

"Shannen, that's wonderful," Mum said, smiling brightly.

"It's not," Jade called through the curtain. "He's poor."

I placed my glass down on the table to avoid snapping the delicate stem in irritation at her words.

Judith's brow furrowed, and my mum watched me carefully. She'd clearly sensed my annoyance, but she never got involved in my disagreements with Jade unless it was completely necessary.

"Poor?" Judith said as if I'd just confessed to farting during a church service.

"He's... a painter and decorator." The hesitation wasn't because I was embarrassed about Cal's job, it was because I was anticipating the derogatory laugh Judith was already struggling to suppress.

"Really, darling?" she asked. "How on *earth* did you meet a painter and decorator?"

"She's not dating an alien, Judith," my mum said, an amused smile on her face. She turned her attention back to me. "So, you've been together for a few weeks. When can we meet him?"

That was a bridge I wasn't ready to cross, more for Cal's sake than anything. He seemed to view my family as if they were royalty, and the idea of meeting them made him break out into a sweat. However, I smiled at my mum for not recoiling at the idea of me seeing someone 'different'.

"He'll have to find a babysitter first!"

"For God's sake, Jade!" I snapped, standing up and pacing the room. None of this was for her to share. Not one word of it. She could have just let me say I hadn't picked a date for her wedding yet so I could tell my mum about Cal in my own time. As always, though, she had to make a big thing of it.

"He has a *child*?" Judith asked, her eyes bulging out of her head.

I ran my hand through my hair. This was Jade's day. The day she chose the dress she would marry the love of her life in. I had to calm down.

"Yes, he has a child," I said. "But this isn't important right now. Let's just..."

"Tell them how his kid is in your class!"

The next laugh that shot out of Judith was even more patronising than the first. "Oh, you can't be serious!"

"Shannen?" Mum said, and I turned around to look at them both. Judith's face was filled with a mix of horror and incredulity, while my mum merely looked curious.

"Yes. He has a child. Who is in my class."

"Did you meet him at work?" Mum asked.

I shook my head. "No. I met him in a pub. It was just a coincidence that I happen to teach his son. Look..." I sighed. "I don't want to talk about this here."

It was bad enough dealing with Jade's bitchy comments about Cal. I didn't want to add Judith's too.

"No. No, of course not," Judith said. It might have sounded like she was trying to save me, but her body language screamed that she was embarrassed for me; as if I had something to be ashamed of.

Even with years of dealing with this kind of thing, my insides simmered with rage. I wanted to leave, but the earache I'd get for walking out wouldn't be much less painful than what I was already enduring.

Mum gave me an understanding smile, but I knew she wanted to find out more. "Shannen, can you come and look at a dress with me? I saw it earlier and I need a second opinion."

Without another word, she stood up and led me by the hand across the shop to the mother of the bride outfits that were on the opposite side from the fitting rooms. Since the whole space was open, no corners to hide behind, Mum reached for a navy blue floor-length dress and took it off the rail, showing it to me.

"So, when were you going to tell me you're in a relationship with a painter and decorator you met in a pub who has a child in your class?" she asked, holding the dress against her as if it were the real reason she'd dragged me away.

Keeping up the charade, I took a small step back and nodded, then reached forward to touch the silky material. "I'm sorry," I said. "You weren't supposed to find out that way."

It stung that Jade hadn't thought for a second about how I'd feel about her blurting everything out like that. It wasn't her place, and her mocking tone and Judith's judgement had put a dark cloud over what should have been a good afternoon. Okay, due to my and Jade's recent drifting, I hadn't been overly excited about it, but I thought her focus would have been on dresses and maybe bridging the gap between us a little. I hadn't expected to be thrown into the spotlight so harshly.

"Is it serious?" Mum asked as I let the material slip through my fingers.

I glanced up at her, and unlike Judith, there was no horror in her expression. "I don't know yet." I moved along to look at another dress. "Would it be a problem if it was?"

"No, sweetheart," she said softly. "Not if you're happy."

I smiled up at her. "I'm happy."

Mum placed the dress she was holding back where it came from, continuing to browse with me. "So, what's he like?"

I let out something between a sigh and a laugh because... where would I start? I didn't want to lead with any of the not-so-good things. Did my family even need to know about Cal's past? It wasn't like he was still struggling to get himself on his feet.

After a few teething problems, he and Aiden had settled into their own place well. Aiden was much calmer now Cal could pick him up from school a few times a week, and now he'd seen that he could still spend time with Guy and Helen. All around, he was more content and his behaviour was improving week on week. Because of that, Cal was more relaxed too, and there hadn't been any major drama since they'd moved.

Instead of saying anything, I took my phone out of my jeans pocket and unlocked it, scrolling to a selfie I'd taken of Cal and me the week before, when we'd finally gone out for drinks at the Quay. Holding up the phone to her, I waited.

"Oh my goodness," she said, her eyes widening. "He's gorgeous!"

I smiled and turned the phone to look at the photo. Mostly it was our heads that were visible, but the collar of Cal's leather jacket was showing. His stubble was trimmed, and his brown eyes smouldered.

"Yeah," I said, putting the phone back in my pocket. "I sometimes find myself staring at him, not quite able to believe I get to be with him." A flutter rippled through me at the thought of getting out of the bridal shop and back to him. A feeling that hadn't faded since I'd met him. In fact, it grew stronger with each day.

My mum smiled. "That sounds quite serious."

Nodding slowly, I said, "I like him a lot, but it's still new. But also..." I paused, taking a deep breath. "What Jade said... she doesn't know anything about him beyond his job and that he's a single parent, but he *is* different from anyone I've been with before. He doesn't come from the same kind of background as us. He doesn't live anywhere fancy, he drives a van, and he doesn't have a highly paid job." I shrugged. "I don't care about any of that, but Jade and Judith clearly do, and I'm sure others will have something to say about it too."

My mum placed her hand on my arm to stop me idly brushing my hand along the expensive garments in front of me. "Shannen, is he good to you?"

I nodded again. "He is. We don't get to go out much, and when we do, it's simple things like going to the pub or out for dinner somewhere. I've only just spent a full night and day at his place with his son knowing I'm there because we've been taking things slowly, but yes. He's good to me. I like what we have."

I wasn't sure 'being good to me' meant the same to me as it did to her. And definitely not to Jade. Although my mum wasn't a hardcore snob, I was sure she was asking if he took me to nice places and bought me things, but I didn't care about that. He made a great lasagne and the sex was out of this world. I'd happily trade an evening of wining and dining for mindblowing orgasms.

"Then that is all that matters," Mum said. "You know we've never been into all that country club gossiping that goes on. I know you've felt there was a lot of pressure on you and your sister to do certain things, but this is your life, Shannen. If he makes you happy, then we're happy."

"But people *will* gossip, Mum. Especially if Jade allows me to bring him to the wedding."

When I'd first met Cal, I'd been as convinced as Jade that we would never last that long, but that had changed, even more so when I'd woken up in Cal's arms that morning. Aiden had giggled when he saw me emerge from the bedroom with Cal—fully dressed, might I add. Then, he smiled brightly at us and asked if we could make pancakes for breakfast. And we did. Pancakes smothered with maple syrup and bacon because that was Aiden's favourite. Everything about it had felt right. There was still so much about Cal I didn't know. In fact, beyond the basics of all that had happened with Aiden, I knew nothing aside from tiny snippets of info I'd gleaned from conversations we'd had. But we had time. This was more than just a fling now.

"That is a bridge to cross later," Mum said. "For now, just tell Judith you're bringing a plus one, and if that is your new man, they'll all just have to deal with it."

I looked at my mum, searching for signs of doubt on her face, and when I found none, I smiled. "Thanks, Mum."

"Now," she said, reaching for the first dress she'd shown me. "Is this the one for me or not?"

The rest of the afternoon passed by with limited drama. Neither Jade nor Judith offered any apology for their words earlier, and although I'd played my part of the helpful bridesmaid, my heart wasn't in it. Jade had picked her dress—the first one she had tried on—and I'd found my bridesmaid's dress. I wasn't going to be the only bridesmaid, of course, but as the best friend, I was the one to get the first pick. I'd made sure to choose a colour and style that would work for everyone, and I was sure the others, all six of them, would be happy with it.

On the drive home, I thought about the things Jade had said. The way she'd opened me up to criticism from her mum, and possibly even my own. She'd always been pretentious and lacking in tact, but she'd never really hurt me before, and that was how I felt about the blatant disrespect for my relationship with Cal. Long-term or not, it was mine, and it wasn't for her to expose or make jokes about. I was used to her trying to have a say in my decisions, and I'd brushed off a lot of her comments in the past, even if they'd irked me. This was on another level, though. One that made me wonder why I continued to put up with it. I'd never been a doormat who rolled over and did what she wanted. In fact, it was a rare occasion when I let her pressure me into anything, no matter how hard she pushed. But there had been times when I'd got sick of her trying to throw her opinions at me and make not-so-subtle digs about my life choices when I should have told her to back off.

In the lead-up to her big day, her Bridezilla potential was huge. I wouldn't create drama by stepping down as her bridesmaid, but when it was all over, I would need to think about whether this was a friendship worth working on.

When I walked into Cal's flat with the key he'd let me borrow for the afternoon, it was strangely quiet. There was almost always some kind of sound, whether the TV or Aiden's tablet. Maybe they'd gone out for a bit. Cal did say they might go to the park for a while as I wasn't sure how long I'd be. That was perhaps for the best. My tension levels were high, and I wanted to relax for a bit before going out again later. However, as I entered the living room after taking off my coat and putting my bag down, I saw Cal sitting on the sofa. No TV, no video games playing. Just Cal on his own, and he turned his head to look at me as I walked in.

"Hey," he said, smiling.

"Hi." I glanced around. "Where's Aiden?"

"Guy came over to drop off some stuff I need for work on Monday, and he asked Aiden if he wanted to go out for a game of football. Guy said he'd watch him until we go over later."

I hadn't been expecting to have Cal to myself yet. The realisation caused the frustration inside me to squirm in my stomach.

"Are you okay?" Cal asked. "You look... stressed. Did Cinderella not find her perfect wedding dress?"

He'd learned enough about Jade to know exactly what she was like, but I wasn't ready to talk about how the afternoon had gone. What I wanted to do was forget about it. To pretend I wasn't best friends with such a pretentious cow.

She might not have respected what I had with Cal, but he was what I wanted.

His gorgeous brown eyes watched me, waiting for me to speak. But I didn't want to speak.

I wanted to ease my tension.

The satisfying way.

Without a word, I walked towards him, lifting my jumper over my head, and dropped it on the floor at his feet. His gaze heated as I straddled his lap, wound my arms around his neck, and kissed him hard.

There wasn't even a second of hesitation before he kissed me back, his arms circling my waist to drag me in closer. His tongue probed my mouth, and I pressed my hips against him, feeling his hardness against me already.

This, right here, is the only place I want to be.

I pulled back from him just for a moment to unclip my bra, flinging it to the side and enjoying the way Cal's eyes flashed at my move.

He leaned in, capturing one of my breasts in his mouth while his hands rested on my hips. I moaned at the sensation of his tongue gliding smoothly across my nipple, the bud stiffening instantly, but it wasn't enough.

I needed hard and fast.

Weaving my fingers through Cal's hair, I pushed him against me, urging him to take more of me while my free hand alternated between rolling my other nipple between my fingers and cupping my entire boob, squeezing at the soft flesh.

Cal's eyes darkened, and knowing he was watching me made my movements more exaggerated. Each tweak and brush of my skin shot tingles through me, yet somehow, it still didn't feel like enough.

Cal bucked his hips underneath me in approval, and I writhed against his hardening dick, my knickers already damp with arousal. His tongue flicked harder across my nipple, sparking my need for him higher. He pushed my hand away from my breast and his took its place, his touch rough across the delicate skin. His teeth grazed at my peaked bud, pulling it between his teeth, his fingers kneading my other breast almost punishingly. The moan I let out made Cal growl hungrily, sending a vibration through me that made me shudder.

I tugged at his hair, pulling him back from my tits so I could kiss him and get my hands on his chest. I slid my hand under his t-shirt, my fingers splayed out as I explored him, then scratched my nails lightly down his stomach. My breasts ached in the most delicious way from his touch, and I moved one of his hands back to my chest, my hand over his, encouraging him to squeeze even harder than before.

I needed it. Needed him to be rough. I wanted his hands, and his tongue, and his lips on every part of my skin. Wanted him to bite me, bruise me, fuck me, leaving me aching, shaky, and satisfied.

Cal's lips left mine, trailing along my jaw and down my neck, finding that sensitive spot that made my entire body shiver.

Reaching between us with my free hand, I flicked the button of his jeans open and slid his zip down. He put a hand under my ass to support me then raised his hips so I could pull his jeans and boxers down, freeing his now rock-hard dick. His mouth was demanding on mine as I undid my own jeans and lifted myself enough that I could get them and my soaked knickers down my legs. Once I'd wriggled them past my knees, Cal yanked my jeans off, then used both hands to tear my panties right off me, tossing the ripped material over his shoulder.

Before I could fully register the hotness of that move, he placed both hands on my hips again. I shifted my knees on either side of him, opening myself wide and moving a hand between my legs to rub at my wet, aching centre. I looked deep into his eyes as I moved my fingers across my slick core, and I could feel the heat coming from him as his gaze dropped to watch me. His chest heaved and his hand dragged down from my hip to my thigh. My fingers moved to my throbbing clit as he easily slipped a finger inside me. He didn't move, holding my other hip firmly as I squirmed, trying to get some relief. My lower stomach coiled, my pussy practically vibrating, willing him to fuck me.

Cal tilted his head, his breath hot against my throat, and whispered, "I'm in charge now."

The words fluttered across my skin, making me shiver with desire, and he moved my hand from my clit and back to my breast. I stroked my wet fingers across my tits, loving how tender they were from our touches. I was lost in the moment, weak with neediness and so desperate for him that I couldn't think straight.

"Harder," he said, his voice commanding.

I was hypnotised, totally under his control, and I loved it.

I did as he told me, but his hand moved from my hip, and there was a hard, sharp slap against my ass cheek. The sensation shot a bolt of pleasure through me, and I cried out, wanting more. Wanting to feel the sting, the pain. I wanted him to hurt me in that delicious way that made my body come alive.

"Harder!" he growled, his mouth enclosing one of my nipples again and biting sharply. My thighs grew slicker as I squeezed my breast, eager to please him so I could get what I wanted so badly.

"More," I mumbled, throwing my head back, and I cried out again as he slid another finger inside me, and I pushed myself down on them, my core tightening.

"You like that?" he whispered against my skin before grazing his teeth and stubble across my nipple while I rode his fingers, my legs trembling as I tugged at his hair.

"Yes!" I cried out, feeling myself racing closer to the edge. My body was so damn hot. So aroused as my movements sped up, the sensations overwhelming me until I felt dizzy.

Nothing else existed. Just me, him, and *this*.

"What do you like?" he asked, his voice gravelly.

"I...I..." I panted, closing my eyes. "I like your mouth on my skin. And when you... when you bite me."

His teeth gripped my nipple, tugging on it hard, and the spasm in my core almost tipped me over. I wanted the pleasure, but the build-up was so fucking intoxicating.

He pulled his fingers from me and I cried out again, watching as he sucked them into his mouth, eyes on me. My core throbbed, and I tried to form words, to beg him to take me, to let me come. The torture was too much. Too overwhelming.

I could barely breathe.

Cal put a hand on the back of my head, kissing me deeply, his tongue pushing against mine like he was claiming me. Letting me know I was his.

As he pulled away, his teeth nipped my lower lip. "Wallet," he said, nodding to the side of me.

He'd left his wallet on the table at the side of the sofa, and I reached over for it. I could barely see straight as I fumbled to find the condom. My body quivered with the need to have his hands all over me again. I didn't care where, as long as he touched me. Once I had the condom, I handed it to him, my chest heaving with the anticipation of having him inside me. Cal's breathing was heavy as he opened the packet and rolled the condom over his dick. I watched his every movement, wondering what it would be like to fuck him without anything in the way.

He eyed me for a moment as I stared at his thick cock standing proudly.

That was a mystery I'd solve another day.

With a growl of desperate need, I moved back over him, but just as I was about to sink onto him, he gripped my hips hard to stop me. He smirked cockily as I trembled. "What do you say?" he asked, licking his lips slowly, like he was still savouring the taste of me on them. My breath hitched and he slapped my arse again. My hips rocked involuntarily, small movements just to prolong the tiny tingles that were already racing through me. Cal rested his hand over my wet centre again, lightly teasing my folds until I was panting.

"Please," I cried, trying to grind against him. "Please!"

Without a word, he took his hand away and nodded towards his dick.

I sank down, immediately sliding onto him and gasping with relief, my arms back around his neck and his hands on my waist. I could feel his eyes on me as I rode him hard while he watched the bounce of my tits and the place where our bodies joined.

I was close. Getting closer, but the connection was so good I didn't want it to end. His dick twitched inside me, and his fingers found my swollen clit, pressing against it and causing my body to erupt in waves of satisfaction that pulsed out from my core to the tips of my fingers and toes.

The sound I let out sounded alien even to me, but I continued to ride him, crying out over and over until he reached his own release, thrusting his hips up as his balls emptied. He growled before tugging me into him and holding me tight against his chest.

Our breaths were heavy, and it had been such an epic release that I wanted to cry.

"Cal," I murmured into his neck. I didn't even know why. There was nothing I needed to say to him in that moment. It was more like I was reassuring myself that he was real. That he was with me. His hands were tight on my back, his dick still inside me.

The tightness slowly left my muscles, every bit of me shaking as I came down from the high.

"Shan," he whispered, his breath tickling my neck. "Talk to me."

It took me a few minutes to calm before I could move. I just stayed pressed against him, the rest of my tension draining away as I clung to him.

Taking in a deep breath, I finally lifted myself off him. I kinda wanted to go and clean up, and I knew he'd want to deal with the condom, but he sat me down on the top of his thighs and held me close to him again.

"Sorry," I said, resting my head on his shoulder. "I... I don't know."

"Why are you sorry?" he asked, his fingers playing with my hair in that way he did that I found comforting.

"I didn't intend to pounce on you the second I walked through the door," I said with a small laugh. I was sure he could feel the warmth of my cheek against his skin that wasn't solely due to exertion.

"You can do that anytime you want. That was the hottest thing I've ever seen." There was a huskiness to his tone, and a part of me cringed again at how bold I'd been. But a bigger part of me felt free.

Safe.

Cal made me feel safe to just be me. Whether that was to lounge around in my comfy, unflattering clothes or to beg him to bite me and touch myself in front of him... I was safe. Something I hadn't experienced with anyone before. Other men I'd dated had been financially safe, but in every other way, I'd been insecure. I hadn't felt emotionally supported. Hadn't felt able to ask for what I wanted in case I was called needy or high maintenance. And sex? Whatever I'd had before Cal could barely be called that. Previously, it had been mildly satisfying at best. At worst, it was a disappointing act done to satisfy my partner's needs while mine were unfulfilled.

With Cal, there were no expectations. He didn't need me to be a certain way to impress the 'right' people The only thing he'd ever asked me to give him was my time.

And it made me want to give him everything.

"What happened today, Shan?" Cal asked, interrupting my thoughts. "I know you weren't excited about going wedding dress shopping, but I thought you'd enjoy it when you got there."

The mention of the source of my frustration made my high deflate. It was *supposed* to be a good day, but my best friend had managed to ruin it. "Me too. But I should have known better."

I blew out another breath, knowing this conversation wouldn't exactly make his day. I hadn't thought about whether I'd tell him about all of it because I hadn't expected us to be alone. It wasn't a conversation to have in front of Aiden, and so if Cal had asked how the afternoon had been, I'd probably have just said it was fine. It wasn't that I thought I had to shield him from the snobbery that was such a big part of my life, more that I knew he already felt inferior. Not with me, but whenever mentions of my family or friends came up, he visibly stiffened. He felt pre-judged because of Jade's reaction to him. Maybe if I'd known we would last longer than two weeks, I might not have been quite as honest about

Jade's opinions. Then again, one meeting with her and it would have become clear anyway.

I pushed my hair back out of my face. "It all started okay, and it was good to see my mum. But then Jade's mum asked me about who I would be bringing to the wedding as a plus one."

Just as I'd expected, I felt the immediate tightening of his muscles. I was certain he wouldn't want to be anywhere near that wedding, but if we were still together by then, he was the only one I'd want to bring.

"As you know, I hadn't told my parents I'm seeing you yet," I said. He also knew that wasn't due to any level of embarrassment on my part. Simply that I wanted to give us a bit more time to see where things went. I'd tell them soon, as the weekend with him had shown me this was where I wanted to be. But I didn't want it to happen the way it did. "But Jade... she brought you into the conversation and kept saying things about you that weren't her place to say." I shifted my position so he could see my face fully because I didn't want him to misunderstand. "I wanted to tell my parents about you myself. To explain that you have a son, and that he's in my class, and... it wasn't for her to do. But Jade and her mum... they're awful. Jade's mum looked at me like being with someone who already has a child was the worst thing in the world."

"Come on, Shan," Cal said, also shifting so my ass scooted further down his legs. "Their judgement wasn't about me having Aiden, it was about me not being born with a silver spoon up my arse."

He wasn't upset with me, just pissed off that there was this one very real thing, this difference between us that had the potential to change people's opinions of me if I stayed with him. Not the good people in my life like Gaby and Nova, but certainly the friends I'd grown up with and maybe some of my family too.

"For them, that's part of what it is," I said honestly. "But I don't care about their opinions."

"Then why were you so upset when you came in?"

"I told you why." I leaned back a little. I knew this conversation would trigger his insecurities, but not to the point where he didn't believe what I was telling him. I *didn't* care about their opinions. Well, not in the way he was thinking. I cared because they were unfair to him, not because I thought he wasn't good enough for me.

Cal nodded, and I could see guilt at his tone mix with the worry about whatever else was stirring in his mind at that moment. "What did your mum say?" His jaw was tense, and I smiled.

"She was fine. The only thing she cares about is that I'm happy. And I am. I told her that."

There was a beat where he just looked at me. His eyes fixed on mine like he was looking for a sign that I was bullshitting him, and when he didn't see it, he loosened up a bit. "Why do you put up with Jade?" Cal asked, not for the first time.

"That is a good question," I said with a sigh as he pulled me back to him again, kissing the top of my head. "And I think I'm done. She apparently still wants me to be part of her wedding, and if I step back, it will cause all kinds of drama. Not just for me but between her mum and mine potentially, and since our two families have always been so close... it's just not a good idea. Plus, she should be the centre of attention in the lead-up to her wedding. I don't want the stress of knowing this big event is looming and being the one to disrupt it. But once it's over, I'm out. I can step away slowly and maybe nobody will even notice."

Cal raised his eyebrows. "Are you doing this for me? Because you shouldn't."

I shook my head. "It's not for you. I mean that in the nicest way possible," I added, and he chuckled. "It's just, being with you has made me see how much she tries to dictate every part of my life. She doesn't get away with nearly as much as she would like to, but when it was just me, I could ignore her. Now, I have you to think about. And not just you, but Aiden too. I don't want her toxicity and judgement around any of us. A normal best friend would be pleased I'd found someone. But all she can think about is how things look to others. I could not care less. I just want you."

Another pause, and then Cal tilted my chin with his finger and pressed his lips to mine before looking into my eyes. "I'm not good enough for you, Shan. I'm not. But I will do everything I can to deserve you."

It hurt me every time something like that fell from his lips. It didn't happen often. Mostly, it was flickers of doubt that showed behind his eyes if I talked about my parents or my friends. I knew some of the reasons he was so down on himself, but he'd admitted the mistakes he'd made when he was younger and they didn't matter to me. He'd confirmed there were things I still didn't know, but how bad could they be? He had Guy and Helen in his life, and if he was as bad as he thought, would they have his back? Helen didn't like him, but she had defended him all those weeks ago when everything had blown up with Aiden. If there was anything that terrible lurking in his past, she would never have allowed him into her home or around Aiden.

"I don't know why you continue to think that you somehow don't deserve me, but I'm really not that different from you. People are people, no matter where they came from. Do you think there aren't people I grew up with who haven't fucked up their lives beyond recognition? Or that people who came from shaky upbringings haven't gone on to become millionaires? It's just money, Cal. Money and circumstance." I placed my hand on the back of his neck. "I. Want. You. That's it."

He softened under my touch. "I know you do. I know."

"Do you think..." I began, but then stopped. The words had started to slip out of my mouth before I had even finished the thought. And it hardly made sense when I'd just told Cal that, after the wedding, I would distance myself from Jade. Honestly, the idea that had popped into my head was illogical, my brain still addled from the epic high I'd just been on. But now Cal was looking at me questioningly, and I wasn't sure I could backtrack.

"What?" he asked, his eyes on mine.

"This is a terrible idea, but I know you won't let it drop now, so... would you maybe consider meeting Jade?" His eyebrows rose comically, and I held up a hand. "I know. It's ridiculous. But I just thought... maybe if she could meet you, she'd see that she's not being fair." Even as I said the words, I knew they weren't true. Maybe the idea wasn't even about how she viewed him anyway. What I wanted was to know that, if I asked her to, she'd make an effort. For me. For our friendship.

"You know that wouldn't happen," Cal said quietly. "If you wanted me to meet her, I would. But it won't change anything."

If he'd said no, I wouldn't have minded at all. *I* didn't want to see her most of the time these days, but the fact that he'd said he would do it without pause filled me with warmth. The thing I so badly needed from my best friend was coming from Cal. The reassurance that he'd try to bridge the gap between the two of them if it mattered to me.

"It probably won't," I admitted with a sigh.

"Ask her," Cal said, resting his hand on my cheek. "If she's up for it, I'll go. And I'll be nice. But I won't put up with any shit from her either."

I smiled. "I wouldn't expect you to."

Chapter 16

Cal

Shannen and I walked down Guy's front path, Shannen holding a bottle of white wine in one hand, whilst her other was wrapped around mine.

After she came home from dress shopping with Jade and she'd subsequently fucked me senseless on my couch, things had got tense for a while. It didn't happen often, but talk of her family had made me edgy. I didn't care that she hadn't told her parents about me before because I wasn't anywhere near ready to meet them anyway. What I did care about was her prissy friend whispering in her ear about how bad I was for her. She wasn't wrong, but Shannen didn't seem to mind. If it continued...if Jade kept pushing her, would it matter then? I'd told Shannen I'd meet Jade. I wasn't crazy about it, but if we were going to stay together, at some point, our paths would have to cross.

I didn't doubt that Shannen wanted to be with me. What I wondered was how long it would be until the differences between us got too big. And how long before she got sick of reassuring me? I needed to stop showing how insecure all this stuff made me, but she'd done something to me. She'd made it okay for me to be a mess. It was a relief and a hit to my masculinity at the same time. That was also the reason I hadn't been a good dad to Aiden. I'd fought between telling him it was fine to be sad and the nagging voice of my father, who firmly believed that crying was a sign of weakness. I'd stayed in limbo for a long time, not teaching him anything either way, and that was why he was emotionally all over the place. Because I just let him be. Let him see me vent my frustration in an unhealthy way. I knew better now. I had to learn fast when I was the only one responsible for him, but I still felt like I was failing at almost everything.

And yet, I was happier than I'd been since I was a kid.

I wasn't good at figuring out how my brain worked, but what I knew for sure was that I wanted Shannen. I wanted more weekends like the one we were having.

More of her fucking me on the sofa wouldn't go amiss either, but I pushed that thought away because I didn't want to arrive at Guy's with a boner.

"You didn't need to bring wine, you know?" I said as we reached the door. "It's only Guy and Helen, and we're having a takeaway. They won't expect anything."

Shannen turned her head towards me and smiled. "I know they don't expect it, but it's the polite thing to do. They said they would pay for a takeaway for all of us tonight, so it's just a nice gesture." I shrugged, and she laughed out loud. "Cal, really? All the times you've come over here for food and you've never taken anything with you to say thank you?"

"No. Because they don't expect it."

Shaking her head as I rang the doorbell, she teased, "No wonder Helen wanted you gone. It never occurred to you to do something nice for them?"

I laughed. "Listen, I could offer her a six-week cruise, a million quid, and a basket of puppies, and she still wouldn't be happy. The only thing she wants from me is to never have to see me again."

"And yet, here we are. Invited."

Her smile made me want to kiss it from her lips, and I would have if I didn't hear footsteps approaching. "Guy invited us. Helen tolerates us."

When Shannen laughed again just as Guy opened the door, I pushed the conversation aside. The truth was, Helen didn't mind Shannen. They had only met a couple of times, most of them briefly as we dropped Aiden off at their place, but she was warmer to Shannen than me. I was surprised when they'd invited us over, but Guy had assured me it wasn't so Helen could kick off about something I'd done. His words, not mine. She apparently just wanted to get to know Shannen better.

Guy welcomed us inside, closing the door, and Aiden rushed out from the living room, a wide smile on his face. He hugged us both at once, one of his little arms wrapped around each of us, and I ruffled his hair. Once again, Shannen gave me a side smile at his affection towards her, and I wound my free arm around her, squeezing her waist.

"Hey, buddy. Have you had a good afternoon?" I asked.

"Yeah. Me and Guy played football, and then we came here and Helen and me made cupcakes!"

"I hope you saved some for us," Shannen said, and Aiden beamed at her.

"We did. Helen said they can be for dessert."

Shannen laughed. "I have never had room for dessert after a Chinese, but maybe we can take some home with us."

She tensed as the words left her mouth, and my heart started to beat harder.

Home. She said home.

119

She didn't mean that your home is her home, you bellend. She meant she is going to your home tonight. Your and Aiden's home, not hers.

My heart wasn't hammering because I hated the idea of it being her home, though. It was the opposite. I just hadn't expected to hear those words, nor to like them. To like the idea of having a home with her one day.

It's been six weeks. The naggy voice of doubt whispered in my ear. I wasn't a guy who dived in feet first, so I wouldn't start now, but I also couldn't pretend I didn't feel something beyond basic lust for Shannen. There was no way to tell if we'd even see another few months out, let alone more, but I did know that I wanted it.

"I didn't..." she began, her voice croaky as she looked at me, her cheeks red. "I meant..."

I tried to ignore Guy concealing a laugh, and I smiled. "It's okay. I knew what you meant."

But her eyes met mine, and I could see a small part of her had the same thought as me. That she had thought about a future where that could happen. Perhaps more than I had from the blush on her face, but still. Another sign this was getting real. Another reason for my brain to fight about when and how to talk to her about all the things I was still hiding. The closer we got, the less I could excuse keeping secrets.

"Come on," Aiden said, tugging my hand and dragging me into the living room. I winked at Shannen before I disappeared down the hallway, knowing she needed a minute. Guy was with her, and he'd calm her down.

In the living room, Helen was sitting on the sofa, watching some game show on TV, and Aiden bounded over and sat beside her. I offered her a perfunctory hello before taking off my jacket, and she answered with equal effort. I hung my jacket on one of the chairs at the back end of the room, and seconds later, Shannen and Guy joined us.

"Shannen brought wine," Guy said, holding up the bottle to show Helen as Shannen came to stand beside me.

Helen raised a brow. I wasn't sure why she was surprised. She hadn't let up about the fact that Shannen was better than me since the day they met.

"Thank you," Helen said, smiling softly at her. "That'll go down nicely with the Chinese."

"I'm starving," Guy said. "Shall we grab a menu and see what we want?"

"I know what I want," Helen said, and Guy smiled.

"Chicken curry with fried rice and a side of chips," he said, and she nodded. Guy turned to me. "I assume Aiden will have a chicken chow mein?"

We didn't have Chinese takeaway that often, but he liked noodles and chicken, so it became his go-to order.

Once everyone's orders were noted, Guy phoned it through and we all sat down. Guy sat on the other end of the sofa from Helen and Aiden, and Shannen and I sat close together on the other sofa. The TV continued to play in the background. I knew from living there for so long that Helen was competitive, and she and Guy always made a game out of trying to answer any quiz questions first.

Aiden remained by Helen's side, content watching the TV. Within a few minutes, the questions were coming fast.

"In what year did Tony Blair become the British Prime Minister?" the quiz show host asked.

"1995," Helen answered quickly.

"No idea." Guy's brow wrinkled.

"I'm telling you," Helen replied not taking her eyes off the screen. She was unusually focused. Normally, when they had people over, the TV was off and she would be chatty with their guests. Since it was her idea that we came over, I was surprised she had barely looked away from the quiz show, but I'd long ago given up trying to understand her.

Beside me, Shannen twitched, and when I glanced at her, she was biting her lip.

"You know the answer, don't you?" I asked quietly. Shannen nodded. "Is she right?" I jerked my head towards Helen, and she shook hers. "Go on, Shan. Show her who's boss."

She snorted out a quiet laugh, and Guy whipped his head towards us. "What?"

"Shannen knows the answer," I singsonged, and Guy laughed at me.

"Come on then," he prompted with a smile.

"It's 1997."

Helen and Guy exchanged a glance.

"What can I say?" Shannen shrugged. "My parents are into politics."

The game show host revealed Shannen was correct, and I squeezed her leg. Not in a condescending way. I just enjoyed seeing her getting one up on Helen. I never joined in with these things because I didn't know shit. My general knowledge skills were terrible, and anything I learned while watching these shows I forgot about the moment they were over.

Now Shannen had joined in once, she was on a roll, and she frequently beat Helen to the answers, much to my amusement. Helen wasn't bothered by Shannen's input. In fact, she seemed to find it entertaining and started to loosen up. After a while, she said, "Maybe we should set up a team for quiz nights at The Lucky Jester."

"That might be fun," Shannen said, looking at me. "You want to?"

I gave her a questioning look. "You did see me not answering any of these questions, didn't you?"

"Doesn't mean you don't know them."

"He doesn't," Helen said with a smirk. "We might need an extra person since Cal will be no use. I'm not even sure how big teams need to be."

Shannen bristled at how quickly Helen had dismissed me, while I didn't even flinch.

"Plus," Helen went on, "we can't all go out. There'd be nobody to watch Aiden."

The tone of 'it's about time he looked after his own kid' was clear to everyone and totally unnecessary. The only times I hadn't been with Aiden since we'd moved out were when I was at work and the few times Guy and Helen had offered to have Aiden for the night. I think in all that time, I'd asked them once. The rest was all them.

"I guess that idea's out then," Guy said, quickly trying to smooth things over.

"On second thoughts," Helen pressed, looking at me, getting into a bitchy stride, "it might be good if you came to a quiz night. You might learn something."

Shannen's fingers wiggled as if to lessen the tension in them. I placed my hand over hers without looking at her because I didn't want to draw attention to it. This was just Helen's way when it came to me. She always perked up when she got a chance to make a dig at me. Nothing she'd said had ever hurt my feelings because I didn't like her and I didn't care what she thought.

The doorbell rang, interrupting both the conversation and the quizzing. Guy jumped up.

"Helen, give me a hand, please." His shoulders were rigid, and I eyed him questioningly, even though he wasn't looking at me.

Was he pissed off with the way she'd spoken to me? He tended not to get involved unless she went too far, but we didn't usually have an audience.

Helen slid out from beside Aiden, her mouth set in a thin line, and once they were gone, I turned slightly towards Shannen, whose jaw was still clenched.

She breathed out slowly.

"You'll get used to her," I said quietly, squeezing her hand again.

She shook her head. "What is her problem?" she hissed. "She doesn't like you, I get that. *Everyone* gets it. But it's like she purposely chooses the conversations just so she can attack you."

"It's just how she is with me." I shrugged, rubbing my thumb across her knuckles.

She shook her head, confusion making her eyes narrow. "How can you be okay with it?"

Something clicked inside my brain at her words. She was so annoyed on my behalf, but I knew exactly how she felt because I'd felt it too. Not for myself but for her.

I shuffled closer to Shannen, my voice remaining low so as not to disturb Aiden, who was still watching the game show. "Shan, how you feel right now is how I feel every time I know Jade has been saying stuff to upset you. I wonder why you put up with her the way you wonder why I put up with Helen."

Shannen dropped her head onto my shoulder. "Maybe we both need to stand up for ourselves."

"Or get new friends," I suggested, making her laugh lightly.

"That's an option. We're not giving up Guy, though. He's good."

I smiled. "Yeah, he is."

Although Shannen and Guy hadn't spent a lot of time together, they always got along well. I thought it was because of whatever he'd said to her that first time they met, when he'd spoken to her outside in her car. Neither of them had ever told me exactly what they discussed, but they seemed to have a lot of respect for each other, and that made my life easier.

The sound of a plate smashing in the kitchen made all three of us jump. Shannen and I looked at each other and then at Aiden, who froze as Helen yelled, "Then why don't you just go!"

Guy and Helen rarely argued, and aside from Guy looking stressed a minute ago, there was no indication of anything being wrong.

Aiden flew across the room to sit with Shannen and me, just as Guy yelled, "I'm so sick of this! This can't keep happening!"

"Well, maybe it wouldn't if you acted like you cared! This matters to me, Guy!"

Aiden curled in against me, but I kissed the top of his head before shifting him onto Shannen's lap and standing up. Aiden was used to hearing me go off, but he wasn't used to hearing Guy and Helen, and clearly, it had affected him. I needed them to stop.

Shannen tightened her arms around him, and I heard her speaking softly to him as I left the room, closing the door behind me. Guy and Helen continued to yell as I walked quickly along the hallway. When I reached the kitchen, I saw the shattered plate around their feet, and they stopped yelling when they saw me.

Guy ran a hand through his hair like he'd just realised how loud they were being, and Helen glared at me.

"What?" she snapped.

"Your yelling is upsetting Aiden," I said, my voice as even as I could make it. I was sick of her shit, not just because she'd scared my son, but because her mood had annoyed Shannen, and she'd just been screaming at my best mate, who deserved a medal for putting up with her.

"Well, you know where the door is!"

"Helen, for fuck's sake!" Guy turned to her. "Can't we just have a drink and calm down?"

"Calm down? Calm *down*?" She looked murderous, and we both took a step away from her. Shaking her head, she said, "You need to leave. All of you." She stared at Guy, making it clear she meant him too.

His jaw tightened, and he swallowed. "I'm not going anywhere."

What is going on here? Guy and Helen bickered, usually good-naturedly, but I'd never seen anything like this between them. As much as I disliked Helen, and as much of a bitch as she could be at times, she'd never lost it like this. She was always on my back about *my* temper, so whatever had happened must have been big for her to shout.

"We'll go," I said, trying not to smell the Chinese food that still sat in bags on the counter. I was starving, but I couldn't exactly ask for our orders to take home. We hadn't paid for it anyway.

"Not like you to take a hint," she said, once again unable to resist taking a swipe at me.

And that's me reaching my limit.

Turning towards her, I coldly said, "Listen, you hypocritical bitch, I don't know what is going on, and right now, I don't care." I raised my arm, pointing towards the living room. "My son is upset in there because of you. You scared the hell out of him, and he doesn't need to hear you screaming at Guy. And you might want to re-think throwing Guy out because if he's got any fucking sense, he won't come back."

Normally, at that point, Guy would have jumped in to defend her, and the fact that the only thing he did was flash me a look of thanks told me I might not have been far off the mark.

Guy had never mentioned there were any problems between them. Most likely because he knew I'd have told him to get away from her, which wouldn't have been very useful. To be fair, even I wasn't that much of a prick. He loved her and I couldn't imagine him with anyone else. The idea of them not being together shook me in a way I hadn't expected. Probably because, once, they were the only stable thing in my life.

"That's fine with me!" Helen raged at me. "After all, I'm just a hysterical female who needs to 'calm down'. Maybe I'll be able to do that without him around!"

The sheer hatred in her eyes nearly knocked me off my feet, so I had no idea what it was doing to Guy. He stared at her, their eyes locked, and I knew Guy was about three seconds from flipping. He wasn't just pissed off. He looked... upset wasn't a strong enough word. His whole demeanour looked wrecked and tired. Where had it even come from? He'd been fine. Not just that day, for weeks, but whatever had caused this didn't feel new.

"Hey."

Shannen's soft voice broke the rising tension, and we all turned to her. She stood in the doorway, Aiden in her arms with his head buried into her shoulder. Helen let out a small sob at the sight of him and turned away, leaning against the counter, her head down and shoulders shaking.

"Do you guys want to take Aiden home?" Shannen said, and this time, she didn't squirm over the word 'home'. Her eyes were practically begging us to do it, but I wasn't sure what her plan was. "Guy," she added gently, and he looked up at her. "Take your car and take them home. I'll drive back in a bit."

"You're staying?" I asked, shock making my voice louder than I intended.

She nodded. "Just for a bit. I'm going to help Helen clean up in here." It was obviously just an excuse as it would take thirty seconds to clear away a broken plate. Not a two-person job.

Shannen stepped past me and handed Aiden to Guy, and Guy instantly relaxed, holding him close. Aiden wrapped his arms around my best mate's neck.

"Come on, buddy," Guy said gently. "Let's take our food and go home."

Thank fuck.

I had a quick look through the bags, figuring out which containers were ours. Once I had it organised, I picked up the bags then headed for Shannen as Guy carried Aiden towards the front door.

"Are you going to be okay?" I asked her, though I hoped my eyes were saying, *'Why are you doing this?'*

She nodded. "I won't be long, I promise." She smiled up at me, and I really didn't want to leave without her. Helen wasn't screaming anymore, but I still didn't want Shannen to be alone with her.

After a short pause, I kissed her on the cheek before following Guy to the door. As he opened it, Aiden lifted his head and reached out his hand.

"Shannen!" he said, and my heart leapt. I was pretty sure Shannen felt the same way, and she walked over to him and linked his fingers with hers.

He'd adored her as a teacher, but over the weekend, when she'd shared her favourite childhood movie with him and they'd made pancakes and played games together, it had changed something. It had been happening very slowly over the time we'd been seeing each other, but the last couple of days had cemented his affection for her.

"Wait up for me, okay?" she told Aiden. "I'll be coming over soon. And don't eat my Chinese!"

Aiden giggled as she winked, and I grinned at her.

She smiled back, and Guy turned his head. Letting out a deep sigh, he gave her a grateful nod before heading out the front door.

Chapter 17

Shannen

I stood in the kitchen doorway as Helen leaned over the counter at the far end of the kitchen, her shoulders shaking.

Less than ten minutes ago, I'd been on the verge of marching across the living room and throttling her for the way she was talking to and about Cal.

Now, my heart ached for her.

I'd heard the words 'I'm just a hysterical female' after she'd screamed at Guy that *'this'* mattered to her, and I began to put some pieces together in my mind.

My gut feeling told me I was right.

Unsure how to broach the subject, I walked tentatively into the kitchen and lightly touched Helen's arm. She stiffened but didn't turn around or push me away. She just continued to cry. After another moment, I gently lifted her wrist from the counter and turned her to face me. Tears streamed down her cheeks, her eyes were sunken and dull, and her blonde hair hung around her face.

Even though I didn't know her well and she was incredibly hard to warm to most of the time, I wrapped my arms around her and pulled her in for a hug. She collapsed against me, her body trembling as she sobbed and clung to me.

"It's okay," I said gently, holding her tight. "It's okay."

I kept a hold of her until, eventually, her tears slowed and she stopped shaking, straightening up and using the sleeve of her white jumper to dry her face.

"Coffee, tea, or wine?" I asked.

Helen paused for a second, then said, "Coffee."

She looked exhausted, her eyes puffy and red, and she pointed me in the direction of the mugs and sat down at the kitchen table while I made the drinks.

Once they were ready, I took them over to the table and sat down in the chair opposite Helen's. She'd calmed, but her face was pale and tear-stained. She'd tucked one leg underneath her and wrapped her arms around herself like she was cold.

"How long have you been trying?" I asked quietly.

Her head lifted to look at me. "How did you know?"

With a shrug, I said, "I guessed. My sister took a while to get pregnant, and I saw her have monthly breakdowns when it didn't happen. That and some of the things you shouted made me think that's what it is."

Helen nodded. "I thought this month was it," she said. "My period was five days late, and we were going to get a pregnancy test on Monday, but this morning..." she trailed off. "Turns out, we don't need to." With a sigh, she pushed her hair back out of her face. "It's been a year of trying. I had a miscarriage two years ago, which scared me off from trying again for a while, but for the last year, I've really wanted to start a family. I've been doing everything the experts recommend to stay healthy and active, and we've been having sex at the perfect times of the month to increase my chances, but... nothing." Helen drew her mug towards her, wrapping her hands tightly around it as if it would somehow ease her pain.

"I'm sorry," I said softly. "But, you know, in the grand scheme of things, a year isn't that long."

"I know." Helen sighed again and began turning the mug slowly around in circles on the table. Her eyes focused on it as if the repetition comforted her. "But with each month it doesn't happen, I'm getting more disheartened. Like, what the hell is wrong with me? What kind of woman can't get pregnant?"

"Don't do that." I reached across and placed my hand over one of hers. "Don't blame yourself for something that isn't your fault. There could be all kinds of reasons it isn't working out."

"Well, I wouldn't know because Guy refuses to come to the doctor with me. I want us to get some tests to make sure everything is okay with both of us, but he says that since I got pregnant before, there can't be anything wrong." She shook her head, tension building around her again. Her jaw clenched. "I just... I feel like I'm in this on my own sometimes."

Knowing Helen better would be really useful right now...

I could only guess based on the few times I'd met her, and she hadn't been particularly likeable on most of those occasions. She might have been lovely when she wasn't heaping stress on herself, though. According to Cal, she was a bitch most of the time, but I very much doubted Guy would be with a woman who was so prickly on a regular basis. Plus, I'd seen glimpses of her softer side now and again.

"Does Guy want this too?" I asked.

Helen shrugged. "He says he does, but then he tells me to just relax, and it'll happen when the time is right. I believe he wants a family, but I don't know if he wants it as much as I do. If he did..." she trailed off, shaking her head.

"What?" I pressed.

She leaned back in the chair, picking up her cup to take a sip of coffee. "I just want him to understand how I feel. He acts like I'm an overemotional pain in the arse, and it's getting old. I'm thirty-three, and Guy and I have been together for almost eight years. Where's the commitment?"

I had to fight not to raise an eyebrow. In my world, eight years without at least a proposal was a lifetime. However, in the real world, I knew that getting married and starting a family wasn't the only way to live a fulfilling life. There were plenty of couples who had children but didn't get married, or who got married and never had kids. There were men and women who worked on their career, or travelled the world, and didn't do anything in the traditional way.

"Have you told him how you feel?"

"Yup. Many times. It's not..." she paused, looking up at me. "He's never *called* me an overemotional pain in the arse. It's just that he always wants to brush the way I feel aside. He doesn't want to listen when I want to talk about it."

From his reaction to her yelling, it didn't seem like he exhibited the behaviour of a man who didn't care. When he left, he'd looked as tired and drained as Helen.

Placing my hands around my own cup, I said, "Listen, I don't know either of you very well, so I'm just guessing here, but have you thought that maybe he's finding it hard too?"

Helen blew across the surface of her drink to cool it. "If that were true, he would talk to me. That's why I lost my temper tonight. He was going on at me about laying into Cal, and all I could think about was how he doesn't show the same consideration for the way *I* feel. Today of all days."

My hackles rose at the mention of her behaviour towards Cal. Because hurting or not, attacking someone else was a shitty way to deal with it.

"What?" she asked when I didn't speak for a moment. "You agree with Guy."

It wasn't a question.

Letting go of my cup, I rubbed at my forehead. "This isn't about Cal. That's not why I stayed."

She shrugged. "Why did you if not to defend your man?"

Standing up, I turned away from her for a moment, taking a deep breath. "If this is how you are with Guy, I'm not surprised he doesn't say anything. Do you always turn everything into a confrontation?"

Guilt shot through me almost immediately because she was in pain, but she was so damn difficult.

Shaking my head, I wished I could take a break, but I'd held this in for weeks. The glares in Cal's direction, the mumbled remarks. The stares full of judgement aimed at me just for being with him. I was tired of it all. Cal and Guy both said

Helen liked me, but she had a weird way of showing it. I *wanted* to like her, yet she made it so bloody hard.

Turning back to face her, I said, "I hoped I could be here for you. So you could talk to someone other than Guy. But it always leads to the same thing. Any chance you get, you can't stop yourself from going at Cal. Even when he isn't in the room. I hoped... God, I thought maybe we could be friends. Guy told Cal that you wanted to get to know me, but instead, you had to lash out and make everyone uncomfortable. Just because Cal isn't affected by your words, that doesn't mean the rest of us are immune. How about some respect for me, and for his best friend? Most especially for his son, who was sitting right beside you while you were saying that stuff."

I realised I had done the thing I'd said I hadn't intended to do. I *hadn't* stayed to defend Cal, but irritation had got the best of me.

The mention of Aiden made Helen bristle, and her eyes narrowed. "Better he finds out sooner rather than later that his dad's a disappointment."

"What is your problem with him?" I asked, throwing my hands in the air. "I could kind of see it when he lived here, when he was under your feet all the time. Especially in the beginning, when he had nothing and had to rely on you and Guy for everything. But he's been gone for weeks. He hasn't relied on you in any additional ways since he left. In fact, you're doing less now he's able to finish work early some days to get Aiden from school. So, what is it? What about him makes you hate him so much?"

Her eyes filled with tears again, but there was no other sign of upset in her expression. She still looked like she wanted to snap at me, to scream at me, but she didn't.

As the first tear slipped down her cheek, she threw her head back for a second, closing her eyes. Letting out a long breath, she looked me straight in the eye and said, "When Cal first came here, he was a waste of space. He had nothing, he didn't show any sign of wanting to do anything, and he was just always *there*. When Guy said Cal wouldn't be here for long, I believed him, but then he mentioned Cal needed a stable home and a job so he could get Aiden back." Her blue eyes glazed over for a moment. "Guy and I almost split up over it. Cal wasn't who he is now. He was angry *all* the time. He had no patience, no drive. I told Guy he wasn't our responsibility, but Guy refused to give up on him. It got to the point where I threatened to leave, but Guy begged me to stay. To give Cal a chance and help him. So I did."

I walked back over to the chair and sat down again, but I didn't say a word.

"Guy gave him a job," she went on. "And once he had that, he was better. He wasn't in my way all the time, and he had his own money, so he actually paid for things instead of sponging off us. And then he got Aiden back." Helen swiped at her tears again. "Cal was so awkward with him in the beginning, and Aiden wasn't a picnic either. Aiden was quiet and unsure, and sometimes he would flip out over the smallest things. Cal didn't know how to deal with him, so at first, a lot of that fell on me and Guy. We took care of him, and the more we did that, the more Cal pissed me off. He didn't try hard enough with Aiden for a long time, when Aiden needed it most."

Cal had admitted that to me himself, but he and Aiden were closer now. Their relationship was better. Why was Helen always so fixated on the things Cal had done wrong instead of the things he'd done right?

"He's come a long way," I said. "Both of them have."

Helen nodded. "Yeah. A long way."

"So why do you still hate him?"

Swallowing hard, she said, "Cal had Aiden by mistake, and he couldn't look after him. When Aiden came here, I couldn't understand how Cal could have ever let him go. How he could drown in his own misery instead of sorting himself out for his child. Aiden needed someone to love him, and Cal failed him over and over."

I bit down at the anger that bubbled up at her words. Cal had made mistakes, but there wasn't a parent on the planet who hadn't. Not everyone's were as serious as Cal's, but being responsible for a child doesn't come with a handbook. Cal loved Aiden more than anything. He'd always loved him; that was why he had such a hard time forgiving himself for everything that had happened. It ate away at him all the time, making him feel like a failure.

Maybe her words did affect Cal more than he let on. A lot of the things he'd said about himself sounded an awful lot like Helen.

"That's not a reason for *you* to hate him, though," I said. "And it's not a reason for you to make him feel worse for something he already hates himself for."

Helen shook her head, her tears falling harder.

"I know, okay?" Her shoulders slumped forward, and she wrapped her arms around herself again. "I know Aiden needs to be with his dad, and I know Cal can take care of him. I just wish... I wish he was better at *being* a dad."

I didn't know what it was like to want a baby so much that it took over everything else. I didn't know how Helen must have felt wanting a child and having one who needed her in her house while his father couldn't cope. But I did know that when my sister struggled to conceive, she'd told me that the whole situation was made worse when she got envious of couples with children. She didn't begrudge them their happiness, she just wished she was in their shoes.

I stood up and then knelt on the floor beside her, wrapping my arms around her again.

"Why are you being nice to me?" she asked, her tears soaking into my shoulder.

"Because I finally feel like I understand something about you," I told her. "And it turns out, you might not be so bad after all."

She gave a choked laugh. "Well... thanks."

I laughed a little too as I pulled back from her. "Helen, you and Cal might never get along, but I swear to you, he is trying so hard to be the best dad he can be. This weekend, I got to see them together in their own home for longer than a couple of hours and they're doing great."

"I know." She nodded. "I know. I just... I miss having Aiden around. It was easier for me not to stress when Aiden kept me busy."

"Then why are you still always nagging at Cal to look after him?"

She grimaced. "Habit, I guess." Wiping her eyes, she said, "Even I know I owe him an apology for tonight. But I can't help the way I feel about him. I still see what he used to be and know it could only take the smallest thing to send him back there."

Her words were unfair, but she felt how she felt. If seeing how much Cal had changed since she first met him wasn't enough, nothing I could say would help.

The conversation with Helen hadn't clarified a whole lot about whether I liked her or not. She was defensive and judgemental, but she was also suffering in her own way too. *Could* we be friends? I hadn't completely ruled it out, but I wasn't sold on it either. It didn't matter much either way when it came down to it. Cal had maintained a friendship with Guy despite being unable to get along with Helen, so if that was how it had to be for me too, then we'd make it work. The last thing I needed in my life was another 'friend' who didn't like Cal.

Which brought me back to Jade. I'd been thinking about the afternoon with her, and about her meeting Cal. It sounded like a terrible idea; I knew that. But I had tolerated Jade's fiancé, Scott, for years. He was smug, and rude, and I couldn't stand him, but I put up with him without a single complaint because he made her happy. If she couldn't do the same for me, what was the point?

Letting out a long breath, I stood up. "I should go, but... give yourself a break. Stop blaming yourself for things that aren't your fault."

Helen nodded, a hint of gratitude showing in her eyes. "I'll try."

With a single nod, I headed out to the hallway to get my things. As I went, I typed out a text to Jade.

> Hey. I've been thinking, and it's time you met Cal. Let me know when you're free this week and we'll go out for a drink. You need to give him a chance x

Within twenty minutes, I was back at Cal's apartment, waiting for him to open the door.

I felt... exhausted. The entire day had been draining to say the least. From the disaster with Jade, to the most satisfying tension release with Cal, to then walking on eggshells at Guy and Helen's... I just wanted to eat and then snuggle up with Cal and Aiden for a while before bed.

The scent of the Chinese food hit me immediately when Cal opened the door, and Aiden ran down the hallway and flung himself at me before I even got inside.

I laughed as I lifted him up, and he wound his arms around my neck. Cal smiled at me as I cuddled Aiden, and a wave of happiness washed over me when he held on tight as if he hadn't seen me in years.

This. This is what people mean when they say their heart is full.

Being around Aiden for the full weekend had worried me a but I wasn't sure how he would deal with his teacher being in his home for so long. We'd got along well all the other times I'd been with him and Cal, but this was very different. A full weekend with no break instead of a day here or a few hours there. But it had been great. Aiden was so different now from the troubled and challenging boy he'd been when he'd first stepped into my classroom. He still wasn't an angel, but he'd been less disruptive since he and Cal had moved. Knowing what I knew now about Guy and Helen's relationship, I couldn't help but wonder if, in part, Aiden had picked up on some discomfort between the two of them that had unsettled him, or if he was simply happier now he could spend more one on one time with Cal. Either way, the changes in him were huge.

"Hey, Aiden," I said, stepping inside. As Cal closed the door behind me, I reached up to briefly brush my lips across his.

"Are you okay?" Cal asked, wrapping his arms around both of us and increasing the feeling of warmth running through me.

"Yeah." I nodded. "But I'm starving."

"Me too!" Aiden said, and Cal and I laughed as we walked down the hall to the living room.

Guy sat with his Kung Po Chicken on a plate in his lap, poking at it with his fork. Aiden's chicken chow mein was on the coffee table in its plastic container, abandoned as he was still wrapped around me, and Cal's shredded crispy beef and chips were piled high on a plate that rested on the sofa.

I put Aiden down, and he ran back to the coffee table and sat on the floor to tuck in.

"I'll get your food, Shan," Cal said, and I smiled gratefully before he went to the kitchen.

Once he was gone, I shrugged out of my jacket and took off my boots, putting them in a neat pile by the living room door before turning my attention to Guy.

He must have felt my eyes on him because he looked up at me. Taking one look at my face, he said, "She's hard work, isn't she?"

I tried hard to hide an embarrassed smile because I didn't want to be horrible about his woman, but I failed, and Guy huffed out a laugh. The sparkle was missing from his eyes, though.

"Are you all right?" I asked him.

We both glanced at Aiden, who was feasting on his meal, and Guy shrugged.

"How much did she tell you?" he asked.

"Not much. She said you were trying to…" I trailed off, not wanting to go into details with Aiden there.

"Yeah." Guy sighed, continuing to push his fork through his food. "How is she doing?"

Grimacing, I said, "You guys need to talk."

He raised his eyebrows. "That's your advice? You've just tried that for half an hour, and you look like you need a stiff drink."

His tone told me he was kidding, but there was some truth at the heart of it. She *was* hard to talk to. She held grudges and attacked as soon as she felt threatened. But she did love Guy. That was clear in how badly she wanted to have a family with him.

"Do you want what she wants?" I asked him, and his smile faded, his eyes glazing over.

He nodded. "Of course I do. I just don't want it to take over our whole lives. Things haven't been fun for a while. Every time we… you know… it's for a purpose. I just want things to be relaxed again. But that's difficult when she's pissed off all the time."

Cal came back into the room with my chow mein and sweet and sour chicken balls on a plate. He put it down on the coffee table before lifting his own plate from the sofa and sitting down. He didn't start to eat, though, and I had a feeling he'd been listening to our conversation from the kitchen.

"I don't know if…" I began but then trailed off, trying to find the right words. "She's struggling, Guy. Would you consider seeing the doctor with her? It might just put both of your minds at ease." I glanced over at Aiden, who was looking at something on his iPad while he ate. He might have been listening, but he seemed too engrossed in swiping something across the screen.

Guy sighed. "I really don't think anything is wrong, but we can't go on like this. I'll talk to her about it when I get home." He offered me a grateful smile. "Thanks for checking on her."

"Not a problem."

My phone vibrated in my pocket as I walked around the coffee table to sit down, and I pulled it out of my pocket.

> **Jade: Scott and I are both free on Thursday night at 7.30. I don't think meeting Callum will change any-thing, but we'll slum it at your local and see xx**

Thanks for the effort, bestie.

As I sat down, I turned the phone towards Cal to show him the message, and he rolled his eyes.

"Shall we do it?" I asked him, already knowing if this was her approach, there was little chance she would even try to get along with Cal.

He nodded, looking over at Guy. "I know this is a crap time to ask, but can you watch Aiden on Thursday night for a couple of hours?"

"Sure," he answered, finally taking a mouthful of his food. "It'll just be me because Helen will be at work. What time?"

"Can you get here for seven? I'll make sure Aiden's ready for bed by the time you get here."

Aiden still didn't pay attention, even with the mention of his name, and Guy said, "Yeah, I can do that. Where are you off to?"

I stabbed my fork into a chicken ball and dipped it into the sweet and sour sauce, swirling it around. "I'm going to attempt to stop my best friend from running Cal down all the time by introducing them." There was no disguising the cynicism in my tone.

Guy raised an eyebrow.

I lifted my chicken ball, letting the excess dip fall back into the polystyrene pot. "You know how much Cal dislikes Helen?" Guy nodded. "Well, it's like that, except it's based on absolutely nothing."

With a snort, Guy said, "Maybe we need to get new friends."

I glanced at Cal, and we both smiled. "Yeah, we said that earlier. You'll be pleased to know we decided to keep you, though."

Smiling properly for the first time since I'd got back, Guy said, "Well, that's something. Now, I just need to find out if Helen still wants to keep me."

We ate, making small talk, and Guy went home almost as soon as we'd finished eating. Once the plates were cleared up, Cal and I put Aiden to bed together before going to Cal's room.

It was super early for either of us to be in bed when we hadn't gone there with the sole purpose of getting naked. I knew we would later, but in that moment, all I wanted was to lie with him and enjoy one more night together before I had to go back to my place. There was one more week until half-term, and I hoped we'd spend some of that week together too. If this weekend was an indication of how things would go, I figured the chances were pretty good.

Cal wrapped his arms around me, pulling me in closer, while I let my hand drift idly up and down his bare chest.

"Hell of a day, huh?" he said, and I laughed lightly.

"It was eventful, that's for sure."

"Are you really okay?"

I tilted my head to look up at him and shrugged a shoulder. His eyes watched me closely, a hint of scepticism lurking there. It was sweet of him to ask when his day had been worse than mine. What he'd witnessed between Guy and Helen earlier had rattled him. To him, they were a solid team, and he saw their foundations were shaken. But even with that weighing on his mind, he was still worried about how I felt. How I was coping with the possible imminent breakdown of my longest friendship.

It never failed to surprise me that, in spite of all the differences between us, our lives held some strange parallels.

Cal had been cruising through life when I met him, neither happy nor unhappy. I'd been doing the same.

He was sick of feeling like a loser in Helen's eyes. I was sick of being looked down on by my best friend.

Now, Cal might lose the normality of Guy and Helen. Because, like her or not, Helen was still a big part of his and Aiden's life. And me? I was about to flush a twenty-five-year friendship down the drain.

The only difference in that last scenario was that I had a choice. Cal might not. Either way, all of these similarities strengthened my belief that good relationships could not be forced. Shouldn't be created because a pairing might be *good for business*. My life wasn't *quite* that intense, but it did happen. As far as I was concerned, it made no difference where people began or how they met. If it worked, it worked.

"I'd be feeling a lot worse if I wasn't here with you," I told him, smiling softly. "How about you?"

Cal glided his hand gently down my side, my skin tingling at the movement. "I'm glad you're here too. I wasn't expecting the easiest time at Guy's, but I didn't see *that* happening."

"Did Guy tell you what it was about?"

He nodded. "Yeah. But he'd never mentioned them trying for a baby before, so I didn't know there were any problems between them until tonight." His eyes dimmed, glazing over as if lost in thought. "It was weird. You know I can't stand Helen most of the time, but I felt bad for her. For both of them."

If only she could have heard that.

Helen assumed because Cal said nothing, he felt nothing, and it just wasn't true. What I didn't understand was how she couldn't see that, especially when she spent so much time spouting off about how clueless *he* was.

Sliding my hand up to the back of his neck, I said, "Guy wasn't wrong when he said Helen is hard work, but all relationships are sometimes."

Cal's focus switched back to me, his eyes meeting mine and his fingers moving lightly across my bare stomach.

"This isn't hard work, Shan," he said quietly. "Me and you."

"No." I pressed my lips gently against his. "It isn't hard work."

When he smiled lazily, his hand still drifting across my belly as I teased his hair with my fingers, that feeling of being safe with him surrounded me again. The worst days we'd had when we first met were still better than any relationship I'd been in before. Even with Matthew—my longest relationship to date—a man I'd loved even though I always came second to his studies, it was never this good.

Cal leaned forward and captured my mouth with his, tugging me gently closer, and my bones turned to jelly as I surrendered to the kiss.

His soft touches mixed with the intensity of his lips across mine at the end of a day that had been a rollercoaster of crazy made my heart swell.

I'd tried to take things at a steady, sensible pace with Cal, but I'd realised something that afternoon.

When the day had gone to shit, all I'd wanted to do was go back to him. Cal had become my person. The one I wanted to talk to at every possible opportunity. Who I wanted to share the good and bad parts of my day with. When we weren't together, I missed him, and when we were, I didn't want to leave him.

There were still a million things I didn't know about him, but I trusted him. Knew he would tell me the things I needed to know when he was ready.

Six weeks wasn't that long.

But it was long enough to know how I felt.

Chapter 18

Cal

My first full weekend with Shannen had thrown me.

I knew it would be fine. That we'd have a good time. My main concern was that Aiden might stress at having Shannen there the whole time, but that didn't happen.

What happened was that, even though I never meant to be with Shannen for longer than a few weeks, we were on our seventh, and I had no intention of giving her up.

And fuck if that didn't scare me.

She had wound her way into every part of my life. She'd made friends with Guy, and she'd even made an effort with Helen. Aiden thought she was the best thing ever, and she looked at me like I actually fucking mattered.

I'd been certain that Shannen's snooty best friend would convince her to dump me, but that hadn't happened either.

Which meant I was in trouble.

With every day that passed, the things I needed to tell her weighed on me. I still wasn't sure which bits she needed to know. Whether she needed to hear every fucked up thing in my past, or if I could hide the most shameful bits.

My failure to properly take care of Aiden when he was a baby would always haunt me; Shannen knew that already. But that still wasn't the worst thing I'd ever done. Not by a long way.

As Guy and I headed towards Aiden's school, I was the most unsettled I'd been for a while. My past fuck-ups were on my mind, not helped by the fact that it was the night Shannen and I were going out and I'd get to meet her best friend, who already hated me. If there was ever a time not to highlight my flaws, this was it, not when her mate would do it for me. Shannen had tried to ease the pressure of the evening by asking her co-worker, Nova, and her boyfriend to come along too, but I didn't think anything would make it better. The only way I'd look forward to the evening would be if Jade decided not to come.

"Who pissed in your cornflakes today?" Guy asked as we walked. The street was lined with parked cars, all full of people going to the same place we were. Knowing what school time traffic was like, I always walked to collect Aiden instead of taking the van, but the slowly increasing drizzle made me regret that decision. I pulled the collar of my leather jacket up, even though it did nothing much to protect me from the rain.

It was one day before half term, and parents had been invited into the school to see what the kids had been learning since the beginning of the year. Guy had come with me since Helen was working—not that she would have come with me anyway—and I clearly wasn't doing a very good job of hiding my dark mood.

"I'm fine," I said, keeping my eyes straight ahead. This was the first time I'd seen Guy all day as we'd been working different jobs.

Guy was way too good at reading me, so lying was a waste of both of our time.

"Cal, who do you think you're talking to? What's going on?"

Blowing out a breath, I said, "I don't want to talk about it, mate." *I'm just trying to keep it together.*

"Come on," Guy pressed. He pointed towards the school building that loomed ahead. "You can't go in there looking like that. You'll scare the kids."

"Just leave it."

"Hey." Guy gripped the top of my arm, forcing me to stop walking, and I shrugged him off, glaring in his direction. "Talk to me."

His eyes stayed on mine, and I knew he wouldn't let it drop. Rubbing a hand across my forehead, I said, "I need to tell her everything. About... you know."

Guy's eyebrows rose. "Everything?"

I dropped my hand to my side in frustration, shaking my head. "I don't know. I just... I don't think it's right to keep so much from her. But I also don't think she'll stay with me once she knows."

The fear struck me harder than I was comfortable with. Getting close to people was dangerous, especially for someone like me. Even more so when the person I was getting close to deserved better and actually had something to lose.

People were beginning to get out of their cars to head into the school, and we'd stopped right in the middle of the path. Guy ushered me to stand to the side out of the way, the rain getting heavier and causing passers-by to shriek and walk faster.

"I think you're underestimating her," Guy said. "She isn't stupid, Cal. She knows you're keeping things from her. Has she still not asked about your family?"

"Nope. I can tell she wants to. But she hasn't pushed it."

Sometimes I wanted her to, so I was forced to explain. Other times, I hoped she never asked. There were days when I liked that there were things she didn't know about me. Then I could keep convincing myself that what we had was just casual. That she didn't care enough to dig deeper. It was a load of crap because she *did* care. But that was another level of scary I wrestled with.

Why does she want me?

Is this just a bit of fun for her?

Fun is all I do anyway.

But she means more to me than that now.

I should end it.

But I don't want to.

That was the loop. Round and fucking round. So I just did nothing. Changed nothing and waited in some constantly worsening limbo.

"At the very least, Shannen needs to know about your mum and Luca," Guy said. "And your dad too."

"And what about the rest?" Every stupid decision I'd made in my late teens rushed into my mind, along with the one thing I never wanted anyone to find out about me. It still gave me nightmares twelve years later.

Guy sighed. He was the only person in my life who knew every single thing about me. Helen didn't even know most of it. Guy also understood the magnitude of any admission I made to Shannen. Not just because of what I'd done, but because anyone I gave that information to would have to mean a lot to me. Aiden's mother didn't know it, and we'd been together for the best part of two years.

"That's up to you," Guy said. "It depends on how honest you're willing to be."

Blowing out a breath, I said, "The only thing she ever asked is for me to be honest with her, but... I don't know if I can. Not about all of it."

Guy placed his hand on my arm in support. "Tell her about your family, then take it from there. But I don't think there is anything that woman wouldn't understand. Look at how she handled everything with Aiden. Not to mention her keeping an eye on Helen this past week when she hasn't exactly been the nicest."

He was right; I knew that. Shannen had the patience of a saint. Even though Helen had been a first-class bitch, Shannen had checked in with her. They'd even swapped numbers. They hadn't spoken a lot, but she'd reached out. Something Guy had been especially grateful for since he and Helen were still on shaky ground.

Knowing time was ticking to get into the school. Guy and I started walking again, caught up in hordes of other parents and family members going the same way.

"I think I just want to get tonight out of the way first," I said. "Meeting Shan's friend is going to be enough drama for one day."

Guy chuckled. "Yeah, I heard she's a piece of work."

"And her fiancé is worse, so Shannen said."

I loved a night out whenever I could get it, but being scrutinised and judged by some privileged princess was not my idea of a good time. I told Shannen that we'd have one drink and get the hell out of there, and she'd agreed. The only reason she wanted to do this at all was to see if her friend would climb out of her own arsehole long enough to support her. We both already knew the answer, and I thought it was a waste of time, but Shannen needed it. Proof that her best mate was no kind of mate at all. It would hurt her more than me; nothing Jade could say or think about me would be a problem. But for Shannen, it would suck. That wasn't just me being cynical. Shannen knew how this would go down too, but I planned to be around to pick up the pieces.

"Just... keep your cool, okay?" Guy said. "It's going to be hard enough for Shannen to be in the middle of you two. Try not to make it worse by losing your shit."

His comment made me bristle. I had no plans to lose my temper, but if something triggered it, I couldn't easily control my response. And I wouldn't if the little bitch said anything to upset my woman.

"I'll do my best, but I make no promises."

We rounded the corner through the school gates, following the train of people on their way to the classrooms of the school's youngest students.

I was kind of looking forward to seeing her at work. I had never seen her in teacher mode aside from the day she'd called me in. Then, we'd both been so blindsided by her being Aiden's teacher that her normal job rules flew out the window. This time would be different. She'd be interacting with the kids and their parents, and I'd get to see her in a way I hadn't seen her before.

As we filtered through the doors into the building, a lady with a clipboard took our names, and then Guy and I made our way to Aiden's classroom.

The last time I'd been in there, I hadn't seen anything other than Shannen, knowing the confrontation that was coming. Now, I stepped through the door and the first thing that hit me was the warmth. The second thing I noticed was how bright everything was. The walls were covered in eye-catching displays showing the alphabet and simple times tables, along with what I guessed were projects they'd worked on. Mostly artwork. The small tables were covered in various art supplies, and some of the kids were gathered around them with their adults, all eager to show them what they could do.

I spotted Aiden standing by the edge of a table where some of his classmates were colouring shapes on pieces of paper, and when he saw me and Guy, he beamed and ran over to us. He took our hands and dragged us across the classroom.

"Come and see my drawing!" he said, pulling us to a less busy table. There were only two other kids sitting there, but no other adults were around.

Aiden flung himself into a chair and then picked up the piece of paper. I glanced around for Shannen but couldn't see her. The class teaching assistant was there, buzzing around and helping anyone who needed anything, though.

"Cal, look!" Aiden said, and I shook my head and turned my attention back to him. Guy held Aiden's drawing. Aiden tugged on Guy's hand to make him lower the paper, and he pointed at each figure. "That's me, and that's you," he said, looking at me. "And that's Shannen. And look! We're eating popcorn and watching *The Brave Little Toaster*!"

As I studied the picture more closely, my heart flipped over. He'd drawn all three of us sitting on the sofa like we had at the weekend. We were all so close in the picture, and he'd even drawn the coffee table with drinks on top, and the TV with a toaster on the screen.

"This is great, buddy," I said, and I felt Guy's eyes on me. He was grinning when I looked at him.

"Miss Morgan told us to draw what we like to do best," Aiden went on, and I thought my fucking chest would explode.

It wasn't just that he'd decided that spending time with me and Shannen was what he liked best; it made me sure of his happiness. With me. Settled. We still needed to work on the *dad* thing, but this seemed like a massive step forward.

I knelt down so I was at his level.

"Well, I think we'll be able to all watch movies together again next week when you're off school," I said. "Does that sound good?"

Aiden's smile was wide, and he nodded.

All of a sudden, I got the feeling someone was looking at me, and I turned my head to see Shannen across the room. She smiled as she watched us, her eyes bright and full of... something. Happiness? Fondness? Whatever it was, I liked it, and I straightened up as she walked towards us.

"Hi," she said, and I found it hard not to wrap her up in my arms. She wore a plain black skirt and a simple blue T-shirt, with black tights and low-heeled black shoes. Her hair was tied back into a loose bun, and she looked like every schoolboy's fantasy of a hot teacher. She was sexy without even trying, and not being able to touch her bordered on painful. Although the head teacher and some of Shannen's colleagues knew about us, nobody else did. Shannen was worried that making it public while Aiden was still in her class might mean she was accused of favouritism, and I didn't want my kid getting picked on because the others knew their teacher spent time with him outside of school. In five months' time, when the summer holidays hit, it would no longer be an issue, but until then, we planned to keep it low-key. Aiden had promised not to tell anyone, and while I didn't like him having to keep it a secret, it just felt easier than more people finding out and airing their opinions about how incompatible we were.

"Hi," I said, smiling at Shannen in a way I hoped let her know how hard I was going to kiss her later. "Aiden has something to show you."

She looked down at him with a grin, and Guy handed her the drawing.

"It's us," Aiden said enthusiastically, but not loud enough for anyone to hear.

Her eyes glistened as she looked at the picture, then she shifted her gaze to my boy. She knew what it meant since she was the one who'd set the task, and she glanced at me before looking back at Aiden.

"This is brilliant," she told him, that fondness in her eyes again. "You can take it home if you want to. Maybe your dad will put it on the fridge."

I laughed because several of Aiden's pictures had been stuck to our fridge with magnets. This one would be the new favourite, though.

"Can we?" Aiden asked me, eyes wide.

I nodded and ruffled his hair. "Course we can."

"Hey, Aiden," Guy said. "Come and show me what else you've been doing."

Aiden took his hand and pulled him to a different table, chattering away and leaving me and Shannen alone. Well, as alone as we could be in a class full of kids and their parents.

"I think this is for you," she said, handing me Aiden's masterpiece. "This is the cutest thing I've ever seen."

Her smile made me grin. "It's definitely going on the fridge."

Lowering her voice and taking the tiniest step towards me, she said, "I hate that I can't hug you right now."

Her words triggered that part inside me that nobody else had ever reached. The one that made my chest feel tight, but in a good way.

"Well, you could," I said. "But then you'd have to hug every other parent in here so they didn't feel left out."

She laughed lightly. "I guess I'll just wait until later. I'll come to yours just before seven. Nova and Donovan said they'd meet us early so we can have a drink before Jade and Scott arrive."

I nodded, my mood slipping at the mention of our night out. I'd have much preferred Shannen just came to mine for a few hours instead.

"It'll be fine," she said, meeting my eye. It was the only way we could connect without touching each other, and I nodded again.

I was about to speak when I heard Aiden call to me. He was showing Guy some books that had been laid out, and Aiden waved me over.

Shannen grinned. "Go. I'll see you later."

With one last look letting her know how much I couldn't wait to get her alone, I wandered over to Aiden and Guy, feeling her eyes following me.

I just hoped I'd survive the evening.

Chapter 19

Shannen

"THIS IS GOING TO be okay, you know?" I said to Cal as we sat in his van in the pub car park, both of us bracing ourselves for the evening ahead.

I'd dreaded it all day, in spite of the fun I'd had at work, and the tension in Cal's jaw told me he felt the same. The words I'd uttered were said with hope, not certainty, and they were as much for my benefit as Cal's.

Jade had messaged me earlier in the day to tell me she and Scott wouldn't be staying for long, which was fine with me. Cal and I had already agreed to one drink, but if they left first, then maybe we could enjoy some extra time with Nova and Donovan.

I'd practically begged Nova and Gaby to come with us, just to ease the focus away from Cal. He'd find it easier to relax if there were other people to talk to besides just Jade and Scott. Gaby was fuming that she couldn't come because she already had plans with another friend. She knew all about Jade, and she would have cut her down with her sharp tongue in an instant. However, Nova had mentioned Donovan was back in the country for a couple of weeks and that they'd love to meet Cal, so at least we'd have some people in our corner.

"I just want it over with." Cal had barely said anything on the drive over, the rain lashing at the windows the only sound to be heard. I knew he was feeling the pressure, even though he said he wasn't. The pressure wasn't coming from me; all I wanted was for him to be himself. But as much as he knew he would hate Jade, I got the feeling he still wanted to make a good impression for my sake.

"Cal." He turned his head to look at me, his eyes already a little defeated. "Thank you. For doing this for me." He offered a single nod, and I said, "Come on. Let's go in and get a drink."

With another nod, Cal opened the door on his side, and I picked up my bag before climbing out of the van.

I was straightening out my thick winter coat and wishing it had a hood when Cal appeared in front of me and pressed me back against the van door, making me gasp.

One hand held onto my hip and the other slid around to the back of my neck. My heart was pounding as hard as the rain as I looked up at him, surprised by his move. I could feel his own heart beating fast, and after our eyes connected for a moment, he leaned down and kissed me. His lips were gentler on mine than I'd expected, but I felt more in that kiss than I could have heard in any words he said. It was worry and apology, mixed with need and care, and it made my head spin.

For someone who wasn't good at expressing his emotions verbally, he certainly knew how to express them with his actions.

He rested his forehead against mine, placing one more peck on my lips before determinedly saying, "Let's do this."

Smiling at him, I entwined my fingers with his, and we hurried across the car park to the pub.

Warmth enveloped us as we entered, a comfort after the cold rain. Although we weren't soaked through, water dripped off the ends of our hair, and we both laughed in relief at being somewhere dry.

Looking around the quiet pub, soft pop music playing in the background, I spotted Nova and Donovan at a four-seater table, but it had a two-seater beside it so Jade and Scott could fit in when they arrived. I waved as Nova spotted me, and I gestured to the bar to let her know we were going to get some drinks.

There was only one other person standing by the bar—an older man wearing black jeans and a blue denim jacket covered in tiny pin badges. The ones I could see looked like band logos, and I wondered if he'd seen all of the bands or if he just liked them.

"What do you want to drink, Shan?"

I'd been so busy checking out the man's accessories that I hadn't realised a barman had come to serve us.

"White wine spritzer, please," I said. If I didn't have to work the next day, I would have strongly considered knocking back a couple of shots. Jade and Scott wouldn't be there for another half an hour, but now we'd arrived, a wave of nerves swept through me. I needed to calm down. I had to relax so Cal would too.

Cal ordered my drink and a Coke for himself.

I raised an eyebrow. "Not even one beer?"

"Nah." He looked down at me and shook his head. "Not tonight."

Considering what he was likely to endure later, I was impressed. I wouldn't have blamed him for wanting a drink to take the edge off. I'd asked if he wanted to get a taxi to the pub so he could have a couple of beers, but he insisted on driving. Having never seen him drunk, I wasn't sure if alcohol made his temper quicker than usual, or if he simply wanted to have a totally clear head. I didn't know if he even got drunk anymore after the drinking binges he used to go on a few years ago.

Another question on the list of things I still didn't know about him, but I wasn't worried. He hadn't been pissed anytime we'd been together, and if he wasn't tempted now when he was so uncomfortable, it seemed unlikely anything else would tip him over the edge.

Smiling up at him while we waited for our order, I said, "This is the first time we've been back here since we met."

Finally, another tiny crack in his tense expression. Cal's lips curled up at the corners, and he reached up to softly stroke my cheek. "Yeah. We should come back soon, just the two of us."

I nodded. "We should." Reaching up, I whispered in his ear, "Next time, I won't be so shy around you." My face heated at the memory of how nervous he'd made me the night we met.

Cal's eyes lit up, and he smirked. "From what I remember, you weren't *that* shy when I got you alone."

My cheeks warmed further at his words. I wasn't embarrassed, just instantly aroused as I thought about how very *not* shy I'd become since we'd been together.

Cal's shoulders relaxed a bit more, and he lightly brushed his lips against mine just as the barman placed our drinks down on the bar. Cal tapped his card on the reader to pay, then we picked up our glasses and headed over to Nova and Donovan.

As we approached, they both stood to greet us. Nova looked gorgeous in black jeans and a burgundy long-sleeved top with a tie-front. Her light brown hair was pulled back in a loose ponytail. Donovan, who I'd seen briefly in December, was extremely good-looking with his dark hair, sun-kissed skin, stocky build, and short beard. He wore blue jeans and a charcoal grey button-down shirt open over a white t-shirt. I couldn't help thinking what an attractive group we were. Underneath Cal's leather jacket were a dark green shirt and blue jeans, and beneath my long coat, I also wore blue jeans teamed with a grey ruched neck chiffon top with a leopard print pattern around the bottom. I didn't often wear animal print. Perhaps I was trying to subconsciously convey that I wasn't going to take any crap. Hopefully, Jade would get the message.

Once introductions had been made, Nova pulled me in for a hug and whispered, "Oh my God, Shannen! I know you said he was good-looking, but he's something else!"

I giggled and whispered back, "You're one to talk!"

She chuckled as we pulled apart, and we all sat down, me opposite Nova, and Cal opposite Donovan.

"So, what's it like being back in the UK?" I asked Donovan, resting my hand on Cal's thigh.

He was home for a week and a bit from the Maldives, and Nova had told me she hadn't expected him back so soon. However, both of them were struggling with being apart, so Donovan had asked his bosses if he could pop home to see his woman and spend a bit of her half-term break together. Luckily, his employers were family-oriented and had allowed him some time out.

Donovan smiled, and his handsome face became even more so. His eyes had a sparkle to them, and they crinkled at the corners with his lopsided grin. I shifted my eyes to Nova, and she raised her eyebrows as if to say, '*I know, right?*'

"It's great," Donovan said. "Today is the first day I've been able to function after the jetlag, but it's been great being back with Nova and seeing my nan."

Nova had met Donovan when he'd come to stay with his grandmother over Christmas, and his nan lived next door to Nova. As it turned out, though, Donovan and Nova had known each other as kids, and they spent the Christmas holidays getting reacquainted in a way neither of them had expected.

"Where have you been?" Cal asked, pausing to take a drink.

"I work in the Maldives," Donovan answered. "I have a job over there for a few weeks, helping the owners of a new resort to get the word out about it on social media."

"Donovan's a travel blogger," I said. "Super big following online."

Donovan smiled again, but there was a slight grimace with it. "I still think it sounds wanky when I admit what I do."

Cal sat back in his chair, all tension gone. "So, are you one of those people who does crazy dances on TikTok?"

Snorting, Donovan said, "No. My followers would disown me if I did that. They like me because I'm more... sarcastic and honest."

Cal chuckled, and as they drifted off into their own conversation, I turned my attention to Nova and mouthed, "Thank you." Without her and her super friendly man, waiting for Jade and Scott would have been like waiting for our own execution.

Nova nodded and said, "How are you feeling about tonight?"

I hadn't known her for that long, but I'd got to know her through Gaby, and she was fast becoming one of my best friends. She knew all about my struggles with Jade, and she'd been only too happy to come along for moral support. Now Donovan and Cal were hitting it off, I was really glad I'd asked them.

"I'll be happy when it's over," I admitted. "Jade said they wouldn't stay for long, so that is what I'm holding onto." I shook my head. "I know that sounds terrible. She's my oldest friend, but..."

Nova held up her hand. "You don't need to explain. From what you've said about her, that feeling is understandable."

A ripple of guilt still ran through me. Something born from my polite and respectable upbringing that told me I should never speak badly of people.

Too bad Jade and her family didn't think the same way.

The twenty minutes Cal and I spent talking to Nova and Donovan was exactly what we needed to calm the anxiety. Cal had built up a rapport with Donovan, and we made a plan to get together again before Donovan had to leave. It was an additional relief to me to have another couple to spend time with. I loved Guy, and Helen was okay in small doses, but to be with people who hit it off immediately was something different. I hoped a time came when Donovan would settle back in the UK with Nova because they were perfectly suited, and I'd never seen her so happy.

As the time drew closer for Jade and Scott to arrive, I found myself glancing behind me at the door. I tried to be subtle so I didn't make Cal feel uncomfortable again, and a part of me kept hoping they wouldn't show up so we could keep on enjoying our evening. But they had to. The point was for Jade to do something for me. Even so, when she and Scott finally arrived, tension wound its way through me.

Here we go...

I nudged Cal lightly, letting him know they were here before standing up to greet them. I blew out a breath as they walked over to us. The Lucky Jester was a nice place, but it seemed like Jade and Scott had gone out of their way to make themselves look *more*. More than the rest of us 'commoners'. More than the establishment's regulars. They were dressed casually, but the kind of casual that suggested they had *far* more money than everyone else in the bar. Jade was wearing Louboutins, for God's sake. Honestly, I was surprised she allowed them to touch the carpet of a place she clearly considered beneath her.

Swallowing down my frustrations, I forced a smile on my face as they reached us. "Hi!"

With a sigh, Jade pulled me in for our usual hug, which I returned, even though she was making it difficult since her blatant irritation was on full display. As we parted, I offered Scott a polite nod. It was the best I could do. He was unbearable at the best of times, but tonight, he would be especially so. I'd never liked him, and he felt the same about me. I found him obnoxious and boring. He considered me, and I quote, 'unworthy of my privileges if I refused to take advantage of them'. Wealthy as his family was, I'd never worked out why he had chosen to work in law enforcement. I often wondered if he was one of those corrupt officers who brandished their badge like a medal of honour while doing underhand, sketchy things in the background. As he stood there, his beady blue eyes surveying me critically, I wanted nothing more than to leave to escape his judgement. I hated everything about him, from his stupid smirk to the way he slicked back his blonde hair as if it made him look cool. It didn't. Instead, he looked like he was desperately trying to hold on to the dying embers of his youth.

"Jade, Scott..." I gestured to my friends first. "This is Nova and Donovan. Nova works with me at Oakwood Lane Primary School, and Donovan is a travel blogger currently working in the Maldives."

Jade and Scott offered friendly smiles and greetings to them, and then it was time to do the thing we'd come for. "And this is Cal." Just before I turned to him, I caught Jade's eyes widening slightly as she looked at him.

Even she couldn't deny he was good-looking, and the realisation made me grin.

However, when I turned to look at Cal, his posture was rigid again, probably because he realised he was being assessed and analysed in every single way. I reached for his hand, and he glanced down at me and swallowed hard before looking over my head at Jade and Scott.

"Hello," Jade said, nodding once before breezing past him to sit at the table beside ours. Cal turned to look at her and said hi before looking back at Scott, whose eyes were narrowed. I wanted to kick him in the shin for the way he was so blatantly measuring Cal up.

"Why don't you go and get some drinks?" I suggested to Scott, glaring hard at him.

As he cast his attention to me, his eyes brightened and an arrogant grin spread across his face. "Good idea." He shot one last look at Cal before heading to the bar, and I stared after him, inwardly cursing his rudeness. What had he found so amusing anyway?

Turning back to Cal, I found him clenching his jaw so hard I thought it might break. I couldn't blame him. While Jade had been dismissive of Cal, Scott had looked at him as if he was something he'd scraped off his shoe, and it obviously hadn't gone unnoticed.

"Hey," I said softly, slipping my arms around his waist to bring his focus back to me. "Are you okay?"

His body tensed again, but he nodded. "Yeah, I'm okay."

I wasn't sure that was the truth, as he never usually missed a chance to put his hands on me, but he didn't even attempt to touch me. I offered him a warm smile, and he took in a deep breath before I let go of him and we sat back down.

I glanced at Nova across the table, and she mouthed, "You got this."

Of course, Jade didn't notice because she'd immediately pulled out her phone and was scrolling her thumb over her screen, her momentary interest in Cal over.

Smiling at Nova, I put my hand back on Cal's thigh and took a large gulp of my drink. He placed his hand over mine and squeezed it as if I were in danger of disappearing. All I wanted was to get out of there. Jade and Scott's less-than-stellar greeting and all-round lack of friendliness was already pissing me off, and their appearance had made everyone uncomfortable. Even Nova and Donovan, who had both slipped into the silence that surrounded us.

Nobody said a thing until Scott came back with the drinks for him and Jade and sat down opposite her. Rather awkwardly, that placed him close to Cal, and I could feel the waves of dislike bouncing between them without a single exchange of words.

"So, how did you two meet?" Jade asked, placing her phone down on the table and turning her attention to Nova and Donovan.

I liked that she was making *some* effort, but I'd also hoped it would be directed at Cal.

Nova smiled up at Donovan. "I got him for Christmas."

I chuckled at the truth of that as Nova went on to explain how they got together. Jade squealed with delight as each detail unfolded. From the corner of my eye, I kept glancing at Cal. His hand was still on mine and his grip hadn't loosened, but he was listening to Nova, as he hadn't heard their story before either.

"That is just adorable!" Jade said when Nova had finished. "It's lovely that you were reunited, and at such a magical time of year too! I wanted to get married at Christmas, but Scott said it would be too cold and nobody wants to attend a wedding all wrapped up in winter clothes." She turned to look at him as if he were the best thing ever, her eyes shining with love for him.

"We're getting married in September as a compromise," he said, looking back at her with a smile. "If I had my way, we would have had a summer wedding. It's much more appropriate, but at the same time, many of our friends take long holidays in July and August, and we didn't want anyone to miss out."

"So, will it be a big wedding?" Donovan asked.

He had been pre-warned by Nova what he was walking into here. While his tone remained pleasant, a glimmer appeared in his blue eyes that suggested he was mocking Scott's self-indulgent chatter about when was an 'appropriate' time of year for a wedding. I'd seen some of Donovan's TikTok videos and read some of his blogs, and he was the most down-to-earth guy you could ever want to meet. Much like Cal, he would never be impressed by how much money a person had; he had his own anyway. He seemed far more interested in people's personality and integrity. Two things Scott severely lacked, and Donovan had quickly picked up on that.

"Oh my God, it's going to be huge!" Jade stated, tapping her hands on the table with each word. Excitement poured from her, and the part of me that had once loved her couldn't help smiling. The dream wedding was all she'd ever wanted, and she was actually going to have it. "All of the most important people in the city will be attending. It'll be the wedding of the year!"

Cal shifted in his seat, and I tangled my fingers with his.

His shuffle must have caught Scott's attention as he moved his focus from Jade. "So, Callum," he said. "What is it that you do for a living?"

Callum? Nobody called him that, and that wasn't how I'd introduced him, but this was typical of Scott. Always had to be superior.

Jade's eyes fixed on Cal too. She already knew the answer to the question. To her, his job was the lowest of the low, and she'd used it to insult me and him frequently. I had a feeling Scott knew too, and this was all part of some idiotic ploy to make Cal feel small.

Cal turned his head towards Scott. I couldn't see his expression, but I imagined it was nothing like the way he looked when interacting with Donovan. "I'm a painter and decorator," he answered. "What about you?"

Scott smirked. "I'm a superintendent here in Exeter. I've worked in various places within the area, but I'm right in the heart of the city now."

I watched the back of Cal's head as he nodded slowly. "Good for you."

His voice was stiff, and Scott continued to eye him with distaste.

"Do you find decorating fulfilling, Callum?" Jade asked, and my head snapped to her. I guessed it was her turn to take a shot.

Cal turned his attention to Jade but didn't correct the name she used. I recalled when I met him he'd said he was Cal to his friends, and there was absolutely no chance these three would ever be that.

"It pays the bills," he said, his tone cool.

"But don't you ever want something more from your life?" she asked, tilting her head to the side with genuine curiosity. "Shannen is my best friend in the world. She deserves the best."

And there it is. The change of pitch wasn't subtle, nor was the critical eyebrow raise as she looked him up and down, letting him know that, in her eyes, he was *not* the best. She'd only said two things to him, and already, irritation prickled at my skin.

"Can't argue with that," Cal answered, though his jaw ticked. If she didn't let up, there was every chance that twitch would lead to him flipping out. I hadn't seen Cal lose his temper often, but often enough to know the signs.

"So, why don't you do something about it?" Jade pushed.

"Jade, stop," I said, keeping my voice low to convey an air of calm. In reality, my patience was reaching its limit.

"What?" She shrugged, tucking her blonde hair behind her ear. "You asked us here to get to know him. How can we do that without asking questions?"

Donovan got to his feet, picking up his empty pint glass. "Cal, come and give me a hand getting some more drinks." He didn't wait for a response, just slid out from behind the table, shooting a glare at Jade on the way. He was clearly unimpressed with her, and I threw him an apologetic smile. Donovan gave me a subtle wink as Cal stood up and the two of them headed for the bar. I stared after them for a moment, watching as Donovan patted Cal on the shoulder and said something to him that I couldn't hear.

Turning back around, I said to Nova, "He's a keeper."

She smiled. "He is."

"Well, that was rude," Jade said. "But I suppose he doesn't know any better." She rolled her eyes, a small grin on her lips.

Slamming my hand down on the table so the glasses and bottles rattled, I leaned towards her and hissed, "Enough!" Luckily, we were tucked away and the music was loud enough to drown it out. "I don't ask for much from you, Jade. I never have. The only thing I needed from you tonight was for you to make an effort to get to know Cal. To show a non-judgemental interest in the person I'm dating because he's important to me. Apparently, even that was too much for you." Shaking my head, I stood up. "This was a mistake. It's pretty damn clear that how I feel means less than nothing to you, and neither I nor Cal need to spend another minute watching you two getting off on making him feel like he's below you."

"Someone's over-sensitive," Scott murmured, and I whirled around to look at him.

"Not over-sensitive, Scott. I'm pissed off. Both of you have no right to look down on people the way you do. You said way more tonight with your glares and scowls than you did with words. Neither of you had any intention of giving Cal a chance."

I took my coat off the back of my chair and put it on while Jade stared at me with wide eyes and Scott continued to smirk. As I picked up my bag, I turned to Nova. "Thank you so much for being here tonight. I'm sorry you had to waste an evening witnessing this."

She shook her head, standing up too and picking up her jacket and bag, as well as Donovan's coat. "It wasn't a waste at all. I enjoyed meeting Cal, and I'm looking forward to seeing you both next week."

What the hell have I been doing with my life? Why have I only ever had friends that weren't real friends until I started my job?

Maybe because Jade was my main frame of reference. I hadn't known what I was missing until I met Gaby and then Nova.

But that wasn't totally true. I'd always inherently seemed to understand what being a good friend meant, even without being shown or having that friendship fully returned. Growing up with a sister probably helped, though.

Before I became a full-time teacher, almost all of my friends had been people I'd known since I was a child. Many of us had gone to the same private schools and we stuck together, right up until we went our separate ways for university. Well, some of us did. Others, like Jade, immediately began looking for a rich husband. For them, everything was about appearances and money. I'd never been into that. Not the desperation to settle down, nor the need to be with someone wealthy, and definitely not the two-faced bitching that some of the women engaged in. My mother and sister weren't like that, and I'd never wanted to be either.

Until Nova and Gaby, I hadn't had the kind of friend who would go to bat for me. Jade? She continued to prove that what other people thought was more important than anything else, including our friendship.

"You're really leaving?" Jade asked, brows furrowed.

I nodded. "Yup. If you want to give Cal an actual chance, let me know. If not, I guess I'll see you at my mum's birthday dinner in a few weeks."

Without giving her a chance to respond, I waited for Nova to round the table, and we headed towards Cal and Donovan at the bar.

Nova linked her arm through mine as we walked, which was good because my entire body shook from the suppressed tension that had been released with my outburst. "Are you okay?" she asked quietly.

Nodding again, I said, "Yeah."

It was half true. Jade had done everything I'd known she would that evening. I'd prepared myself, and while I'd planned to sit through it and wait for it to be over, after ten minutes, I'd had enough. She and Scott hadn't said much, but between the looks Scott had been shooting and Jade's less-than-subtle remarks about Cal's job, I was done. Jade just didn't seem to get that by making digs at Cal, she was equally insulting me. Letting me know that she had no respect for my choices or my relationship.

Either she would apologise and try to make things right, or she'd stand firm and let our friendship turn to dust. It was her choice now.

Donovan, slightly taller than Cal, saw Nova and me approaching, and he nudged Cal and nodded in our direction. As Cal turned, concern and something that looked like regret were etched into every part of his face. I had no idea what had caused it because he hadn't done a thing wrong, but Nova released my arm and I went straight to Cal and wrapped my arms around him.

"What happened?" he asked as I buried my head against his chest and breathed in deep. Leather, aftershave, and the sweet scent of the Coke he'd been drinking wrapped around me, making me feel safe again.

"We're leaving," I said. "Unless you already bought drinks."

Cal's body seemed to relax, and he wound his arms around my back. "We didn't. But why are we leaving already?"

Raising my head, I said, "Because Jade is a bitch, and Scott's a prick, and I'm sorry."

His eyes... They seemed to both soften and intensify all at once, resulting in his deep brown gaze swathing me in warmth and security. "Shan. You don't need to be sorry."

"I should never have suggested this," I said, shaking my head. "I..."

Cal's lips silenced me, his arms tightening around me. "It's fine," he whispered, his forehead against mine. "It's fine."

In that moment, I'd never felt more protected. My dating history was nothing to be excited about. If I really looked at it, it was a list of men who wanted someone respectable to bring home to their families. Someone who knew how to behave at social events and could schmooze their colleagues or talk them up in front of potential connections.

Not Cal, though. Cal had stepped up for me and done something because I'd asked him to. And that knowledge had made me want to protect him right back.

"Can we please go home?" I said.

Cal nodded. "Yeah. I can take you home."

"No." I shook my head. "Can we go to yours?"

I knew I wouldn't be able to stay over and I'd have to get a cab back to my flat because I'd left my car at home, but I just needed to be with him. To apologise again for making him so uncomfortable and subjecting him to so much scrutiny in the hopes my friend would actually take us seriously, even though I knew she never would.

"Yeah, of course," he said. Pressing a kiss to my forehead, he let go of me and took my hand.

Nova was standing by the bar with Donovan, his arm lightly around her waist, and as we turned to them, I said, "I'm so, so sorry about tonight."

"Stop apologising." Nova smiled, reaching over and taking my free hand. "None of this was your fault."

"Plus, the only other plans we had tonight were watching soaps with my nan," Donovan added, and we all laughed. I knew he was trying to ease the tension; he was staying at Nova's, not his nan's. "I say we try this again next week. We could go out to eat."

At that, I grinned. "The Smugglers for a carvery?"

Nova giggled. "It is good, but maybe we could go to The Boathouse at Dawlish Warren instead. There's a play area there which would be great for Aiden."

I glanced at Cal, and his eyes brightened at the thoughtfulness of her suggestion. She'd included his child. Jade and Scott couldn't even be bothered with Cal, let alone his little boy.

These are our people.

"Sounds good," I said.

We stood for a few more minutes, chatting, and in that time, Jade and Scott sidled by, glaring our way as they left.

And it stung. It stung that I had wasted so much time on a one-way friendship. Once, she truly *had* cared. She'd always been superficial and stuck-up, but she used to show an interest. It seemed the more she'd got caught up in moving to her new fancy house and the upcoming wedding, the more everything else slipped. I was tired of being the only one trying.

I wasn't sure where things would go after this, but right then, I didn't want to think about it. All I wanted was to go to my favourite place.

The exact same place Aiden had chosen as his favourite too.

Chapter 20

Cal

Numb.

That was the only way to describe how I felt after meeting Jade and Scott.

There were a lot of ways I'd thought the night might go down, but being confronted by my past was not one of them.

Jade's bitchy comments barely registered because all I could think about was how her fiancé could blow everything for me with just a few words.

The look on his face when he saw me. It was like he'd won the lottery. I had no clue how Shannen hadn't noticed. Maybe he was always that much of a pompous dickhead.

Yeah, he was *always a pompous dickhead.*

He hadn't taken his fucking eyes off me, laughing silently that he knew something about me that Shannen didn't. And he knew I hadn't told her because, if I had, she wouldn't have still been with me.

On the way back to my flat, I made small talk with Shannen, but it felt... I didn't know what the hell the word was. All I knew was that she hurt because of her shitty friends, and while I wanted to keep her with me to make her feel better, my gut churned because I was going to hurt her too.

The phone call from Jade was coming. The one that would see Shannen cutting ties with me forever. If I didn't tell her, Jade would. It would be better coming from me, or as 'better' as it could be, but how was I meant to do that? I'd been trying to figure out what she needed to know and been back and forth over letting her in on everything from my past, but I hadn't expected to be backed into a corner over it. And this *was* a corner.

I was still dazed when Shannen and I entered the flat, dripping wet from the rain. We took off our coats and shoes in the hallway, and as we walked into the living room, Guy looked up at us in surprise. He sat in the armchair, playing a game on the PS5.

"I know you said you wouldn't be long, but I didn't think you'd be that fast," he said. It had barely been an hour since we left.

Shannen let out a humourless laugh. "Didn't even get as far as a second drink." She rubbed at her forehead, swiping away some stray raindrops. "It was a disaster."

Guilt and panic surged through me again, and as Guy looked over at us, he must have seen something on my face because his eyes narrowed slightly in question. "What happened?"

Shannen, still oblivious to my internal meltdown, dropped her bag down and said, "Pretty much what I expected. Scott wouldn't stop sneering at Cal, and Jade started asking questions that were designed to make Cal feel like crap. I'm sure they pre-planned their moves because they both looked very pleased with themselves, and then Jade had the nerve to seem surprised when I said we were leaving." She shook her head, letting out a sigh. "I just... I should never have suggested it."

Her eyes glistened with unshed tears, and the knife in my gut twisted more as she looked at me. Her thoughts were written all over her face. While I stood there holding onto the secrets that would destroy us, Shannen was hurting because she thought I was upset about the things her friends had said to me.

And I couldn't bring myself to correct her yet. Whether I told her the truth or not, I was the cause of her pain and I hated it. Hated myself.

"I'm sorry," Guy said, putting the controller down and standing up. He was still watching me with concern, and I needed him to stop because between his looks and the ache in my chest, I felt like everything was slipping away from me. I didn't get out of the pub virtually unscathed for Guy to raise Shannen's suspicions now.

Not that it mattered. My past was going to come out one way or another.

Shannen glanced up at me. "Where can I find some towels to dry off?"

"In the bathroom. The cupboard under the sink," I told her.

With a nod, she offered Guy a tired smile and headed for the bathroom.

Once she was gone, Guy turned to me. "What the hell happened tonight?" he asked quietly. "Because I know you don't give a shit what some posh bird and her fella think of you."

My stomach dropped the way it had when I first saw Scott walk into the pub, the memory making me feel sick. The severity of the situation hit me again, and I drew in a deep breath. "Shannen's friend's fiancé. It's Scott McCalden."

Guy looked blank for a moment, until he remembered, and his eyes widened. "As in Sergeant McCalden?"

"Superintendent McCalden now."

Guy had been at university in Liverpool when I found myself on Scott's radar, but he learned about it when he came home and Scott kept showing up everywhere I was, watching me, looking for any reason he could to get me in trouble. It was years later when I told Guy the full truth, but by then, Scott had long since given up on me and neither of us expected to cross paths with him again.

"Fuck," Guy hissed, pushing a hand through his hair. "But... I mean... Shannen doesn't know anything yet, right? She..." he trailed off.

He didn't need to finish. She wouldn't have been in my home if she knew.

"Cal, you need to tell her. You said earlier today that you'd been thinking about it."

"Thinking about it, yeah. But doing it..." I shook my head. "Guy. I can't lose her."

I hadn't had her for anywhere near long enough. Forever wouldn't have been long enough with her. I'd only just allowed myself to admit that I wanted to be with her. That I'd thought about a future with her. Now, she was going to slip through my fingers because of things I'd done when I was an angry, fucked-up teenager, and there was no way to stop it.

Shannen's footsteps halted our conversation, and Guy stepped back.

"Has Aiden been okay?" I asked him, needing a subject change. Shannen re-entered the room, rubbing one-handed at her long curls with a blue towel. Her other hand carried a white towel, which she offered to me. The defeated look in her eyes as I took it intensified the pressure in my chest.

You're going to lose her. You're going to lose everything.

"He's been fine," Guy said, disrupting my thoughts. "I checked in on him about ten minutes ago and he was fast asleep."

I nodded, using the towel to dry off my hair. "Thanks for watching him."

"Anytime, you know that." After eyeing me for another moment, Guy said, "I'll head off since you're back. But I'll see you tomorrow." Nodding again, I turned to see him out, but he said, "It's okay. Stay here and get dry."

He offered me and Shannen a small smile, then headed out, closing the living room door behind him.

Once Shannen and I were alone, Shannen sighed. "I'm really sorry about tonight."

I flung my towel over the back of the couch, then took hers from her hand and threw it on top of mine. "You don't have anything to be sorry for."

"I think I do." Shaking her head, she turned away from me. "I knew she would never give you a chance, but I just-"

"Shan," I interrupted, putting my hands on her shoulders and stepping close behind her. "Stop." I ran my hands down her arms and then held both of her hands. "I wasn't expecting Jade to like me, so this isn't a big deal."

Aside from the part where her fiancé fucks this up for me.

Letting go of my hands, she turned to face me again, tears in her eyes. "It's a big deal to me. I basically threw you into the lion's den."

"Do you really think her comments are the worst thing I've ever heard? Shannen, I lived with Helen for over a year. She makes Jade look like an amateur when it comes to making people feel bad about themselves."

In spite of herself, Shannen laughed, and I pulled her in close to me. Her arms slipped around my waist, and her body against mine eased my fears. We could get through anything, couldn't we? If I told her everything, it would be okay, wouldn't it?

Just. Fucking. Tell. Her.

I would. I had to. But I needed to find the right words, even though I knew deep down she wouldn't understand my justification. Also, with Aiden sleeping... it just wasn't the right time. It had to be when we had a solid few hours alone. I'd have to call in another favour from Guy because, when Shannen inevitably walked away from me, I was going to need to spend a night getting shit-faced, and I couldn't do that while I had my boy in the flat.

"Shan?" I said softly.

"Yeah?"

"Can you please stay tonight?"

She looked up at me, her blue eyes soft on me. "I can, but I'll need to sneak out because I don't have any clothes to change into."

I brushed my lips across her forehead. "That's okay. I just want you here tonight."

Tomorrow, I'd tell her everything because I owed her the truth. I just hoped Jade wouldn't beat me to it. Until then, though, I had to keep Shannen close and soak up every second I had left with her.

Reaching up, Shannen pressed her lips to mine. "Why don't you go check on Aiden, and I'll go and get ready for bed."

"It's not even half past eight." My lips tipped up in a smile.

She nodded. "I know it hasn't been long since our last early night, but I can't think of anything I want to do more than snuggle up with you."

That ache in my chest throbbed at her words. She was so goddamn sweet. Way too good for me.

"Okay," I said, reluctantly dropping my arms from around her. "I won't be long."

With a smile, she turned and headed for the bedroom, while I went to Aiden's room.

I carefully opened the door, and I heard *Toy Story 3* playing on his iPad. He had it face down beside him, and he was fast asleep. I smiled to myself as I watched him for a moment. He lay on his stomach, his head turned to the side, and his black hair all messy.

"Sweet dreams, kid," I said quietly, before stepping out and closing the door.

Before going to my room, I double-checked the front door was locked, then went back to the living room to turn off the PS5 and the TV and make sure I'd turned off anything else I needed to.

When I finally entered the bedroom, I found Shannen sitting cross-legged on the end of the bed. She'd taken off her jeans and top and thrown on the t-shirt of mine she liked to wear when she stayed over. It was just a simple black t-shirt, but it made her look sexy as hell. Her dark curls hung over her shoulders, and she smiled as I approached her.

"Is Aiden okay?" she asked, uncrossing her legs and pulling me in between them, her arms tight around me.

I nodded, sinking my hand into her hair and hating the continued pain in my chest. The worry that I was going to lose her soon weighed heavily on me. I just had to get through one more day before I told her everything, and then? Who knew what was going to happen?

"He's asleep with *Toy Story 3* playing," I told her, and she chuckled. "And he's only watching that because he doesn't have a DVD player in his room so he can keep watching *The Brave Little Toaster*."

"I'm sorry." Her eyes sparkled with a hint of joy, though. She'd left her DVD at our place so Aiden could watch it again, and I knew she loved that he'd liked it so much. "I didn't mean to create another obsession."

She pressed her cheek against my stomach, and I closed my eyes and bent down to kiss the top of her head. The sweet smell of honey drifted around me, and I couldn't stand the idea that I might not have this, her, for much longer.

I heard the sound of a gentle vibration and stiffened. My phone was in my pocket, so it wasn't me.

Shannen pulled away and reached behind her for her mobile, and I clenched my jaw so hard I thought I might break my teeth.

That would be Jade. She was going to tell Shannen before I could.

A light laugh eased the tension, and I glanced down to see Shannen smiling. "It was Nova," she said, looking up at me. "Just checking if we're okay."

I gave a single nod, and Shannen typed out a reply while I tried to get a grip on myself.

Just tell her now. Get it done.

But I couldn't.

Not tonight.

I needed one more night with her because nothing would ever be the same once I told her the truth. I had to do it the next day and suck up the consequences, but right then, I wasn't ready to face losing her.

Once she'd finished her message, she tossed her phone carefully behind her again so it landed on her pillow, then shuffled back up the bed. Moving her phone to the bedside table, she said, "Come here."

Her smile made it impossible for me to refuse her, and I pulled off my shirt before I joined her on the bed.

Shannen turned on her side and faced me, and I didn't miss the way her gaze travelled down to my chest before she looked back up at me. "Thank you for tonight," she said. "I know it went badly, and we both expected it would, but I appreciate that you did it for me."

"It was no problem," I said, though it was obviously a lie. Not that I minded doing it for her, because I didn't. But it was uncomfortable, and not just in the ways she knew.

She shook her head. "I don't think you understand." Her hand slid across my stomach and rested on my waist, stroking the skin there before she slipped it around to my back, where her fingers lightly moved up my spine. "I haven't been in a lot of relationships," she went on. "A couple of serious, long-term ones and one or two short-lived things. Do you know what they had in common?"

"Big... bank balances?" I smirked, and she laughed.

"No. Well, some did. But that wasn't what I meant." I pulled her in closer to me, my hand resting on her hip as she said, "The thing they had in common was that none of them did for me what you did tonight."

Frowning, I said, "What did I do?"

Her eyes lit up as she smiled softly. "You didn't want to meet Jade and Scott. You knew they'd be awful, but you still came because I asked you to. I've never been with anyone who put me first. With other men, I was the one who had to compromise and do things I didn't want to do, but if I asked them for something, there had to be something in it for them. You're not like that, though. You did this just for me."

Closing my eyes because the way she was looking at me filled me with guilt, I pressed my lips to hers. "I would do just about anything for you."

The admission was the most honest thing I'd ever said, which only made me feel worse about what was to come. The idea of this being over made every muscle in my body tense. I'd never felt anything like it before—wanting to be with someone so badly it hurt. And I loved it and hated it in equal measure. While it was great now, soon, it wouldn't be, and I wasn't sure how to handle it.

"I'm still sorry, though," she said quietly, and I opened my eyes to look at her again. "I should never have put you in the position of being stared at and judged like that. She is... was... I don't even know anymore... a friend. And you would have met her eventually anyway, but I just wish she had really tried to get to know you."

"Shan, I don't care what she thinks of me. I don't need her help to feel bad about myself. I've had years of experience with that."

She flinched as if I'd lashed out at her, and she said, "I hate it when you do that. When you say things about yourself that aren't fair or true." She moved her hand down to the waistband of my jeans, her eyes dropping for a second. "Like when you say you aren't good enough for me."

"That's a fact," I said, my hand slipping down to her bare thigh. "I'm *not* good enough for you."

As her eyes met mine again, she said, "Well, that could be a problem."

"Why?" I asked, holding her gaze.

"Because I love you."

My sharp intake of breath at her words was quickly followed by my body stiffening.

The fight or flight mode inside me had been triggered again, and my brain screamed at me to get away from her. To push her right away and protect myself from the inevitable pain that comes from those words.

Nobody had said that to me in a long time.

Not since I was fourteen years old.

And those people were gone now. That was why I never said it anymore. Not to anyone. Not even Aiden, which I was fully aware made me a shitty father. But the risk was too big. I'd already lost him once, and I couldn't do it again. I was taking care of him. Making him feel safe. Actions meant way more than words anyway.

So, why did Shannen saying it make a lump form in my throat and my heart beat so fast?

As she looked into my eyes, I wasn't sure what to do or say. I hated that I couldn't speak. All words had completely left me.

This beautiful, kind, sweet, sexy woman had just told me she loved me, and I couldn't say it back.

Not because I didn't want to.

Because I actually *couldn't*.

For a second, her eyes dimmed. It made me hate every screwed-up bit of myself. Not hearing those words back hurt. I knew that because I'd been there. Not in a romantic relationship, but a familial one. It felt like rejection, and that was the last thing I wanted to make her feel.

Say something, you useless twat.

Shannen ran her hand along the waistband of my jeans, her expression somewhere between disappointed and thoughtful.

"Shan," I began, my voice croaky.

"It's okay," she said softly. Her eyes met mine again, and right in those blue depths, I could see that even though I'd given her nothing to explain, she understood. She'd taken hold of the tiny insights I'd shown her and put together a picture in her mind. It must have had a lot of blank spaces, but she'd figured out enough to know that my lack of response didn't mean I didn't still want her.

Because, *fuck*, I wanted her.

Moving the hand that was on her thigh up and underneath the T-shirt she was wearing, I leaned in and kissed her. If my lips couldn't speak the words, I'd keep on kissing her until she understood.

Shannen shuffled her hips closer to mine, stroking her fingers up and down my back again. The light touch made a shiver run through me, and she knew it. Knew that I loved the slow trace of her hands all over me. *Almost* every part of me softened under her fingertips, and when her full lips trailed across my stubbled jaw and down my neck to my shoulder, my heart clenched in my chest.

Her hands, her lips, the warmth of her breath... it didn't matter how or where she touched me. Everything she did, each movement told me she meant what she'd said. She'd been silently telling me for longer than I was ready to admit or accept because *those words* scared the hell out of me.

I slid my hand higher, over her perfect, curvy hip to the soft skin on her waist, and carefully rolled her onto her back. I used both hands to push her T-shirt up, my grip slow and firm, and she shifted so I could take it off and drop it to the floor.

She lay there, in her matching lacy white underwear, her chest heaving as she watched me, and she had never looked more freaking stunning.

"Cal." The word was almost a plea, and I moved over her, my lips on her neck as she snaked her arms around me again.

I breathed in deep the honey smell of her hair that fell around her shoulders as my mouth blazed a trail from her neck down to her breast. I pulled the straps of her bra down, and she let go of me to slip her arms out while I reached behind her to unclip it. She tugged it out from between us and flung it aside before winding her arms around my back as my lips drifted to her perfect tits. Flicking my tongue slowly over her nipple and sucking lightly on it caused it to stiffen in my mouth, and I grazed my teeth across the hardened bud, eliciting a small moan from her. I kissed over her soft flesh, then lavished the same attention on her other breast. She squirmed underneath me, reaching in front of me to unzip my jeans.

My dick had been ready for her since she'd whispered my name, but this wasn't about me. I needed this to be about her. To show her the things I couldn't say.

I continued to rain kisses down her body to her stomach, loving the soft roundness that she told me she hated. I didn't want washboard abs, all hard and unwelcoming. She was slim, but not so toned that nothing moved. The bounce of her tits and that tiny bit of extra flesh on her stomach drove me crazy. The things she saw as imperfections were the things I liked the most, especially her sexy, shapely hips that she was pressing against me. She thought they were too wide; I thought they were gorgeous, and I held them firmly as I slid her knickers down a little.

From my position at her lower stomach, I looked up at her, watching the flush covering her skin, her hands clutching at the duvet because she couldn't reach to touch me anymore.

She. Is. Perfect.
And you can't keep her.

Instead of letting that thought settle, I continued to pull her knickers down her legs. When I reached her feet, her underwear now on the floor, I leisurely kissed back up her leg, from her ankle up to her damp thighs. Her wetness made my dick throb with the need to sink inside her, and I swiped my tongue across her glistening entrance, needing a taste.

She moaned again, opening her legs more for me and lifting her hips off the bed. Unable to resist an invitation, I plunged my tongue inside her, and the breathy gasp she gave almost had me shooting my load. My fingers dug into her hips, and I licked all the way to her clit, then circled my tongue around the sensitive bud. As she bucked against me, I slipped one arm under her ass, holding her hips up so she was more open to me, allowing my tongue deeper inside her.

She began to pant, her legs trembling as I took her closer to the edge. She tasted fucking divine, and the wetter she got, the harder I pushed until she let out a cry that shot straight to my cock. Slowly, I lowered her hips, her skin shining with a sheen of sweat as she came down from her high.

But I didn't want her to come down from it. I wanted her a hot, writhing mess until she couldn't take any more.

I wanted her to know that her satisfaction, her happiness... it was all that mattered.

Even though my dick was ready to explode just looking at her, I would take that torture because I deserved it. I deserved to suffer, while she deserved the goddamn world.

"Cal," she breathed. "I need..."

"What do you need?" I asked, moving back up her body so my face was in line with hers.

"Kiss me."

A grin pulled at my lips as I hovered my mouth close to hers. She lifted her head towards me, but I moved back just a little so she couldn't reach.

The desire in her eyes was like nothing I'd ever seen, and I knew why. When I kissed her after my tongue had been in her pussy, she loved it. She loved that I'd tasted her, and the bad girl inside her was aroused by how dirty it felt after a lifetime of men who would have got up to clean their teeth before kissing her again.

Still high from her orgasm, she wrapped a hand around the back of my neck. "Please," she begged.

"Tell me what you want."

Just like I knew they would, her cheeks reddened, but she looked me in the eye and said, "I want to taste myself on you."

With one more smirk, I covered her mouth with mine, swallowing her moan as our tongues found each other. I could feel her heart pounding, and she pushed my jeans down. I helped her by shoving them past my knees and wriggling out of them while she slid her hands inside my boxers and gripped my arse.

The whole time, our lips never parted, and as I eventually pulled away from her, I said, "What else do you need, Shan?"

"I just... I need you inside me," she said. "I just want you."

Those words meant so many things, and my inner demons fought to escape. To remind me that my time with her was temporary.

But I had to silence them for now. Had to let her know what she meant to me in the way that was easiest to me.

I pressed my lips to hers once more before shuffling over to the bedside table to sort out the all-important mood killer that would protect us both. The whole time, my hands were shaking, desperate to get back to her, and the second I was ready, I paused for a moment to just look at her, the way I often did when she was naked in front of me.

With anyone else, I'd never taken the time. They were just a quick fix to relieve some tension. But even from the first night with her, I'd wanted to take in every aspect of her. To memorise every bit of her because she was beautiful.

After what she'd given me, what she'd said, I needed her to know that there had never been anyone else like her and that, if I was honest with myself, even though I'd tried to pretend, she'd never been a quick fix.

Moving back over to her, I placed my hands lightly on her ankles and moved her feet up the bed a little so her knees were bent. Parting her legs, I slipped between them on my knees, my hands on her hips again. Her eyes were intense on me, like she was searing her gaze into my skin.

"Lift your hips, Shan," I said, guiding them up.

Once they were fully raised, I slid my hands around to her ass and raised her just a bit more so most of her back was off the bed, her arms flat on the mattress to help support her.

In that position, the view of her, completely under my control, was something I knew I'd think about on nights when she wasn't with me. The glow of her skin, the need in her gaze, her chest heaving with the anticipation.

I couldn't wait any longer.

I lowered her hips slightly and adjusted my position to sink inside her.

The warmth of her walls around my dick was something I'd never get enough of.

Her eyes widened, her mouth falling open for a moment as I pushed all the way in. I moved slowly at first, letting her get used to the depths I was reaching. As her body relaxed, she straightened one of her legs, resting it on my shoulder and adjusting her angle so I could go even deeper.

Still supporting her with both hands, I sank into her again, a little faster now. Shannen closed her eyes, pushing her head back into the pillow as I squeezed her arse, drawing her closer to release. Her hands gripped the duvet as she squirmed under my grasp, trying to encourage me to speed up.

Even though her eyes were closed, mine were on her, watching the flush on her cheeks that travelled down her neck to her chest. The way she tried to conceal her gasps as I pushed into her. The way her whole body trembled as moans fell from her lips. My balls tightened, my dick throbbing more with every thrust.

Supporting her with one arm under her hips, I glided my other hand up her stomach, and she cried out as I took one of her tits and squeezed before tweaking her peaked nipple between my fingers.

Her breaths were shallow, her body tense, and I drove harder and faster into her, my fingers tormenting one nipple then the other.

The moan of sheer pleasure she let out as she came was enough to trigger my release, and a string of nonsensical curse words fell from my mouth as my body shook and my dick pulsed, my balls emptying inside her.

My limbs weakened, and as I pulled out of her and gently lowered her back to the bed, wrapping her up in my arms, the final thought I had was simple.

Please don't leave me.

Chapter 21

Shannen

I had never been more ready for the last day of term. Going out on a work night wouldn't have been so bad if it hadn't included being with people who drained me. I truly felt like I'd had the life sucked out of me when I'd got back to Cal's the night before. Some idiotic part of me thought Jade might text an apology for being such a monumental bitch towards him, but my phone remained silent.

And then there was Cal.

He'd stepped up for me, and in the midst of the disappointment caused by Jade's rudeness, his actions cemented what I'd known for a while.

He was everything I never knew I was missing. It didn't matter that we hadn't been together for long. It didn't matter that there were gaping holes in the things I knew about him that still hadn't been filled yet.

I was in love with him.

And even if he didn't say it back, I knew he felt the same.

It didn't take a genius to figure out that expressing emotions wasn't his strong point. That had always been clear, but I didn't know why. What had caused it? What he didn't say with words, though, he showed in other ways. Not just with orgasms, although I couldn't deny they were great. It was the way he looked at me. The way he considered my feelings and had right from the start. The way he wanted me near him as often as possible, and how he'd allowed me to be part of both his and Aiden's life.

I couldn't say I wasn't disappointed he hadn't uttered the words to me, but I hoped they wouldn't be too far away.

He was worth waiting for.

"Morning, gorgeous!"

I looked up from the paperwork on my desk to see Gaby standing in the doorway, grinning. "Morning. How was your evening?"

She waved a hand dismissively as she walked into my classroom and leaned her hip against the desk. "Fine, fine. I need to know about yours, though. I haven't seen Nova yet, so I came straight to you. How did it go? Did anyone need to slap Jade?"

Snorting out a laugh, I said, "I suspect you'd have been tempted if you'd been there." Not that Gaby was violent in any way, but she *was* fiercely loyal.

Gaby's face pulled into a grimace. "What happened?"

I sighed, dropping my pen down on top of the work I'd been doing. "We left after Jade and Scott had been there about ten minutes. Scott was just... he looked at Cal as if just because his job doesn't pull in high five figures, he wasn't worthy of being in his presence. And Jade... she basically went at Cal like he was at a job interview. Honestly, I'm surprised she didn't have him draw up his five-year-plan."

Gaby chuckled. "Sounds like fun. What about Nova and Donovan? Did they leave with you?"

I nodded. "Yeah, and we're planning a double date next week. Cal and Donovan hit it off."

With a wiggle of her eyebrows, Gaby asked, "And what was Donovan like?"

Smiling, I said, "Oh, he's absolutely stunning. Nice guy too. I can see why Nova is so taken with him, and he clearly feels the same way about her." Nova had told us a lot about Donovan, and Gaby and I had been desperate to meet the man who had turned our friend into a mushy romantic. He did *not* disappoint.

"Ah, young love." Gaby sighed as she straightened up. "I miss those days..."

"Oh, stop." I laughed. "It's not like you're ready to draw your pension." Gaby was thirty-four; not old by any means.

She grinned. "No. But the only thing I've pulled in the last year is a muscle, so I'm going to have to live vicariously through you and Nova."

Even though she joked about dating, both Gaby and Nova had been happily single for a while until Donovan came along. It was one of the foundations of their friendship initially. Even with Nova and me both in relationships now, Gaby was still content to be on her own.

"You're welcome to join us next week," I said, standing up because it was almost time to let the children in. "We're going to Dawlish Warren, and Aiden will be coming too."

"Ha!" Gaby said as I rounded the desk and we headed out of the classroom towards the playground. "It's one thing Aiden spending his weekends with one teacher, but three might be a bit much for him."

"I think he'd be okay with it," I said. "It would be great if you could come too."

"I'll think about it," she replied as we walked through the reception area. "But I'd rather protect you from Jade if the opportunity arises again. Ten minutes with me and she'd never piss you off again."

Laughing out loud, I couldn't disagree.

Just as we were about to breach the doors outside to the playground, my phone vibrated in the pocket of my black trousers. I paused to pull it out and there was a text on the screen.

> **Cal: Guy and Helen are watching Aiden tonight and Helen will pick him up from school. Come over about seven? Need to talk to you. xx**

My brows drew together. That message two minutes before work started wasn't helpful. I needed more info. Was it a good talk or a bad talk? Did he ask Guy and Helen to take Aiden specifically for this talk to happen? Or was it a happy coincidence?

There had been no sign of anything being wrong when I'd snuck out of his place at six o'clock that morning. Cal had been a little quiet, but he'd just woken up, and he was often grouchy first thing.

"Everything okay?" Gaby asked, waiting for me in the doorway.

I text back a quick 'okay, see you later x' to Cal and slipped my phone into my pocket. "I think so."

As I headed out to greet my class, I tried to put my concerns aside, but I couldn't shift the unsettled feeling in my stomach.

By the time lunchtime rolled around, some of my unease had calmed, and I made my way to the staff room to meet Nova and Gaby as I usually did. I wanted to see Nova, to thank her again for the night before and to hear her full thoughts on the disaster that was our evening. However, as I passed the reception desk, Charlotte, one of the receptionists, called my name.

I paused, wheeling around to face her.

Charlotte smiled up at me from her desk. She was as new as me and had also started at Oakwood Lane in September, so we'd bonded over that. Charlotte was fresh out of university and this was her first full-time job. Already, she was popular with the other staff and the parents due to her sunny and understanding nature.

"The head would like to see you in her office asap," she said. "I know it's lunchtime, but she says it's important."

With a frown, I said, "Any indication of what it's about?"

Charlotte shook her head. "No, sorry."

My stomach rumbled, but I thought it best to go and see what she wanted before I ate. Iris Braithwaite's office was just next to the staff room, so, after thanking Charlotte, I continued the way I'd been heading.

Iris was the kind of gentle headmistress any parent would want at a primary school. Stern when needed, but mostly welcoming, and she took the time to get to know her staff and the children in her care. She was in her late fifties and had been the head of this school for ten years, and when I'd become part of the Oakwood Lane team, she'd done everything she could to help me settle in.

I knocked on her door and waited for her to call me inside. When she did, I opened the door, and she looked up from her desk with a strained smile.

And there's that unsettled feeling again.

"Hi, Shannen. Take a seat."

Her light brown greying hair was tied back in a bun, and her glasses perched low on her nose. As I sat, she pushed the mouse she'd been using to do something on her computer to the side and fixed her attention on me.

"You're making me nervous," I admitted, wiping my sweaty palms on my trousers. This wasn't normal. Usually, Iris greeted me much more warmly, and the notion that something was wrong grew.

Offering me a more welcoming smile, she said, "Sorry. That wasn't my intention." She paused, tapping her left index finger on the desk as if trying to find the right words. I drew in a breath and held it as I waited.

"Shannen, am I right in thinking that you are still in a relationship with Mr Lewis?" Iris began, and I nodded, frowning slightly.

"Yes, I am. Why?"

Her hands slowly flattened in front of her, and she said, "I'm aware that Mr Lewis had a few personal issues some time ago that led to Aiden being in foster care for a while. However, I was wondering if you were aware of any other issues he may have had in his past."

The knot in my stomach tightened. I knew he had something of a drinking problem for a while and that he'd been with more women than I liked to think about, but that didn't seem like the kind of issue I'd be called into the office about.

Shaking my head, I said, "No, nothing."

With a slow nod, Iris sighed. "This morning, I had a visit from a Superintedent McCalden."

My entire body stiffened. What was Scott doing at my workplace?

"He said he's a friend of yours," Iris continued, and her brows rose for a second. "Although, admittedly, a real friend would have spoken to you first."

"He's my friend's fiancé," I explained, although I used the word 'friend' loosely there too. I could feel the wrinkle creasing my forehead as strongly as the churning in my gut while I awaited more information.

"Superintendent McCalden expressed concerns that Mr Lewis is known to him for a very serious assault on a man that took place eleven years ago."

My blood ran cold at her words. "What?"

Another slow nod. "Clearly, you weren't aware."

Not only was I not aware, I was completely blindsided. *A serious assault?* On who? Eleven years ago would have made Cal nineteen. That was before Aiden. Before the drinking... maybe.

And just like that, the mountain of things I didn't know about him seemed sinister. I'd never pushed him for information, but he also never offered it. Was he hiding some kind of violent past from me? He had a short temper for sure, but violence was not a thing I associated with Cal. I'd known him to throw things and shout but never lash out.

"When you say a very serious assault, what exactly are we talking about here?" I asked as panic began to trickle through me.

"According to Superintendent McCalden, Mr Lewis was never charged with the assault, but there is a record of his arrest. I don't know the details."

"So, he might not have even done anything?" I asked, my head tilting to the side.

"I think perhaps that is something you need to speak to Mr Lewis about," Iris said, her eyes softening as she took in my obvious confusion. "The reason I called you in here wasn't just to ask you if you're aware. With this coming to light, my first concern is for your safety. Have you witnessed any sign of violent behaviour from Mr Lewis?"

"Absolutely not," I answered without hesitation. Again, though, my thoughts were brought to his quick temper. It had been clear to me for a while that something had happened somewhere in Cal's past that had traumatised him. I still hadn't forgotten how he'd frozen when I'd mentioned him having a brother, and how he talked about his mum in past tense. I'd surmised that perhaps he'd lost his family, though I didn't know how or when. But did whatever happened lead to him being violent? Was this something else he'd moved past, like the other bits of his old life that he'd left behind?

"Okay," she continued carefully, pushing her glasses back up her nose. "As you know, what you do in your personal life is not my business. The only time it would be is if you were living with someone who had the potential to put the children here at risk. As I said, though, I do care about you and your career. You need to have a chat with your young man and find out more about this. I don't know what your *friend* was hoping to achieve by bringing this to my attention, but my feeling is that it wasn't for a good reason. And if he decides to make Mr Lewis's record of arrest common knowledge, there's a chance the parents here..." she trailed off, raising her eyebrows.

She didn't need to complete the sentence.

If Cal had been arrested for a violent crime, guilty or not, the 'no smoke without fire' claims would pour in, and that would have an impact on me. It might not be a huge impact, but there was always a chance it could lead to questions about the company I kept and whether the children in my class were safe with me.

Scott had done this, not out of concern for me, but to force Cal's past into the present. It suddenly dawned on me why Scott had been staring at Cal in the pub, and why he'd looked so amused.

Prick. Iris was right; Scott was no kind of friend. Not that I'd ever considered him one, but if he *was*, he would have told me himself instead of marching into my workplacc and telling my boss.

And Cal. He hadn't been so quiet because he was bothered by Jade and Scott's behaviour. He'd recognised Scott too, and instead of telling me, he'd taken me home with him and given me the best sex of my life.

But why wouldn't he have told me unless...

Unless it was true.

This had to be the reason for Cal's text earlier. He wanted to tell me about it, and if he thought it best that Aiden wasn't present for the conversation, it suggested he was expecting it not to go well.

A dull ache began to throb at my temples, and I ran my fingers across my forehead.

With a quick nod, I turned my focus back to Iris and said, "Thank you for letting me know what Scott said. I need some time to process all of this."

"I understand." She reached over and gently squeezed my hand. "If this blows up, and it's a big if, I will do all I can to support you, but the court of public opinion is often loud and unstoppable."

That much I knew. What I didn't know was what that would mean for me and my future at this school or as a teacher.

"Go and get some lunch," Iris said. "And enjoy half term. You are more than welcome to reach out to me over the break if you need to."

I gave her a grateful smile, even though the dull ache was already blooming into a full-on headache. And I still had another half a day to get through. "Thank you."

I stood up and turned to the door, walking towards it. As I reached for the handle, my mind swirling with thoughts, I stopped and turned back.

"Iris, I would never be with a violent man. And if I thought either Aiden or I were in danger, I wouldn't let it continue. But that isn't... that just isn't the man I know."

Again, her eyes softened, but the empathy in her gaze was too much for me, and I turned and left the office before her kindness made me cry.

Once outside the office, I leaned back against the door for a second, but I knew I couldn't stay there. At lunchtime, teachers and teaching assistants were in and out of the staff room, and someone would pass me and ask what was wrong if I didn't move.

Instead of joining Gaby and Nova as I'd planned, I straightened up and marched out of the reception area and back to my classroom. I used the key in my pocket to unlock my desk drawer, where I always put my handbag to keep it safe, and pulled it out. Slinging it over my shoulder, I took out my car keys as I walked back through the halls and reception area, then out to my car.

As I pulled out of the car park, I wasn't entirely sure where I was heading yet. All I knew was that I needed to be alone. Any hunger I'd felt had disappeared, taken over by a sensation of nausea. There were so many questions. So many things to think about.

Scott had known something about Cal, and instead of telling Jade or me right there in the pub, he'd just sat there, smirking like the arrogant arsehole he was. Realistically, he couldn't have known for sure if I knew what he knew, but he *did* know that by taking it to my workplace, he could make it into an issue. If I hadn't had such a decent head teacher, I could have been in for a potential lecture and possible judgement. He'd attempted to mess with my good reputation at a job I had worked my arse off for.

It was then I realised I was heading for Jade's house before consciously making the decision. It was a fifteen-minute drive, and I only had an hour for lunch, but there was no way I'd have concentrated on work for the afternoon if I didn't deal with the simmering rage that coursed through my bloodstream.

When I pulled up in the driveway of Jade's house, I couldn't help but stop and shake my head in amazement at the sight of it, just as I always did. The place was beautiful. It had six bedrooms—three en suite—plus two other bathrooms and a shower room. The kitchen, lounge, and dining room were huge, and the garden looked like it could hold a small football pitch, not to mention the added bonus of their indoor heated swimming pool. Frankly, I didn't know how she kept up with it all, but there was never so much as a speck of dust to be found anywhere. Anytime I went over there, I half expected to be vacuumed up by an overzealous maid.

Getting out of the car, I didn't bother locking it because I wasn't planning to be there for long. I marched to the front door and hammered on it, hoping Jade was home. Their double garage concealed their cars, so I couldn't tell if she was in from the outside.

After a minute, Jade came to the door, and her eyes widened on seeing me. She probably hadn't expected me to show up in the middle of a school day, and as she took me in, her face paled slightly.

Before I could speak, I heard footsteps approaching, and Scott appeared behind her.

The arrogance on his face was enough to make me want to swing for him, but the last thing I needed was to get myself in trouble for assaulting him.

"What did you do?" I spat, and he grinned.

"I was just doing my job, Shannen," he said. "I have a duty to make sure local residents are safe, and that includes the children you teach. Your principal deserves to know that someone responsible for teaching five-year-olds has jumped into bed with a known criminal."

His words caused bile to rise up in my throat. With one sentence, he'd turned my relationship into something that sounded disgusting and seedy. Like I was getting a kick out of sleeping with a convict.

Except Cal wasn't convicted of anything.

"You went into my school and told the head that you were concerned for me!" I snapped, and his grin grew. "What you were actually trying to do was make me look bad! Why didn't you just tell me what you knew instead of bringing my job into it?"

Scott shrugged. "Like I said, I felt she needed to know."

"Know what?" I exploded. "I still don't even know what you're talking about."

This time, he bellowed out a laugh. "Oh, this is gold!" He looked down at Jade. "I told you he'd kept it from her." As Scott looked back up at me, he said, "It's okay, Shannen. You don't need to be embarrassed. You weren't to know. The man's a liar and he always has been. But at least you know now."

Unable to stand looking at him anymore, I fixed my attention on Jade, who stood rigidly in front of Scott. "Did you know what Scott was going to do?" I asked. "Did you know he was going to take this to my workplace?"

She nodded, some strands of her blonde hair slipping from her loose ponytail. "Yeah." With a one-shoulder shrug, she added, "I thought it was for the best. You wouldn't listen to me when I told you he was no good for you."

"So, instead of calling me last night, you thought the best course of action was to humiliate me?"

"You are worth more than him!" she argued. "If I'd told you, you'd have found a way to make excuses for him. This way, you'll have to deal with it. Just get rid of him and keep your career safe."

Blinking rapidly, I tried to process what she'd just said. She didn't care about my career. She never had. Jade hadn't understood why I wanted to study, to make a life for myself that didn't involve relying on a man. Her mother married a rich man and lived off him, and that was all Jade wanted for herself too. Anyone choosing a different path just didn't compute for her.

Jade's response to whatever Scott had told her all came back to one thing.

"Let's be honest here, Jade. You never wanted me to be with Cal. It didn't cross your mind for a second that you could be wrong about him. That's why you started talking crap about him in front of our mums, and why the only effort you made towards him last night was to make him feel like he wasn't good enough. The truth is, you don't care about me at all. All that matters to you is having friends who wear the 'right' clothes and date the 'right' men and fit into this weird little box of perfection you try to force people into. We've been friends for twenty-five years. And we've disagreed about a lot of things. But never until Cal came along have you tried to control me."

A lump lodged in my throat at the reminder of just how long we'd been in each other's lives. Jade could be unbearable at times, but long before she became judgemental, we were just two little girls who loved to play with dolls, put on dance shows for our families, and talk about all of the amazing things we would do when we grew up. As I stared at her now hardened face, I saw the adorable kid with pigtails who I told all my secrets to. The one who had confided in me and had, at one time, been the most important person in my life.

I loved her.

And even as we grew up and material things took precedence over her innocent hopes and dreams, we found a way to bridge our differences.

But somewhere over the last year, those differences had gotten bigger, the gap widening until she no longer seemed to care about anything except what was happening in her world. Everything else was an inconvenience, including me.

"Control?" Scott scoffed. "Nobody is trying to control you here. What we're trying to do is make sure you don't end up an outcast because of your shitty taste in men."

Fixing him with a firm look, I said, "I will happily be cast out of anywhere that doesn't accept who I choose to be with."

"So, you're still going to keep seeing him?" Jade asked, her mouth agape.

I opened my own mouth to speak, but Scott interrupted, "Let's just be clear, Shannen. If you choose to stay with a man who half-killed someone, a man who has kept his fucked-up past hidden from you, you will no longer be welcome here. And especially not at our wedding."

Half killed?

Scott had to be wrong about the details. If Cal had really done something so terrible, he would have been charged, but he wasn't. I wasn't oblivious to the fact that guilty people *could* get away with horrible crimes, but I just couldn't see Cal doing something like that.

But then, he must have had some connection to a violent crime, something that linked him to it, or he would never have been arrested in the first place.

This was the part of the equation I hadn't got around to dealing with yet. Didn't have a clue where to start.

One problem at a time, Shannen.

I glanced at Jade, waiting to see if she would fight for me. To tell Scott that I should have some time to think before making any big decisions. To say *anything* in my defence.

I was met with silence.

Tears pricked at my eyes. I hadn't truly believed Jade would stand up for me, but that didn't stop it from hurting.

"Okay," I said, my voice clogged with emotion. "I'm out. Whatever I decide to do about Cal is irrelevant because I don't ever want to see or speak to either of you again. Screw you both, and screw your wedding."

I spun around before the first tear fell and headed back to my car.

I genuinely had no idea how I made it through the afternoon at work.

Gaby had messaged me when I was on my way back from Jade's to see where I was, and when I'd parked back in the school car park, I text her to tell her I'd explain later. I still wasn't ready to talk about it. Instead, I plastered a smile on my face and focused on the sweet yet overexcited faces in my classroom. The last day before the end of term was always somewhat more relaxed, and the kids had a lower attention span, so I reverted to playing games that were educational but seemed like fun. This time, Aiden behaved brilliantly, even when he wasn't winning, and pride swelled within me at how much he'd changed.

It wasn't just Cal I adored. Aiden had come so far in the last few weeks. He wasn't an angel in the classroom or at home, but he was substantially calmer and less easily riled. Spending time with him outside of school had made me better able to understand him, which made teaching him easier. I was very careful not to treat him differently to any of my other students, but I couldn't deny that I'd grown extremely fond of him, and that added another layer of anxiety to my already edgy state.

While at the end of the day, and especially at the end of the week, I usually stayed behind to make sure everything was tied up before the weekend, that day, I just wanted to go home. I hid in my classroom, gathering my things while my teaching assistant saw the children out. I didn't want to see Helen, and I wasn't ready to speak to Gaby or Nova yet either. I did, however, send a message to our group chat to let them know that I had to rush home and I'd speak to them over the weekend.

As soon as I got into my flat, I was finally free to let all of the thoughts and feelings I'd been forced to block rush through me.

I stood with my back against my front door for a moment, my head resting against it.

What a day.

My mind was still reeling from the things I'd learned, but mostly from the things I hadn't. The information from Scott's bombshell was minimal, and it left my brain to fill in the gaps.

And yet, no matter how I tried, I couldn't. All I knew was that Scott had claimed Cal had been arrested for 'half-killing' someone. But he was never charged. So, did he get away with something he did, or did someone incorrectly point the finger at him?

If Cal's arrest became public knowledge—innocent or not—questions would still be asked, and even more if anyone found out that a primary school teacher was in a relationship with a man who had had his own child taken away. Few people would look at the turnaround Cal had made and celebrate that. They'd only look at the negatives, and it *would* reflect on me.

Letting out a frustrated sigh, I straightened up. No part of me truly believed Cal was dangerous now, but what if, when he was younger, he didn't have the tools to keep his short fuse in check? What if he *had* hurt someone?

My mind was all over the place.

I'd just severed a lifelong friendship over a man who had been keeping a huge secret from me. As much as Jade had hurt me, cutting off someone who had been a part of me for so long was painful, and I hadn't even begun to deal with my feelings about that yet.

I had to talk to Cal, and I couldn't wait until seven. I'd waited long enough. He'd be at work for another hour or so at least, which gave me time to shower and figure out exactly what to say to him.

How would I even approach it, though? Earlier, when Iris told me what she'd learned from Scott, my wrath had immediately been directed at him for being so underhanded. Whereas Cal... I'd just been confused. This wasn't my libido overriding my common sense. The idea of him badly hurting someone just didn't seem right, but what the hell did I know about what he was like more than ten years ago?

With a shake of my head, I took off my coat and shoes, dumping my coat over the back of the sofa. I was about to head for the bathroom when I heard my phone ringing in my bag. I didn't want to talk to anyone, but I scooped it up to at least see who it was before I went to wash the day from me.

Mum.

My heart sank with dread before speeding up and pounding against my chest. It wasn't unusual for my mum to call me, but it *was* unlike her to call before six on a weekday because she knew I often didn't leave work until well after four. It was only four-thirty now, which suggested either something was wrong, or once again, Jade had let her know something about my life I wasn't ready to tell her.

"Hello?" I said, trying to sound as normal as possible.

"Shannen, I just had a hysterical phone call from Judith about how you've ruined Jade's wedding by pulling out of being her maid of honour because you've fallen out over the man you're seeing. What on Earth is going on?"

That sounded right. Only Jade could have her fiance interfere in *my* life and still make it my fault.

"What exactly did she tell you?" I asked, trying to control my hands, which had already begun to tremble with my irritation. I leaned back against the sofa, telling myself to stay calm. We weren't children anymore, and yet the first thing

Jade thought to do was have her mummy tell my mummy that I'd ruined her big day.

"She said Scott found out something about your boyfriend, and you got angry with him and Jade and told them to screw their wedding."

Ha. Semi-accurate.

"Yeah, she missed out the part where Scott said that if I continue my relationship with Cal, I wouldn't be welcome at their house or their wedding. So, yeah, I did tell them to screw it," I explained bluntly.

"Shannen, Judith said that the man you're dating has a criminal record."

There was no anger in her voice. Not even judgement. More confusion.

"Mum, I have had the day from hell. At lunchtime, I was called to see the headmistress because Scott had been to my workplace to report that Cal was arrested when he was nineteen for an undisclosed violent crime. Arrested, but not charged. This is something I knew nothing about. I still don't know anything because I haven't had a chance to speak to Cal yet. All I know is that Jade knew about this and instead of coming to me, Scott tried to stir up trouble at my school. If Judith is hysterical about her daughter's ruined wedding, maybe she needs to have a talk with Jade about not marrying such an underhanded, judgemental arse."

So much for staying calm.

Taking a deep breath and blowing it out slowly, I said, "Sorry, Mum. It's just... it's been a long day. And I don't know what to tell you. I don't even know what Cal is supposed to have done yet. The only thing I'm sure of is that I don't want Jade in my life after the way she's been lately. She'll have no problem finding a new maid of honour. If their family wants to make an issue of my choices, so be it. I'm sorry if any of that reflects on you, Dad, and Sadie, but this is my life. The only person who decides what I do is me."

Mum was silent for a few moments, but I could hear her soft breathing down the line. "What will you do if Scott's claims are true?"

I hadn't allowed myself to think about that yet. How could I when I had no knowledge of the alleged crime? The words 'violent' and 'half-killed' were uttered, but what did that mean? Was it a bar fight that resulted in some broken bones, or did Cal outright attack someone randomly and seriously injure them?

And would any admission change how I felt about him now?

"I don't know," I said with a sigh. "There are a lot of variables here. I can't guess how I'll feel until I hear him out."

"I understand," Mum said softly. "I know tonight you probably just want to talk to Cal and find out what's going on, but I'd like us to talk over the weekend so you can tell me more about what's been happening. I'm going to have a word with Judith about Scott because taking a private issue to your workplace is low. And after the way Jade was on the day we were wedding dress shopping, I understand your decision. She's supposed to be your friend and I saw how hurt you were by her behaviour. So, Judith and I will come to some agreement that doesn't involve Jade dragging your name through the mud. And just to be clear, if Judith allows that to happen, that will be the end of my friendship with her too."

"Mum, no," I said, my voice wobbling at her fierce protection of me. "This is Jade's and my issue." Mum and Judith had known each other since they were kids. I may have found Jade's mother to be rude and snobby, but she was still my mum's best friend and I didn't want that to suffer because of Jade and me.

"When her family tries to mess with my daughter's career, it becomes my issue too," Mum said gently but firmly. "But Shannen... your father doesn't know about any of this yet. If Cal is responsible for a crime, charged or otherwise..."

She didn't need to finish the sentence. My dad was old-school. He would have been relatively okay with me dating a working-class guy, but someone with any kind of criminal activity in his past was a no-go. His strict upbringing made him extremely firm in his beliefs. In his mind, even the smallest illegal *indiscretion* was inexcusable.

And I hadn't considered that. The only thing on my mind was talking to Cal. Anything else was a problem for later, including my family.

"I know," I said quietly. "I'll call you tomorrow, once I've got some actual information."

"Okay, sweetheart. If you need me, though, you don't have to wait until tomorrow. Call me in the middle of the night if you need to."

A tear slipped down my cheek, one that had been threatening since I heard her voice. "I will. I love you."

"I love you too."

As I hung up, I brushed the tear away and took a deep breath. Then, I pulled up Cal's messages and typed:

> I've spoken to Scott. Come over as soon as you can. x

Chapter 22

Cal

I knew this would happen.

I knew he'd tell her before I could.

Now, I was standing outside Shannen's flat after having the fastest shower and change ever, my whole body tense as I waited for her to open the door.

I'd held my breath all day, hoping I could just get through it so I could talk to Shannen before Scott or Jade did, but deep down, I knew they'd beat me to it.

Maybe I should have told her the night before, but I was too selfish. The reason I didn't *was* partially because Aiden was in the flat and it wasn't exactly a quick chat over coffee kind of conversation. But mostly, it was because I needed one more night with her.

No part of me believed we would still be together once she knew everything. So, I'd kept her close to me while I could, before it all slipped away.

It seemed to take forever for Shannen to open the door, and as soon as she did, I wanted to run. To avoid this conversation because the idea of losing her... it made my head light and my heart heavy. If we never talked about it, then she couldn't turn me away. Couldn't walk away from what we had. I wouldn't have to hear her say what I'd half-expected her to say since we met.

It's over.

She looked perfect. Her long hair was damp and hung over the black hoodie she wore. She also wore plaid red and black lounge pants, and as was her preference, her feet were bare.

Her eyes trailed from my face down to my feet, then back up, like she was trying to familiarise herself with me. As if we hadn't spent the last seven weeks learning about each other.

As if I was already a stranger to her.

My jaw ticked, and my teeth clenched. My defences were rising, and I internally counted to ten, trying to calm down. If she was upset with me, she had every right to be. My past was my business, and we hadn't been together long enough for me to be ready to explain it all, but once I saw Scott, I knew my hand would be forced and she *should* have heard my story from me.

Surprising me, Shannen took my hand and gently pulled me inside to the living room.

Once we were in the warm, cosy room, she looked up at me again. The tears glistening in her eyes intensified the self-loathing that had been building in me all the way to her place.

"I don't..." she began, then sighed. "I want to hug you, but I don't know..." Again, words failed her, and she shook her head and turned away from me with a sigh.

Before she could get too far from me, I grabbed her hand and gently pulled her to face me again. I wasn't sure if she wanted it, but I *needed* it, so I let go of her hand and wound my arms around her waist, crushing her against me. As I buried my face in her hair, breathing in that fresh honey scent, I felt her hands on my back, holding me just as tight.

I didn't ever want to be anywhere else, or with anyone else. Only her. Like this.

"What's going on, Cal?" she asked quietly after a while, her words muffled against my chest.

Something seemed to lodge in my throat as I tried to speak, and I swallowed hard before saying, "What did he tell you?"

Stupid question. He would have told her the truth. Everything I didn't want her to know. If he hadn't, she wouldn't have been so tense.

Shannen pulled away from me a little, looking up at me again. "He didn't tell *me* anything. He told the headmistress at my school that you're a dangerous criminal."

Blinking as she let go of me, I said, "He what?"

Shannen's lips pulled together in a thin line, and she shrugged. "Apparently, telling me directly was too easy. Instead, he decided to try to cause trouble for me."

Her chin wobbled, like she was trying to hold in her emotion, and I wanted to find that prick and knock his teeth out.

"Did he?" I gritted out. "Did he cause trouble for you?"

She shrugged again. "Not yet. But that doesn't mean he won't try again."

I met her gaze, but she flicked her attention to the floor, like she didn't want to look at me. Like she didn't know who I was anymore. It made my blood run cold; I didn't want that from her. I wanted the way she usually looked at me. The brightness in her blue eyes, the sparkle when she smiled at me.

But there was no way I could get it back now. I was someone different to her.

I *was* a dangerous criminal. I had been since I was a young teenager. Even Detective Dickhead didn't know that much about me. Nobody did. It didn't matter that I'd turned my life around. For most of it, I'd been a waster. A fucking pathetic excuse for a man, who couldn't be arsed to get it together. Not even for my own kid.

That was the real me. I was a fraud, living life as a responsible adult, when inside, I was still a kid, unable to stop my father from beating my mother. An angry youngster, pissed off with the world and hating everyone in it.

For just a moment, I had this amazing woman. One who made me believe life wasn't so bad.

Except now, my mask was off. She could see the ugly; she had to. I felt it pouring out of me, the side of me that deserved nothing. It seeped from me, wrapping itself around her so all she could see was the bad. The man I'd tried to put behind me.

But you can't outrun badness. Someone always knows. Someone will always remind you.

"Don't," Shannen said quietly, and I snapped my focus to her. She wasn't even looking at me. She had her hands on the back of the sofa and was looking right ahead while I stood by the living room door, contemplating making a run for it.

"Don't what?" I asked her.

"I can hear you over there, telling yourself you're no good. You need to stop it."

I hadn't spoken out loud, but she'd proved my point. My bullshit was obvious to her. My unworthiness clear.

Or the unthinkable had happened and I'd let her in too far.

Slowly, she turned to face me again, and the confusion and pain in her eyes made my knees buckle. I wanted to go to her, to hold her again, but I couldn't move, paralyzed by the weight of the situation.

"Cal, I have no idea what you're going to say, and I'm scared."

The lump in my throat that I'd tried to shift rose again, and I took in a deep breath. "Of me?"

She shook her head, but the moisture in her eyes glimmered, causing my jaw to clench again. "Of what you're going to tell me."

"Do you really not know?" I asked, my brow creasing. She had to know *something* or she wouldn't have called me over, and she wouldn't be so afraid.

"Scott told the principal at my school that you'd been arrested when you were nineteen for a serious assault, but you weren't charged. He said you were known to him. And even though I've spoken to him myself, I still don't know the details. All I know for sure is that he doesn't want me anywhere near him and Jade as long as I'm with you."

Her words came out a little croaky at the end, and my gut twisted. "What did Jade say about that?"

She shrugged. "Nothing. She knew what Scott was going to do. She didn't warn me, and she didn't make any move to defend me, so... we're done."

Shannen tucked her hands inside the sleeves of her hoodie and wrapped her arms around herself as if she was cold. I walked over to her, gently tilting her chin up to look at me before sliding my hand to the back of her neck.

I wanted to tell her she was better off without that pair of arseholes in her life, but she was upset. Not over Scott, but over her friendship with Jade. As far as I could see, Jade wasn't worth the upset. She was a bitch who only wanted things her way. But they had been friends since they were kids, so maybe it was their history she mourned.

"I'm sorry," I said. "I'm so sorry I made this happen. I should have told you last night."

She shook her head. "You didn't make this happen. Scott had no idea if I knew the things he knows. He went to the school intending to cause trouble. Admittedly, it would have been a tad better if I wasn't blindsided by it, but ultimately, it wouldn't have made much difference. It certainly wouldn't have stopped him. He just wanted to humiliate me into ending things with you."

She still hadn't pushed me away yet, so I braved another step towards her and used my free hand to circle her back. Her arms dropped to her sides, and although she didn't put them around me, she stepped closer, so her body was pressed against mine.

"Shan... your job..." I began, praying to God that this didn't screw up her career.

"My job is fine," she interrupted. "For now, anyway."

I wasn't sure what she meant by that. Too afraid to ask because I suspected it might depend on whether or not she wanted to keep seeing me.

"I need you to tell me everything I need to know." As she pulled back from me, she looked up.

I still saw it there in her eyes. That thing she said to me the night before that I hadn't been able to say back. But behind it was confusion and worry, so the bright blue was dulled, even behind the sheen of tears she tried to keep at bay.

There were many ways I'd imagined having this conversation, but none of them started with Shannen already being on edge. Whenever I'd thought about it, about what I'd say, I assumed it would be long after I'd told her about my family, so she would have at least had a chance of understanding what led to my arrest. Now, I had to explain it all at once, and I didn't know where to start.

I dropped my hands from her and walked around to the sofa. She followed me, and as I sat down at one end, Shannen sat at the other, crossing her legs in front of her and facing me. She picked up a cushion and hugged it to herself like a shield, protecting her from whatever I was about to say.

I hated the distance, but I also wasn't sure I could hold her through this. I definitely didn't deserve any comfort from her.

Taking a deep breath, I dropped my head against the back of the sofa, trying to work out where to start when all I wanted to do was turn back the clock and handle all of this differently.

Lowering my head again, I turned to look at her, expectant eyes on me.

"When I was fourteen, I was responsible for the death of my mum and brother."

Chapter 23

Shannen

I heard the words Cal said, but no part of me understood them. I'd braced myself to hear about something he'd done when he was nineteen, so how had he begun with something different?

All I could do was stare at him as he sat there, watching for my reaction, but I had nothing. I'd been stunned into silence.

While I'd waited for him to arrive earlier, my mind spun with thoughts about what he could have done. It had made me on edge so that when he got to my place, I wanted to simultaneously hold him and keep him at arm's length. I was afraid of what he was going to say, but every time I looked at his perfect face, all I could think about was how much he meant to me. How hard I'd fallen.

Even now, with the words he'd just uttered, my heart twinged, and I wanted to crawl across the sofa and into his lap because the pain and fear in his eyes clawed at my insides.

But I was frozen.

Cal must have realised I couldn't speak, as he blew out a long breath. "When I was young, my life was great. Normal. I had parents who spent time with me and my brother. They took us swimming, and to the beach, and on day trips. My mum taught us how to cook, and my dad took us fishing. But when I was ten, my dad had to give up his job. He worked in holiday camps in Exmouth, sang at weddings, and did pub gigs. Back then, he was happy. But he developed a condition that affected his voice, and he had to give it all up. He was only qualified to sing, so Mum had to get a full-time job to cover the money we lost. There was nothing else my dad ever wanted to do, and unable to do what he loved, he didn't want to do anything." There had been a sparkle of fondness in Cal's eyes as he'd spoken about his parents at first, but it lessened, and he let out another deep exhale. "Mum tried to encourage him to find a new job, but all he could think about was the thing he couldn't do anymore. He started drinking, and after about a year of being unemployed, he hit my mum for the first time."

My stomach twisted, and now I *really* wanted to get closer to him, but I didn't think he'd appreciate the comfort. He'd see it as pity. I uncrossed my legs and tucked them under me instead, unwilling to interrupt.

"My dad never laid a finger on me or my brother, but Luca and I... we heard every time our parents had an argument. Heard the slaps to her face. The times he threw things around, sometimes aimed at her and sometimes not. Luca used to come into my room every time a fight started. The first few times, he hid under the bed or in my wardrobe as if that would help to block it out. He soon realised it didn't make any difference. After that, he would sit next to me wherever I was. Sometimes I would just lie on the bed, trying to ignore it, and sometimes I'd play a video game and turn the volume up to drown out the noise. Luca would be at my side no matter what, though. I guess it made him feel safer." He paused, running his hand across his forehead wearily. It was like the memories he recounted had taken him back, and I wondered if he'd ever spoken about this before. I was aware he was only giving me a summary, and what he'd been through likely ran a lot deeper. His words were almost robotic in tone as if giving me the basics because delving into the specifics would tip him over the edge.

"My dad went from fun and happy to depressed and mean," Cal went on. "He had no time for any of us anymore. From almost the moment he lost his job, he had no patience, and everything any of us did was wrong. For some reason, I was on the receiving end of most of his bad moods. Mum got the physical attacks, and I got the yelling, being told I was useless, and things being flung at me. He was never truly aiming for me, but he would throw things to the side of me to scare me to do as I was told."

An ache began to form in my chest as I listened to the snippets of Cal's childhood. No wonder he found it so easy to call himself a waste of space. If he'd heard that and things like it from his own father, it made sense that he'd revert to those thoughts as soon as he felt like he'd done something wrong.

It also went some way to explaining why Cal tended to throw things when his temper got the best of him. Aiden had seen Cal throw things once in my company, but I wasn't sure how often he'd seen it before or since. And Aiden had his own issues with his temper sometimes. The cycle *was* breaking. Cal was trying to break it, but I couldn't help wondering how much of the things Cal had been through were already emblazoned in Aiden's five-year-old brain.

"One evening, when I was fourteen, I wanted to go to Guy's house," Cal said. "Dad said I couldn't because it was a school night, even though I'd done my homework. By that time, I was sick of the way he was and just cocky enough to start pushing back. I didn't do it often because if I didn't behave, he'd take it out on Mum. But that night, I was done, and he raised his hand to me for the first time. He didn't hit me because I was too fast, and I ran out of the house to Guy's place." Cal stopped, flexing his fingers a couple of times before clenching his fists in his lap. "I was too scared to go home, so I stayed at Guy's place until late, and then I planned to sleep there. But around eleven o'clock that night, my dad came to get me. I heard him from upstairs, telling Guy's mum that there had been an accident and we needed to go to the hospital." His head lowered and his entire body shuddered as if a shiver had shot through him. "Shan, I can't go into all the details because I..." Trailing off, he shook his head and then sighed like the memories overwhelmed him, and I swallowed back a sob. "My brother was dead already when we got to the hospital, and my mum was gone within the next couple of hours. When we finally got back to our house, my dad lost it. He tore up the entire living room, screaming at me that it was my fault they were dead. He said if I hadn't been so selfish, there wouldn't have been an argument. Because he'd almost hit me, Mum had told him she'd had enough and was leaving him. The few bags she'd packed were found in the car she crashed. On the way to pick me up."

He blinked, his fists clenched so hard his knuckles were white, and his whole body began to shake again, but this time, it didn't stop.

"When I was fourteen, I was responsible for the death of my mum and brother." The words he'd said suddenly made sense.

Shifting quickly, I moved across the couch towards him, as close as I could get without climbing onto his lap, and rested my hands over his.

"Cal, no," I said. "Look at me."

He shook his head again, his jaw tight, and I tugged at his fingers, trying to unfurl them before he drew blood from his palms. I succeeded, but he was still trembling, and I weaved my fingers between his.

"He said I killed them," Cal said, his voice low and strained. "If I'd just done as I was told, it wouldn't have happened."

"There is no way you can know that," I said gently. "There's no way to know that your mum wouldn't have chosen that exact time to go out in the car for a drive, or to pick something up from the nearest shop, or for any number of reasons. And if she'd left five minutes earlier or later to come and get you, it wouldn't have happened. It wasn't your fault."

"It *was* my fault." He pulled his hands from mine, clenching them again immediately. "If it wasn't for me, she would never have driven that way. There would have been no need for her to. But she did, and she ran right into the path of some idiotic boy racer trying to prove how cool he was. You know what injuries he got from that crash? A bump on the head and a couple of cracked ribs."

As if the torment of his memories was too much for him, he got to his feet and paced around behind the sofa, walking a path from the edge of the living room to the kitchen door before stopping and thudding his back against the wall there. He dropped his head against it, looking up at the ceiling.

"My dad got worse," he went on, his voice now void of emotion. "When he didn't have my mum to beat on, I became his new punchbag. My mum was always smart with money, and she had life insurance, which paid off the mortgage on our house, but my dad sold it a year after she and Luca died. He bought us a cheap, shitty flat that he didn't have to put any work into, and the only thing he did for me was ensure I had the basic things I needed. Clothes, shoes, school supplies. He didn't cook, and the food shop consisted of beer, bread, milk, teabags, and microwave meals. He didn't talk to me unless it was to tell me he hated me. If I'd left that place, he'd only have noticed the next time he needed to take his anger out on someone."

I bit the inside of my cheek, trying hard to halt the tears that had filled my eyes, but I wouldn't be able to hold them for long. I still wanted to go to him, but right then, he was too far lost in his own mind, and I didn't want to feel the sting of rejection I'd felt when he pulled away from me before. For now, I had to stay strong, listen, and keep my distance, even if it hurt because what I felt was nothing compared to what telling me this was doing to him.

"I gave up on school," he went on, finally turning his head to look at me. "I went, but I wasn't interested. My grades got worse, and they weren't great before. I scraped through my GCSEs with nothing above a C, and when I left school, I did nothing, just like my dad." Straightening to stand, he said, "I was a petty thief who nicked food when I was hungry and spent as much time out of the flat as I could. So, all those times I've said I'm not good enough, Shan? All those times I've told you you're better than me, I was right. You should be able to see that now."

I wasn't sure if that was a reflection of how he felt about himself or a dig at my privileged upbringing. We *were* different. Our childhoods and families were different. But I'd never looked at him or treated him as anything other than an equal.

"Why?" I challenged, not moving from my place on the sofa. "Because your dad told you you weren't good enough? Because you didn't get the best grades? Because you were left with a parent who let you down? None of that is your fault, Cal."

"I *am* him!" he roared, his stature rigid as he stared at me like he needed me to believe something that simply wasn't true. "I'm him! I don't deal with things, I run from them! I let my kid down, just like he did with me, and when I couldn't cope, I started drinking! If it wasn't for Guy, I'd probably still be drinking myself to death in a council flat!"

I flinched at the raise of his voice, and he hung his head, his eyes dimming further.

"Is that what your dad did?" I asked quietly. "Did he drink himself to death?"

186

Cal shrugged, looking back up at me. "Don't know, don't care. He started spending time with some woman who also drank too much, and he moved in with her and left me on my own when I was twenty. I haven't seen him since the day he walked out. He *could* be dead for all I know."

I nodded slowly, trying to absorb the enormous amount of information that had just been thrown my way.

It wasn't hard to see how he'd reached his conclusions. He had a father who had homed in on his insecurities and then used them to torture him. He'd lost his mum and his brother in one cruel hit, and he had nobody else to turn to. No mention of other relatives. Presumably, if there had been anyone else, things would have been different.

And when he had Aiden, and he didn't know how to handle the responsibility of being a single parent, he'd done just what his dad had taught him to. He hid behind alcohol because he hadn't been shown any other way to deal with pain.

But he *wasn't* his dad. Not even close.

"Cal?" I said, turning around and leaning on the back of the sofa as he began to pace again.

He stopped and looked at me, his eyes dark and heavy with the things he'd shared.

"You're not him," I said firmly.

"I was," he argued. "I couldn't get myself out of my own mess any more than he could. Maybe if he'd had someone to check on him, he would have got it together. But neither of us could have done it on our own."

Shaking my head, I said, "I don't think that's true. When Aiden was put into foster care, you didn't give up on him. You kept on seeing him when you could have just let him go."

"Maybe I should have," he muttered. "Better than having to explain the shit-show of a family he comes from."

I bit down on my instinct to remind him Aiden was happier now than he'd been in the entire time I'd taught him. That he'd been better since they moved out of Helen and Guy's house. He knew it, but right then, he'd got himself caught up in the things I guessed he never let himself think about. At least not consciously. It seemed like all of that negativity and toxicity ran through his veins at low levels all the time, getting more noticeable any time life got hard.

Lowering one foot to the floor behind me, I pushed myself to stand and walked around the sofa to stand in front of him. Cal looked down at me, a hint of a challenge in his eyes.

I ignored it because even with what I'd heard so far and the amount of rage coursing through him, I wasn't scared of him.

Stepping forward, I wound my arms around his waist and held him tight. He didn't feel right, all tense and solid, but I didn't let go. Wouldn't. Not unless he asked me to.

I rested my head against his chest, listening to the fast beat of his heart. He didn't touch me, but I stayed right there as the thudding of his heartbeat calmed and his muscles loosened.

"I told you before, Shan. I'm a mess."

"Yeah, you did tell me that. I didn't run away from it last time and I'm not running now."

"Don't make promises you can't keep. There's more to tell."

Chapter 24

Cal

Having Shannen's arms around me was more than I deserved. I wanted to push her away. Not because I didn't want her there—I always wanted her there—but because I knew this couldn't last. The longer she held me, her warm body pressed to mine, the harder it would be when this all went to shit.

It didn't matter that she said she wouldn't run.

She would.

Letting out the extent of my dark side would be too much for her to handle. I'd had years to process it, and *I* still couldn't handle it.

And even knowing that, I wrapped my arms around her waist because I didn't ever want to let her go.

When she felt my hands on her back, she softened against me and held me tighter.

Fuck.

Fuck everything I'd done that meant I couldn't keep this woman in my life.

"Can we sit down again?" Shannen asked.

I would have much preferred not to have to look her in the eye for the next confession. The last confession. Pacing and not watching her feelings for me drain away seemed like the better choice, but I also *needed* to see her. To see if the things she said matched up with the way she looked at me. There was no way she would see me the same way after this.

Instead of answering her, I slid my hands down to her hips and then took one of her hands in mine. She led me back to the sofa, but instead of settling far away from me, this time, she sat next to me and kept hold of my hand.

Before I'd even started talking, her face paled a little. She knew from the vague hints I'd dropped and my insistence that she wouldn't like what she heard that this wasn't going to be pleasant. More than that, she had probably worked out by now that my arrest wasn't just a mistake. She'd likely spent the day hoping that was the case, and I was about to disappoint her.

Shannen's jaw had clenched, mirroring my own expression, but she rubbed her thumb across my knuckles, letting me know she was with me—for now, at least. Those blue eyes of hers were piercing through me, and I tried not to think about this being the last time I saw them.

After a moment of mentally preparing myself, I said, "The person who rammed into my mum's car was an eighteen-year-old who had only been driving for six months. He wasn't drunk or on drugs, but he *was* speeding. My mum was also speeding, according to witnesses. And there were a few since the crash occurred close to a residential street. My mum pulled out of one street too fast, just as this kid was bombing it down the street she turned into. The collision shunted my mum's car down the road and..." I paused, gritting my teeth because I didn't want to say the words. I hadn't been there to witness the crash myself, but I'd envisioned it. Saw it play out as if I were both an observer and as if I were in the car with my mum and Luca. Each version made my blood run cold, and while those visions of how it had looked had lessened over the years, there were still times when I had nightmares about it. Bad dreams that took me back to that time. I'd even had dreams that I was the one who'd been driving the car that had killed my family.

It didn't matter how many times Shannen or Guy told me it wasn't my fault, it was. My mum would never have been on that road if I had been at home. Or if I hadn't caused the argument with my dad that led to their fight in the first place. Didn't matter how I looked at it, it was all because of me and that would never stop haunting me.

Shannen gently squeezed my hand, and I realised I'd zoned out. A tension headache started to form because my body was so taut from the onslaught of memories and the fear of what would happen once Shannen knew everything.

Swallowing as best as I could with a dry mouth, I continued. "My mum was driving recklessly, so the fact that the man who crashed into them was also driving like a prick was slightly cancelled out. That and his driving inexperience got him a lighter sentence. Five years. He was out within four."

I risked a glance at Shannen, and sadness was written across her face. I figured she was still processing that my mum and brother died in such a horrific way, and I was about to drop the truth that I was a piece of shit on top of all that.

Letting go of her hand, I shifted uncomfortably in my seat, that familiar feeling of disgust starting to crawl all over me, but I had to push through. Had to keep going.

"You already know what my life was like with just my dad," I said, wiping my hands on my jeans as if I could wipe the shame off me. I couldn't, though. I'd tried for eleven years. "I was angry. At my dad for the way he was, and at the man who killed my mum and brother, and at my mum and Luca for leaving me, and at myself for being the reason they died."

"Cal, you weren't-"

"Don't," I interrupted, more harshly than I meant to. I glanced up at her and she blew out a breath. She wasn't upset that I'd cut her off. Her eyes were filled with the burden of my self-hatred. I'd seen it before. Every time I said something bad about myself, it was as if I'd said it to her instead. She took on the pain I inflicted on myself. The difference was, when I said those things, I didn't feel it anymore. I was numb, completely accepting of how fucked up I was. For Shannen, it was still new. She didn't understand the depth yet.

"One day, I was in the city centre and I saw him," I went on. "The person who killed Mum and Luca. It was five years after they died. He was walking around the shops with some other man. I didn't think I'd recognise him, but I *had* spent a long time staring at his social media photo after his name was known to me. Obviously, he was older and looked a bit different when he got out of prison, but I knew it was him. And I followed him. I wanted to see where he went, what he was doing. What kind of life he had after he'd been in jail. Turned out, he'd got a job. He went into a coffee shop with the person he was with, disappeared through a back door, and came back out in a uniform." The memory of that time, of how messed up I was, caused every muscle in my body to coil. That was how I'd always felt back them. Edgy, tense, and full of pent-up rage. "He'd never seen me before, so he had no idea who I was. A few times, I followed him after he finished work, and then when I learned where he'd parked, I borrowed my dad's car and followed him home. He lived in a ground-floor flat. Not a very nice one, but I hated that he had it. That he had a job and a home while I had nothing left."

My hands balled into fists on my lap, and I inhaled deeply, trying not to let my mind go too far back. I had to tell Shannen what I'd done, but I didn't want the dark side of myself to be set free again in the process. I'd had to work hard to let that hatred go. For myself and for *him*. If it got me now, I wasn't sure I'd be able to shift it again.

"The anger... it was eating me up. From the first time I saw him, I couldn't stop thinking about what he'd taken from me. All the fun times I'd missed out on with my brother. All the things I could no longer talk to my mum about. The way my dad had got more and more violent and nasty since they died. I had no-one, and he had a home and a job and a car!" I ran a hand through my hair, fighting the urge to get up and start wearing holes in Shannen's carpet again. I hadn't chanced a look at her in a while, but I didn't think I could until I'd got all of this out.

"I wanted to hurt him," I said. "I wanted to destroy him the way he'd destroyed my family. So, I started to keep track of his shift patterns. When he'd be home.

When other people would be around. I studied him for weeks until, one night, I broke into his flat while he was at work."

I waited in the dark, sitting in one of his armchairs like I belonged there, just biding my time until he got home.

I'd waited for this moment for a long time. Since I was fourteen, really.

He nearly crapped himself when he flicked on the front room light and saw me there.

Which only made me laugh.

"Wh... who are you? And how did you get in here?" Edward Firth asked, his face paling as he stared at me with unease. He looked tired. Dark circles sat under his eyes, but it was past ten, and he'd been on his feet at work all day. His brown hair was messy on top, and his blue eyes were flickering with fear.

Good.

"Take a seat, Eddie, and I'll tell you all about it," I said with a dangerous edge to my voice.

It was probably shock that made him comply, and he sat down at the other side of the room, trying to stay as far away from me as he could in the tiny space.

He slid his hand in between his leg and the side of the chair, but I pretended I didn't notice that he was attempting to reach for his phone, keeping my eyes on his face.

"You can take anything you want," he said, eyeing me cautiously. "Please just don't kill me."

"Me kill you? Killing is more your speciality, isn't it?"

His eyes widened, his face becoming almost transparent. "Look, mate, I know I did a terrible, terrible thing, but it was years ago and it was an accident. I've done my time. I just want to-"

"Just want to what?" I roared, launching myself out of my seat and getting in his face. "You want to live your life and forget about what you did? Huh? Well, that's too fucking bad, mate."

His words made me curious, though. Had other people remembered him as the kid who'd killed a mother and son? Did he regularly have people lurking in his flat in the dark, ready to give him a beating?

My eyes flicked down as his hand slowly tried to move to his jeans pocket, and he saw that I'd spotted him this time. I didn't think it was possible, but his cheeks grew whiter as I stared him down.

"You won't be needing your phone," I said, my voice eerily calm now. "Turn it off and hand it over."

With now shaky hands, Edward slid his phone out of his pocket. He fumbled with it as he pressed the button to switch it off, and once the screen had turned black, he placed it in my outstretched, gloved hand. I took it from him and flung it across the room into the chair I'd sat in before.

"What do you want?" he asked, his voice croaky. He didn't take his eyes off me, like he was staying alert in case I made a sudden movement he needed to block. I barked out a laugh; he didn't stand a chance.

"What do I want?" I asked, straightening up and taking a step back. "I want to tell you a story."

A crease formed on his brow as I sat down on the coffee table in front of him and offered a fake friendly smile.

"Once upon a time," I began, "there was a little boy. He had a great family. They were the best. But after a while, it all turned to shit. The dad became an alcoholic and started beating up the mum. The little boy and his brother were scared that one day, he might kill her and then kill them. After a few years, the mum decided she'd had enough. She was about to leave the dad behind and start a new life with her sons. But here's the thing. As she was driving away, frightened for her life, her car, with her youngest son inside, was hit by some cocky prick who was showing off in his new ride."

Edward's eyes widened, realisation filling them, but I wasn't done.

"The mum and the brother died," I continued, "and the cocky prick? Barely a scratch on him. All of a sudden, the little boy was left alone with a violent, alcoholic father. And since the dad didn't have a wife to beat anymore, he used his child. That little boy became the reason for every bad thing that happened until he reached the point where he didn't care about anything anymore, and he got angry. Really. Fucking. Angry."

My stare was cold and focused right on him.

"You're Alessandra Lewis's son," he said, swallowing to ease the croak in his voice.

"Yes, I am. And for some reason, you seem to be allowed to walk around freely. Have a job, a home. No worries at all."

He shook his head. "Well, that's not really true. I-"

"I'm not interested," I shouted, getting to my feet again, the move making him jump. "Four years in jail, and you get your life back! Four years, and everything goes back to normal! Not for me, though! You killed my family, and just because of your driving inexperience and the fact that you showed remorse, you get to move on!"

"I haven't moved on," he said quietly, and instead of looking afraid, he looked... accepting? Almost like he knew it would be pointless trying to reason with me. "I have to live every day of my life knowing that because I thought I was cool with my new car, I killed two people. I shouldn't have been speeding. If I'd been driving at the right speed, I'd have seen your mum's car and been able to at the very least slow down, if not stop completely, and they'd probably still be here. I am so, so sorry. I thought about reaching out to you so many times, but I know sorry isn't enough. I know it won't change anything, but for the rest of my life, I have to carry what I did with me. And it's fucking heavy."

I felt myself sneering at his words. How the fuck dare he sit there and try to make me feel bad for him? I was the one who had lost everything. I was the one who'd suffered at the hands of my father, and with the constant knowledge that I was just as responsible for the deaths of my mum and brother as Edward was. I knew the weight of guilt better than anyone.

But he did kill them. And his punishment wasn't enough.

"I knew one day this would happen," Edward went on, tears filling his eyes. He tried to wipe them away with his sleeve, but more came. "Even after five years, people don't forget. There are people who still know what I did and glare at me with disgust. I knew one day that one of those people would be you."

"Am I supposed to feel sorry for you?" I snapped. "Because of you, I have nothing!"

He shook his head. "I didn't know. But I truly am sorry. I wish there was something better I could say."

"There is nothing you can say. Nothing you can do. Not ever."

I stared at him as tears ran down his face, and I hated him. Couldn't stand how pathetic he was. Maybe he did feel bad about what he'd done, but he didn't have any idea how much suffering he'd caused. The nights as a fourteen-year-old when I cried myself to sleep thinking about how scared Mum and Luca must have been in that moment when they saw a car hurtling towards them. Wondered if they'd felt it. Luca died almost immediately, so hopefully, he didn't get a chance to even know what was happening. And my mum. She had so many injuries that she couldn't fight them.

"Get up," I said coldly, watching him.

He gave a single nod, even though he was still crying.

Fucking prick.

He was making it too easy. I wanted to make him suffer. He looked at me like he knew he deserved this, and true or not, I didn't want him to accept it. I wanted him to feel the fear I'd lived with every single day since he destroyed my family.

He wiped his eyes with his sleeve again as I took a step towards him.

"What did you do to him?" Shannen asked, her voice shaking.

I felt a tear drip down my cheek, and it wasn't just Shannen who was shaky. My whole body shivered as the heaviness of my admission threatened to crush me.

"I was picked up at my flat the next day by the police," I said, swallowing thickly. "Edward's brother found him that morning. He went over to see Edward and couldn't get an answer. He was worried, so he got his key and let himself in. Edward's nose, jaw, and ribs were broken, his face and torso were severely bruised, and he had swelling on the brain."

Shannen closed her eyes, taking in a long, deep breath. She shuffled back from me ever so slightly, and the knife in my gut didn't just twist. It pierced right through me, and I dropped my head back, knowing the end of us was coming.

Shannen had grown up in a world where everything was *nice*. People were friendly—at least to each other's faces. They didn't live on their anger, battering people for revenge.

This was it. The time she realised I was right all along. I wasn't worthy of her and I never could be.

Because I could never take back what I'd already done.

"What happened to him?" she asked, her eyes still closed.

"He was in hospital for a while. The swelling on the brain caused some damage, although he did recover eventually. But I..." I paused, swallowing again. "He was alive when I left him, but when the police picked me up, I was sure he must have died. If his brother hadn't found him when he did..." I trailed off again, not wanting to say the thing that continued to torment me.

I almost killed someone. A couple more hours, and I wouldn't have only avoided jail. I would have literally got away with murder.

Would it have been fair if I had killed him? One life for the two he took from me?

When I was nineteen, I wanted him dead. But I didn't want to be a killer.

The thing I had never forgotten was that Edward didn't struggle. He continued to look at me as if he'd earned every blow to his body until his eyes finally closed. He didn't make a single sound the whole time.

If he had died from what I did to him... it would have finished me too.

What I did to him wasn't who I was. It never had been, and I knew my mother would have been so fucking ashamed of me. She didn't bring me up to be someone who took revenge. Without her guidance, or any guidance, I'd just wanted someone to suffer the way I was.

"So, Scott was the one who arrested you?" Shannen asked, finally looking at me again.

It was better when her eyes were closed because now, she just looked confused. Disappointed. Hurt.

Our seven weeks together must have felt like a lie to her. I had always been willing to open up to her, but there was no winning for me. I'd let her fall in love with me knowing this would be the eventual outcome. Knowing she'd one day look at me in a way that told me I'd broken her trust.

And maybe her heart.

Running my hands through my hair, I growled, tugging hard at the ends because I hated myself.

Every. Single. Bit.

I wasn't worth shit.

"Cal," she pressed as I got to my feet.

"Yes, Scott arrested me," I answered, turning my back to her. "Edward's brother was asked by the police if they knew of anyone who might want to hurt him. Like Edward had told me, there were people who remembered what he'd done and had made comments to him, but what I didn't know was that his brother had seen me hanging around his coffee shop a few times. Saw me glaring at him. He told the police that he thought I was the 'Lewis kid' because of my eyes. I have the same eyes as my mum and brother, and when their accident was in the news, their photos were everywhere. He did say he wasn't certain, but he called it a gut feeling. Through the magic of social media, which I no longer use, the police pulled up a photo of me, and when the brother confirmed it was me, I became suspect number one. So, they arrested me."

"And then what?"

"They questioned me for hours. I admitted to being in the coffee shop. To knowing who and where Edward was. I even admitted to following him home once, but there was nothing that tied me to the scene of the crime. I wore gloves when I entered the house, in the pitch black, in the winter, so nobody would spot me. His back door lock was useless, so I didn't even have to break a window to get in. And anything I wore into his flat was set on fire and then disposed of. Even my shoes."

I risked turning around to face her again, and she visibly shivered, wrapping her arms around herself. She wasn't looking at me anymore. Her head lowered slightly, like she was lost in her own thoughts as I spoke.

"I told the police I was at home with my dad all night," I said. "But I also added that he was a drunk and probably wouldn't remember. When they went to ask him, he lied to them. Said he'd had a few drinks, but he'd seen me in the kitchen around eleven, which was when Edward was attacked, they estimated. Scott did not believe a word either of us said, and he did everything he could to shake me. But door to door questioning of Edward's neighbours didn't lead to any information. Scott swore that when Edward woke up, he'd know for sure it was me, and then he'd finally get me. It took a long time before Edward was able to say anything, and when he did, he told the police he didn't see his attacker's face. I don't know if he just remembered it wrong or doing the same as he did when I hurt him; accepting that he deserved it. But either way, there was nothing anyone could do to pin it on me, and Scott was pissed off."

"Do you think he deserved it?" Shannen asked, her voice almost a whisper as she wiped a tear away before wrapping her arms around herself again. Her expression was blank now, almost like she was in shock.

You did that to her. You fucking broke her.

I exhaled deeply. "At the time? Yeah, back then, when I was messed up, I believed he deserved it. Right up until the moment I thought I'd killed him." My palms grew sweaty and my vision blurred as I remembered the panic when I'd opened my front door to two police officers. I'd almost thrown up because in the cold light of day, I felt terrible about what I'd done. "It was like getting all of that anger out had cleared a space in my head, but what it showed me wasn't anything good. It showed me I was just like my father. Using my fists when I was pissed off because I didn't know any other ways to handle things. If I cried, even when my mum was still alive, he'd tell me to cut it out. Boys had to be strong and not talk about how they felt. Just had to get on with life and knock down anything that got in their way."

It had been a long time since I'd heard my dad's voice in my head, but it echoed out loud and clear.

"For fuck's sake, Callum. What kind of a man are you? Stop your pathetic crying and grow up."

Because that's definitely the right way to handle a grieving, scared teenager, Dad. But I couldn't say that to him. Not unless I wanted a black eye or a couple of broken bones. I wasn't a man then. I was a child, being forced to deal with death way before I should have.

Shannen looked up at me, and the fact that I could still see any affection in her eyes had me sinking back down onto the couch, my head in my hands.

It wasn't real. That affection. It was dying. Once she fully took in all I was telling her, she'd want me gone. Far away from her forever.

"Do you know..." she paused, her voice cracking. "Do you know what happened to him? To Edward?"

"Yeah. Because I saw him again." Running my hands through my hair, I said, "I never looked for him again, but I did see him. Sometimes, when things got too much, I'd go to the cemetery and sit by Mum and Luca's grave. One day, he was there. This was a couple of years later. As I got closer, I heard him talking to them. When he saw me, he didn't even look scared. He said he'd spent ages trying to find the right grave because he'd been having nightmares about the crash and he felt he needed to find the place they were buried. Said he'd been having nightmares since the day it happened, but they were getting worse. I told him I had nightmares too. We just stood there for ages, not speaking. Eventually, he patted my arm and left me alone. It was like he was telling me he understood why I did what I did, but I didn't even apologise. I think he knew I was sorry, though."

Guy, who knew everything else about me, didn't know any of that. Not that I'd seen Edward at the cemetery. I had never told anyone about it. For nine years, I'd kept it to myself to the point where I sometimes wondered if it had even happened at all.

My stomach lurched, and I pulled at the ends of my hair again, trying to distract myself from the sickness that threatened at what came next.

"Three weeks later," I said quietly, "my dad showed me Edward's obituary in the local paper. He'd overdosed on pills and alcohol."

I'd thrown up on hearing the news, earning myself a sharp slap around the head from my father before he shoved me to the floor into my own vomit, telling me I should be glad he was dead. And I just lay there for ages. Maybe even hours, thinking about how I'd caused *another* person's death.

Out of what felt like nowhere, a roar of pain and guilt and grief ripped from me, and I slid from the sofa to the floor as everything overwhelmed me.

I'd just... lived with it. The grief over my mum and Luca, the hatred and fear of my dad. The embarrassment of being a 'man' who couldn't defend himself against my father's beatings, even though I was just a kid. The blinding rage at the man who'd taken my family from me. The twisted joy I'd got when I'd got revenge, only for it all to turn to terror when I realised what I'd done. More guilt and shame over what my mum would have said if she knew I'd become a monster. The ache of regret and disgust for what I did to Edward, eventually culminating in the sadness of his death.

Because what was really so different about us?

He never set out to kill anyone, and we both carried the pain of that one night that changed both of our lives.

So, anytime Shannen had ever looked at me like I meant something, I knew better.

I didn't deserve her, and Aiden was probably better off without me because at some point, I'd only screw them both up.

She was wrong.

Now, I'd opened the box that contained sixteen years' worth of suppressed feelings, and I didn't know if it would ever close.

Right then, I wasn't a thirty-year-old man with a job, and rent to pay, and a son who depended on me.

I was a fourteen-year-old child, wondering where his mum and brother had gone.

And I sobbed.

Chapter 25

Shannen

My heart had just broken.

That was the only way to explain the shattering, splintering pain in my chest as Cal crumpled to the floor, huge sobs wracking his body.

His guilt was almost tangible in the room, filling the space around us until I couldn't breathe. The atmosphere felt thick with it, and I slid down onto the floor beside him, wrapping my arms around him.

Cal shook his head, taking hold of my wrists and pushing me away, but instead of letting him, I shifted quickly, lifting my leg over both of his, straddling him and placing my hands on his tear-streaked face. His gaze dropped, refusing to look at me. I brushed a couple of his tears away with my thumbs, my own now falling too, then wound my arms around him again, holding him tight against me.

I hadn't even begun to deal with everything I'd learned. All I knew was that my man was hurting, and no matter how tight I held him, I couldn't fix it.

I'd figured out a long time ago that he didn't have a family, but the truth about why was worse than I could have imagined. His childhood had been a short time of happiness followed by years and years of trauma and abuse, and he'd just carried it around with him. I assumed Guy knew about it, but this wasn't a thing Cal spoke about often, especially not the circumstances surrounding the death of his mum and brother.

Everything I knew about him made a lot more sense now. Even more so the way he struggled with Aiden. Cal was a good dad, but that was in spite of his upbringing, not because of it. What kind of role model had he had? And yet, he still kept trying to make things better between him and Aiden.

To hear Cal compare himself to the man who had done nothing but break him down tore at my heart and made my insides twist because he was so, so wrong. He was nothing like that.

But then... he hurt someone.

Not just hurt them but almost killed them.

And I didn't know how to process that.

As Cal's tears soaked into my shoulder and mine dripped into his hair, every instinct inside me told me that the man who had sought revenge and the man I had been dating were two very different people.

Because a man who still held so much malice wouldn't have fallen to the floor in such obvious pain over what he'd done. A man who held onto anger would have stood by his actions and defended his right to hurt someone who had hurt him.

Cal had never truly wanted that. He'd wanted to lash out because he was still a kid who'd had his grief repressed, and the only thing he knew back then was violence.

Did I like that he was ever capable of that? Of course not. What he did was so calculated, from watching Edward Firth, to figuring out his routine, to the timing of the attack and the disposal of everything he'd worn... the revelation had made my blood turn to ice.

Did I think he could still be capable of it?

Maybe under the right—or wrong—set of circumstances, he could be. If pushed. If someone he cared about was threatened.

But did I think *I* was in danger? Or Aiden? Did I think Cal would actually turn into his father?

Not a chance.

And maybe I was naive. Perhaps my safe, comfortable life meant I didn't understand what people were truly capable of when pressed to their limits. Because I doubted Cal's mum expected her husband to become what he did.

But I just couldn't see it happening with Cal. Not after he had already lost so much and fought to get as much back as he could.

After what felt like forever, Cal's arms wrapped around my back, his sobs easing and his head still on my shoulder.

I was too scared to move. I wanted to pull back, to look him in the eye, but even though he was holding me, a huge knot of tension sat in my stomach.

Along with his guilt, I could almost feel the self-loathing oozing from him now; it was why he'd tried to push me away. I had to say something. Something to reassure him. But I was still trying to let all of the information filter into my mind.

Within twenty-four hours, I'd gone from the happiest I'd ever been to the most lost I'd ever been. Cutting Jade out of my life was done with ease because of Scott's actions, but that didn't mean it didn't still hurt. Then, there was the worry of whether Scott would keep pushing what he knew about Cal and make it public knowledge. I doubted the parents of the children in my class would trust my judgement if they knew I was in a relationship with a man who had done such a violent thing.

And there was also my family to consider. I didn't care about family friends and people in our circles who judged me. But I was worried about my dad. Even my mum would find it hard to support me if she knew the truth. Could I sit with them and lie to their faces about the crime Cal committed? Could I tell them he was falsely accused? I didn't believe I could. I wasn't a liar, and I'd definitely somehow give myself away if I tried.

That would mean Cal would always feel uncomfortable around my parents. If they would even understand my choice to be with him.

And that *was* my choice. Maybe I was stupid and trusting him was a risk, but nothing had changed for me. I still felt the same way I had before.

I loved him.

Or maybe I was still in shock and had no idea what I was thinking.

Running my fingers through his hair, I tried to piece together all the things I knew about Cal before with the things he'd just revealed.

He was the man who had made me feel safe.

But he was also the man who had almost ended someone else's life.

He was the only man who had ever truly made me a priority.

But he was also the man who had lied to the police and covered up a vicious assault. And been calculated enough to plan it out so he wouldn't be caught.

"Shan."

It wasn't until Cal whispered my name that I realised how hard I was crying. No sound had left me, but my body was vibrating with my sobs, and Cal's hair was now soaked with my tears where my cheek had been resting.

Cal's arms tightened around me. "I'm sorry," he whispered against my neck. "I'm sorry."

I wanted to tell him it was okay, but I didn't know if it was. I didn't know how to explain the sheer volume of thoughts in my head, so I just held on to him.

Time lost all meaning while his arms were around me. At some point, my sobs calmed, and my body stopped shaking, and still, we sat there. Me still straddling him, and him keeping me close.

My eyes felt heavy, exhausted from the emotion of the day, and all I wanted to do was take his hand, lead him to my room, and fall asleep wrapped up in his arms.

Because somewhere, amongst the tears and the whirling thoughts, I'd made a decision.

Cal was mine. He'd been mine since the first night I brought him home.

Was seven weeks enough to know for sure? Maybe. Maybe not.

But was I willing to throw what we had away over a thing he'd done when he was eaten up with grief and pain? A thing he had never repeated. There was no more violence in his past because, if there had been, Scott would have thrown it in my face. All he had was one incident.

Unless...

He'd got away with it once, so perhaps he'd managed to get away with it more times.

But for what reason? He had one very solid reason for his attack on Edward and he'd punished himself for it ever since. Cal blamed himself for things that weren't even his fault, so why would he give himself another burden to drag around?

I wasn't playing down the severity of what he'd done because it made me sick to know Cal had caused such damage to another person.

But he'd done even more damage to himself.

"I just need another minute with you, Shan, then I'll go. I promise. Just one more minute."

Cal's words cut through my thoughts. Reality had been blocked out for the last... God knew how long, but as he spoke, I realised how dark it had got. It was still daylight when Cal had arrived, but now, the only light was what little poured in through the windows. Even though the heating was on, the darkness made the room feel cold.

"Where are you going?" I mumbled, still not quite out of the fog my mind had clogged with. I blinked a few times, trying to bring myself back as Cal's hold loosened on me. Trying to ground myself, I let my fingers dance lightly, slowly up and down the back of his neck. The warmth of his skin, his scent, helped to pull my focus back to the here and now.

I felt his deep inhale at my touch, and he gently moved my hands, unwinding me from him. I looked down at our still joined hands and then up at his face. His eyes were red-rimmed, and his face appeared drawn and tired. I had no doubt I looked the same, and it just added to the feeling of wanting to curl up in bed with him and sleep away the stress.

As his gaze met mine, he squeezed his eyes shut, letting go of my hands. When he looked at me again, his brown eyes sparkled with unshed tears. Something in them looked... wrong. I couldn't place what it was, but something was different somehow. I could still see the affection, but shining through was the torment he'd shown when he was telling me all the things he'd done and been through.

Of course. Nobody could open up about so much and then just bounce back as if everything was okay. But I wasn't sure why he was pulling away from me when I wanted to keep him close.

Cal ran his hands down my waist to my hips and began to lift me, but instead of moving with him, I clamped my legs more tightly around him, forcing him to stop and lower me again.

Noticing the furrow of my brow, he dropped his head back. "Shannen, please."

I'd intended to speak, but his use of my whole name threw me off. I didn't think he'd called me Shannen since the night we met.

Keeping his voice even, he said, "You need to let me go."

The finality in his tone made my hands shake again. Not only my hands, but all of me. I felt cold. Not just the kind of cold you feel when the temperature drops, but the kind that chills you from the inside.

And yet his hands remained on my hips. Not lightly, but like he wanted to hold on.

My heart was thundering in my chest and Cal didn't speak for what felt like forever, just looking at me, still tangled up in the mess inside his mind.

Eventually, he said, "Shan, I don't want to lose you. But I've already lost a lot. And you... if you want this... us... there might be things you lose too. I am not worth your career or your family. I'm just not. I can't let you risk any of it for me. So, I need you to think about this. About what you might lose if you decide you want me. And for you to do that, I can't be here. "

My insides twisted, nausea swirling in my gut at the idea of losing anything. Him, my family, my job.

I'd been in serious relationships with a trainee doctor, a software developer, and the CEO of a recruitment company, and none of them gave me what Cal had. None of them made me feel half of what he did, and none of them had truly cared about me either. Cal, though... every single day we'd been together, I'd never needed to question whether I could trust him. Never had to worry that he didn't really want me. Never thought he wanted anything from me other than just for me to be myself.

But as much as I didn't want him to go, I needed to consider everything he'd told me. My heart was pretty damn set on keeping him, but my head... I had to use that too before I made a promise I couldn't keep.

I buried my face into his neck and held him tight as my heart continued to crumble. I wouldn't be able to think straight if he stayed, but I was afraid that without him, I was going to fall apart. That if he left, *he* would fall apart.

"I don't want you to be alone." I lifted my head to look at him, hoping he could see in my eyes how worried I was. I didn't think he was at any risk of physically hurting himself, but I was concerned about what his mind would do to him if he was on his own.

"I'll go to Guy's," he said. "If Aiden's still up, I'll take him home, and if not, I'll see if I can crash there too."

I wanted to go with him more than I wanted to breathe. I wanted to snuggle up with Cal and Aiden and just block out everything I'd learned for a while. I'd even have put up with Helen's snarking if it meant I could stay with Cal.

But that wasn't going to happen. We needed some space.

"Okay," I said with a sigh. "But... what... what do we do here? Can we talk later? Or tomorrow? How long do you want us to stay apart?"

Letting out a sigh as deep as mine, he said, "I don't know. I think tonight, we need to take a break. Call Nova or Gaby. I don't mind if they know, Shan. If you need to tell them, it's fine. I just... I don't know how much time you need."

"Tomorrow," I told him. "We'll talk tomorrow."

Resting his forehead against mine again, he said, "Okay. But Shan... please, really think about this. I need you to do what's best for you. I don't want to hold you back from anything."

And that's how I know...

The pain etched into his face and the way he was putting me first told me everything I needed to know about the man he was now.

But the man he used to be... I had to be absolutely certain I could accept him too.

Chapter 26

Cal

I NEED A DRINK.

The thought pounded at my skull, the only thing I let myself feel as I sat in my van in the car park outside Shannen's block of flats. My insides felt empty, as if offloading everything bad I'd done had left a hole inside me. I'd thought it would be a relief to get it out. To let Shannen know what I'd kept hidden, but relief wasn't even on my radar. I felt... exposed. More than that, I was scared.

Because what if, after sleeping on it and taking a look at what she would lose just to be with me, she decided I wasn't worth it? She was right, but I didn't want it to be over.

But how could I not give her space? Right then, if I'd stayed and accepted that she wanted me before she'd thought it through, I would have been on edge, waiting for her to see how bad I was for her. I was on edge anyway, but at least this way I could prepare myself for her rejection.

Not wanting to lurk in the car park like a weirdo, I started the van and drove away, with no idea where I was going.

I was never planning to go to Guy's like I'd told Shannen, though I would call him to check on Aiden and let him know what had happened. Home wasn't an option either. Too quiet. Too much potential to explode.

Too tempting to get drunk, and in the mood I was in, that was dangerous. Drinking when life was going well was no problem, but when I felt like I was losing everything... it was much more risky. Getting stuck in the fucked-up rut my dad had got into would have been so easy. A quick escape from the pain that was trying to force its way through me. While alcohol would help keep the hurt away, it would also unleash the person I'd fought to escape from, and I'd left him behind a long time ago.

The look on Shannen's face as I walked out of her front door. I'd never seen her so defeated and broken. Her eyes were red-rimmed, and she looked exhausted. Just thinking about it made my grip on the steering wheel tighten, and my heart hammered in my chest. I did that to her. Not just me. Scott had a hand in it too, but I was the one who'd hurt her the most. I'd let Scott have that power when I could have just told her myself, but that was only a small part of it. The thing that had caused the damage was that she now knew how much of a monster I could be. That somewhere inside me, no matter how hard I tried to keep it contained, there was a dark side. There wasn't a single part of me that believed I would ever hurt Shannen, just like I wouldn't hurt Aiden. Did *she* know that, though? Something like this probably seemed like a threat to her. She'd seen me lose my shit a couple of times already. Would that play on her mind? Or would knowing that I'd never lashed out at anyone actually help my case?

Except I'd lashed out at Edward. It may have been a long time ago, when I was a different person, but it was still me. Something that lurked in the depths of me. Just because she hadn't seen it meant nothing.

Have a drink. Have a drink. Have a drink. That'll make it all go away.

I shook my head, deciding on a destination. It was a strange whim. I hadn't been there since before Christmas. Guy's place would have been the more logical choice, but I wasn't thinking about logic. Adrenaline and fear were driving me now.

When I pulled up outside the cemetery gates after a thirty-minute drive, I jumped out of the van, wishing I had my jacket. I'd been in too much of a rush to just get to Shannen that I'd gone home, changed, and hurried straight out. Ensuring the van was locked, I hunched up my shoulders, trying to block out the cold as I entered the cemetery.

Mum and Luca had been buried in a different part of Exeter than where I lived now, closer to the flat my dad had moved us into. After he'd disappeared, I used to worry that I'd bump into him right there at their gravesides, but I never did. I wasn't sure anyone came but me, and I didn't do so regularly anymore. Christmas, birthdays, and when something was bothering me, which was a lot less often than before.

The silence of a graveyard at night should have seemed creepy. However, I'd been going there after dark since I was a kid, and it never bothered me. I was safe next to my mum and brother. The light from the lampposts cast a ghostly glow over the headstones, but Mum's and Luca's were just out of the way of the main beam. Not that it mattered because there was nobody else around, but the shadows kept me concealed. There was shelter in that small patch of darkness.

I slumped down on the damp grass between the two graves of my family members, resting my back against Luca's headstone, my feet towards my mum's.

When I was younger, I used to sit and talk to them. Tell them about Dad. About how much I hated living with him. There had been times when I'd considered jumping in front of a train or walking out into traffic just so I could be with Mum and Luca again. Not many because I was too stubborn, but on the hard days, when my dad had been extra violent, I wanted it all to end.

I flicked my eyes towards my mum's headstone.

"I messed up, Mum," I said, dropping my head back against the cold, solid slab that marked Luca's resting place. "People say that those who are no longer with us watch over us, but I fucking hope you haven't been watching me. Not with the mistakes I've made."

I'd killed people. Not myself, with my own hands. But I'd had a part to play. With Mum and Luca, and with Edward too. When he'd taken his own life, it was long after I'd attacked him, but the way I'd felt about him had likely made his own guilt worse. I hadn't cared about his feelings the day I'd broken into his house and beaten him half to death. It wasn't until my red mist had shifted that Edward's words had sunk in. That he was traumatised by what he'd done. My telling him what I'd been through after can't have made that any better. I'd wanted him to know, to suffer, but once I'd made it happen, what did it achieve? It didn't bring my family back. It didn't make my dad nicer. It didn't make my life easier.

"I met a girl," I went on. "You both would have loved her. She's a teacher, and do you know what I've learned from her? That even though I'm a mess, I may not be a completely lost cause. Well, I might be now, but up until tonight, she made me feel like I wasn't."

"If you were here, Mum, you'd be able to tell me what to do. Luca... you'd take the piss out of me the way you used to. You were always a cheeky little shit."

I huffed out a laugh as I thought about the way—before life got serious—he'd always tried to wind me up. I wondered what he'd look like now. He'd probably have been doing some kind of important job, wearing a suit to work. He was cleverer than me, paid more attention at school than I did. Even if nothing had gone wrong in our lives, I doubted I would have been that different, at least not job-wise.

If Mum and Luca hadn't died, I'd have had way less issues with trust, and with feelings, and with... everything.

"She said she loves me," I said, acknowledging Shannen's words out loud for the first time, my chest tightening painfully. "And I didn't say it back. The stupid thing is, I'm sitting here talking to you, so I know that not saying it enough... that's a bad thing. I don't know if I told you guys enough when you were here. The thing I've learned, though, is that when you let yourself love someone, you're probably going to get hurt. And when you tell them you love them—because I know I told you sometimes..." I paused, remembering I threw the words, 'love you, Mum' over my shoulder as I ran out the door the last time I saw her. "...I don't know. Maybe it's just inviting something bad to happen. Shannen told me she loved me, and then... boom. Disaster."

I may as well have been drunk with the amount of crap that fell from my lips, but there was too much swirling around my head, and letting it tumble out as I thought it was all I could do out there in the cold. Although, I didn't really feel the plummeting temperature now. The numbness had crawled back over me, and I was glad.

"I'm the problem, I know," I went on. "I should have told her the truth when I realised I..." Stopping myself, I swallowed back the words I refused to say out loud. "When I realised how much she matters to me. I was with Katie for years and I never felt anywhere near as much for her as I do for Shannen. But that's why I was afraid to tell her. I *would* have told her, soon, not because I was forced to but because she deserved to know. I guess it would have come to this one day anyway, with or without Scott's 'encouragement'. I just hate that she found out the way she did, and that I have to let her go."

I lightly thudded my head against Luca's headstone over and over as I admitted what I'd known all along.

That she wouldn't choose me. Not over her family and her job. That I cared about her enough to *make* her pick them over me if I had to.

I'd allowed my son to be taken away when I couldn't give him what he needed. And then I'd done all I could to be better for him so I could get him back.

Now, I'd allow Shannen to walk away for the same reason.

I just wasn't sure fighting for her would ever be the right thing to do when she had so much to lose.

Chapter 27

Shannen

I had barely slept.

I'd gone to bed almost as soon as Cal had left, completely wiped out from the prolonged extreme emotions that had shot through me since lunchtime, when the principal had called me in. Anger, confusion, shock, fear, grief, panic... they'd run rampant for hours and it had drained me.

But I'd just lay in bed, light off, staring at the ceiling as thoughts and images circled my mind.

Cal had given me too much to process. I had a feeling it would take longer than the twenty-four hours I'd hoped it would take. I didn't want to make him wait and I didn't want to be away from him for longer than that. At the same time, though, I didn't want to tell him something I wasn't sure of. My entire heart ached at the idea of not being with him anymore. But he'd asked me to think things through, and if I'd called him first thing and told him I'd decided, he wouldn't have accepted it, so I kept the distance he'd insisted on.

I'd sent Gaby and Nova a long voice note to give them a brief rundown on how I was feeling without fully explaining everything. That would require a phone call, but I knew they had been worried about my quietness. So, I told them what Scott had said without getting into all of the details of Cal's crime, albeit one he wasn't convicted of. I *would* tell them. I promised them I would call them over the weekend, but I didn't want to take up too much of their time, especially Nova, as she had limited time with Donovan before he had to leave again. My stomach knotted as I thought about the day out we'd semi-planned that might not happen now.

What I needed more than anything was my mum, so I drove down to Plymouth to my parents' house. If I were to make a decision, I had to know what they thought about the things I'd discovered. Whether they'd accept the way I felt for him, even knowing everything.

Whether they'd accept *him*.

And if they wouldn't... I'd worry about that later.

I sat with my mum in her conservatory on comfy grey rattan chairs, a huge latte in my hands, looking out at the dull, grey day. The weather matched both my mood and my energy; miserable, dark, and sluggish.

"You look tired," Mum said, eyeing me over her cup of herbal tea.

Even on my best days, I wasn't as well put-together as her. She wore close-fitting blue jeans and a white button-up blouse, even though I was the only one visiting. I'd thrown on a pair of comfortable black bootcut jeans and a black jumper, my hair slung back messily with a hair tie.

"I am tired," I answered, raising my glass mug. "Hence the caffeine."

She smiled softly. "So, what happened last night?"

Inhaling deeply, I launched into some of what Cal had told me the night before. About his parents, and how he felt responsible for the death of his mum and brother. Then I told her what he did to the man who had actually killed them, and how he felt about it now. I even told her about him losing Aiden for a while because they were all parts of him I wanted her to understand. To show that he'd done some bad things, but he didn't do them anymore. Mum listened on with the empathy I was hoping for, and when I was done, finishing with how Cal and I had left things, she sighed. Both of our cups were empty now, and a chill ran through me as I waited for what she would say.

"What do you think you'll do?" she asked, tucking her hair behind her ear and shuffling a little in her seat. I wasn't sure what my expression showed, but hers told me she already knew my answer.

"What do you think you'll do about what?"

Mum and I jumped at the voice behind us, and we turned to see the tall and slightly imposing frame of my dad in the doorway. I jumped out of my chair to hug him.

"What are you doing home so early?" Mum asked as Dad wound his arms around me and kissed the top of my head. I breathed in his familiar, musky Giorgio Armani cologne and instantly felt comforted. I was and always had been a daddy's girl, even though he'd worked long hours and he hadn't been at home as often as we all would have liked when I was growing up. His time with us had been limited, but when he was with us, he'd always given one hundred percent.

"Leon had to get back because Shona, Marty, and the kids are going over for dinner, and Nancy wanted him back to help get things ready," Dad said.

Leon Addison was one of Dad's surgeon friends, and they rarely got a day off together. From the way my dad was dressed, in loose-fitting beige trousers and a green polo shirt, I assumed they'd been out for a round of golf.

"To what do we owe the pleasure of your company?" Dad asked as I pulled away from him. We both sat down, me where I was before, and Dad on the chair next to Mum's. He leaned in to kiss her cheek and she beamed at him.

They were nauseatingly adorable, but I loved it.

Before answering my father, I glanced at Mum for help. She offered a reassuring smile to me then turned her head towards Dad.

"Shannen needs to talk to us about something," she said. "But... you need to keep an open mind, okay?"

A crease graced his forehead and his brown eyes narrowed. "Sounds ominous." He focused his attention on me, and I sighed. If I'd known he was going to come home, I'd have waited and told them together instead of having to relay the entire story again. This was where Jade would have been useful. Her skill of blurting things out would have made this much easier. Though, thinking about it, her saying, 'Shannen's new boyfriend is a criminal,' might not have improved the situation.

I explained everything once more, in substantially less detail, because I didn't have the strength to go into all the intricacies of the story. Leaving some things out wouldn't help my case, but knowing my dad's feelings on crime and violence, nothing I added would make much difference anyway.

While I spoke, the frown on my dad's face grew. He didn't interrupt, but it became increasingly clear that he wasn't happy with what he heard. When I was finished, I braced myself for his response.

Dad eyed me across the room with a stare so intense that I felt like he was scanning my brain for information, and it took all my effort not to fidget under his scrutiny.

"I presume since you're telling us this that you want to keep seeing this man?" he asked eventually.

I nodded. "Yes."

Dad returned my nod with a thoughtful nod of his own, and he leaned forward, resting his hands on his knees. "Shannen, you know your mum and I have always let you and your sister do your own thing. We've encouraged you to forge your own paths in life, but what I need to ask you is whether he is worth losing anything else for. You've already lost Jade and-"

Mum held up her hand, interrupting him. "Before you finish that sentence, Steven, do you not think Shannen made the right decision under the circumstances?"

My dad turned his head to look at her. "Jade was a long-term friend, and that friendship wouldn't have been severed if not for this man."

His second use of 'this man' made my skin prickle; he knew Cal's name. Mum had told Dad about him the day she found out I was seeing him.

"Cal wasn't the reason for it," Mum replied calmly. "If anything, being with him just showed Shannen how toxic Jade can be. And how petty."

"Perhaps," Dad said, leaning back again, turning his attention back to me, "but the fact is, this relationship has the potential to affect your career and other friendships. That's not my main concern, though. Shannen, you are involved with someone who has a violent history. He grew up in an abusive household and he was responsible for causing serious harm to someone. Is this really the kind of person you want to be with?"

Shaking my head, I said, "That's not who he is now."

"Can you be sure of that?"

This was one of the many questions that had kept me up all night. Cal and I had been together for less than two months, which meant we were very much still in the 'honeymoon phase'. However, in that time, we'd already leapt over a fair few hurdles, and I'd learned a lot of things about him very quickly. When Cal had told me about Aiden being taken into foster care, I'd only known him for one weekend. I'd witnessed a glimpse of his temper then. I saw it again the night Guy had called for Cal to come home because Aiden was having a meltdown, and that time, I'd seen him throw something across the room and been on the end of his harsh words. While it had given me pause at the time, my gut feeling and Helen's reassurance—which I knew for sure now she wouldn't have given if she didn't truly believe it—had brought me to the conclusion that he wasn't dangerous. Even knowing what I knew now, I still didn't believe he would hurt me because he didn't have a whole list of violent crimes to his name. Scott would have delighted in producing Cal's criminal record if he had one. As it stood, there was nothing beyond this isolated incident that had occurred after years of pent-up grief.

"I'm pretty sure," I said.

"And if Jade and Scott make what he did public?" Dad questioned. "People will want to know why, after a whole lifetime of friendship, the two of you aren't speaking and why you aren't going to be part of her wedding. I don't imagine they will hesitate to tell the truth."

"Well, then I won't go to any social events until everyone has got over it," I said with a sigh. Truthfully, I didn't want to be anywhere near people who would judge Cal, or me for being with him. If that meant no more country club membership and fewer fancy gatherings, that was okay with me.

"I will not allow that girl to make you look bad," Mum said, and I smiled softly at her.

"Thanks, Mum, but if Jade starts telling people about Cal, there's nothing you or anyone can do about it. I... I'm past caring what people think."

I'd never fully fit into the ass-kissing and fakery that so often went on. Anything I attended was for my parents, or whichever suit I was dating at the time. I could count on one hand the people whose opinions I cared about and most of them were my immediate family.

My dad silently watched me for a moment as a wave of tiredness washed over me. I didn't want to be there, discussing this. I wanted to see Cal. I wanted to hear his voice, see his face, feel his arms around me.

Even with everything I knew, nobody had ever made me feel safer.

"Annie," Dad said, shifting his focus to my mum. "What do you think about all this?"

It was Mum's turn to sigh. I hated the furrow of her brow that let me know that, as supportive as she was trying to be, she was concerned too.

"I think that, as you pointed out, we always let our girls make their own way in life," she said, "so we have no right to be upset when they do just that."

"*Are* you upset?" I asked her, my heart clenching at the thought.

"No, darling," she said, shaking her head. "Not upset. Just worried about you. I can see how much you feel for Cal, but I can also see how much our opinion matters to you, and I don't want you to be torn between us."

"Does that mean if I stay with him, you won't be okay with it?"

This was the situation I didn't want, yet I knew the answer before either of my parents spoke. A nice, responsible man from a different walk of life would have been fine, but they didn't consider Cal to be that. He was a scary, angry man to them, and I understood why that was all they could see because that was all they knew about him. Yes, I'd told my mum he treated me well, but this new information tainted that. For them, it tainted everything.

"I think it's a mistake," Dad said bluntly. "Obviously, you are my daughter and I don't think anyone will ever be good enough for you. But a man like this, with such a turbulent past... you deserve more."

My head bobbed slowly, almost without me thinking about it as I turned to look at my mum, waiting for her input.

"Shannen, I don't know, sweetheart," she said. "I do trust your judgement, but I'm afraid that maybe he's only showing you his best side."

Why do people keep saying that to me when he has literally just confessed to almost completely beating the life out of someone?

Helen had said it too, or something similar. If he was only showing me his best side, I wouldn't know any of what I knew.

"His best side?" Dad asked, giving a voice to my thoughts. "If this is his best side, I'd hate to see how much worse it could get."

I got to my feet, frustrated and hurt by my dad's words. I knew he wouldn't take any of this well, but I'd hoped for just a bit more understanding. They were my parents, and they wanted the best for me, but it stung that they refused to look past the uglier parts of Cal's life.

"You have no idea what he's like, or what he's been through to get where he is now," I said, keeping my voice calm, even though I wanted to snap. "We haven't been together for long, but I've never been afraid around him. Not once."

"Never?" Dad challenged with a raised eyebrow.

I was unable to control a wince. "I've never felt afraid for my safety," I reiterated. Because I wasn't. His temper had startled me and made me reconsider if he was someone I wanted to be with, but it was fleeting, and he'd only ever shown me that my instincts that he wasn't dangerous were right.

"What happened?" Mum asked with a frown.

Shaking my head, I said, "It was the end of a horrible week and he lost his temper and shouted, but it wasn't a big deal. It happened once, and he apologised immediately. I told him I wouldn't accept being spoken to like that and he never has since."

Mum and Dad exchanged a look as if they were having a private conversation without words, and I hated that I couldn't decipher what they were thinking.

"Can we meet him?" Mum asked, looking at me again.

Memories of Cal meeting Jade flashed through my mind. That was pretty much how we'd landed in this situation. Or at least, that was the reason it had got so out of hand. With the cynicism in my father's eyes, I couldn't see this meeting going any better.

"No," I said. "I mean, one day, of course. But I'm not bringing him here for an interrogation. He's nervous enough about meeting you as it is."

"It wouldn't be an interrogation," Mum said, still with that tone of understanding. She was trying, and I trusted that she wouldn't grill him. I couldn't say the same for my dad, though.

I shifted my gaze to my dad for his confirmation, but he shook his head.

"Shannen, you're our daughter," he said gently. "We need to make sure he's good enough for you."

I was so sick of hearing those words. Who decides who is 'good enough' for another person anyway? The only person who should decide who was good enough for me was me.

Running my hand through my hair, I sighed. "Dad, what does that even mean? Good enough by whose standards? Do you mean someone who treats me well, or do you mean good enough to parade around in front of pretentious people, most of whom we don't even like? Because Cal isn't the kind of man I have ever been with before. He won't be comfortable at huge social occasions. With us, our family, he'd be fine because we aren't stuffy and pretentious. And that is all I care about. That he fits in here. I don't need him to be anything other than who he is. He wouldn't, and I would never ask him to be. I don't know what you want, Dad. Like you said, you encouraged me and Sadie to go in our own directions, but it seems that means we can't go as far as we like. All I want is to be with someone who isn't going to be at work more than he's with me. Who makes me feel comfortable and happy."

Dad studied me for a long moment. "Can you really overlook what he's done?"

I sighed. That question was the biggest reason for my sleepless night. I had fallen in love with Cal before I knew any of this stuff. I understood a whole lot more about him since learning about what happened to his mum and brother. So many things made sense now. More so when he explained how awful his father had become.

Did I know anyone who would have done what he did? Probably not.

Did I understand what drove him to the point he'd reached? To a degree.

Did it scare me that he had it inside him to *plan* to hurt someone?

Yes. Because there was no pretending that what he did wasn't highly calculated. He had plotted out the best way to get to Edward and ensure he wasn't caught. His dad had even offered him an alibi, so if Edward *had* told the police what he knew, there was nothing to tie Cal to the scene. No witnesses. No evidence. At most, Edward reporting Cal would have seemed like he was clutching at straws to make someone pay, but there was nothing concrete to prove it.

The thing was, Cal had immediately regretted the attack. When he'd understood that Edward wasn't living some happy life, that they shared some of the same demons, Cal knew he'd made a mistake. And that had led him to shoulder another load of guilt on top of the weight he already carried.

His pain, so clear when he broke down, showed me that if he could go back and change it, he would. But that didn't alter the fact that he could hold that much rage inside him.

"I'm not overlooking it," I said eventually. "I can't overlook it. But it was eleven years ago. He's never done anything like that again. Never."

My mum hadn't said anything for a while, and I glanced at her. She had been super understanding of my feelings for Cal, even when she'd heard what he'd done. She had also warned me of my dad's reaction. I'd just hoped my dad would see that Cal's actions had been the result of the horrendous circumstances he'd been through. He wasn't a horrible, heartless thug who went around attacking people out of nowhere. He'd been in so much pain that he'd honestly believed that 'revenge' would be the only thing that made him feel better.

"Shannen," Mum said gently, "do you truly believe you're safe with him? Do you believe that what he did all those years ago was just a bad decision that he regrets?"

"I *know* it," I told her emphatically, the image of Cal's sob-wracked body and his tear-stained face filling my mind and making my stomach clench.

Mum nodded. "Okay. I trust you will make the right decision."

Offering her a warm smile, which she returned, some of the worry about my parents' response lifted. But only some. Because when I looked at my dad, it was instantly apparent that he was not going to accept the decision I'd already made.

"I can't be okay with this, Shannen," he said. Even though I could see how much those words hurt him to say—because he wasn't a monster—another ripple of anger shot through me. "I know you believe that he has changed, but in my experience, most people who can do something that extreme will always have it inside them. I can't be happy about you being with a man who has been so violent, and who has known mostly violence through his formative years."

Tears bit at my eyes. I knew his words were coming from a place of parental love and concern, but it stung that my father wouldn't give me his support. His trust. He was my *dad*. The man who I had always looked up to. Who had given my sister and me everything we needed. Not always everything we wanted, but what would make us into the people we had become. He'd raised two headstrong women, and I respected him for everything he did for our family. He was my protector. The man who'd taught me how to ride a bike and swim. Who had told me that whether I wanted to be a teacher or a brain surgeon, I could do that. He'd always believed in me to make the right choices, but this? Wanting a man who had done such a horrible thing? That was too much for him.

Maybe I was blinded by the whirlwind Cal and I had been caught up in. But no matter how much I analysed it, spun it around in my head, I couldn't imagine Cal falling so far back, being so filled with hate, that this could ever happen again.

"So... what does this mean?" I asked with a tremor in my voice. "I understand your worries, but he's not what you are imagining. I have spent all night thinking about everything he told me. I've thought about how I feel about it, and how, while I hate that he did it, I can see past it." Pausing, I shrugged. "He might not be who you would have chosen for me, but nobody has ever made me happier."

Tears shone in my parents' eyes, and my mum turned towards my dad. "Steven. Can you please try to give him a chance?"

My dad shook his head, swallowing hard. "I'm sorry, Shannen. You will always be welcome here, but I can't accept you being with someone like that."

My head lowered as I battled to fight my emotions. Rather than support me, my dad had chosen to isolate the man I wanted to be with. Sure, I could go and visit, but if Cal wasn't welcome, then I wouldn't be there. I would see my mum, and maybe she could meet Cal, but anything that had my dad involved was out.

Standing, I said, "Okay. I can't change how you feel. But I can't change how I feel either, so I guess... I'll see you when I see you."

My dad offered a single nod, and I knew this wasn't easy for him. Knew he was thinking about what he wanted for me, and that Cal was not it. Perhaps, with time, he would come around, but for now, we were at an impasse.

I heard my mum say my name, but I had to go. I needed to get out before my tears fell.

I'd been tired when I got to my parents' house, but after speaking to them, I felt exhausted. Too much emotion. Too little sleep. And I still had to drive home.

As I left my parents' house, promising myself a caffeine hit before I left the city, the only thing I wanted to do was get to Cal.

I'd upheld my side of the deal. I'd thought about what I wanted, and my answer hadn't changed. Now, I just needed to find out if he'd allow me to stay in his life.

Chapter 28

Cal

> **Guy: Please can you come and pick Aiden up? Helen is itching for a fight, and I'd rather he wasn't here for it.**

That message had been sent at ten a.m. on Saturday morning, but because I'd spent most of the night shivering my arse off at the cemetery, rambling at my dead relatives, I didn't see the message until half past eleven, when I woke up.

My head ached like I'd been on a drinking binge, even though not a single drop of alcohol had passed my lips. I thought I deserved a medal for not giving in after the few days I'd had, and Guy's message was a sign that things probably weren't going to get any better.

But my boy needed me, and as much as I wanted to wallow, to fall back to sleep and block out the pain of knowing Shannen and I were almost over, I rubbed my eyes and dragged myself out of bed.

As I grabbed some clean underwear from my drawer and then rummaged in my wardrobe for a T-shirt and some jeans, I used my free hand to call Guy.

He answered after just two rings. "Hey," he said, his voice strained. "Are you on your way?"

"I will be in two minutes. Sorry, I've only just woken up." I'd spoken to Guy from the cemetery to let him know how things went, and that Shannen now knew all there was to know about me. He was way more confident than I was that things between me and her would work out. I thought she would speak to her parents and that would seal my fate, but Guy was always more optimistic than me.

The idea of losing her was too big a thought for the amount of time I'd been awake, so I tried to shake it off to focus on the call.

"I thought you'd sleep late after last night," Guy said, his voice apologetic. "I wouldn't usually mind, but... things aren't good."

They hadn't been right since the week before when everything had blown up between him and Helen over the whole wanting a baby issue. I'd expected things would calm down between them, but it seemed like the tension hadn't gone yet, and Aiden didn't need to be around it.

"You okay?" I asked as I began pulling on my clothes as best as I could with one hand. Shaking my head, I put Guy on speaker and put the phone on the end of the bed.

"I've had enough," he said sharply, and I guessed neither Helen nor Aiden were in earshot. "I agreed to do what she wants. We have an appointment with the doctor next week, but somehow, that still isn't enough. It's like having a baby is all she can think about, and I don't understand how it's suddenly got so much bigger over the last few weeks."

Because she hasn't had Aiden around to distract her. That was my best guess anyway. She liked having Aiden around, and with him gone, it had just shown her what she was missing.

"I don't know what else you can do," I said. "I wish I did, but she wanted you to go to the doctor, and that's what you're doing."

"She seems to think trying to jump me at every opportunity is going to help, but her mood doesn't exactly make me want it. The time Aiden's been here is the longest she's stopped throwing herself at me in weeks. And I know having a woman who wants to have sex every hour of the day sounds like a dream situation, but it's not. Everything we do, from our diet to exercise to the things she wants us to do to reconnect is about her getting pregnant. I've tried talking to her. Tried to make her see that all of this stuff she's trying to change about us is killing us. I just want things to go back to the way they used to be when she wasn't stressing over dates and food and vitamins."

Not a great weekend for relationships in our world. I felt like a dick for asking them to have Aiden so I could wallow in self-pity while Guy and Helen were having their own problems.

"Sorry," Guy said, interrupting my thoughts as I pulled on my jeans and zipped them up. "I know you've had a tough night too. Are you okay?"

Huffing out a laugh, I said, "I was just thinking that I haven't been a very good mate, and you're over there thinking the same thing."

Guy chuckled. "It's easy to get self-involved sometimes, but you know I've got your back."

"Same," I told him, heading out of my bedroom to get my shoes. I was still barely awake, and I took a detour to the kitchen to grab a bottle of water. "So, what are you going to do about Helen?"

"I don't know. All I can do is what I've been doing. Keep talking to her, keep listening, and hope she calms down once we've been to the doctor and got things moving." With another sigh, he said, "Have you heard from Shannen yet?"

I unscrewed the cap on the water bottle and took a drink, enjoying the cold water sliding down my dry throat. "No, but I wasn't expecting to yet. I told her to take some time to think, and I need her to do that. I need her to be sure about what she wants."

While I'd sat out in the dark, cramped between my mum and brother's headstones, I'd felt every single emotion, including ones I never usually let myself feel. But overriding them all was guilt. I'd done too many things I couldn't forgive myself for, and instead of recognising a pattern, I just kept on doing more things to feel guilty about. I'd gone back and forth most of the night over whether or not I should have just let Shannen go. I could have taken away all the worries she faced about her job and her family by ending what we had, but I was too selfish. And she was too stubborn to allow me to walk away.

If it came down to me or her job, or me or her family, I would make the decision for her because I refused to ruin someone else's life. The way I'd ruined Edward's, and Aiden's, and even Katie's. Yeah, it takes two to make a baby, and Katie had wanted Aiden—or she said she did at the time—but still, without me in the picture, she wouldn't have had him, and she wouldn't have felt the need to walk away from him and never look back.

All of this was what had fucked me up. Looking at all the shitty things I'd done and knowing Shannen didn't need any of it in her life but not wanting to be without her. I was stuck. There was no winning for me because if she stayed, then I would always be holding her back and she'd one day hate me for it. If she left, even though I only wanted what was best for her, I'd be pissed off that she didn't fight to stay.

All this whole experience had done was solidify to me that the 'L' word was evil. Every single time it's uttered, something goes wrong. The word wasn't the only issue; I was the other one. But all of it together reminded me that getting close to people was too fucking painful.

"If she comes back and says she's done with you, I'll let you live at the flat rent-free for a year," Guy said.

I snorted. "I'm glad you're confident." I put the cap back on the bottle and then headed for the hallway, trying to focus only on what I needed to do right then, which was to go and collect my son. "Right, that's me dressed. I'll see you in a minute."

When I got to Guy's, a weird feeling came over me as I approached. Surely I couldn't feel the tension from outside the front door? I couldn't hear any arguing, but I couldn't shift the idea that something was off. I knocked and waited, and it was barely a minute before Helen answered, her hand on Aiden's shoulder as she ushered him out the door, his blue backpack over his shoulders. Her face was stony, her eyes dark. I saw a glimpse of Guy in the hallway just before she slammed the door behind Aiden without a word.

What the fuck?

I was tempted to knock again and make sure Guy was okay. From what I'd seen, he looked fine, just pissed off. I hadn't even had time to thank them for watching Aiden.

Trying to ensure I didn't look as confused as I felt, I knelt down to him, both of us still on the front step. His face was drawn down into a frown.

"Helen didn't say bye," he muttered.

The sadness in his eyes made me want to hammer the door down and make her apologise for upsetting Aiden, but instead, I took one of his hands in mine. "It's okay, buddy. I think she just had some things to do and she forgot to say goodbye because she was really busy. I bet she will say sorry next time you come over."

It wasn't okay at all, it was fucking rude, but I couldn't explain to a five-year-old that Helen was about to go and have a fight with Guy. I knew that look on her face, and she was going to explode as soon as we'd driven away. I'd seen the expression many times when I'd pissed her off. I wasn't sure whether Guy had truly done anything to cause it, but that was for them to sort out. My immediate concerns were getting some coffee and cheering Aiden up.

Aiden just nodded, his lower lip jutting out.

"How about me and you get in the van, drive to Dawlish, and go for a walk on the beach?" I asked.

"But it's not sunny."

It was kind of overcast but not as cold as it had been, but there was never a bad time to go to the beach as far as I was concerned. "We'll go and get a hot chocolate. With cream and marshmallows?" I offered, and the first signs of a smile crossed his face.

"Okay," he said. "Can I have a cake?"

Giving him a mock glare, I said, "Don't push your luck," and he giggled. The sound was better than any sunny day, and I straightened up, keeping a hold of his hand as we headed for the van.

On the way, I heard my message notification, and I took my phone from my pocket, my heart rate increasing. It had to be Shannen. She and Guy were usually the only ones who messaged me regularly. Nobody from work messaged at the weekend, and since Guy was otherwise engaged, it had to be her.

Shannen: Please can we talk soon? I'm done thinking. Need to see you. xx

That was a good sign, right? Unless...

She was the kind of person who would break up with someone politely and in person, so perhaps I wasn't safe yet.

Taking a breath, I typed back:

> **I have Aiden and we're just going to Dawlish for a hot chocolate and a walk on the beach. Do you want me to pick you up? xx**

I hoped that whatever she had to say could be said with Aiden nearby. Once we were at the beach, he could run off and play on the sand if the tide was out, so we would have some space to talk.

As Aiden and I got to the van, I put my phone in my back pocket, opened the passenger side door, and lifted him up and into his car seat. Just as he was secured, my phone went off again, and I grabbed my phone before shutting the van door.

> **Shannen: I'm just about to leave Plymouth so I'll be about an hour. Can meet you there? xx**

If she'd been in Plymouth, that meant she'd been to see her parents. And that also meant that she'd done what I'd asked and maybe even talked things over with her mum and dad.

She still wanted to see me, though, and that was the thing I would try to hold on to until we could talk.

It would only take me twenty minutes to get to Dawlish, but Aiden and I could kill a bit of time in the arcade until she arrived. I'd taken him once in the summer and I'd had to fight to get him away from the 2p machines. I rounded the van and jumped into the driver's side.

"Hey, Aiden, do you want Shannen to come with us today?" I asked, already knowing what his answer would be.

The last of his sadness fell away, and he grinned and wiggled in his seat, making me laugh. "Yes!"

This will go badly if she ends things with you...

He'd already felt rejected by Helen that morning; he didn't need any more of that. Shoving that thought aside and looking at the bright smile on my boy's face, I said, "Okay, I'll let her know. We can go and play some games for a while until she gets there and then we'll go for a walk and get our hot chocolate."

"I like it when we do things with Shannen."

That was clear from the picture he drew at school, which was now hanging on our fridge as promised, but it was reassuring to hear his confirmation. Closing my eyes and breathing deeply before the next negative thought could penetrate my brain, I ruffled Aiden's hair and shut the van door before texting Shannen back.

> **Sounds good. I'll meet you at Harrison's Amusements?**

She confirmed within seconds, and with another deep breath, I started the van.

One way or another, by the end of the day, I'd have some idea of what was next for us.

⁕⁕⁕

Aiden had the best time in the arcade. He fleeced me for fifteen quid in the half an hour we waited for Shannen, most of it on the 2p machines and a couple of quid on the claw machines, but he did manage to win a small cuddly tiger. We also had a game of air hockey, and by the time Shannen found us, I was ready to get out of the arcade before he bankrupted me.

The moment Aiden caught sight of Shannen, he flew across the space to greet her, and she smiled brightly as she bent down to give him a hug. Even amongst the noise of the music and machines, I heard him telling her about the toy he'd won, which I had tucked under my arm as I walked towards them, my stomach knotting with each step.

As Shannen straightened up, Aiden clinging to her hand, she smiled again as her eyes met mine.

The knots in my stomach loosened when I saw that the way she looked at me hadn't changed. The sparkle was still there, although I could see a deep underlying... something that I would ask her about as soon as I could. There was no sign of her *not* wanting to be there, though. No indication that she was done with me.

"Hi," she said, though she stood a bit awkwardly. It was like we'd just met all over again, when neither of us quite knew how to be around each other.

I wanted to lean down and kiss her like I always did, but even seeing how her gaze was still bright, I wasn't sure if she wanted that. I was also very aware of Aiden looking up at both of us as if waiting for us to do *something*.

"Hi."

It was all I could manage. Still holding Aiden's hand, Shannen took a step towards me and slipped her free arm around me, snuggling against me. I even heard her breathing in the smell of my leather jacket. I wound an arm around her, resting my chin on the top of her head. There were so many things we needed to talk about, so much to figure out, but for that moment, I just wanted her close to me.

We couldn't stay like that for as long as I wanted to because I could still feel Aiden's eyes on us. He might not have understood what was going on between Shannen and me, but he had to feel the strange vibe in the air. The relief of being together mixed with the uncertainty of where the day was going to lead.

I stepped back from her, but not before placing a kiss on her forehead.

"Can we get a hot chocolate now?" Aiden asked, making us laugh.

"Sure can," I told him, taking his other hand, and the three of us made our way outside and towards the beach.

We walked along the sea wall, pausing for a moment to zip up Aiden's coat against the cold breeze, then heading for the bit of the beach that was tucked away behind the huge red cliff. Guy and I had found it by mistake when we were out walking one time. We thought the wall just reached an end as it curled around the corner near where a few small rowing boats lay, but as we neared, we found the path continued to what looked like a secret beach. Much smaller than the main one, and far away from the crowds that took up the rest of the area in the summer. There was also a mobile cafe type thing that served drinks and snacks around there with some tables and chairs set up, and that was where we were headed.

All the way, Aiden chattered about his weekend, and he told Shannen and me that while he'd been at Guy's, he and Helen had taken him to McDonald's for tea, and then Guy had played with his Lego with him for a while before Helen read him a story when she put him to bed. Despite the weirdness that had existed that morning, Aiden had, thankfully, mostly had a good time.

As we got closer to the Cove Cafe, Shannen laughed. "Well, look at that."

She nodded towards the seating area, and sitting there with a hot drink each, was Nova and Donovan. Shannen had mentioned that Nova lived in Dawlish, so it wasn't that surprising that we'd bumped into them. They weren't the only ones there; an older couple sat at another table, and a woman was standing by the wall, looking out at the sea.

I wasn't sure if Shannen had spoken to Nova about me and all the things I'd told her, and she must have noticed me tense because she said, "She doesn't know much. Not the truth of what happened, anyway. Last night, I just... I wanted to think things over."

Nodding, I said, "Will you tell her?"

I glanced down at her, and she said, "If you don't mind, then I will. But if you'd rather I didn't, I don't have to."

I shrugged. "It's up to you. If you want to talk to her and Gaby about it, it's your choice. I'm not in control of what you say to people, Shan. If you need to talk about it to your friends, I said last night that I don't mind." That came out harsher than I intended, but it was the truth. What she told her friends about me was her business. I wasn't going to tell her to keep her feelings to herself. If she needed to talk, then she needed to talk.

"I know, it's just... it's not information you give out freely."

Before I could answer, Aiden let go of our hands and ran ahead of us to the wall. It was low, but he was still just a bit too small to easily see over it, and he rose up on his tiptoes, watching the waves. His quick movement caught Nova and Donovan's attention, and Nova's eyes widened as she recognised Aiden and looked our way.

"Small world," she said with a grin.

When we reached the table, Nova stood to give Shannen a hug, her ponytail whipping around in the wind, and Donovan smiled at me. "Didn't expect to see you again so soon," he said.

I opened my mouth to answer just as Aiden sped over, halting when he spotted Nova. Shannen laughed. "Hey, Aiden. You know Miss McKay from school, don't you?"

Aiden nodded, looking up at Nova like she was a unicorn spotted in the wild. Clearly, spending time with Shannen outside of school didn't stop his surprise at seeing another teacher out of the classroom.

"Hi, Aiden," Nova said, looking down at him. "Shannen was just telling me you've come to get a hot chocolate."

"Yeah," he replied, nodding. "And a cake."

"Kid's going to put my bank account in negative figures today," I said with a laugh.

Nova grinned, her eyes lighting up as if she understood. "The dangers of seaside towns. What do you want to drink? My treat."

"You sure?" I asked, and she nodded. "Just a coffee for me, thanks. Do you want some money for Aiden's hot chocolate?"

"No, it's cool." She smiled again as she hooked her arm through Shannen's and they went to order, while Aiden ran back to the wall to have another look out to sea.

"Take a seat," Donovan said, and I sighed.

I felt like the time between Shannen arriving at the arcade and us getting to the cafe had been a blur. I'd walked with her and Aiden, but I didn't feel settled, and I didn't think I would until Shannen and I had talked properly. Maybe I should have just asked her to come over to mine after Aiden had gone to bed instead of trying to have an important conversation with him in tow, but I'd missed her. It wasn't like we had never spent a night apart before. We'd spent more evenings apart than together because of work and Aiden, but an emptiness had settled inside me the second I left her flat the night before. I just wanted it to stop.

I pulled out the metal chair and sat next to Donovan, trying to think of something to say to make conversation. He was a nice guy, and I wanted to be sociable, but words were failing me.

"Listen," he began, "I don't know what's going on, and it's not my business, but if you want to grab a pint sometime before I leave, I'm up for that. As someone who spent a long time pretending not to feel anything, I recognise the signs. Just saying, I'm here if you need a different perspective on anything."

What the hell was I portraying that suggested I needed someone to talk to? Probably my inability to string a sentence together. Or maybe Nova had said something to him. Donovan and I had barely spent an hour together in total, but talking to him in the pub a few days ago was a nice change of pace. He was the first person I'd met other than Guy who seemed to get me. The lads I worked with were great, but none of them had become friends. Donovan had something different about him, though. I didn't know what it was, but he seemed like someone I could consider a mate.

"Thank you," I said. "I might take you up on that. How long until you have to go?"

"My flight leaves from London on Wednesday night, so I'll have to be on my way from here on Wednesday morning."

His shoulders dropped a bit, and I nodded. "It's a shame you can't stay for longer."

"It is, but really, I'm lucky my bosses allowed me to go away at all so soon after starting the job. They told me they were sick of seeing me moping around and put me on a plane." He chuckled. "Long distance is hard."

"I can imagine. One or two days without seeing Shannen is hard enough." I glanced over to see what Aiden was doing, but he still at the wall. He'd sat his toy tiger on the ledge, moving it around as if showing the tiger what was in the distance, and the woman standing nearby watched him with a smile on her face as he played. I shifted my attention to Shannen. She stood with Nova, talking while they waited for our order to be ready.

We might not have had a long-distance relationship, but there was definitely something that had caused a disconnection. A wedge between us that needed to be dislodged and I wasn't sure how we would do that without the time and space to be alone.

As if she'd felt me looking, Shannen smiled at me, and the chaos inside me settled, but there was still something else in her eyes that told me she wasn't completely okay. I just didn't know whether it was because of me or something that had happened with her parents.

Chapter 29

Shannen

This is a weird day.

Cal, Aiden, and I were sitting by the sea with Nova and Donovan, chatting about everything and nothing while sipping on hot drinks. On any other day, I would have relished every second of it. While it was lovely to see them and spend time with them, there was a strange undercurrent running between Cal and me that made it hard for me to enjoy it the way I usually would. There was too much still unsaid between us.

We hadn't split up. But Cal had asked that we had some space and we'd done it so well that it remained there, separating us. He was waiting to find out what conclusions I'd reached, and I wasn't sure he would accept what I wanted to tell him.

But when we were close, when our eyes met, for that split second, we were still *us*, and I held onto that the whole time we sat there.

"You know, Aiden," Donovan said once our drinks were finished, "when I'm travelling to other countries, I like to spend time on the beach and look for pebbles and shells to take home. Do you want to come with me and Nova and see if we can find any here?"

If it had been appropriate, I would have kissed him. It was obviously apparent that Cal and I needed a minute to ourselves, and Donovan and Nova had given us an opportunity to do that.

Aiden's eyes widened in excitement, and he glanced at Cal. "Can I?"

Cal shot Donovan a grateful smile then turned his attention back to Aiden. "If you want to. But behave, though. No running off too far, and when Donovan and Nova say it's time to stop, you come back without arguing. Okay?"

"Okay!" He stood up so fast he almost knocked over his chair, and we all laughed at his enthusiasm.

Donovan and Nova got to their feet too, and Nova said, "Let's see what cool things we can find to show your dad and Shannen." She held her hand out for him and he took it without hesitation.

They were just going to be a short distance away, down the small ramp to the sand, so if we stood, we would see them over the wall. Cal was happy for Aiden to go with them since Aiden already knew Nova, and as they walked away, Aiden skipping, I said, "Gotta love friends."

Cal smiled. "Yeah. They're good people."

We watched until the trio was out of sight, and once nothing remained to distract us, Cal finally turned to me. I shuffled my chair around the table so we were closer, and I allowed myself to really look at him.

Now I was studying him, I could see how tired he looked. Dark circles sat under his eyes, and I imagined I looked the same. I'd cried some of the way home from my parents' house, but I hoped that the tear stains on my cheeks had gone by the time I got to Dawlish.

Even exhausted, Cal was still perfect. I'd spent many, many hours talking to him, taking in his features, and it still always took my breath away when I saw him. His thick black hair rippling with the breeze, his deep brown eyes, his sensual lips, and a smile that had captured me from day one.

I would not give him up. Not ever.

If he was going to fight me, I'd just fight harder.

"Cal," I said, after a while. "Are you okay?"

He shrugged, a slight frown on his face. "I've been asked that a lot today. I don't know the answer."

"After everything you had to relive last night, I'm not surprised." I reached over and took his hand in both of mine, hating the distant look in his eyes. I could almost feel his fear at what I was about to say, and I needed to eradicate it as quickly as possible so we could get back on track.

On the drive home, my father's words and my feelings tumbled around in my brain, and it didn't matter how many different ways I looked at it, no part of me believed that there was any merit in my dad's worries. I understood them, but I didn't buy into them. It just didn't add up to me that Cal could ever slip so far back.

"Not talking to you again last night was one of the worst things ever," I told him. "I wanted to call you, to make sure you were okay, and because I missed you. But you asked me to think, and I did." Running my fingers across his knuckles, I added, "I don't feel any differently about you than I did before Scott interfered,

Cal. I spent all night turning over everything you said, and how I feel about it. I don't like what you did. I'm not going to tell you that the depth of it didn't scare me, but it was such a long time ago. You were someone different then."

Cal shook his head, his shoulders slumping as he pulled away. "That's just it, Shan. The reason I didn't want you to know. I always knew, or hoped, you'd understand, but if even for a second you were afraid of me... everything's changed."

"No, it hasn't." I leaned forward, closing a little of the gap between us and shivering as a cool gust of air hit me. "I'm not scared of *you*. I just... it was a shock, you know? That there was a time when you had so much anger inside you."

He ran a hand through his hair then let it fall into his lap with a sigh, defeat filling his features.

I was messing this up. Saying all the wrong things when I was meant to be reassuring him. I never expected this conversation to be easy, but it didn't help that he had come almost seeming pre-prepared for a rejection. He'd let me hold him, let me touch his hand, but he wasn't all the way with me, and my words seemed to only make the distance wider.

"Do you really think I've changed?" he asked without looking up at me. "Come on, Shan. You've seen me lose my temper more than once. I'm not that different."

I was so goddamn tired. From not sleeping, from the emotion of the night before, and from the hurt of my dad's inability to accept me being with Cal. As I tried to catch Cal's gaze, I could see how torn he was. Between wanting to accept my words and wanting to push me away. And as always, pushing was his default. His tone was baiting me to fight with him, or maybe *for* him, but I didn't have the energy for games now. I just wanted him back.

"You don't think you're different?" I asked, keeping my voice low. "Do you think the nineteen-year-old version of you would be sitting here having this conversation? Do you think he'd be working for a living and raising a child? Would he have admitted he'd fucked up? Been able to calm himself instead of resorting to violence?"

Cal shook his head again. "You're not looking at the bigger picture."

"No, *you're* not looking at the bigger picture," I said, reaching for his hand again and pulling it towards me to get his attention. "Sometimes, when you look at me, you see someone privileged who always had the best things in life. I can see it in your eyes some days that you don't understand certain things about the way I grew up. But most of the time, you just see me. Just Shannen. The person you want to spend time with, and who you trust with your son, and who you care about. We're different, Cal. We always have been, but it's always worked. I *see* you. All of you. And you see all of me, beyond the things that you don't get about some parts of my life. You might have done some things that haunt you, but that isn't all you are. You're thoughtful, and fun, and you work hard, and you take care of me, and you don't pretend to be something you're not. *That's* the bigger picture."

Cal's eyes glazed with tears as he stared at me, and I could practically hear him rejecting my words, so instead of saying anything else, I just stared right back, willing him to hear me.

"What about your parents?" he asked eventually, and I swallowed, trying not to flinch.

"Can we just deal with us first?"

Pulling his hand away again, he said, "No. Because this isn't only about us, it's about you and what you could lose."

I ran a hand across my forehead, wondering how I was ever going to make him see that he mattered more to me than other people's bias. It wasn't that I didn't care about my dad's opinion because I cared a lot. It was breaking my heart that I didn't have his blessing to be with Cal, and that everything with Jade had gone wrong, and that Scott had tried to sabotage my career. It was all too much.

I didn't want to lose anything else.

"I guessed you went to see your mum and dad when you said you were in Plymouth," Cal said.

I nodded. "Yeah. It was... disappointing." Once again, hurt trickled through me.

Cal's demeanour, that had been stiff the whole time we'd been talking, shifted. Maybe because he'd seen the tears I could feel burning my eyes. Tears were the last thing I wanted right then because any sign of my pain would only seal Cal's warped logic that he was bad for me.

"What happened, Shan?"

"Can we walk?" I asked. We wouldn't be able to go too far because Nova and Donovan wouldn't know where we were, but I needed to move. Maybe stare out at the water and hope it calmed the storm inside me.

Cal nodded, and we both stood. As I was about to turn to slide out from between the chairs, he reached for my hips and pulled me against him. One arm wrapped around my back, and the other moved up and slid into my hair, capturing me in his warmth. The tears I'd tried to stop spilled over as I snaked my arms around him, my head against his chest. His jacket was zipped up, so he wouldn't feel my tears on his shirt, but he knew I was crying because my body was trembling. Through sadness, through fear, through exhaustion. I remembered the night before, how I'd just wanted to curl up in bed with Cal and hold onto him while we both slept, and I felt the same way now.

"I'm sorry," he said gently, his fingers softly playing with my hair. "I'm sorry I'm hard to talk to today. And I'm sorry things didn't go well with your dad. I just... I hate what all this is doing to you. I spent all night thinking, telling myself that if your family weren't okay with you and me, then I'd walk away. But I can't..." As he trailed off, I looked up at him. He was doing that thing he always did when he was serious. Not looking at me, but looking straight ahead. It was like he hoped by not looking me in the eye, I wouldn't see the truth in his, but it was always clear. Well, almost always. Right then, he wasn't torn anymore. He knew what he wanted to say.

So I waited.

"I can't be without you, Shan," he said. "As much as I know I'm ruining your life, I can't let you go. I'm too selfish to force you out. If you wanted to go..." he paused again, taking a sharp breath in. "If you wanted to go, I would let you, but I'm done pushing people away. And that's weird for me. Because I know you'd be better without me."

"Hey," I said, reaching up to put my hand on his cheek. He lowered his gaze to look at me. "I'm not better without you."

"What if you lose your job over what Scott told your principal?"

"I won't." I couldn't. Not just on the grounds of being involved with a man who was once arrested for a crime he, according to his record, didn't commit. Scott could make some noise, make it public knowledge, and if he did... there was no legal grounds for me to be fired. It could make my life, and my principal's life, difficult, but I could ride that out. Plus, I didn't fancy Scott's chances if my mother found out he had anything to do with risking my career.

"What about your family?" Cal asked, his eyes still on me. "Am I worth losing them?"

What a question. Yes? No? He always wanted a black and white answer, but not all situations had one. Not when I refused to choose one over the other. Family is important. The people who raised you, taught you, guided you. But then you grow up, and you find someone you want to be with, and they become family too. Not by blood but by choice. Things between Cal and me were still new, so perhaps siding with my family over him should have made some kind of sense, but not to me. I knew him well. Better than I'd known anyone else I'd been with, who I'd dated for longer. From the first night we met, there had been something about him I couldn't shake off. He was *real*. No two-faced, false persona for me and a whole different one for every person he spoke to. He was who he was, and as much as I loved my family, I wouldn't put them ahead of him because he meant too much to me now.

"Cal," I whispered, closing my eyes for a second. "You are worth everything." He pulled me in tighter, and I moved my hand to the back of his neck, stroking the soft skin there. "I love you."

He visibly tensed under my touch, just like he did the first time I said it. I wasn't sure why those words triggered him, but it wasn't because he didn't feel it. I was sure of that. He lowered his head a little, brushing his nose against mine and then kissing the tip before his lips lightly caressed my mouth.

"*You* are everything," he said, kissing me again, deeper this time.

I didn't care that we were out in the open, people milling about around us. All I cared about was that I had Cal back. That even though we still had things to talk about, he wasn't running from this. He was still in. Things with my dad would settle, I hoped, but until then, I would enjoy being with this man because there was nowhere else I wanted to be.

Chapter 30

Cal

Shannen and I walked and talked for a while longer after she'd made it clear that she hadn't changed her mind about me. She told me what had happened when she went to see her parents, and that her mum had been understanding, while her dad had basically told her to get rid of me.

Was I pissed off about that? Not as much as I would who thought because I'd expected it. At least her dad hadn't cast her out completely; it was just me that wasn't allowed within their fancy family circle. I'd always wondered what it would be like to meet Shannen's family, and the idea had me wanting to reach for the beer. I could never measure up to what they wanted for her. The most I'd ever hoped for was that they would put up with me for her sake. But it looked like that wasn't the case for her dad. And I got it. *I* knew I wasn't worthy of Shannen, so they were bound to notice.

But she was happy. And when I thought about Aiden growing up, the only thing I wanted was for him to be happy. I hadn't been for most of my life, and I didn't want things to be like that for him. Maybe that was too simple a way to look at it, but when you've grown up with almost nothing, happiness means more than a high-powered job and a big house.

Aiden had a great time on the beach with Nova and Donovan, and we'd arranged to meet them on Monday as we'd half-arranged the night we met in the pub. Aiden had a pocketful of pebbles in various shapes and colours, which he studied and chatted about all the way home.

Shannen and I had driven to Dawlish separately, but she invited us over to hers for a while. Aiden hadn't been to Shannen's place before, and he wanted to go because, *"She might have some more movies for me to watch."* Since *The Brave Little Toaster* had been such a hit, I hoped she had something else he might like or he'd get bored fast. Although, the stones and the toy tiger did seem to be keeping him pretty well entertained.

As it turned out, Aiden was happy to play with his tiger, and Shannen had taken a soft grey bear and a tiny black cat toy from inside her wardrobe, so he sat in the living room making up some kind of game with them. Shannen and I sat together on the sofa with a cheesy TV movie on that we weren't watching. What we were doing was enjoying being near each other again. We didn't need anything more than that.

At just after half past four, we were disturbed by a call from Guy. I had been waiting for it after how uncomfortable things had been that morning at his house. I hadn't told Shannen about that yet because we'd been too busy sorting our own shit out. I figured he'd catch me up as soon as Helen had gone to work.

"Hey," I said, as Shannen leaned away from me just a little, probably so as not to overhear what Guy was saying. It was a waste of time as I would tell her anyway.

I pulled her against me the way she had been, and she smiled up at me, then rested her head back on my shoulder.

"Hey, man," Guy said, his voice low and rough-sounding. "Are you busy?"

"Me and Aiden are at Shannen's. You okay?"

"No." There was a pause. "Helen's gone."

From his tone, I didn't think he meant just to work, but I needed to be sure. "Where?"

"She packed a couple of bags and she's gone to her mum's. She will only be coming back to get the rest of her stuff in a few days."

Shit.

I hated her. And I didn't use that term lightly. She had never given me a break, and the only thing I could give her credit for was how she looked after Aiden. The way she had been acting lately-and perhaps for longer than I'd even known about—treating Guy like a dick on a stick—was messed up, and I wouldn't miss her one bit. But Guy loved her, even if things had been horrible over the last few weeks.

"I'm sorry," I said. "What can I do?"

Guy sighed. "I don't know, mate. I don't even know what to do. She left over an hour ago and I've just been sitting here. I don't really know how I feel right now."

"Can you give me ten minutes?" I asked, knowing I needed to get to him. He'd always been there for me and there had never been anything I could do for him. He was always so *together*. He had his life in order, unlike me. But now he needed me. I just had to see if Shannen could watch Aiden so Guy wouldn't be on his own. "I'll call you right back."

"Sure," Guy answered. "Talk to you in a sec."

He disconnected right away, and I glanced down at Shannen. "Did you catch that?"

She nodded, worry in her eyes. "I hoped it wouldn't come to this."

"Me too." For Guy's sake, anyway. And Aiden's. I wasn't sure how I would explain to him that the main female figure in his life would no longer be around. He liked being around Shannen, and although Helen had hurt his feelings earlier, she was the one who'd been there for him when he'd come home to me. The one who had looked after him the most. I'd worry about that later. I had to see Guy first. Besides, even though he'd told me she would only be back for her stuff, there was always a chance they might change their minds. They'd been together a long time. I didn't want to tell Aiden she was gone, only for her to be back in the morning.

"Go to him," Shannen said. "I can look after Aiden."

"You sure?" I asked. "Because... this is new." I wasn't worried about leaving Aiden with her, just realising that this was yet another step forward. She looked after Aiden every day at school, but this was me asking her to watch my son as my girlfriend with no idea how long I would be gone.

Shannen smiled softly, a faint blush colouring her cheeks as if she also saw the significance. "It is. But I'm happy to take care of him."

"I could be a few hours. Is that okay?"

"Yes," she said, nodding. "It's fine. I'll feed him... if there's anything here he'll like."

Laughing, I said, "You know he'll eat pretty much anything. He isn't allergic to anything."

"Can I order a Burger King?"

"I heard Burger King," Aiden said, jumping up and making us both laugh.

Kissing Shannen on the cheek, I stood and walked over to Aiden, where he was bouncing on the balls of his feet with a grin on his face. "Listen, I have to go out for a bit. Will you be okay here with Shannen?"

He jumped up and down, flapping his arms, his smile widening. "Yes! Is she taking me to Burger King?"

"I'm going to order it to come here so we don't have to go out when it's getting dark," she said, moving across the sofa and leaning over the arm to look at us. "Is that all right?"

Aiden nodded. "Yeah! Can we watch a movie while we eat?"

The excitement my boy had at staying with Shannen, and how pleased she was about it too, made the last of the day's stress slide away. I'd been so close to walking away. To letting her go so she could keep everything that mattered to her.

But *we* mattered to her too.

I had no problem fucking up my own heart, but hers and Aiden's? That wasn't an option.

While the two of them talked about what they were going to do while I was gone, I put my shoes and jacket on, and when I was ready, Aiden had given up on his toys and was sitting on the sofa, flicking through Netflix with Shannen. Like before, my chest fluttered at the two of them having fun together. If it had been anyone other than Guy who needed something, I'd have blown them off for this. For the kind of family life I'd lost.

"Okay," I said before that thought could take hold and eat away at me again. "I have to go."

Shannen and Aiden turned around and looked at me over the back of the sofa, and again, my heart stuttered. Aiden had a mischievous look on his face, and Shannen's smile hit me square in the chest.

Everything about us felt right.

I walked back over to them and placed a kiss on Aiden's forehead and then Shannen's.

I love you.

The words I'd been too afraid to even think pushed to the forefront of my mind, but I swallowed them down. Still wasn't ready to let them out. They were right there, ready to fall from my lips, but they'd lodged in my throat.

She knew. I knew she did. And Aiden? Well, as shitty as it was, that was still a work in progress. I would have thrown myself in front of a bus for my kid, but telling him I loved him? My issues still made that hard.

"Cal?"

Shannen said my name gently, and I blinked, realising I'd been staring at them.

"Sorry," I said, shaking my hands out to rid myself of the weird feeling that had come over me. "Better go." I looked at Aiden. "Be good, please. I don't want to hear that you've been giving Shannen any trouble while I'm gone or we won't be going out with Nova and Donovan next week."

Aiden's face fell at the idea. He'd taken a shine to Donovan, who'd apparently been telling him about different places he'd been to. On the way home, Aiden had even asked me if we could go to the 'Philiminnes'. He'd be lucky if we could afford a wet weekend in Bognor Regis, but I liked that he was interested in learning about other countries. He was smarter than me, that was for sure.

"I'll be good," Aiden said. "I promise."

Chapter 31

Shannen

"What's that noise?"

Aiden's words pulled me from the game of Uno we were playing, and then I heard it. The faint buzz of my phone which I'd left on vibrate.

"Thank you for hearing that," I said, jumping up from the floor to see where I'd left it. It was around the sofa, and I dug my hand down the side of the cushion, my fingers finding the device. Cal's name was on the screen, and I answered quickly.

"Hi," I said. "Sorry, my phone was hiding."

He chuckled, though it was a bit strained. "That's okay."

"How's Guy doing?" I asked, holding a finger up to Aiden to let him know I'd just be a minute, then wandered through to the kitchen so he didn't hear anything he shouldn't.

Cal sighed. "I don't know what to do, Shan. I don't think it's sunk in that she's not coming back. He does seem relieved that the fighting is over, but also... he's just broken up with someone he was with for seven and a half years, so he can't be okay."

"Do you know what happened?" I asked, leaning against the kitchen counter. "Was it a mutual decision, or..."

"Sort of. He didn't throw her out, but when she said she was leaving, he didn't ask her to stay. He said he was sick of being treated like her personal sperm bank, and she didn't react well. But he said that was how it felt to him. He feels bad that if she wants to start a family now, she's another step behind because she doesn't have someone to do that with, but she'd made it difficult for him to want to be with her."

"Is this really just something that's happened over the last few weeks?" I asked. Because it was a lot to give up after a short rough patch. Nobody throws away seven and a half years over a blip. Cal and I wouldn't give up seven weeks, let alone years.

"Apparently not." He sighed again, and I could imagine him pacing, his hand running through his hair the way it did when he was stressed. "It's been worse over the last few weeks, but it's been going on for over a year. He said it started with her just being upset about how hard it was for them to have a baby, but over time, it made her angrier and more pissy with him. She said he wasn't supporting her enough, but apart from not going to the doctor like she wanted because he thought it was too soon to worry, he didn't know what else he was doing wrong."

I couldn't speak for what Guy had done right or wrong, I just knew that even when I'd gone to Helen with the best of intentions, she'd made it really freaking hard. Her treatment of Cal had never made her very popular with me, but I'd still felt for what she was going through. I wondered if she was as difficult with Guy as she was with everyone else. Either way, both of them were going through a lot.

"So, what's the plan?" I asked. "Do you need to stay over there for longer?"

"That's why I'm ringing." He sighed again. "I think he'll be okay, but... Shan, when everything was crap for me, Guy stayed up with me all night, talking, helping me figure things out. I want to do the same for him, but I've got Aiden to think about. Can you keep him until about nine? It's later than I want him to be up, but I can't leave Guy yet."

This was a moment I wished my dad could see. These were not the actions of a dangerous, angry, selfish man, they were the actions of someone who cared about people.

"If you want to stay with Guy, I can keep Aiden for the night, but we might need to go to yours to get some of his things because there's nothing here for him. No clean clothes, and he'll probably want his iPad or a book to read before bed or something. As long as Aiden doesn't mind, obviously."

The offer was made without hesitation because Cal needed me, and I didn't mind Aiden staying with me. Guy *did* need someone to be with him. I didn't like the idea of him being alone.

"Are you sure?" Cal asked. "I can come and get him if it's easier for you."

"It's up to you. I'm cool either way, just let me know and I'll do whatever you want me to do."

He laughed again, but not as stiffly. "If you can repeat that next time we're in the bedroom, I'd appreciate it."

"Cal!" I couldn't help laughing too, though. With the events of the last day, *that* had been the last thing on my mind.

Now he'd mentioned it, though...

I shook my head to rid myself of the dirty things he might ask me to do. "Focus."

I could almost hear his smile down the phone. "Sorry. Okay, let me talk to Aiden and we'll see what he would prefer to do."

And that was how, at nine-thirty, Aiden and I were having a living room sleepover at my place.

Cal had gone home to get Aiden's PJs, clean clothes for the next day, and his iPad, and then dropped it over to us in a little blue backpack.

The moment Aiden had said he wanted to stay at mine, we'd set up the living room by dragging my duvet from my bedroom and the one from the spare room out. I'd pushed my two armchairs together to make an almost-sofa-sized bed for Aiden while I would sleep on the actual sofa, and I'd put the small table lamp on instead of the main light to make it a bit less bright. On the table, I'd laid out some snacks, and Aiden's iPad was charging on the arm of the sofa. I figured he might find it easier to sleep if I turned the evening into an 'adventure' rather than putting him into a strange room alone.

Cal had taken one look at the room and I could see in his eyes how much he wished he could stay. He'd held onto me for a long time, and Aiden told him we could do the living room sleepover with him another day. I suggested during the week, maybe Monday night after we'd been out with Nova and Donovan, but that didn't change how little he'd wanted to leave us behind.

"Shannen," Aiden said from his armchair bed, all snuggled up under his quilt.

"Yes?" I was still sitting up with a cup of tea, TV off now, and I looked over at him.

"When Cal picked me up from Guy and Helen's house today, Helen wasn't very nice to me."

This kid doesn't miss a trick.

Cal and I had tried to keep our voices down when talking about where he was going, and especially why, but Aiden was a bright kid, and way more sensitive than Cal realised sometimes. He got upset about things easily, but he could also pick up when someone was sad, and I couldn't help but think it explained Aiden's temperamental moods when they'd lived with Guy and Helen. Cal might not have noticed the tension, but Aiden was around Helen a lot. He'd have noticed, even if he didn't tell anyone.

"What happened?" I asked gently.

He turned onto his side to face me, cuddling his new toy tiger. "She said that Guy was making me go home early, but then Guy said he wasn't, and Helen said something about him being shellfish, whatever that means, and she pulled me into the kitchen. She hurt my arm."

It was hard not to giggle over the 'shellfish' comment, but Aiden was so lost in the memory that his lower lip jutted out. Plus, the mention of Helen hurting him, even if by accident, took the humour out of his words.

"Did she say sorry?" I asked, and he shook his head.

"You told me at school that if I hurt someone then I have to say sorry to them, but she didn't say sorry to me. She told me to hurry up and get ready to go and..." he stopped, his dark eyes filling with tears.

I leaned forward, putting my drink on the coffee table, then went to Aiden and sat down on the floor beside the chairs. "What is it, sweetheart?" I rested my hand on the edge of the chair, and Aiden pulled one of his arms out of the covers and tucked his hand in mine, causing my heart to swell.

How did this boy go from being the nightmare in my class to someone I wanted to protect? In my job, I wanted to protect all of the kids in my class. There wasn't a single one I wouldn't have put my life on the line for if it came to it, but Aiden... spending so much time with him, understanding how much he'd been through, and that he belonged to the man I was in love with... when he was hurting, it hurt me too, and I just wanted to make it better.

"She said that Cal would be late to pick me up anyway because he was probably fighting with you. But then Cal came and Helen didn't even say bye to me."

One of the tears that had welled in his eyes dripped down his cheek. Cal had mentioned to me that Helen had upset Aiden that morning by shoving him out the door, but he thought Aiden was over it. Knowing it still played on his mind showed me how much he cared about her, but also that he felt like she had shown him something he didn't like.

"Sometimes she's mean," Aiden went on. "She shouts at Guy a lot. He never shouts back. He talks to her nicely, but she always yells. And she's always mean to Cal."

I wasn't sure if he was looking for answers, and I hoped not because he was way too young to learn that some people are confusing and not always what they pretend to be. But also, I didn't know what the truth was behind whatever Aiden had witnessed. What mattered was that he *had* witnessed it, and it had messed with his head. He didn't understand how someone could be so nice to him but not nice to Cal and Guy.

I gently squeezed his hand. "How does all of that make you feel?"

He shrugged. "Sad. I don't like it when people are mean, like when Cal gets angry sometimes, but he doesn't say bad things to people. He does say bad words sometimes, though. And he doesn't get angry as much now. Helen is always angry, but it makes me sad because I think she doesn't like me anymore. I don't think I like her sometimes."

With my free hand, I softly wiped the tears from his cheeks. "Helen has been sad too," I told him. "Sometimes people shout when they get upset because they don't know how to talk about things."

"Like Cal does. He told me that. And he told me that I should tell him when I feel upset so I don't have to shout. But if I'm upset then I cry."

"That's okay too," I told him with a smile. "Your dad is right, though. You should tell him when you're sad."

"Can I tell you too?"

I nodded, my heart melting further. "Of course you can." Aiden gave me a tiny smile, and I said, "Are you ready for sleep yet?"

Aiden screwed up his face in thought, and I chuckled. "Please can you read me a story?"

Giving his cheek one more gentle swipe to erase the last of his tears, I said, "Absolutely."

Aiden slept brilliantly, but he snored like a fully grown adult, which meant I didn't get as much rest as I would have liked. I was now running on two nights of minimal rest, but I didn't mind. At least the reason for my lack of sleep this time was a good one and not due to stressing over my future. It was amazing how much difference twenty-four hours could make. I glanced at Aiden's sleeping form and smiled. Things could have gone so differently, and I was grateful that Cal and I had figured things out. Or at least as best as we could with the limited amount of time we'd had to talk. In spite of his best efforts, Scott hadn't managed to break me and Cal. He had, however, opened up a rift between me and my parents and dug up a whole load of Cal's trauma, and we would be dealing with the fallout from that for a while. What mattered most to me, though, was that Cal was still with me. We'd work through everything else together.

A gentle tapping on my front door scared the life out of me, and I looked at the clock on my phone. It was almost one a.m.

Slowly and quietly climbing out from under my duvet, I wandered out to the hallway as the tapping sounded again.

Thank God for peepholes.

I opened the door to Cal, who had a dopey grin on his face, and I quirked an eyebrow. "I hope you didn't drive here."

He shook his head. "I did not. I got a taxi. Guy passed out on the sofa, so I left some paracetamol and water on the coffee table and then came to see you."

Chuckling, I opened the door wider for him and he came inside. "How much have you had to drink?"

Cal smiled. "Not as much as I thought I would. I've had four beers, but it's been a while since I drank anything at all, and I'm knackered, so I guess I'm a bit drunker than I would usually be, but not enough to affect my conversational skills."

"I don't know," I teased. "I've never heard you say 'conversational skills' before."

When I smirked, he reached out for me, pulling me flush against him. His eyes travelled across my face, studying me as if he hadn't seen me in years. The intensity of his attention always made me feel like I was the most special person in his world, and a small sigh of sheer joy escaped me. "I want to kiss you, but first... is Aiden all right?"

Pulling myself together from the trance he had me in, I said, "Can you not hear that snoring? He sounds like a chainsaw!"

Cal laughed, running his hands up and down my back. "Yeah, I should have warned you about that. Did he go to bed easy enough?"

"He was fine. We played a couple more rounds of Uno, ate some crisps, then we had a chat before I read him a story and he fell asleep."

"Thank you for taking care of him." Cal brushed his lips across mine, and I could taste the beer on his breath. It reminded me of the first time he'd kissed me, when the scent of the alcohol had intoxicated me, and I could feel the same effects happening now. Except it was better. Because when he kissed me now, I knew exactly what to expect, what his lips, hands, and filthy words could do to my body.

He pulled away from the kiss, his eyes roaming over my face. "Fuck, Shan," he murmured. "I've missed you."

He didn't just mean the few hours we'd been apart that evening. And he didn't just mean that he'd missed physically being around me. He'd missed the same thing I'd missed. That closeness we'd always had that had been frayed by our own fears that we wouldn't make it through all of his revelations. For him, the worry that I would decide to end things with him, and for me, the concern that he would keep pushing me away so hard that I actually went.

And I knew because I felt the same way.

It didn't seem right that such an intense and potentially damaging few days had made us closer. Somehow, though, the possibility of the end had cemented how much Cal meant to me, and I had a feeling that Cal seeing what Guy was going through made him glad he wasn't going through it too.

"I missed you too," I told him, moving my hand up and into his hair.

He let out a soft growl at the sensation of my fingers curling into the strands. "I did not come here just to have sex with you, Shan, but I would really like to. Even in your Care Bears pyjamas."

His mouth on mine cut off the response I was forming, his tongue lightly teasing mine and making my core clench with need. I didn't care about his playful mocking of my PJs; they were adorable and I'd needed something sensible to wear with Aiden in the flat.

What was it about leather, alcohol, and Cal combined that made me want to take off my clothes?

I was so, so tired, and yet being around him was like an electric shock to my libido. We had got so close to losing each other that now we hadn't... we needed to reconnect. To throw off the last of the hangover we'd been left with from the last few days.

"Besides," he went on, his mouth moving close to my ear, "earlier you said I could tell you what I want you to do."

His husky tone and the heat in his eyes made my knickers dampen immediately. He rarely told me what to do in the bedroom; he talked dirty sometimes, asked me what I liked, but he'd never taken total control, and I wanted it so bad I was almost panting.

"Cal," I breathed as his lips danced across my neck, causing shivers through my whole body. "We can't. Aiden..."

"He's asleep." His teeth grazed my earlobe. "And if you can't be quiet, I can always put something in your mouth."

The moan of need that slipped from my lips made him chuckle darkly, and he let go of me and dragged me to my room.

Chapter 32

Cal

By ten o'clock on Sunday morning, Shannen, Aiden, and I were up, dressed, had had breakfast, and had put the living room back to its normal state, all bedding and evidence of snacks gone.

After I'd had the most fun I'd ever had with Shannen in the bedroom, we showered, and then slept on the sofa together, keeping the living room sleepover alive.

If I'd had my way, I would have kept her in the bedroom all night, watching as I made her drive herself to the brink over and over, never quite letting her over the edge. Her skin flushed, damp with sweat, her hair a mess as she writhed under her own touch.

There was just something about her touching herself... it triggered a need in me to make her wait until she was begging me to let her come.

And she did beg.

The wait was worth it. Because when I was finally inside her, every part of us connected, the high was euphoric. Her taste, her smell, her warmth... she surrounded me and I held onto her so fucking tight because I'd come so close to losing her. To losing the feeling she gave me that nobody else had or could ever give me.

I'd told her the day before that she was everything, and she was. Regardless of what I'd done and how her family felt about me, she was mine. She wanted me. Even the fucked-up parts.

And falling asleep knowing nothing could break us now was the best feeling ever.

Shannen was just in the kitchen with Aiden, making him a drink, when there was a knock at the front door.

"Can you see who that is?" Shannen called out. "I won't be a sec."

"Yeah," I called back, though I hoped it was someone I knew. It would have looked weird if I ended up staring blankly at one of her friends who I hadn't met before. Besides, if I didn't know about them, they might not know about me either and then we'd just be standing there awkwardly.

Without checking to see who it was, I opened the door, and I was met by a tall, well-built man with thinning brown hair. His head retracted very slightly in surprise when he saw me, and he looked me up and down carefully.

There was no disguising who he was. His eyes were the same gentle blue Shannen's were. He wore fitted blue jeans and a dark green shirt with thin black stripes down it, and his clothes looked expensive. Good quality.

"You must be Cal," he said.

His voice was deep, intimidating, and had he been anyone other than Shannen's dad, I would have squared up to him. I still didn't like authority figures, and while he wasn't exactly authority, he did have that rich-person way of surveying people, like he was judging their worth. But as I eyed him back, refusing to *look* intimidated, he relaxed a little. Maybe, based on what he knew about me, he was expecting me to be covered in tattoos and piercings; the stereotype of the kind of look upper classes assume means trouble.

"Yeah," I said. "I'm Cal." I offered him my hand, and he took it, shaking firmly.

"I'm Shannen's dad, Steven. It's nice to meet you."

His tone suggested that wasn't true, but I nodded anyway. "You too."

Stepping aside, I let him come in, shutting the door behind him as Shannen called out, "Who was it?" from the living room.

I didn't want her to freak out, but I gestured for her dad to go on ahead of me, which he did. As I turned into the living room, Shannen stared at him as he stood by the door. I paused in the doorframe, looking to see where Aiden was. He sat at the dining table, paper and a ridiculous amount of coloured pens and pencils spread out in front of him. A small glass of orange squash perched on the table, and I hated that I was going to disturb him when he looked settled in for hours of drawing. However, the tension in the room had built up fast and I didn't want to be in the way of whatever conversation was about to begin.

"Shan," I said, drawing her attention away from her father. "If you give us five minutes, we can get out of the way so you can talk."

"No, you don't have to go." Shannen flicked her gaze back to her dad before looking at me again. "Please."

I glanced at him, and for such a big man, he looked... uncomfortable. I had no idea if he'd come to apologise or to try to force her to ditch me, but either way, I didn't think Aiden or I needed to be there.

"It's okay," Mr Morgan—it didn't feel right to call him Steven, even in my own mind—said, turning to look at me. "I came to talk to Shannen, but you don't have to go."

Still, he was saying the right words, but it didn't sound genuine.

Shannen's eyes darted between us again, confusion all over her face. Not so much about what to do, but more about why he was there. There wasn't a hint of hope on her face that he had somehow changed his mind about me; she'd told me he was stubborn. So, I could understand why she was on edge.

"Can I make you both a drink or something?" I offered, unsure what to do. I wanted to support Shannen, but I also didn't want to make anything worse for her by saying something stupid, or that would embarrass her. He already thought I was beneath her, and I didn't want his opinion to sink any lower.

Shannen smiled gently at me, some of her tension easing. "Actually, that would be great. Can I have a latte, please?"

"That's all you," I said, shaking my head with a chuckle. "Because the last time I tried that, I almost broke your coffee machine."

Damn coffee pods. Her fancy machine had exploded and shot milk all over the place, and she'd politely asked me never to use it again; something that had clearly slipped her mind in the moment.

Her smile widened at the memory, and I stepped into the room as she said, "Good point. Tea will be fine. Dad?"

We swivelled our heads to look at him, and he'd been watching our exchange with interest. I held back a smirk because I saw the way Shannen looked at me, and her dad had too. And I was pretty sure I was looking at her the same way.

"Tea for me too, please. No sugar."

I nodded to acknowledge his drink order, smiling again at Shannen in a way that I hoped said I would be there for her no matter how this went down. As I walked towards Aiden, he lifted his head from his drawing. "Come and look!"

He pushed his piece of paper towards me across the table, and I leaned down to see. In pencil, he'd drawn a cowboy hat, and I chuckled. "Another Woody picture?"

"Yeah! I already did Buzz Lightyear pictures yesterday, so it's Woody's turn today."

"I'm surprised you haven't drawn The Brave Little Toaster yet."

Aiden's eyes widened like that hadn't even crossed his mind. "I'm going to do that instead! And the lamp, and the radio, and everything!" Aiden shoved his Woody drawing aside and reached for a fresh piece of paper. "Who's that?" he asked, loud enough for Shannen and her dad to look up.

"This is my dad," Shannen said from across the room. "Dad, this is Cal's son, Aiden."

Aiden eyed him suspiciously. My kid was a good judge of character, he just wasn't subtle about checking people out. After a moment, Aiden offered him a hesitant wave.

Mr Morgan smiled for the first time since he'd arrived, his body relaxing. "Hello, Aiden."

Was he expecting my kid to be a thug also? I might not have been good at much, but I did teach Aiden to have manners.

"Do you want me to draw you a picture?" Aiden asked, and a quiet laugh escaped me. Even if I was undecided, Aiden had deemed Mr Morgan a decent person. Decent enough to offer artwork to.

Mr Morgan nodded and said, "That would be nice. I like dogs."

Aiden shrugged. "I was going to draw a toaster, but I'll try!"

Aiden got back to work, and shaking my head in amusement, I went to the kitchen to put the kettle on. While I waited, I text Guy to see if he was up yet. After a drinking binge—which didn't happen often—he sometimes didn't surface until at least midday, but he text back right away.

> **Guy: I'm awake. Thank you for leaving the paracetamol. Much needed.**

> **Hope you don't mind that I left. Will come over later with Aiden.**

> **I get it. You needed to be with Shannen after everything that happened. Hope you had a good night.**

> **We did. But her dad is here now.**

I watched the dots on the screen showing Guy was typing, then they stopped before starting again. Eventually, the next text came through.

> **Shit. Let me know how it goes. I'm going back to sleep for a bit.**

Part of me wished I could do that. Crawl back into bed and hide from whatever was happening in the living room. There were no raised voices, and Mr Morgan had settled after Aiden offered to draw him a picture.

Had he honestly expected to find Shannen shacked up with someone who couldn't hold a conversation, with a kid who didn't know how to behave? It was the same kind of judgement Jade had made, and I didn't miss the surprise on her face when she met me. She'd heard the words 'painter and decorator' and decided

I'd be some scruffy dickhead who communicated in grunts. It was fucked up to me that with everything Shannen had achieved in her life, her family and friends thought she was incapable of making a good decision for herself.

I made the tea, not bothering with one for myself, and carried them into the other room. Shannen was now sitting in one of her chairs, her dad on the sofa. I put their drinks down on the coffee table and the conversation halted as I came in. There was less of a weird atmosphere now. I still felt like I shouldn't be there, but I wasn't sure where to go. I hadn't heard anything that had been said so far because of the noise of the kettle boiling.

"Thank you," Mr Morgan said, and Shannen gave me a smile. "Can you come and sit down, please?"

My instinct was to say no. To find an excuse, pretend Aiden wanted my attention or something. Shannen reached for my hand, and I perched on the arm of her chair as she tangled her fingers with mine. Her body was a little stiff, her features set as if prepared for this to go badly. She wasn't open like usual. I squeezed her hand gently and she clasped mine right back.

"I was just saying," Mr Morgan began, a serious expression on his face as he reached for his cup of tea, "that I wasn't expecting you to be here. I wanted to talk to Shannen about what she told me yesterday, but it's perhaps a good thing you're here too."

"Dad," Shannen interrupted. "I'm glad you want to talk, but Cal being here doesn't mean you can ask him questions and make him uncomfortable. That's why I said no to you meeting him. This is my home, and if you're planning to grill him... please, just don't."

This fucking woman. She sat there, dressed in a pair of black leggings and a massive oversized blue top that swamped her, her thick curls messily tied up in a ponytail, facing her father, who thought I was a piece of shit, and told him not to attack me. Even though it wasn't the first time she'd gotten annoyed on my behalf or defended me, it always surprised me.

She is in love with you.

I'd never doubted that. Questioned her sanity, yes. I didn't doubt her feelings, though. It still scared the crap out of me, but hearing her side with me over her father made it clearer than ever.

"That isn't what I want to do," Mr Morgan said, causing me to look over at him, though his eyes were on Shannen. "But you have to understand, you are my daughter, and I'm concerned, so I do have some questions."

Shannen's fingers squeezed mine again, and I gently stroked my thumb across the back of her hand to calm her down. "If you ask him what his intentions are with me, I swear to God..."

Mr Morgan's lips twitched. "That wasn't the question."

No kidding. If I'd said I wanted to marry her, he'd have had a heart attack. *Although...*

Nope. If I took that idea any further, *I'd* have a heart attack.

"Shannen," Mr Morgan began, "I've thought a lot about what you said yesterday. And about how we move forward from here. Your mum had a chat with me about the way I reacted, but this is hard for me." He looked at me. "You have a son. You probably understand what I mean when I say that I want what's best for my daughter."

"I do," I said, nodding slowly, "but your idea of best and mine are going to be very different. I want my son to be happy, whatever that is for him, because I didn't have that for very long when I was a kid. I don't want him growing up believing that nobody cares about him or having to steal crisps from the corner shop because he's hungry. I don't want him to feel like there is nothing for him and that he can't do whatever he wants to do because he isn't good enough."

Mr Morgan and Shannen both flinched at those last words, and it wasn't hard to know why. We all knew he was implying *I* wasn't good enough, and he at least had it in him to shift with discomfort about being called out, even if not directly.

"Okay," Mr Morgan said. "You're right. We might have different views on what the best means. What I don't want, though, is to have to worry for Shannen's safety. I know you didn't have the most stable childhood-"

"Dad, stop," Shannen interrupted as I forced myself not to react to his words. I wasn't sure if he was attempting to *get* a knee-jerk reaction from me or just really bad at getting his point across, but I wouldn't give him anything he could use against me.

"My childhood isn't the point," I said after a moment, grasping Shannen's hand again. "I am far from perfect, Mr Morgan. And even further from being the best thing for your daughter. She's beautiful, she's understanding, she's patient, she's thoughtful. She is the best person I've ever known. Yet you keep talking to her as if she's not intelligent enough to know what she wants. I might not be what you wanted for her, but nobody will work harder to make her happy than I will. I'm never going to be rich or wear designer clothes, but she is safe with me. She will be safe with me for as long as I'm lucky enough to be with her."

I could feel Shannen looking at me, her fingers gripping mine tightly, but I kept my focus on her father, our eyes locked as he assessed me. My words weren't fancy or well-presented, and I'd just told him he was treating Shannen like an idiot, but I was honest. If he didn't like that, we were never going to get anywhere anyway.

After a while, Mr Morgan nodded thoughtfully.

"This is what I was trying to tell you yesterday," Shannen said. "I just want to be happy. You liked the other men I was with because it looked like they were treating me well, but they weren't. Not really. I've spoken to Cal more in the last two months than I spoke to most of the other men I dated combined because they were never around. And when they were, they didn't want a conversation, they wanted to talk *at* me. What you want for me is not what I want. I don't care about anything other than feeling safe and cared for, and that is how I feel with Cal."

Mr Morgan put his cup down on the table and shuffled across the sofa a little closer to us. He looked like he was struggling to figure out what to say next, and after a minute, I said, "I heard my father beating my mother for years. Saw the bruises all over her and how she had to tiptoe around him just in case she caught him at the wrong time and he flipped. I tried to protect my little brother from it, but I never could because they were so loud. I could hear my mum crying some nights in her room while my dad was out getting drunk because she didn't know what mood he would come home in, or if he'd come home at all." I let go of Shannen's hand and stood up, hating how I had to go through all of this just to make my point, but I did it for her. She was sitting right there, risking her father walking away by putting her faith in me. The least I could do was explain why it was so easy for me to promise I would never let her down. "I've been the child of a parent who was beaten, and I don't want that for my son. I don't want him to grow up knowing his father is a bully, or to be scared of me, or to resent me for making his life miserable. And I've lived as the person who was beaten. Not just physically. I was verbally attacked almost every day when I was a teenager and I wouldn't wish it on anyone." Fixing my eyes back on Shannen's dad, I said, "I don't have a degree, don't own property or even a proper car. But I work hard and pay my bills and my rent on time. I have a shitty temper. I might get frustrated or shout, and I might even say things I don't mean sometimes. But I would never hit your daughter. If there came a day when I even raised a hand to her, I'd make her leave me because I would rather let her go than be responsible for causing her pain. So, when she tells you that she feels safe with me, it's not just words. It's fact. I have got way too much here to risk losing it."

I glanced back at Shannen, her blue eyes bright with tears. I didn't care if Mr Morgan accepted me in that moment because the way Shannen was looking at me took over everything.

We'd been through a lot of crap in such a short time, and she still looked at me like I wasn't the mess I actually was.

She stood up and slipped her arms around me, and I held her close, my hands staying very respectfully on her back, even though I wanted to bury them in her hair and kiss her.

Mr Morgan cleared his throat, and a wave of emotion crossed his face. I must have said something right. Or maybe he was simply understanding how much Shannen and I meant to each other. The connection between us seemed to fill the room, and I held her tighter.

"Cal," he said, his voice a little croaky before he cleared his throat again. "I can see how much you care about Shannen. And I appreciate you sharing all of those things with me. I'm sure it wasn't easy." As he continued, Shannen loosened her grip on me and turned around to look at him. I rested my hands on her hips, and she covered my hands with hers. "But I still can't condone what you did. I have seen men who have turned their lives around slip back into old habits when things get hard, and I don't know you well enough to trust that you won't be the same. However, my daughter *does* trust you, and my wife thinks I should give you a chance."

Shannen's body stiffened, like she was holding her breath, and mine did the same.

"My family is everything to me," Mr Morgan continued, his face softening as he looked at Shannen. "And if Shannen wants to be with you, there is obviously nothing I can say that's going to change her mind." Shifting his eyes back to me, he said, "If you swear to me that I won't ever have to hear her crying over something you've done to her, then... I'm willing to give you a chance."

Shannen let go of me and darted across the room to him, throwing her arms around his neck and making him laugh as he fell backwards into the sofa. "Thank you."

As he straightened, he nodded to me over her shoulder, letting me know he was really going to do this. To be okay with me and Shannen and at least try to get over the crap I'd done in the past. I returned the nod, hoping he could see how much I meant what I'd said before.

He wrapped his arms around Shannen, both of them finally relaxed as he quietly said, "I love you. And I'm sorry about yesterday, Shannen. I'm sorry."

I didn't hear what she said back, but she didn't let him go, and I smiled as I watched them for a second before sitting back down on the arm of the chair while they had their moment.

Shannen had given me the impression that her dad would be hard to get around. That he was so set in his ways that his decision couldn't be swayed easily, and a part of me wondered why he'd come around so fast. My speech wasn't that impressive, not to someone who had such firm beliefs about right and wrong. I hoped that one day he would accept me and Aiden as part of Shannen's life when he saw I wasn't going anywhere and that I wasn't dangerous. I just didn't expect it to happen before I'd had a chance to prove to him that I meant what I said.

But looking at them, it was pretty obvious that his family *did* mean everything to him, and maybe the pressure from Shannen's mum and not wanting to hurt Shannen anymore had made him rethink.

It didn't matter what the reason was. What mattered was that he was willing to try.

And for once, everything was working out.

Chapter 33

Steven

My hands were shaking as I exited Shannen's building and walked towards my car, pulling my phone from my pocket on the way.

I went to visit her thinking we would have some time to ourselves. Time for me to talk her out of being with a man who was entirely unsuitable for her. Violent, dead-end job, single father with no prospects. He was never going to be right for her. Never.

And I believed that right up until the moment I saw them together.

It had been a long time since Annie and I first met, but I saw something between Shannen and Cal that I hadn't expected. I saw myself and Annie when we were younger. I saw it in the way they looked at each other. In the way they communicated. The way they fought hard for each other. There was no hiding the bond between them already. My daughter was in love with that man, and he was in love with her. And his boy... he was sweet, funny, and polite, and he also looked at Shannen with adoration.

She was happy. They all were.

I'd imagined something different. Not someone with no redeeming qualities because Shannen wouldn't go for someone like that. But I thought he would just be a fling. A moment of rebellion that would burn out quickly. I'd hoped that was the case because I was not prepared for my daughter to remain entangled with someone volatile and dangerous. Someone who could drag her down and ruin her life.

And maybe he still had the potential to do that. Maybe he was just a good actor saying the things he thought I wanted to hear to get me on his side.

I was ninety percent certain, though, that I'd made an error. He seemed like a man who had turned his life around and was now fighting to keep everything he'd worked for. It didn't change how I felt about his past. I still hated it, felt disgusted by what he'd done.

But not as disgusted as I felt with myself now.

One meeting with Cal wasn't proof that he would never mess up. But it did prove that my imagination had taken over any rational thoughts because of my need to keep Shannen safe. I needed more time. To get to know him and see if I was right.

Pulling up my recent call list, I hit the name at the top and waited.

"Steven!" the male voice said, glee in his tone. "It's done."

"Undo it," I snapped, fumbling in my pocket for my car keys. "Undo it now."

There was a pause. "What? Why?"

"I think I made a mistake."

You fool.

"Shannen is in love with him," I said, opening the driver's side door and getting into my car. "You need to back off."

He barked out a laugh. "Surely, that should be even more reason to get the ball rolling."

"No!" I spat, slamming the car door shut, my hands still trembling. "Jesus, I knew she cared about him and that she wasn't going to give him up easily, but he isn't what you said he was."

"He is *exactly* what I said he was. He's scum who will drag your family into the gutter. Shannen just needs to see that."

"Yeah, and I thought that too until I met him." I thudded my head back against the headrest, silently cursing myself.

"You met him and you think I'm wrong? Christ, he's more manipulative than I thought."

His words pissed me off. I'd gone to him for information, and in my anger and belief that Shannen was throwing her life away on some waster, I'd let him rile me up more. Told myself that what he was doing was for the best. Getting another criminal off the streets and showing Shannen Cal was all wrong for her.

"Scott," I said coldly, "If you ruin my daughter's life, I will end you."

Scott chuckled. "Me? I might have been the one who started it, but you encouraged it. Begged me to get Cal away from her. You knew what this would do. What the effects could be on her and her job, but you still told me to go ahead."

I had. I had known exactly what would happen, but I convinced myself any fallout would still be better than me one day hearing my daughter had been beaten to death by her headcase of a boyfriend. I wanted her safe. I only ever wanted to protect her, so much that I'd acted irrationally.

I could practically hear Annie scolding me. *"Why do you always have to rush ahead? Why can't you just slow down before making stupid decisions."* Not that I could ever tell her about this. If anyone ever found out...

"And now I'm telling you to call it off," I snarled. "I'm serious. I just need a bit more time."

"There is no time, old man. Like I already said... it's done. And so is he."

Oakwood Lane Series

You can read the rest of Shannen and Cal's story in Oakwood Lane Book 2 – Only With You!

If you enjoyed reading about Nova and Donovan, you can read their beginning in Re-Writing Christmas.

About the Author

Kyra Lennon is a UK-based romance author who writes love stories with heart, heat, and emotional depth. Her books often feature small-town settings and characters navigating real-life challenges on their way to their happily ever after. Kyra's stories are full of raw chemistry, complex emotions, and the kind of romantic tension that lingers long after the final page.

A lifelong storyteller and unapologetic daydreamer, Kyra believes in messy feelings, imperfect characters, and the magic of a well-timed kiss. When she's not writing, you'll find her chatting with writers in her online community, overusing heart emojis, and plotting her next book with a latte and loud music!

If you would like to keep up to date with all of Kyra's latest news, you can follow her on Facebook or sign up to her newsletter for news, book recs, and freebies!

Other Books by Kyra Lennon

You can find free content for the Oakwood Lane Series here!

Razes Hell Series
Nobody Knows
Everybody Knows
Chaos and Consent Series
Hear What You Want
Say What You Feel
Take What You Need
Oakwood Lane Prequel
Re-Writing Christmas
Oakwood Lane Series
All Of You
Only With You
Over You
Standalones
Reasonable Doubts
Picture (Im)Perfect
Unintended